loving
at 40

L.B. DUNBAR

www.lbdunbar.com

Cover Design: Shannon Passmore/Shanoff Designs
Editor: Melissa Shank
Editor: Jenny Sims/Editing4Indies
Proofreader: Gemma Brocato
Proofreader: Karen Fischer

Other Books by L.B. Dunbar

Road Trips & Romance
Hauling Ashe
Merging Wright
Rhode Trip

Lakeside Cottage
Living at 40
Loving at 40
Learning at 40
Letting Go at 40

The Silver Foxes of Blue Ridge
Silver Brewer
Silver Player
Silver Mayor
Silver Biker

Silver Fox Former Rock Stars
After Care
Midlife Crisis
Restored Dreams
Second Chance
Wine&Dine

Collision novellas
Collide
Caught

Smartypants Romance (an imprint of Penny Reid)
Love in Due Time
Love in Deed
Love in a Pickle

The World of True North (an imprint of Sarina Bowen)
Cowboy
Studfinder

Rom-com for the over 40
The Sex Education of M.E.

The Heart Collection
Speak from the Heart
Read with your Heart
Look with your Heart
Fight from the Heart
View with your Heart

A Heart Collection Spin-off
The Heart Remembers

THE EARLY YEARS
The Legendary Rock Star Series
The Legend of Arturo King
The Story of Lansing Lotte
The Quest of Perkins Vale
The Truth of Tristan Lyons
The Trials of Guinevere DeGrance

Paradise Stories
Abel
Cain

The Island Duet
Redemption Island
Return to the Island

Modern Descendants – writing as elda lore
Hades
Solis
Heph

Dedication and Inspiration

"Ride" by Chase Rice

And a set of teachers at lunchtime who always knew how to bring the laughs.
Miss you ladies and the occasional gents.

Content Warning

This book contains depictions of issues about gun safety around children in addition to a school shooting situation.

L.B. Dunbar

1

[Jenna]

Someone's been sleeping in my bed, and she's still in it.

I thought I was dreaming. I'd been reading copious amounts of children's tales to my two little girls, and I was convinced the sentences had seeped into my subconscious. I could not get away from being a mom even in my sleep. But slowly, my brain registers that the sound of that final bear's voice was a little too gruff and a little too gravelly and a whole lot of sexy.

My eyes flip open in the dark bedroom, and my heart races. I am not alone in here. My chin is pinned by the power of a thick paw of callused fingertips, and the depth of dark eyes narrowed and focused keeps me frozen in place. His nose is so close we practically touch, and I'd scream if only my vocal cords worked.

"However, she doesn't look like Goldilocks." His eyes flick up to my hair, which happens to be raven black, and he chuckles, rugged and low. "So who the hell are you?"

I swallow, feeling his wrist near my throat as his fingers hold my jaw. Something cold and metallic brushes the center of my chest. *Dear God, don't let him hurt the girls.* The thought speeds up my already sprinting heart.

"Please don't hurt me," I choke out, and his eyes widen.

"What the fuck?" he snaps, startling me even more. "You're in my bed, 'Locks." The incredulous tone roughens his deep tenor.

His bed?

My mind flips through a mental checklist. This is Anna's house. This is Lakeside Cottage. Her folks owned the place, and she inherited it. My daughters and I are her guests. The apartment above the garage was offered to me for a much-needed break. She said her brother—

"Archer?" I croak, wondering if the man holding my jaw is the elusive older brother Anna has mentioned a time or two. He wasn't expected here. At the sound of his name, his hand slowly releases my chin but travels south to my throat. The thick palm isn't squeezing. He

7

just rests it in place like a turtleneck sweater. I can still breathe, but my lungs have stopped working. Despite the dark room, the intensity of his eyes sucks up all the oxygen in the space.

"Who the fuck are you?"

I struggle to find the words to answer him. Maybe it's that strong voice or the fact he's on all fours over me. *How did I not hear him enter the apartment? Or this room? Or this bed?*

"I'm Jenna Davis, a friend of Anna's."

His hand lowers even more, flattening on my chest. I'm certain he can feel my heart thumping under my skin. Wearing pajama shorts and a tank top I bought for this little getaway, I'm loosely covered by a sheet and summer blanket, but I'm all too aware of how thin the material is. The heat of his hand seeps through my flesh just above the swell of my breasts, which rapidly heave in fear. Maybe fear isn't the right word. Is it possible I'm also turned on? Despite not knowing Anna's brother, I was having the most arousing dream before the gruff bear invaded my thoughts, and that dream has my nipples on high alert, especially now that someone's hand is very near them.

However, my head says this is all wrong.

"What are you doing?" I choke because his hand is sweeping lower. My gut reaction is to lift my knee for his balls, which I do. Only, two things happen at the same time. He captures my leg between his thighs before I get anywhere near his precious cargo, and his hand slips lower, squeezing my breast.

"What the fuck?" he says again like sandpaper against rocks.

"What the frickety-frack?" I say at the same time.

"What the fuck is frickety-frack?" That incredulous tone returns, and I finally find enough strength to lift my arms upward and push at his chest. Speaking of rocks, he's missing a shirt, and his smooth pecs are as solid as a boulder. Something silvery and long dangles around his neck. He bitterly chuckles at my weak attempt to move him but shifts enough so I can scramble out from underneath him. He remains on the bed, on his knees, while I slip off the mattress and back up until I collide with the wall.

"I'm not going to hurt you," he says. That rugged voice softens only a sliver.

Crossing my arms over my chest in a giant X, I attempt to cover myself. "You just manhandled my boob," I blurt.

"You were sleeping in my bed. Find a woman in my bed means I get to touch her."

"That's rather assumptive and chauvinistic."

"Those are two big words I can't comprehend in the middle of the night, babe."

I huff again and then think of my girls.

"Tell me you didn't touch my daughters." My heart hammers as the statement stammers from my lips.

"You've got kids?"

I roll my shoulder against the wall, intending to slip from the room through the open door. Only, I misjudge the distance to the entrance and smack into the frame.

My nose explodes in pain and my eyes sting. "Frickety, frack, frack, frack." Instantly, warm hands are on my shoulders, steadying me from behind.

"Where're you goin'?" The seductive sound blurs with the pain radiating across my face, and tears fall.

My voice shakes as I speak. "Just let me go. Just let me get my girls, and I'll get out of here."

His hands peel free of my shoulders, but he doesn't move. His presence overpowers me from behind. Heat wafts off his chest. I sense his strength, but fear no longer holds me in place. His breath tickles the fine hairs on the back of my neck. *Would he kiss me there?* It's the most ridiculous thought I've ever had.

"Look, there's no need to go anywhere. It's the middle of the night. I'm sure this is my sister's fuckup. It's been a long night. I'll just take the couch."

I have no sense of what time it is. This morning, I'd left my hometown of Elk Lake City, roughly three hours north of Lakeside, and arrived midafternoon. That was hours ago. The girls and I needed a change of scenery, and Anna is a friend from college. When she moved here, we promised we'd get together more often.

"No, you should take your bed," I say, spinning to face him, bumping into his firm chest, which remains too close to me. My nose throbs, and tears still prickle my eyes, but those nipples of mine ache as they tenderly scrape the inside of my thin tank top.

"You gonna join me again?" The teasing shift in such a rough voice doesn't compute at first.

"I'll just sleep with my girls." I'm certain I won't sleep after all, but I'm not in the right frame of mind to wake my daughters and carry them out of here. Plus, the time is somewhere past midnight, and the thought of crossing the driveway to wake Anna doesn't feel right. She's been so kind in offering this garage apartment for my two-week stay.

"You weren't supposed to be here," I defend.

"It's still my place," Archer reminds me.

"Yes, but you weren't supposed to be here," I repeat as if that clarifies anything.

"Well, I am." A large arm lifts, and I flinch at the raising of his paw, preparing for a strike. "What the fuck? Calm down, babe." Our eyes meet, and his gaze searches mine for answers I cannot give.

"Do you need to keep saying that word?"

"What word?"

"The frickety-frack word." It took years of training on my part to curb my vocabulary, so I don't drop an f-bomb or two before my girls. I'm conditioned not to swear as I teach high school and need to keep a stern face when I call out kids for language. But I was no saint outside my classroom until I had children of my own. Even then, I'm still not perfect.

Thinking of my two little ones, I need to get out of this room and check on them. Taking a step to the side as Archer's presence is just so . . . present, I kick the doorframe of the opening I still cannot seem to make it through.

"Frick." I hiss as my heel collides with the edge in a fluky spot right where the two pieces of wood corner together. A definitive thud echoes in the quiet of the space.

He chuckles roughly again. "You're kind of a hot mess."

Don't I know it. He doesn't need to know it, though.

"I'm just gonna . . . and then tomorrow . . ." I can't seem to collect words because I inhaled as my breath caught when I kicked the door, and *sweet cherries,* Archer smells good. I can't distinguish any specific scent, but it's strong and musky, and I lick my lower lip. Even in the dark, Archer's eyes dip to watch the motion.

"Girls' room," he says, dropping his voice while focused on my mouth.

I don't know if it's a question or a command, but two hands come to my shoulders, shift me to the left, and spin me to face the wide door opening. I hardly take a step through the space when the door is closed at my back. I race across the living room, but not before bumping into the edge of the couch and then stubbing my toe on the coffee table as I'm unfamiliar with this layout in the dark. Hobbling to the bedroom where my girls sleep, I finally make it to their door and slip into their space, pressing my back against the barrier once I've closed it.

With my head tipped back and my eyes closed, I recall Archer's heavy, thick hand over my breast. Maybe I moved, and it was all innocent. I did try to knee him in the balls, and squeezing my breast might have been more a gut reaction on his part. Still, I reach for the swell and tenderly place my hand over the heaviness, feeling my nipple erect and firm, peaking against the thin cotton of my shirt. Then I stifle a giggle, a ridiculous teenage-girl squeak, at the thought of that large, mysterious man purposely tweaking my breast.

"Oh my God, I need to get laid," I quietly mutter to the heavens in the dark. My lids flutter open, and I lower my head to face two beds and the two little reasons it hasn't happened in years. Taking a deep breath, I sigh with exhaustion and move to one bed, pressing Rosie's little shoulder so she'll roll over. For a tiny thing, she can take up a lot of space when her thin limbs spread in all directions. I won't be getting a wink of sleep with her as she often climbs into my bed at home. I don't mind it much, as the bed feels too large without Ryan, but Rosie has no concept of head on pillow and feet toward the foot of the bed. Eventually, little heels will be pressed into my back, and I'll be forced to the edge of the mattress, hanging on to a sliver of the blanket.

Rosie shifts, and I settle into the bed, pulling the blanket to my throat as if it can hide me, as if it can protect me. My head rolls to the left, and I check the other bed. Talia sleeps soundly on her side, facing in my direction. Her little hands are tucked under her cheek, and her lips part, causing her to snore softly. With not a care in the world, not a fear in her dreams, my little worrier rests.

"Sweet dreams," I say to the dark, wanting only quiet and peace in both my girls' heads as they slumber.

For me, I'll be lying here wide awake until morning when I can escape the apartment of one hot Archer McCaryn.

2

[Archer]

"What the fuck, Anna?" I snap at my sister as we stand on either side of the large kitchen island in our parents' home. *Excuse me*, my sister's home, as she somehow took it upon herself to assume responsibility for this place *and* decided to move into it roughly two years ago.

"Don't take that tone with me, Archer."

"Jesus, you sound just like Mom." My muscles flex as I rest my palms on the countertop, glaring at my younger sibling. With her dark hair and matching eyes, she even looks like our mother. The reminder stings because our parents have been dead for years. In a drive from here to Chicago, a trip our dad could have made in his sleep, a ten-car pileup occurred. Texting and driving kills people. Some punk kid wasn't paying attention to the slowing traffic and rammed into my parents from behind, forcing them forward into a semi-tractor trailer.

At the mention of our mother, Anna's shoulders fall, and mine do as well. I'm the eldest McCaryn, but my sister has always been considered the most dependable one, at least according to our family. No one understands the responsibilities I've had over the years. No one knows because that's the way it was supposed to be. My parents thought I'd abandoned the pack. For their safety, I couldn't tell anyone what I did for a living. Eventually, my dad figured out my work was something dangerous—dangerous but important—so I told him what I could because I needed someone to claim my body if anything were to happen to me.

As I glance around the bright kitchen and sitting room combination, there isn't a trace of our parents' belongings, yet their presence is everywhere. This was our family's second home. Our father was a sausage king in Chicago, and as the wealthy often do from that area, they purchased a place for vacations and weekend getaways in the southwest corner of Michigan. When I was a kid, I hated this place, but I have a different perspective now that I'm older. The house isn't small, but it isn't as large as I remember, or maybe it's just that I'm bigger. Or older. Or jaded.

"That garage is mine," I growl at my younger sister.

"We haven't seen you in years." She pauses.

"I was here for Ben's funeral." The harsh reminder of her husband's passing makes my sister flinch. *Shit.* Rubbing a hand over my short hair, I mutter an apology.

"Where?" She narrows her eyes at me. She didn't see me, but that was the point. I'd broken protocol to pay my respects, but I couldn't linger, and I couldn't be seen. I couldn't explain then, and *right now* doesn't seem like the time for it either.

Her beloved Ben passed away over a year ago, and the loss sucks. He was a good guy. From what I knew of him, he was a decent husband, a great father, and an excellent businessman. He started his landscaping company from scratch after he followed my sister's tail to Chicago. He'd been our lawn boy here at Lakeside. I chuckle at the thought. Sweet, shy Anna ended up with someone my parents considered the help. It was a generational thing on their part and possibly the only rebellious thing Anna had ever done.

"I didn't know you'd be here," Anna says.

"I called you. I told you August." I state the obvious, "It's August." In July, I got the all clear to move forward from therapy. I needed a place to rest and rebuild.

"Yes, but that was last year, Archer. *Last* year."

"Last year? This year? What's the fucking difference? It's August. I'm here, and someone is in my apartment." It wasn't really that simple, and we needed to talk about why I didn't show last August, but I wasn't ready.

I needed to be here. Period.

I don't own the apartment any more than Anna thinks she owns this house. The three of us—myself, Anna, and Amelia—have inherited the property, a beautiful stretch of land on a cliff overlooking Lake Michigan. The land includes this sprawling six-bedroom home and a carriage house of sorts that has a three-car garage with a two-bedroom apartment over it. *My* apartment. Since the time I was a teen, I'd been out there whenever our family came here.

"You have got to stop saying fuck every other word."

"I don't *got* to do anything. I want my apartment. And I don't want some woman with kids in there."

"I can leave." A soft feminine voice comes from my left, and I turn to get a better view of the dark-haired beauty I found in my bed. Last night, it was difficult to make out all her features in the dim light of the room. Only a window offered illumination of her form and what a form it was. She hadn't heard me climb over her body, and that was the intention. Her heart pulsed at her throat. She'd been moaning when I entered, and I wondered what she'd been dreaming about. The soft hum wasn't fear or distrust but more arousal. When I accidentally cupped her breast and squeezed, I got a handful. Her subconscious thoughts were evident from the taut nub of her pert nipple.

The reminder of that heavy swell in my hand makes my dick twitch in my shorts, which is the last thing I need while I'm arguing with my sister. I'd sworn off all women after my last one, and I wasn't interested in this one, but my reaction was a nice reminder that my dick did, in fact, function after all that had happened in the past twelve months.

Because damn, this woman is gorgeous. She checks all the boxes. Long, midnight hair. Dark eyes. Legs for miles and . . . a little head pops out from behind one of those lengthy limbs. Blond curls and bright eyes almost blind me at the reminder that she mentioned something about her daughters last night. Another little person stands beside her as a miniature mirror image of her mother because this woman is a fucking *mother*.

"Good morning, Talia. Good morning, Rosie," Anna coos sweetly.

This is the wake-up call I need. I don't do women with children. I should not be thinking of *this* mother, and most likely a married one at that. Nor am I thinking about her because I am so over women and the bullshit they spew. I scrub both hands down my face to clear all the dirty thoughts I have rushing around in my head.

I will not fuck a *mother*.

"I don't want you to go," Anna says, walking over to her friend and lowering before the little one still peeking around Jenna's legs. *Jenna, that was her name, right?* I'd been too distracted by her racing heart and heaving chest to register the name. The pounding rhythm of her heart under my fingertips did strange things to me. She said something about being Anna's friend, but her mouth—the lush curve of her lips and her sweet breath—stopped my heart. Having a woman underneath me was a position I hadn't been in for a while.

Not going there again.

"I don't want to intrude." Jenna's eyes catch mine across the room while she speaks to my sister. She's standing just inside the kitchen off the large entryway which leads to the front door. Anna reaches out her hand for the carbon-copy little one, stroking over dark hair that matches her mother's.

"You aren't intruding. You're my guests. I asked you to come here." My sister's plea draws Jenna's attention.

"I know, but—" Her eyes seek me again.

In her crouched position, Anna glares at me over her shoulder. Slowly, my sister stands. Her expression hardens as much as it can. She looks so much like our mother, who never could pull off a stern face either. "Archer."

"What?" I have no idea what the hell she wants me to do about this situation. "You're the one who invited her here. You fix this." I wave out a hand. "This house has six bedrooms. What the hell is anyone doing out in the garage anyway?"

"You said a bad word," the blond girl states before disappearing behind her mother's legs again. Those long, tan legs drag to the floor from jean shorts cuffed near the apex of them. My tongue wants to trace that length from ankle to center and then—

"He did say a bad word, didn't he, Rosie?" Anna coos again. "Bad Archer."

"I'm not a *fu*—" I cut the word short as two sets of adult female eyes glare at me. "A dog," I finish. I'm not some errant pooch they're coddling as they insult me. I'm a fucking man who can say whatever the fuck I want. Only, those little eyes peek around her mother's legs once more, and my heart does a little skip.

What the hell?

"Yes, we have six rooms, but the boys are coming back," Anna states, facing me.

"What boys?"

"Mason."

"That's one man." Mason Becker was a friend of Ben's and had a serious boner for my sister when he was younger. Ben was the better man, and he got the girl. Why Ben remained friends with the wanker is a mystery.

"Zack and his boys are going to stay in the house as well," Anna states.

"That's ridiculous. They live next door." Zack Weller is a family friend. Our mothers were best friends from when they were growing up, and the Wellers were our neighbors here at Lakeside until their dad turned out to be a dick. The older son, Noah, is my age, and we've been pals most of our lives. I don't understand all the particulars on how Zack ended up back next door, but he's over there, so I don't know why he needs to stay here.

"And Logan's coming for a few nights as well."

"Logan Anders?" Logan was the final guy in the foursome of Ben's friends. He joined their little crew once the others all went off to college. A little over a year ago, he married Ben's younger sister, which sounds all kinds of wrong until you consider he was forty and she was in her late thirties. They live half a mile down the street. "What the f—" I cut myself off again and catch two little blue beams staring at me. Her thumb has popped into her mouth. Taking a deep breath, I clench my fists and glare at my sister. Through gritted teeth, I ask, "Why would Logan stay here?"

"They promised Ben." The statement is said as if it's all the explanation I need and explains everything, which it doesn't.

"I should really go," Jenna interjects, reminding me why I'm having this argument with my sister. "We can just get a hotel room for the weekend and then head home."

"No." Anna protests as she reaches for her friend's hand. "It's summertime. You'll never find a hotel with vacant rooms around here. Plus, I don't want you to go home. Three hours is too far away. It's also your summer vacation, and school will start too soon. You need this." Anna's voice softens. "I need this. I need you."

I have no idea what she means other than the summer vacation part. My sister is a high school teacher.

Jenna's eyes shift to mine a second before glancing back at my sister. "I don't really want to go either, but . . . ." She side-eyes me again, looking a little forlorn and heartbroken at the prospect of returning to wherever she's from and giving up her time at the beach. Instantly, I recall her flinching as I raised my hand last night, preparing to brush her hair out of her face. I thought she just didn't want my touch, but is it something more? Is she hiding from someone? Is she escaping from him? Protecting others is part of my nature, but it's strange how quickly the need comes as I look at Jenna.

Damn, I hate the idea of someone hurting her or those two little girls standing beside her.

If escape is all she wants, then I understand. I just wanted to come here and get out of my head. The doc said I needed a change of pace for a bit. As Jenna's gaze falls back to me for a second, something in those coffee-colored eyes claws at my chest, and it fucking cuts. It cuts deep, and I should know as I've been stabbed a time or two.

Oh, for fuck's sake. "You don't have to leave," I mutter. Her eyes widen in surprise but quickly narrow in distrust. "We can just share the place."

"She can't stay there with you," Anna defends.

"Why not?" I snap. *What's wrong with me?* Yet even I don't want to answer that question. "It's my place. I'm not leaving."

"I can go," Jenna says, reassuring me, but those eyes—*crap*. She's gutting me with only a look. It's not an intentional look meant to harm, but something in those eyes tells me she needs to stay. I want her to stay. Maybe she needs me. *What am I thinking?* The ridiculous thought is quickly chased out of my head.

"No, Archer can go," Anna says.

"What?" I choke.

"No," Jenna and I respond at the same time. Her head swivels from Anna to me and back, forcing the messy knot on the top of her head to wobble. Taking a second glance at her, I notice a stain on her white shirt and remember all the times she knocked into something last night. Her face on the doorframe and then her heel. I didn't miss the hiss of pain after she bumped into the couch and collided with the coffee table. She'd be horrible at covert missions. She made more noise than an elephant storming through the jungle.

"No, I'll go," Jenna offers once more.

"I want you to stay." *What the fuck am I saying?* The words come out of nowhere and startle both of us. My fingers unfurl and then clench again.

"Really, I can just leave," she argues one more time, but I'm getting tired of this game.

"I can sleep on the couch, 'Locks." The offer is the same as last night. Anna turns her head toward me, narrowing her eyes.

"I can stay in the room with the girls. There are two beds in there." The two-bedroom apartment has two twins in one room with a queen-size bed in the other. In *my* room, where I found little Miss Raven Hair sleeping in *my* bed. I don't own a home or have a place I call one. The apartment over the garage is my haven. Nine times out of ten, I'd crash here between missions once the summer season was finished, and my sister had gone back to her original house. Anna doesn't understand how much I value that apartment space. Now that I'm older, Lakeside is the only place I feel at peace. Once I come down from the high of an assignment, I need this time. I need it now.

Anna glances from me to Jenna. Her eyes are wary as she gazes at the beauty before her. She definitely wants her friend here for whatever reason, and I can't really kick the woman out. I mean, I could—easily— but I don't want her to pack up her kids and go. We're adults, and the apartment has plenty of space. How difficult could it be to share it for a little bit?

L.B. Dunbar

"Stay." My voice catches on the word, and strangely, I mean what I've said. I want her to stay for some reason. When Jenna looks back at me, all cautious and concerned, my brain short-circuits with a memory.

You don't deserve love, Archer. The female who said those words taunts me, and I quickly shake the recall.

"If you're sure . . ." Jenna's eyes soften. If I didn't know better, I'd say I saw relief in her expression.

Was I sure?

No woman would love you like I did. I shake the voice again. I wasn't certain of anything anymore.

"So how long you stayin', babe?" I tip up my chin, telling myself I can do this. I can pretend sharing space with a beauty like her won't be an issue for me. I can handle a woman and her daughters for a few days.

A shy smile lifts the lips that haunted my fantasies last night. The same ones I can't seem to take my eyes off as they slowly curl into a crooked grin and send my dick into all kinds of notions it shouldn't be thinking.

"Two weeks."

Fuck.

3

[Jenna]

He's so frickity good looking. Standing inside the kitchen, he pinned me in place with those eyes, and I couldn't have walked away even if he was begging me to leave. Something was intriguing about Archer McCaryn, and while I couldn't get a read on him, my body definitely wanted a chance to trace the fine lines of his face and the deep divots of his abs which were on display last night. Something closed off rested behind his deep, soulful eyes, and while everything in me screamed to look away, I couldn't. I was drawn to him like I haven't been drawn to another man in over five years.

Maybe it was those large muscular arms caging me in last night. Or the weight of his hand that cupped my breast, the sensation lingering long after I attempted to find sleep. Or possibly, it was what he said in that sandpaper voice of his.

I want you to stay.

I didn't want to read into the simple statement, but his earnest tone along with a fleeting sorrow reflected in those midnight eyes stopped me from second-guessing his sincerity.

"I'm so sorry this happened. I swear he said he wasn't coming here until the end of August. Everyone would be cleared out before he arrived." Anna apologizes again once Archer exits the kitchen, but I still can't shake the way he looked at me.

He wanted something from me, but I couldn't begin to decipher what that might be. I didn't know much about Archer McCaryn, but neither did his sister. He'd been absent every time I'd seen her in the past few years, and I only heard snippets of his name here and there.

Eventually, Anna and I lug the kids, bags of snacks, plus towels and toys down one hundred and fifty stairs to the beach along the lakeshore below, and she explains a few things about her mysterious brother.

"While I was in college, Archer went into the police academy. Once he graduated, he only worked a few years for the department before he disappeared. My mom thought he was into drugs. I thought he was just wayward. A vagabond of sorts, full of wanderlust. I think my dad knew the truth. Archer would show up here on the off-season when the tourist crowds were gone, and the community settled into quiet. He'd be beat up at times. Other times, he'd be wounded more than a street fight. Sometimes, he just seemed weary. He wouldn't talk about what happened." Anna smiles softly as she glances toward the water's edge, where Mila, her twelve-year-old daughter, builds a sandcastle with Talia and Rosie. We sit among a set of sturdy Adirondack chairs facing the massive lake. "Ben might have also known the truth. I don't know why he never told me, though. He would just say Archer can handle himself."

Ben. My heart broke for my friend. It has been a little over a year since her husband's death. She fell in love with him before her senior year of high school, and they dated all through college. Shortly after graduation, they married. He was a great guy with a rambunctious set of friends. I'd seen Mason Becker a time or two as his construction company builds million-dollar mansions in the area around Elk Lake where I live. He's a total player, and I would know as I slept with him once back in college. We brush past the memory whenever we see one another. He still maintains a playboy reputation even in his forties.

During the first two weeks of August, Ben's friends agreed to gather at Lakeside Cottage to remember his passing and celebrate their final vacation with him two years ago. For this first anniversary date, Anna invited me to visit as well.

"I could use a friend who might understand my position."

I'd lost my husband when Rosie was still a baby.

Anna and I had stayed in touch over the years. I'd been down to visit Lakeside Cottage, the family's vacation home, on occasion, but it hadn't been for more than a weekend in the past. When she asked me to stay for two weeks, I hesitated, but that's when she offered me the apartment. I'd have some privacy with my little ones but still be included in the activities when chaos invaded the main house.

"Most events revolve around the guys. Golfing. Fishing. Barhopping. But dinner is a must. Ben wanted his friends to come together and regroup here. Re-center." The request is strange considering the four men went into business together shortly before Ben died, forming a company called Four Points that encompasses design and construction, plus landscaping and real estate legalese. Each man has an expertise in the areas involved.

"I could throttle Archer for showing up like this. It's so like him." Anna sighs. "Are you sure you don't mind staying in the apartment with him? I swear I can kick him out. It might feel good to kick him out." She's teasing. If she hasn't seen her brother in years, she needs to spend time with him. They need to reconnect.

Was I certain I could stay in an apartment with a gruff but attractive man? We're both adults, and my girls will be present. What could possibly happen?

"No. No, I really don't want to be an issue." I'd been looking forward to this respite of sorts since March when Anna invited me to visit. I didn't want to leave, and I didn't want to force Archer to go, so I'd just deal with the awkward setup. Anna had already suggested making some rearrangements with her boys and Mason Becker in the house, but I didn't want to repack my small family's things and inconvenience everyone else.

"Archer will probably just come and go as he pleases." Anna scoffs while squinting out at the lake. "But I really believe he's harmless, as in, he won't hurt you or the girls." A sympathetic glance in my direction is reassuring as she knows my history. My husband had never been the issue. Another man had. "He isn't dangerous or anything."

Instinctively, I don't believe Archer would harm me. I might have been startled last night. Who wouldn't be when an unrecognizable man perches over you in the middle of the night? But hurt me? I just don't get that vibe from Archer despite my initial reaction. He *surprised* me, but I don't fear him, not directly.

"I think we can handle him." I offer a falsely confident wink because my libido is what concerns me. Being around the slightly mysterious, highly attractive older brother of my best friend is more the issue at hand. My body is saying give it to me while my heart is saying what are you thinking?

As I didn't want to go home yet, and I actually couldn't afford a hotel for two weeks, the girls and I will just make do.

How difficult could it be to share an apartment with a man I hardly know but sense could rock my body and spin my heart topsy-turvy?

+ + +

By late afternoon, Ben's friends arrive at the *cottage*, which is much more than the term implies. The main house has six bedrooms, most with private baths, plus various entertainment rooms, but the family spends most of their time in the kitchen, which has a large sitting area.

The boys, as Anna's mother-in-law affectionately calls the forty-something-year-old men, include Mason, Zack, and Logan. I'd met them my junior year of college when Anna and I started hanging out as we shared a major in education.

When Mason Becker arrived, he made himself at home as he had lived here the year Ben was sick. He's model-worthy gorgeous with artfully perfect hair that curls over his ears and along his neck, plus he has a bone structure that says, *I'm an Adonis*. He also knows this about himself.

Zack Weller is now the next-door neighbor, having reclaimed his family home. It's an interesting story, and I look forward to hearing more from the sandy-haired lawyer. Zack has always been a little intense, reserved and guarded against people until he knows them better. He's been Anna's friend for her entire life as their mothers were childhood friends.

Logan Anders rounds out the group. He's newly married to Ben's sister, Autumn. Logan was the sweet, funny guy among the friends, with a personality just as large as his stature. I almost didn't recognize him. He's lost weight, but his face remains innocent and jovial.

"Jenna Babenna," he greets me, reminding me of our college days. I have great friends in Elk Lake City between Tricia Ramirez, a teacher pal, and Britton Scott, who owns the local tea shop where I used to work during summer months off. Still, this reunion of sorts is a reminder of other days when I was a wild child and a proud single lady until I fell in love with Ryan.

"Logan, I didn't recognize you without a beer," I tease him as the party person.

"I'm a changed man," he pretends to whisper behind his hand.

"That's what love does to a person," Mason jokes, slapping his friend on the shoulder and shivering in mock disgust at the emotion. I notice Zack isn't disagreeing. During dinner, I quickly learn about Logan's marriage, Zack's engagement, and the pregnancy of both their women.

"Autumn is pregnant again?" Mason stutters. "You stud." He high-fives his friend across the table. Logan had a baby boy last summer, named Ben in honor of Autumn's brother. She wasn't able to join us tonight for dinner, but she'll join us at the beach sometime this week.

Zack sheepishly grins about his own announcement. He already has twin boys, who are eight, from his first marriage, but Zack and River, his fiancée, are expecting a little girl.

Archer joins us for dinner but remains quiet throughout the meal. Without meaning to do it, I find myself glancing at him from my position at the table. He's seated at the head, opposite his sister, and I imagine it's where Ben once sat. I also wonder how Archer fits into this group. Being older than us, he wasn't present during our college days, but maybe he spent other time with this crew. His silence tells me he's been long absent from this collection of friends, though.

During one of the times I'm watching Archer, he glances up at me and offers a slow, crooked smile that doesn't reach those dark eyes. I don't shift my gaze when I probably should. His eyes are so expressive while the rest of his face is still and hard. The momentary sorrow of this morning is gone, but his eyes are not relaxed. The depth of them pins me in place again as if he's trying to tell me something, but I can't decode what he's saying.

Is he trying to intimidate me? That isn't it.

Is he trying to warn me to stay away from him? That *is* a possibility.

Or is he not pushing but pulling me to him?

My heart beats faster inside my chest. I haven't been this attracted to another man since my husband. I was a late bloomer in the love category but not in the lust one. I played the field like a champ until I met Ryan. He was everything I'd ever desired in a man—passionate, loyal, kind. Considered short and stocky by some, he was a scrapper on the outside but a teddy bear on the inside. He had a goofy grin that gave away how much he enjoyed life. He was also generous to a fault, which often got him in trouble.

Archer is the complete opposite of my late husband. He is equally solid but larger than Ryan in both shoulder width and height. The distribution of his hard form is also different, almost military in manner. With an edge to his cheeks and a sharp jawline, his rugged voice adds to the tough appearance as he sounds like he's on the verge of barking orders. His smile isn't soft but predatory and knowing, like he can interpret all my secret desires with only a glance. He also strategically uses the word *fuck* in his vocabulary as a noun, verb, adjective, and interjection.

When I finally go to bed later that first night, the sandpapery sound filters into my dreams, telling me all he intends to do to me. His fingers. His tongue. His teeth. My hips thrust to encourage his touch, encouraging him to do what he pleases to me. I haven't been touched by another hand other than my own in so long, I can hardly remember the sensation. Wetness pools between my thighs, and I moan, thus waking myself.

I'm disorientated at first, wondering where I am and why I'm dreaming of Archer. We hardly spoke during dinner.

"Give me that." My eldest daughter's tone rouses me further from the fantasy that leaves me panting, dissatisfied, and clutching the sheet outside my thigh, desperate to reach the release Archer's fingers promised to give me. I should not be dreaming of Archer doing something to my body, least of all, giving me a long overdue orgasm. I shake my head, trying to restore my bearings, settle my racing heart, and still the ache between my legs.

Working to calm my breathing, which is coming in short, sharp gasps, I blink at the ceiling overhead. It's morning. My girls and I slept in the same bedroom in the garage apartment. Knowing they are early risers, Talia had strict instructions to wake me when they woke. Although I'd warned my girls not to wander into the other room without me, they are both absent. Even on vacation, I wasn't going to get any sleep.

I explained to Talia how the apartment belongs to Archer, and he was going to sleep in the other bedroom. My eldest girl is suspicious of most things, while Rosie has no fear. Knowing Talia was my worrier, I tried to assure her she had nothing to be concerned about with Archer—at least, I hope not. Anna had repeatedly told me yesterday that she trusted Archer with her life, even though she hadn't seen him in years.

Talia's sharp tone directed at her sister warns me she's gone into mini-mommy mode for some reason.

I'd slept poorly last night, but that was nothing new. Sleep was an illusion at this stage of my life—single mother of two little girls. When Archer had come in late last night, I'd heard him stumble around the living room, curse at a kitchen cabinet, then slam his bedroom door. Wherever he'd been, I envied his good time where he was definitely drinking and possibly carousing. Maybe I projected him into my dream because of where I thought he'd been and what I considered him doing with someone other than me. I have no reason in the world to be jealous of him with another woman. We are opposites. He's all hard planes and sharp edges while I'm long lines and subtle curves. We'd never fit.

Talia peeks her head around the slightly ajar bedroom door. "Rosie has a gun."

"What?" My sleep-deprived, sexual-overdrive brain is slow to process what my eldest daughter is saying. Sluggishly, I sit upright. "Why would you say that?"

My girls know how I feel about guns. I'm open about my fear of firearms, my children's need to be aware of what one is, and that they heed the warning to stay away from them.

"It was laying on the table, and Rosie was curious." Talia tsks like her answer explains everything.

It doesn't.

As I throw back the blanket, my feet tangle in the end of the covers as I try to wrangle myself free from the bed. I fall toward the floor, catching myself with shaky hands before I wrestle my legs from the sheet. I crawl a few paces before pressing upward and rushing into the living room. Once there, I freeze.

"Rosie." I whisper her name not wanting to startle her as she holds a shiny, metal object. My voice croaks. "What is that?" My mind identifies the item, but refuses to accept that my child is holding it, despite what Talia told me.

Rosie's sweet, innocent, sleepy eyes glance over at me while her thumb rests in her mouth. The small military-grade weapon lays in her lap, looking highly out of place against her little body. The dangerous end is aimed in my general direction.

If I could find a stronger voice, I'd scream for Archer, but I can't seem to work my throat. My stomach drops to my feet, and bile invades my esophagus. Brusquely, I push Talia behind my body, shielding her while trying to stay calm, which is the opposite of how I feel. "Rosie, honey, can you put the gun on the table, please?"

Please don't squeeze anything.

"Where did you find that?" I croak next when Rosie doesn't move. Her eyes return to whatever is playing on the television. The dry lump in my throat makes it hard to swallow while my palms are damp with sweat. I don't move because I'm afraid to rush my child and trigger her little fingers.

"It was laying on the table," Talia repeats from behind me. Briefly, I move my gaze in the direction of the television set, flashing a warm glow of light on Rosie in the dim morning hours, wondering what holds her attention. Glancing away before turning back to the image on the screen, I choke. There isn't enough eye bleach to clean my sockets from what I see. *From what my daughter is watching.* Unable to stop myself, I rush for the television to turn it off and cry out Archer's name.

His bedroom door flies open, and he staggers into the living room in dark boxer-briefs. His naked chest is on display along with a silver chain around his neck. With horror and disgust, my eyes meet his briefly before I recall the real issue.

As calmly as I can, I state, "Rosie has your gun." My voice quivers and cracks.

"What the…?" His wide dark eyes blink before shifting from me to my daughter. Still sucking her thumb on the couch. Still holding a gun on her lap. Archer doesn't move for a moment but lowers his rough voice to sugary sweet.

"Hey, baby girl," he addresses her. "Rosie, right? Princess, can you put the gun on the table?"

Only yesterday he accused his sister of talking to him like a dog, yet he's speaking to my child in a similar manner. I'd reprimand him but whatever works at the moment is fine by me.

Rosie stares back at Archer, her innocent blue eyes wide but glossy with remnants of sleep. She shakes her head like she doesn't want to release a coveted toy instead of a dangerous weapon.

Next, Archer addresses Talia. "Talia, baby, go into the bedroom and close the door. Crouch down behind the bed." Talia has been standing just inside the bedroom where we both stood before I noticed the porn on the television.

"Talia, honey," I speak in a trembling warning. "Do as Archer says."

"Rosie has a gun, Mommy."

"I know, baby."

"You told us never to play with guns."

"That's right, baby."

"Was Archer playing with the gun?"

I glance up at Archer, who has his eyes trained on Rosie. His hands are up in the air, and he's moved a few inches toward the back of the couch, which is a barrier between him and Rosie on the second couch, which is ninety degrees to the first.

"Remember what Mommy once told you. Some people own guns. Adult people. But if you see one, you never touch it."

I refocus on Rosie. She's only three. She doesn't know better, but I can't even imagine what prompted her to pick up the forbidden weapon. I also want to know who the hell leaves a gun laying out in the open like this with children present.

"Rosie? Princess, can you put the gun on the table?" Archer continues in his syrupy tone.

Flicking my wrist at Talia, I motion at her to follow Archer's orders. Talia steps back and closes the door, causing Rosie to roll her head on the couch cushion and look in the direction of where her sister disappeared.

In a movement nimbler than anything I've ever seen, especially from such a large man, Archer hops over the couch, slips the gun from Rosie's hand, clicks the top of the weapon to open it, and then shoves the thing into the back of his underwear. Before I know what's happened, Rosie is in his lap, his large hand pressing her head to his chest and his lips settling on the top of her blond curls.

My shaky legs give out, and I collapse to the floor with a sob of relief while my body trembles in shock.

My baby girl was holding a gun.

4

[Archer]

Fuck!

When Jenna fell to the floor, the wail of relief from her feels like having my skin peeled off by rusty, sharp nails. And with the fear on her ashen face, I'd have let someone torture me in such a manner if it meant I'd never see such anxiety in those dark eyes again.

I'd avoided Jenna as much as I could the day before. Our first encounter led to that disastrous decision in the kitchen yesterday morning when I agreed to allow her to stay in the apartment with me. Where I've placed myself in a personal torture chamber because her scent lingers, her stuff fills my bathroom, and my bed has never felt colder without her body heat underneath me.

I frightened her that first night, but she held her ground in the kitchen, squaring off with me, melting the steel cage around my heart just the slightest bit with her soft smile and cautious eyes.

But she's clearly afraid this morning.

Setting Rosie beside me, I slip from the couch and crawl over to Jenna, wrapping her in my arms and tugging her to my chest. "Babe."

"My baby had a gun," she mutters on repeat as I hold her against my naked chest.

With my heart racing underneath my skin, I rock her. "She's okay. You're okay." I repeat the phrase before adding, "I took care of everything."

Her head shakes against my pecs while her body vibrates in shock. I rub her upper arms, hoping to warm the pebbled chill settling over her skin. "It's okay now, babe. Just relax."

Suddenly, she stiffens and pulls back. "I am not your babe." Those dark eyes turn viper sharp. "And who the frick leaves a gun lying around?" Her use of frick would be cute if she weren't so spitting mad, eyes ensnaring me in her anger.

"I—" I *what?* Forgot they were in the apartment? I came home late, drunk and mad at everything because I was sharing my place with a feisty

31

raven-haired beauty and her two baby girls, and I'd had some thoughts of very *unmotherly* things I wanted to do to said beauty. Having energy to expel, I'd tossed my gun on the table after pulling the magazine and checking the chamber for any stray bullets. Then I placed a DVD in the old player. The performance did nothing to settle my raging hard-on and the fact a thin bedroom door separated me from a hot single mom I wanted to fuck.

And I couldn't go there with her.

You don't deserve to be loved. You're a despicable human. The words still haunt me although they shouldn't.

Then this morning, Jenna invades my dreams, giving me another stiffy to rival fence posts, sturdy trees, and sailing masts. Pick your pleasure for comparison. Her strangled voice calling my name interrupted the fantasy of that lush mouth of hers wrapped around my dick. But she wasn't choking on my length or girth like I wanted in my own version of *Naughty Teacher*, the porn video I'd found. Her high voice was distressed, and I knew the difference between pleasure and peril.

Entering the living room, finding her eyes full of fear and her baby holding my gun had my heart racing like propellers on a helicopter. Though I was confident the gun was empty, Jenna's panic-ridden eyes had me second-guessing myself. I'd never leave a loaded gun lying out in the open. Hell, I shouldn't have left the gun lying on the table, period. But the same woman scowling at me right now had me all tangled up inside. I quickly remind myself I should not be interested in her for a multitude of reasons.

"It wasn't loaded."

"That's not an answer," she yells.

Flinching at the sharpness of her tone, I loosen my hold on her.

"I'll put it in the safe." There's one in the main house. I have the magazine in my nightstand drawer, separating the bullets from the firearm, but the look on Jenna's face warns me that anything less than removing all parts of this gun would be unacceptable.

"You're a dangerous man," Jenna spews, and she isn't wrong.

Realistically, this is what I need. I need her to be afraid of me, keep her distance, and decide to get the fuck out of my apartment. I cannot spend two weeks with her. She's burrowed into my head, and I need her to climb back out because I cannot fuck her out of my system like I want.

"I don't like guns," she states.

"You don't say," I sarcastically respond. She's overreacting just a little bit. The gun was safely dismantled, but there is no point in arguing that Rosie was *not* in danger.

Jenna pushes at my chest, throwing me off balance at the sudden display of strength, and I release her, cursing under my breath as my left leg doesn't flex as well as it once did. She quickly stands and knocks into my shoulder with her knee as she rounds my body. Reaching for Rosie still perched on the couch cushion where I placed her, Jenna lifts her child and wraps her arms around her daughter. Rosie slips her little legs around her mother's waist. Squeezing Rosie tightly, Jenna pets her blond hair.

"Rosie, you know you should never, ever, *ever* touch a gun. What were you thinking?"

Rosie doesn't answer. She's crying into her mother's shoulder, unaware of her own danger, or maybe frightened now because of her mother's reaction.

Pressing Rosie back while still holding her, Jenna speaks to her daughter's face.

"Never ever *ever* touch a gun, Rosie. Never."

As Rosie cries harder, puckering her little face and leaning toward her mother, Jenna hugs her daughter again. Without a glance in my direction, she walks around the coffee table, stubbing her foot as she did the other night in the dark. *Damn, she's clumsy*.

And pissed. So fucking pissed.

"'Locks," I mutter at Jenna's back as she heads for the bedroom she shares with her daughters. Whirling around like a spinning top, she glares at me.

"Just what the hell were you thinking?" she snaps. "Who leaves a fricking gun out in the fracking open like that when there are children around?"

L.B. Dunbar

I never go anywhere without my gun, but she doesn't need to know that. Instead, I take her verbal beating even if I disagree with her current upset. She doesn't want an argument from me about how she was safe or how I'd never hurt her child. How I'd never put either of them in harm's way. She just wants to spew venom from those cock-worthy lips, which only turns me on more than it should.

But she was right. Leaving the gun on the table, where anyone could get to it, was a reckless thing to do. "I'm sorry."

"And what were you watching?" Her head nods toward the television, and I glance at the blank screen.

"When?" I choke, not understanding.

"Last night. That . . . *that*." She tips her head toward the set, and slowly, I recall the video I'd found.

"Were you listening?" My eyes squint back at her, mouth going dry. Does the real-life teacher want to live on the naughty side of life? Are there lessons she could teach me? I shake the inappropriate thoughts from my head.

"I wasn't listening, you pervert. My daughters happened to turn on the television, and that . . . that was playing." Her head nods once more in the direction of the set. Her hand presses her child's back like she's clutching a Bible to her chest. She can't even say *porn*, just like she can't say fuck.

"Were you jealous, babe?" I mock. I don't know why I say it and instantly regret it, but I'm riled up just like she is. I'm quick to remind myself Jenna isn't *someone else*. I don't need to play jealousy games with her. And reminding myself of these facts pulls forth something else. Something deep within me wants to comfort and assure her that I'd never hurt her or her girls. I don't want her to be envious either. Watching someone else go down on a guy will not dispel the sudden burn I feel within my belly when I look at her. Porn isn't going to quell the strange ache in the middle of my chest when I see her holding her child in mama-bear mode.

The only reason I put in the DVD I'd found on the shelf below the old player was because I couldn't rid this unrecognizable power the suddenly angry beauty seems to have over me. I needed something to relieve me, and a quick viewing of *Naughty Teacher* giving instructions on a blow job cleared my thoughts—for all of five minutes. Jenna haunted my dreams, wiping away the constant nightmares typically filling my head while I slept.

"I would never be jealous of that," she spits, tipping her head again at the blank screen.

With a body like hers, she wouldn't need to be, but where is her man and why he isn't here taking care of her, satisfying that rocking body and protecting her from idiots like me.

I don't have the chance to ask when she crosses the room with Rosie in her arms and the bedroom door slams, shutting me out, which is where I need to be.

Out of her head. Or her out of mine.

+ + +

"What are you doing in here?" Anna's voice interrupts me as I stand in what used to be our parents' bedroom. This wing was an addition to the main house, built when we were still young although I don't remember the age.

"I need to put my gun in the safe."

"You have a gun?" Anna squeaks, stepping up to me as I pop the picture frame on an old painting of the lake at sunset forward to reveal the safe.

"Yes, I have a gun," I reply, matter-of-factly. I have no idea if Ben ever told my sister what kinds of things I did. He'd been a good guy. I liked him, and I trusted him to take care of my family as I wasn't around much once he entered the scene. Guilt washes over me at the dark circles under my sister's eyes. She's endured too many losses in her young life. Our parents. Her husband.

"Are you into drugs?" Anna's question reminds me of when my mother asked the same thing. Anna even sounds exactly like my mother with that accusatory tone. More guilt presses on me. I should have been a better son and come home more often. I even missed my parents' funeral. Not on purpose, but I'd been on a mission. Only my father and

Ben had a general idea of where I was at any given time. The message of my parents' passing reached me too late. By the time I would have gained clearance to re-enter the States, I missed my chance to say a proper goodbye.

"How does having a gun equate to doing drugs?" I quickly enter the code for the safe but find it doesn't open.

"Are you in trouble?" Concern fills my sister's voice as she ignores my question.

"I'm not in trouble," I snap, growing frustrated as I try the code one more time. "And I don't do drugs." The only drugs I'm involved in are finding the illegal kind, the people who produce them, and investigating how they get into this country. Then shutting that shit down.

"What's with the gun, then?" Anna stands in *her* room with her hands on her hips like she has all day to wait out an answer.

"What's with this safe?" I bark, slowing my thick fingertips to press harder at each number as if that will make the code register.

"Ben changed the number." Anna shrugs. "I have the passcode somewhere."

Turning my head, I glare at my sister over my shoulder. "And might *I* have it?" My brow arcs. What does she think I'm doing here? Playing Tetris?

"Might you explain why you have a gun?" she sasses back as her brow hitches, mirroring mine. Our exchange reminds me so much of when we were kids, going tit for tat at one another. She might have been quiet, but my sister was fierce. I've missed her more than I've allowed myself to realize.

"I just have it." I sigh, deciding now isn't the time to go into the details of being in special ops for the Drug Enforcement Administration. I need to get back to Jenna and apologize. That woman has me all wound up. "But Rosie found it this morning, and 'Locks might feel safer if it's here. In the main house. In the safe." *Which I can't fricking open.*

"Who's 'Locks?" Anna asks.

I clear my throat before answering. "Jenna." She couldn't be Goldilocks because her hair was that midnight sky color, so 'Locks it is.

Anna shakes her head, moving on. "Rosie had your gun?" Her mouth falls open after she shrieks her question. "How the hell did that happen?"

"I left it out."

"You what?" If Anna hadn't punctured my eardrum with the first shrill squawk, she certainly did this time around, and I press a fingertip inside my ear. *Holy hell.*

"I don't need your sass," I bark. "I need the fricking code to this damn safe so I can lock up my gun." *Fricking?* Fuck, she has me doing it now too.

"Archer." Standing beside me, Anna chastises me in tone and body language. Hands on her hips. Scowl on her face.

"It wasn't loaded." The statement isn't an answer or an excuse, but I can't tell Anna the truth. *Because I'm a dumbass who forgot for a moment about the kids while I whacked off to thoughts of their mother.*

"Jenna has a real thing against guns." Anna's voice softens only an octave. "Her husband was shot."

"Fuck," I groan, tipping back my head. "What happened?"

"He was killed when Rosie was a baby and Talia was two."

Fuck. I slam my eyes closed and then pinch the bridge of my nose. "How come I don't remember Jenna?" They both mentioned being friends in college. Anna and I are three years apart, but I still think I'd remember her hot college gal-pal.

"We didn't meet until my junior year. Our friendship began when our education classes started."

I was definitely out by then, off in the police academy, but even if I hadn't been, I would have missed meeting Jenna. In my mid-twenties, I had other things on my mind than settling down with a woman and having a couple of kids. I lacked commitment, and I definitely hadn't desired children. At forty-five, I was in the same position, especially after my recent mission.

So why can't I stop thinking about the woman invading my apartment?

My sister's phone dings from her back pocket, and she quickly pulls it forward to read a text. "What else did you do?" She looks up in horror.

"What do you mean?"

"Jenna sent me a text. She said she's taking the girls on an adventure, and I shouldn't count on them for dinner. She's missing out on Monday manicures and margaritas." She growls. "She needs this break, Archer, so what else did you do?"

"Why the hell is this my fault?" However, I scratch the back of my neck, chagrined, noting once again the darkness under my sister's eyes. *Fuck.* I really screwed up. I swallow hard before admitting the rest of the story. "The girls might have accidentally turned on a porn video."

"What?!" Anna shrieks again, and there goes the other eardrum. "How does a three-year-old accidentally turn on porn?"

"I found a DVD in the television stand and popped it in the old player. I guess the player was still on this morning, and when Talia turned on the TV, the video started up where it left off last night." Once the naughty teacher got the rocks off her student, I was done, so I don't know what happened next.

"Oh, my God, Archer. If Jenna decides not to be my friend anymore, I will never forgive you."

"It wasn't mine," I defend, turning fully to face my sister.

"Then whose was it?" Skepticism drips from the question.

"Mason was the last person to live there," I remind her. Anna scrunches her face, disgusted while concerned. *Yeah, pretty boy has a fetish for hot teachers.* Bet he calls out her name—Mrs. Kulis—forgetting the last name belongs to his best friend. I shiver with the thought. Mason Becker is a prick.

"Look, I messed up. I get it, and I just want to put my gun in this safe, okay? I want Jenna to feel safe." I don't know why I tack on the last sentence, but there's more truth in those words than I'm ready to admit. I don't like what I've learned about her husband. I also don't appreciate my sister scolding me like she's my mother. If we're going to have any kind of relationship, she needs to get over treating me like I'm an irresponsible kid.

"So could we maybe get the code for this thing?" I nod at the exposed safe while Anna eyes me. At one point, my sister and I were close. Zack Weller had been one of Anna's best friends, and his older brother, Noah, had been one of mine. Our group was tight despite the age differences. I had to keep assholes at bay from my shy sister. My youngest one, Amelia, was the wildcat, yet I was the one most people thought caused all the trouble.

"Let me look in Ben's desk."

My head falls forward, realizing this could take a bit. Anna should have codes in a secure location on her phone for easy access or, better yet, memorized.

"Why don't you just know this off the top of your head?"

"I just don't know, Archer. Maybe because I have a million other things up there, and remembering the code to a safe I don't use isn't one of them."

Guilt arrives in another crushing wave. My sister is one of the most capable people. She's always had a quiet exterior, but she's certainly grown a tougher shell over the years. I credit Ben with building her confidence, making her feel strong enough to express herself, and the thought of Ben reminds me why she doesn't recall a simple four-digit safe code. Still, I could do with a little less of her sass.

"I'm sorry," I say, choking on the apology. "Could you *please* find the code?"

"Where is the gun right now?"

"In the waistband of my pants." Readily admitting such a thing isn't something I'd typically do, but I also don't think pulling the piece forward will make my sister comfortable. She takes a step back as if I have presented the weapon to her, though, and wrinkles her nose again.

"Archer," she softly groans, tilting her head at me.

"Anna," I mock back like I did when we were teens. There's more in her name than just sassing her back, though. I need her to cut me some slack here as I'm trying to do the right thing by making Jenna feel safe.

She must sense my frustration because her lips twist like she's fighting between a sly smile and a scolding scowl. "Okay, Ben's desk."

With a touch of finality in her tone, she once again sounds like our mother. Turning on her heels, she spins toward a small room attached to the main bedroom, and I snap the painting back into place to cover the safe. Taking a second, I gaze around the bedroom—once my parents' respite, separate from the rest of the house. Not a trace of their belongings remains, but their presence lingers in the echo of my sister's voice and her appearance. She's our mother in so many ways, and I'd give anything for one more day with my folks. I'd really like a chat with my dad about how to handle a single mother afraid of guns when guns are part of my business.

Then again, minding my own business and steering clear of said woman might be the only sound advice because that hot single mother is the last thing I need.

5

[Jenna]

"Where the hell have you been?" The gruff tone in the dark living room startles me, but the hundred-pound weight of a sleeping child, hardly twenty pounds soaking wet, is weighing me down. Rosie and Talia had fallen asleep in the car after a long day of sunshine and a late-night movie in the park. In order to escape the man snapping at me, we'd driven a few towns over to the state park with a lighthouse to spend the day. The beach offered movies after dark, and Monday evening is kids' night, so we stayed to watch *The Little Mermaid* projected on an inflatable outdoor screen.

Before I even answer Archer's brisk question, he exhales deeply and asks another one with a touch more concern in his tone. "Where's Talia?" He leans forward from his position on the couch, tipping his head as if he can see around me.

"She's still in the car. I can only carry one child at a time." Hiking up the stairs was a challenge, and I was making *Sophie's Choice* when deciding which child to carry up the staircase first. Rosie was easier to maneuver, plus she was smaller, but she was also like an octopus of loose limbs and dead weight. As I'd parked just outside the garage at the base of the stairs, I would only be leaving Talia for a few minutes in the private driveway.

"I'll get her." Archer stands. He moves with that lightning speed he exhibited this morning, and with his stature large and imposing, I flinch at the sudden motion. He winces, and his hand goes to his upper left thigh. He doesn't miss the sudden tension in my body.

"Babe? You don't trust me with your kid?" Not only is his voice rough like sandpaper, but it's also full of defensiveness I don't need at this late hour. It's been a long day of avoiding him and wrestling with my thoughts.

You're a dangerous man. That's what I'd told him this morning, but deep down, I didn't believe it. Irresponsible. Reckless. Maybe even selfish, but not truly dangerous. I'd known a dangerous man once. Then again, I'd been fooled by him. *Fool me once, shame on you; fool me twice, shame on me.*

It won't happen again.

"I—" I don't want to fight with him. I'm exhausted and crabby, and I'd love a hot bath and a stiff drink. "I'd appreciate the help." Swallowing around the admission, Archer's expression softens only slightly from its hard edge. He nods once, and I step toward the bedroom to lay Rosie down on a bed. *How can someone so delicate feel like a sack of bricks?*

No time passes before I have Rosie straightened on the bed, and Archer enters the room with Talia in his arms. She's dead weight as well, but she's plastered to his chest—arms around his neck, legs dangling under his forearm—and for a moment, my heart aches at all that Ryan missed. He didn't get to see how Talia grows smarter every day or how Rosie has his fearlessness. He doesn't know that the dark blob of hair on Rosie's head turned bright blond like his own or how Talia has his nose.

However, there's something about watching Archer placing my eldest daughter on the opposite bed. The grace with which he moves despite his large body. The gentleness he exudes in laying her down. The tenderness he shows as he begins the tasks I was ready to take on to prepare her for sleep. He removes her sandals and smooths down her sundress. After pulling up the light blanket, he sweeps a thick hand over her dark hair, brushing the locks off her forehead. He focuses on her face for only a second, but I'm struck by the idea that I could fall for a man who looks at my child like he is.

Once he stands upright, he catches me observing him, and I chew my lower lip in confusion. I'm still angry with him. The gun. The porn. But my thoughts conflict with the soft kindness he just showed my daughter.

As I've placed Rosie on the second bed, Archer looks around the room. "Where do you sleep?"

"With her." I nod at Rosie, who has commandeered the entire bed with sprawled limbs. It might be sofa-city for me tonight if my roommate doesn't need it for another private porn-viewing session.

Archer tips his head, signaling I should follow him to the outer room. After a final glance at my girls and one more kiss to each of their sleepy heads, I enter the living room. Archer has tossed himself on one couch, slouching into the cushions, and I note the bottle of whiskey and a short glass before him on the coffee table. The television was off when I entered the apartment, but I immediately wonder if he was watching porn again.

"Come here, 'Locks." The depth of his voice in the quiet, dark room sends a shiver down my spine. Not a warning ripple but a rush of heat and longing. Longing for a man to look at me as something other than a mother or a teacher. He playfully pats the cushion beside him, and I lower onto it as he leans forward and pours a sliver of amber alcohol into the glass. Holding the short tumbler up to me, I take it from him.

"I want to apologize for earlier." His gruff voice is softer than normal, and my lower belly is a flock of seagulls taking to the air. "I shouldn't have left the gun on the table and . . . the video. It isn't mine."

I don't ask for clarification of who else it could belong to. This *is* his apartment.

"Anna told me about your husband."

"Jeez. Jumping straight to the hard topics," I mutter before taking a sip of the offered whiskey. The alcohol burns as it goes down, but after the initial shock, the liquid flame instantly warms my insides. It's also an analogy for Archer. He shocks. He warms. He burns. However, fire dies out eventually.

His silence suggests he wants the story, and I swallow around the truth.

"It was my fault." Instantly, I recall the argument Ryan and I had that night.

"That can't possibly be true."

I shrug while tipping my head forward. My hair falls around my face, curtaining me behind the long strands as I stare at the empty glass in my hands. Archer reaches for the bottle and pours me another sliver of alcohol, only the sliver is deeper this round, and I take a dainty sip compared to my previous gulp.

"I was upset he'd been out with friends, and I'd been home all day with the girls. Rosie was only a baby, and I was struggling with the adjustment of having two children." Ryan liked to have a good time, and we had a decent understanding of one another needing a break. He worked at the local marina while I taught high school English, but I was on maternity leave. The transition from one child to two had been difficult for me. "I needed baby formula, and I didn't want to pack up the girls earlier in the day to go to the store. Ryan was supposed to get some on his way home. He forgot, so I made him go back out. The gas station along the highway was open all night, and it was our emergency run location. One canister would get us through the night until I could get to the store the following day."

I take another sip of the spicy alcohol.

"From the report, Ryan entered the gas station while the holdup was in progress. He startled the gunman as he entered and was shot." I close my eyes only briefly before opening them to rid the images that play out every time I imagine what happened. "The gunman was a good shot. Ryan was killed instantly." *Shot through the heart.* The gunman said it hadn't been his intention. He was aiming for Ryan's arm. What was the difference? In my opinion, a man wielding a gun and aiming it at another human being only has one intention.

I take a deeper pull of the whiskey, and Archer brushes back my hair, scooping it around my ear. "I'm sorry that happened to him. I'm sorry it happened to you."

I'm sorry. So many times, those words meant so little. Ryan and I fought and made up as couples do. We'd said *I'm sorry* a hundred ways, but I'd never been truly forlorn until pushing him to go back out for that baby formula. That night was the first time Rosie slept through the night. She'd even slept through the police knocking on my door, and my screams as they delivered the news that changed my life.

Archer's fingers continue to comb down the length of my hair, brushing his knuckles over my shoulder and along my arm. Uneasy with his comfort, I eventually pull away and press my shoulder into the couch back, angling my face to look over at him.

"Thank you." What else can you say when someone expresses their sympathy?

"The gun is in the house, in a safe." He searches my face as he speaks. "I want you to know I'd never hurt you or your girls. I'd protect you against anything ever happening to you. You're safe with me, babe."

It's a nice sentiment, but no one is one-hundred-percent secure. Slipping and falling to your death in your bathtub is reportedly a higher likelihood than being shot in a random gas station robbery along a remote highway. Still, I nod to accept his protective statement.

"So tell me something about you?" I lift the crystal glass to my lips and take a swallow of the fiery alcohol.

"Jeez, going for the hard topics." Archer mocks my statement, but something soft fills that rugged voice of his. "Not much to share." The crack in his voice is subtle but present. He's lying.

"Why do I sense you have lots you *could* share but won't?"

He gives me a knowing smirk. "Because you're right. I won't."

That's honesty. He isn't going to offer any admissions even though I've just told him about my husband's passing, one of the most painful memories I have. I've obviously made a mistake thinking opening up to Archer would crack the façade on him and give me a peek into the mystery he is.

I hum in response and return to thoughts of Ryan. My lids are so heavy, matching the ache in my heart at the reminder of Ryan's absence from my life.

It was all my fault.

Once upon a time, I was a woman who bragged about independence and girl power, but deep down, I'd wanted to settle down. Despite being a wayward woman, I knew I could channel that wild to one person. I'd just need the right man to settle on me. He had to understand me. He had to support me. He had to love me. That person had been Ryan.

We were slightly older by our small town's ideal of *get married young* and *start a family early*. I'd been thirty-six when I met Ryan, and ours was an instant connection. I was growing uncertain I'd have the relationship I desired, but within months, we were married, pregnant, and building a future. My closest friends—Tricia, Britton, even Henry—had all gotten married before me. For Tricia and Britton, they were on their second marriages, and I hadn't even experienced a first. Then Ryan sailed into town, taking over his uncle's marina.

"I was worried about you today." Archer's tight tone breaks into my memories, and my heavy lids lift. His back slouches into the cushions. His bare feet are on the low table before the couch, ankles crossed. He spoke so softly I wasn't certain I heard him correctly. He's fiddling with the medal I've seen dangling off that silver chain around his neck, and I'd love a closer look. Reaching over, I hesitate.

"May I?"

Placing the medallion flat in his palm, he angles his hand so I can see the item better. An inverted sword looks like a cross with angel wings on either side of the crossbar on a circular disc.

"What does it mean?"

"It's St. Michael. For protection."

"The archangel? The slayer of evil."

"The very man."

"The very angel," I tease. "Although I don't ever recall seeing emblems of him like this. He's usually draped in a robe with extended angel wings and stabbing at something, like a snake."

Archer narrows his eyes at the object. "This is incognito. Keeping me safe without giving away which saint is offering protection."

"And you needed protecting?" I arch a brow.

"I was once a police officer. Michael is our patron saint."

I nod, a little confused. "But you need to hide that he's protecting you?"

Archer's head snaps upright, and he stares at me. "I used to be in hiding, but now I'm not." He pauses, staring down at the medallion in his palm. Then he closes his fingers around the sacred item and tucks it back into his shirt. Tipping back his head on the couch cushion, he lowers his lids, and in the quietest voice, he adds, "I'm through pretending."

I have no idea what that means, but my own lids weigh heavy, and after a final sip of whiskey, I can't seem to open them to ask Archer for further explanation. It's been a long day.

I'm drifting in one of Ryan's boats on the lake, and a smile crosses my lips. It's a glorious summer day and hot. So hot, the heat is almost too much. The sunshine permeates my skin, and I breathe in the sunny scent of man. My man.

Only he feels bigger, harder, more defined, and his scent is different. His T-shirt is soft and worn. His chest smooth and firm beneath the cotton. His hand coasts up my back, tugging me closer to him. I can't seem to open my eyes, and I want to look into his, which match the blue sky overhead.

"I'll protect you from anything, even me," he says, but the voice is wrong. The sound too rough, the gravelly tenor not Ryan's.

Again, I want to look into his eyes, but the ones I envision next are dark and deep, like midnight over the water. The tide is suddenly steady, the boat no longer rocking, and a rhythmic beat thumps at my ear, mixing with the lulling sound of the lake waves.

Shaking my head, I will my lids to lift as I pull back from the body holding me.

Suddenly, I realize I'm not adrift in a boat or even in the sunshine of day. The night is still cloaked in darkness, and the body giving off the heat and sunshine has me pinned between him and a couch cushion at my back. My face is buried in the softest cotton over hard pecs and a racing heartbeat that belong to none other than . . . Archer.

6

[Archer]

I don't know why I mentioned the archangel or the protective symbol of the cross at my chest. I'd been given a more traditional St. Michael charm on a silver chain when I first joined the force but quickly had to find something less obvious for undercover work. St. Michael medallions screamed cop. With the sword and the wings, I could say it was any angel to someone unsuspecting, but for some reason, I told Jenna the truth.

I was done pretending. Only I didn't know what exactly that meant.

Lying on the couch, I sense someone watching me, and open my eyes to find the questioning gaze of one hot mama positioned between me and the couch back. Her leg is hitched over my hip, and my hand rests under her thigh, fingers digging into the flesh to tug her closer to my dick.

"Hey." My morning voice is groggy.

After Jenna spilled her story, she wanted something from me, but I didn't know what to give. I didn't want to tell her anything about myself, and suddenly, I realized I didn't know who I was. I had nothing but hard topics with hard limits. I'd been lost in that thought when she drifted off to sleep beside me, still sitting upright, still holding the glass of whiskey on her lap.

She was so beautiful, so exhausted, and so absent yesterday. I'd wrestled with constant thoughts that wavered between concern and confusion. Why had she run away for the day? Where had she been? And finally, as the night grew later, what was keeping her? My imagination ran to the extreme.

I'd been hardened enough in my past to know the worst was never the worst, but still, I already had this strange, strong desire to protect Jenna and her little ones. The longer she'd been away yesterday, the deeper my imagination dug. I hadn't meant to snap at her when she entered the apartment, and I hadn't missed the reacting flinch, similar to the one she'd displayed the first night we met. Her response told me someone had hit her in the past, and if her husband wasn't already dead,

I'd bury him myself. Still, she spoke of him fondly, taking on the burden of his death when it was clearly anything but her fault. She wouldn't have been half as heartbroken at his loss if her man was hurting her, though.

However, women can lie. They could cover up emotions just as quickly as they could express them. My last mission proved such a thing.

"Why am I on the couch with you?" Caution mixes with confusion in her voice, and on reflex, my fingers squeeze the fleshy part behind her upper thigh.

"You passed out on me."

"I did?" Her brows lift.

Maybe not exactly *on me*, which would have been pleasurable. However, we'd been mid conversation. Then again, we weren't talking. We were just sitting beside one another, each with our own thoughts. Being near Jenna was comforting, quiet, and peaceful without any bickering, attempts at jealousy, or blatant lies. I was so tired of pretending—pretending I cared during my last mission when I hadn't. Guilt was what I felt, according to my therapy sessions.

Attempting to move Jenna last night, she'd slid to her side, and I decided to adjust her position on the couch. As uncomfortable as the cushions might be, the old sofa offered her more room than a twin bed shared with her kid. I could have carried her to my bed, but then I knew I'd want to crawl in next to her, which I couldn't do. I had every intention of leaving her alone on the couch.

Then she reached for my tee, holding the thin material like I was her personal life preserver, and she was floating out to sea. She tugged at me with strength I wouldn't have expected from a sleeping body, and I gave in to the temptation to be close to her. I just wanted to hold her. Or maybe I wanted her to hold me. Folding to my side, I curled her into my chest and clung to her like my own lifesaving buoy.

Her palm eventually flattened over my racing heart, and her body sank into the mold of mine, melding her curves against my planes.

She fit. I liked the fit.

"Passed out in the middle of speaking, 'Locks," I clarify.

Her eyes widen. "What did I say?" Her own groggy tone does nothing to settle the raging hard-on in my jeans, standing at attention and begging to salute her. I should get myself under control, but I can't pass on this opportunity to mess with her a little bit.

"You told me your darkest secret," I tease, and her eyes narrow.

"Really?" she says in a smoky morning voice. "And what would that be?"

"You don't know your own deepest thought?" Leaning away only an inch, I give us distance I don't want because all I want is to close my lips over hers and see if she tastes as sweet as she smells. Something fruity and fresh tickles my nose. I want to savor the fragrance, wear it on my tongue, and lick it off my fingers.

"Enlighten me," she quietly suggests as the corners of those lush lips curve upward.

"You want me." Bold, direct, and highly unlikely, I've planted a seed. *Do I want her to want me?*

"Hardly." She snorts. Her cute nose wrinkles, and I can't help myself. I lean forward and kiss the tip. This causes her to pull back, but there's nowhere to go. She's trapped between my large body and the cushion behind her. We're snug with two long bodies on this old couch, but as I've said, I like the fit.

"Yeah. Who'd want a strapping man, ripe with desire to please you and give you what you need." *Why am I flirting with her?* However, her leg hitches higher against my hip, and my fingers dig deeper into her upper thigh. She's flirting with trouble, and that trouble is me.

"Strapping man? Are we living in the 1800s? You sound like Gaston." She's teasing me, dropping her voice as she lowers her gaze to my mouth.

"Should I know what that is?"

"He's not a what. He's a who in Disney's *Beauty and the Beast*, and he's more a beast than the Beast."

"If any of that made sense to me, you might have crushed my ego."

"It's so big, I doubt it'd hurt." Her mouth curls into a delicious smile.

I softly chuckle. She has no idea how much she could hurt me, but I don't hint at it.

You don't deserve to be loved. I chase away the damning thought.

Instead, I hold up a thick hand and pinch my forefinger and thumb together in a teasing gesture. "Maybe just a wee bit."

Jenna huffs again, and I brush back the hairs slipping over her cheek. Watching the motion of my fingers sliding through those silky locks around her ear, I catch another whiff of her fruity scent, and my mouth waters for a sip of her, which is strange because I don't kiss, not on the mouth anyway.

A moment passes before she speaks. "And what is it you think I need? How could you please me?"

Direct and to the point again, I'd say she's in need of getting laid. However, I won't project my own desires on her.

"I'd start by kissing you." Still flirting with her, I drop my voice as quiet as I can with such a deep tenor. Her eyes widen, and her lips part just the slightest bit. My mouth salivates. My heart gallops. *What is this crazy sensation?* I don't kiss lips, but I want to kiss hers. I want to savor her.

"And you think your kiss would please me?" She swallows, and my fingers glide down the column of her throat and under her chin.

Staring at her mouth, I reconsider my hard limit on kissing. "I do." *Or will it please me to finally kiss someone after all these years?*

"You think I need that?"

"Absolutely." *Or is it that I need to be kissed?*

I focus on her lips before stroking up her chin and rubbing my thumb over the plumpness of her bottom lip. What would she taste like? How would it feel? Chewing on my own lip, I lean forward, ready to strike, but pause, hovering over her mouth.

"What are you doing?" Her quiet voice strains between question and desire. Her tongue sweeps over her bottom lip, and I groan.

"Waiting on you to stop me." *Please don't let her stop me.* But I shouldn't be doing this.

"Mommy, I need to go to the bathroom."

Jenna groans, closes her eyes for a second, and then pops upward on an elbow.

"Be right there, baby." Her voice strains.

I lean back, balancing on the very edge of the couch. *Holy shit.* My heart races, and the reality of what I'd almost done hits me. I almost kissed her. I almost broke my hard-and-fast rule not to kiss on the mouth. Not ever.

I should move. I should jump from the couch, giving her a wide berth, but I can't. The wedge in my pants is swollen to aching, extending the zipper enough I might have metal zipper bites on my dick.

"This is why I don't need you kissing me." All teasing from her tone is gone. The flirting is finished. Jenna presses against my chest to lift herself higher, and I roll to my back, hitching her body over mine by my hands on her hips. We're a struggle of limbs in an effort not to fall off the couch, and for a brief second, Jenna straddles my middle. Her thighs spread wide, and her heat hits the throbbing bulge in serious need of relief.

I hiss. "You'll pay for that," I warn while Jenna presses two hands to my chest and lugs her leg over me. Swiping a hand down my face, I meet Rosie's sleepy gaze across the room.

"Morning, princess," I call out to her in a voice full of desire for her mother. I watch Jenna's ass while she crosses the room to her daughter. Shit, I need to get myself together. I was nearly dry humping the woman on the couch with her kids in the next room. Not that I'm opposed to dry humping, but I'm too old for that shit. I want wet and dripping, without kids in a fifty-mile radius. Slowly, I rise, sitting on the edge of the couch with my knees spread wide and my head lowered.

"Why was Mommy sleeping on the couch with you?" My head pops up to find Talia standing on the other side of the coffee table. Her little face scowls, mimicking an expression I'm certain she learned from her mother. She's such a mini-Jenna. The imitation reminds me of my own sister and her copycat antics of our mother.

Struggling to find an answer to her question, I state what I think is the best explanation. "She had a bad dream."

Talia looks over my shoulder to where Jenna has led Rosie to the bathroom. *She's potty trained, right?* I don't know enough about kids, so I can't even guess the ages of Jenna's daughters, but I hope I'm safe to say they both are housebroken.

Talia's suspicious eyes narrow before she glances back at me. "I didn't think Mom was having them anymore."

The comment surprises me. The child before me is wise beyond her years. Not wanting to play into her concerns, I build around my story.

"It wasn't a bad-*bad* one, but she didn't want to wake you."

Talia's hands grip the sides of her nightgown. "She climbs into bed with me when she's scared."

The statement leaves me wondering what frightens her mother. Was there more to the loss of her husband? I recall her flinching behavior. Is she involved with someone now who hurts her? I was ready to kiss the woman without knowing anything about her. I'm physically attracted to Jenna, and that typically doesn't stop me, but Jenna doesn't feel like a kiss and cut out kind of woman. She's the type you plant your roots with, and I'm not into planting. She checks off all the boxes of what I do not want. Commitment. Kids. Complicated sex.

Still not certain how to address the kid before me, glaring at me like I've disturbed some sacred ritual, I'm freed from further explanation when Jenna returns, walking a sleepy Rosie back to the sitting area.

"Early risers," she states, and for half a second, I think she means the stiffy in my jeans. "Let's find you something appropriate to watch this morning."

I turn toward the window and notice the sky lightening. It can't be more than six. "What the hell time is it?"

"You said a bad word," Rosie mutters around her thumb, returned to her mouth for safekeeping. Isn't she too old to be sucking her thumb? I do not know enough about kids to get involved with a single mother. Then again, no one said *involved,* and that's my cue to stand from the couch and slip my hands into my pockets to disguise *my* early riser and excuse myself.

"I'm going to bed," I mutter, leaving Jenna to collapse on the couch and reach for the remote.

"How about *Beauty and the Beast*? That Beast is more strapping than Gaston any day."

I'll show her a beast. I snort at the comparison to some animated character I don't know. When I reach my room, I glance back at the couch, noticing Rosie's head rests on Jenna's arm, and Talia sits close to her mother. The three of them look like a sweet unit, and I'm back to pretending if I ever think I can be a part of their little team.

On that thought, I close the bedroom door and toss myself onto my bed.

+ + +

Anna invites me to spend the day at the beach with her and the reunion crew.

Zack and River. Logan and Autumn. Mason, Jenna, and Anna.

I'm the odd man out.

"Bryce and Calvin haven't seen you since you've returned." My nephews are nearly sixteen and eighteen, and Calvin heads off to college this fall. Remembering when I went off to school, I assume Anna's struggling as our own mother did when I left, especially as I never officially returned home. Although it's natural to fly from the nest, the loss will be another source of heartbreak for my sister. However, she eagerly did the same thing after graduating high school.

Thinking of the boys adds another layer of guilt to the one generated by my long-standing absence. They need a father figure, and I'm certain Ben knew it when he sent me a final message. A few weeks after his death, an email arrived from his sister. It explained how Ben had written his friends each a note to be distributed after his passing. They were the four points of a compass—Ben, Mason, Logan, and Zack—and I was not part of that instrument, but Autumn explained that her brother still had something to say to me.

Be home.

The phrase didn't make sense. He had to mean *come home*. Either way, the message slathered on that guilt even thicker, but my work had been important for the past two decades. I'd helped bring down some bad people, hoping to keep more than one kid off the streets and away from the hard stuff by cutting off the source. I did it so kids like Bryce and Calvin could have a clean future despite their privilege. And let's be honest, they were privileged, which meant they had the means to afford the shit hitting the streets. I didn't want that crap anywhere near my family, though, and I justified my work as a necessity for them. To keep them safe. Despite the distance in years and miles, I did what I did for my family.

The timing of Ben's directive was ironic. I only wish it hadn't been because of his death. He had asked me plenty of other times when I planned to return home, always keeping the door open for me, but the timing never felt imperative until it became the only possibility. After Autumn's email, I sent her the address of a post office box where I could receive the letter. The sliver of cardstock inside a sealed envelope arrived without further explanation. The only information Autumn offered was I had a year to complete the directive. The year was up. I was late again.

The concept seemed like a bunch of hocus-pocus to me until what happened shortly after receiving the note. By then, Anna had moved into the house, and I didn't want to be a burden to her. I needed to get better, *be better*, before I came here. I should just tell Anna what happened to me. Confess everything. The absent years. The current situation. My job. My history. But I wouldn't even know where to begin.

"Yeah, okay," I mutter in response to Anna's statement, knowing I actually do want to learn more about my nephews even if one is about to head off to college. "So, what's the plan today?"

"Day drinking," Mason Becker calls from behind me, and I turn to see the playboy friend of Ben's I've never liked. I didn't understand why Ben kept him around. Anna liked to remind me that Ben saw positive things in people others didn't. I'd often wondered if he saw something in me I didn't recognize in myself. Then again, Ben hardly knew me— not what I did, where I'd been or why—and I didn't need his approval. I was Anna's brother. Blood for life through thick or thin.

"Help carry coolers," Anna directs while Mason helps himself to coffee. I don't have a clue what the other guys received in their letters from Ben, and I don't care what their instructions are as long as it doesn't involve Mason getting near my sister. He was near enough, having lived in my apartment, helping Ben and Anna through Ben's last year.

"I found a few things of yours left behind in my place," I snap at the pretty boy, fluffing his artfully curled hair. I swear he probably used a hair dryer and curling iron on those copper locks.

"Pretty sure I cleared everything out. Even had the place cleaned." Mason winks at me, implying his junk touched my sheets and left behind evidence of his doings.

"It's a video." I level my eyes at Mason, hinting I know his secret, but he stares back at me.

"I don't make videos. You never know where that shit might end up."

Anna drops a water bottle and squeaks as she separates her feet to avoid the jug hitting her toes.

"Dude," I hiss as Mason chuckles at the suggestion of sex tapes.

"What am I missing?" Zack asks as he enters the kitchen area while Anna retrieves the water bottle from the floor and continues to pack a cooler. Noting my sister's activity, Zack rounds the island. "I told you, River and I would handle all beverages. We aren't here to invade."

The soft reminder hints at the reason they are here. The anniversary of Ben's death.

"River's pregnant. She shouldn't be doing anything," Anna counters.

Zack snorts. "Try telling her that and be prepared for a verbal ass-whipping." He reaches out for the water bottle in my sister's hand and gently presses her to the side, taking over the packing of the cooler.

"Make yourself useful," he demands of Mason, who leans his hip against the island, sipping his coffee but eyeing my sister.

"We were discussing Mason's porn collection and how I found a few videos in the apartment," I offer.

Zack stills before standing upright to face one of his oldest friends. "Aren't you a little old for porn?"

"Never too old," Mason jokes. That might be the one thing I agree with him on, although my viewing days are few and far between. Finding that video had been a fluke.

"Must we discuss your sex life so early in the morning?" Anna mutters, busying her hands by rinsing a pan in the sink.

"We aren't discussing my sex life period because I don't have one." Mason speaks with such a serious tone even I almost believe him.

"Please," Zack huffs, chuckling as he returns to filling the cooler.

"I'm serious," Mason argues, but none of us believe him. Not only could he be a male model but he might also be a damn good actor. However, he's in construction. "Isn't that why Jenna's here? You want me to get laid."

Several things happen in unison. Zack groans, "Dude." Anna drops the pan she was rinsing in the sink, and I take a few steps forward, ready to reach over the island and throat-punch Mason.

"That ship sailed," Jenna announces to the kitchen, and my neck cranes, catching her entering the room in a see-through dress which does nothing to disguise her body or the bathing suit underneath. The gauzy material outlines her long, lean form and accentuates those long, lean legs. Oh, hell no, to Mason getting anywhere near her.

"What does that mean?" I growl as she pauses near the kitchen counter. Jenna locks eyes with Mason only briefly before turning to Anna.

"Can I help with anything?"

You can start by telling me what the fuck? Did Jenna sleep with Mason?

"You know you can't resist me," Mason teases, walking over to Jenna and rubbing at her hair like a beloved puppy.

"I resist you every time I see you in Elk Lake City," Jenna deadpans, shifting out from under his touch.

"All a ploy to reel me closer."

"Keep dreaming," Jenna states, glancing up at him with a scowl.

"I do dream. I *so* dream." His eyes follow Jenna, who walks over to Anna, but if I didn't know better, I'd guess his gaze drifts from my woman to my sister. *Wait.* Back that up. Not my woman, my roommate. The woman I dream about, and what a dream it had been when I fell back into bed for an hour this morning. Those lush lips parted. Those tight legs around my hips. The tease of heat over my lap, drawing me into her depths.

Fuck. I need to stop thinking about her.

Slipping my fists into my pockets, I ask, "Where are my girls?" As if I possess Jenna's daughters. Everything in the kitchen seems to stop at my question. Jenna freezes. Anna spins to face me. Zack stills.

"Do you mean Rosie and Talia?" Zack asks, a brow hitching upward.

"Yep. The little princesses."

"They're in the driveway with Mila and Lorna," Jenna answers.

"Party people. Logan in the house." The announcement wallows into the kitchen before Logan is actually present, but his party people persona dies once I see him holding a baby in his arms. The little guy sucks two fingers and glances over his shoulder at all of us before dipping his head into his father's neck. *Baby Ben.* Everywhere is a reminder of my sister's loss, but she crosses the kitchen and ducks her head to speak quietly to the shy child. She's so good with kids—always has been—and it's the reason she wanted to be a teacher.

My gaze drifts to Jenna, recalling she does the same thing as my sister, teaching high school students. Then I shift my attention to Mason, narrowing my eyes and pointing two fingers at my eyes before swiveling my hand in his direction. He good-naturedly chuckles before giving me the middle finger over Jenna's head. He has no idea how much I'll fuck him up if he considers playing with her. And I definitely need to know if he touched her.

"Beach time," Anna announces to the room as she trails a hand down little Ben's back, and I agree it's time for some fresh air.

7

[Jenna]

I shouldn't be self-conscious in my bathing suit. I've had two children, for heaven's sake, which means my breasts sag a bit, and my stomach isn't flat. Not to mention, my hips are more accentuated than they once were. However, the way Archer's eyes keep shifting to me makes me anxious. The one-piece suit is halter style with a deep V between my breasts and large straps that tie behind my neck. The midnight blue material is nothing unique, yet I'd splurged on the suit for this vacation. Now, I'm second-guessing the decision. My nipples are continually erect under Archer's gaze, and I constantly check the breast coverage, hoping a boob hasn't sprung free.

A day at the beach with Ben's friends is entertaining. They razz one another as if they are still twenty-two instead of forty-two, keeping up a stream of insults and jokes. I wait for the moment Ben's shenanigans with these men will turn into sour memories, but it never happens. The laughter continues. The stories inflate, and the time passes with pleasant reminders of their best friend.

My thoughts drift to that first year after Ryan's death and how I felt when people spoke about him. I note that Anna smiles through the teasing tales and encourages details for events I'm certain she already knows by heart.

Then they recall a story about me.

"Remember when we had to come rescue you from that dance?" Logan teases, and I shake my head, eyes drifting to Archer. I don't need these guys telling embarrassing tales about me. "You were such a wild woman, Jenna Babenna. Making all the boys crazy."

I softly chuckle at the reminder of being young, free, and a little reckless, but I don't need a retelling of this story. My eyes meet Archer's across our circle of Adirondack chairs on the beach, and he arches one brow, curiosity in his expression.

"What was that guy's name?" Mason snaps his fingers, and I close my eyes, already knowing where this is leading. Zack laughs.

"Richard Ball," I mutter under my breath, pausing a beat until the name registers.

"*Dickie* Ball," Zack repeats. "I wonder whatever happened to him."

"No," Archer hisses. His face widens into the first genuine smile I've seen on him. It's . . . glorious as his face relaxes.

"He's probably still pining over losing our Jenna," Mason teases, answering Zack.

My face flames, and the bright sunshine is not my excuse.

"Honest to God," Logan raises a hand as if taking a pledge to address Archer's questioning smile. "He had it hard for Jenna."

Jeez. I shake my head. Richard had been one of many bad decisions I made in college.

"Dick Ball," Mason states, dropping his voice. "I heard he had a son named Cockin."

Zack groans. Logan laughs.

"That is not true," I retort, chuckling myself at the poor choice some people make in naming a child.

"My memory might be fuzzy," Mason states, completely serious in tone. Then he snaps his fingers. "Oh wait, that was his other child."

Anna chortles. I shake my head again, fighting a grin.

"He was a cocky little dick," Logan adds. "That's why we had to save you."

My lids lower a second, remembering how I gave my date the slip, telling him I needed to use the bathroom and then called Anna to get me out of that fraternity. I'd overheard him telling his friends how he knew he wasn't going to have any trouble convincing me to sleep with him that night. Then he grabbed his crotch like he was well hung or overcompensating for small things as most braggarts do. That was my hint to get out. Anna brought the entourage of Ben and friends, which added to my embarrassment. I hated to date and dash, but Richard Ball really did have my creep meter rising, and I will not mention rising or his name in the same sentence around these guys.

"I heard they erected a statue in his honor somewhere on campus," Mason continues, and Logan snorts, beer spewing out of his mouth.

"Where? Why?" I ask, unable to imagine a physical homage to the guy, but some alumni turn into major university donors and demand recognition in the strangest ways. When Zack begins to laugh, I realize I've fallen into some kind of trap.

"It's a giant pair of blue balls," Mason teases. "He had them after you left him hanging." Mason points a finger at his groin area like a flashing arrow sign. "Then again, they painted one green and one white, in honor of the school's colors, of course."

"Of course," Zack confirms.

"I didn't leave him hanging," I defend. Escaping Richard as I had wasn't very kind, but a girl had to do what a girl needed to do to get out of a potentially sticky situation. He called me for a week after that dance before he got the hint I wasn't interested. I'm certain Richard quickly moved on.

"Sounds like she was a real heartbreaker," Archer interjects, grinning at the shenanigans while his eyes narrow in on me. He gives me a wink.

"Oh, she's a ballbuster," Mason adds, covering his junk as if protecting them while giving me a wiggling brow. "My balls still feel the pain."

I ignore the salacious grin Mason gives me and the innuendo of Mason and I having once, and only once, been together.

"Really, dude." Zack chuckles.

"I have balls," Trevor, Zack's son, announces from behind me, and Zack groans.

"Not this again," he mutters, lifting his eyes to heaven, before pressing himself upward from his sand chair. "Hey, little man, we talked about this, remember?" Zack speaks to his child as he walks around my chair to approach his son and lead him away from the group to chat privately.

"Dude, you are so much trouble," Logan teases Mason.

"I have a reputation to keep up," Mason proudly states, and thankfully, the subject shifts away from me.

+ + +

After that embarrassing moment, Archer excuses himself to toss a football with his nephews and then toss Mila and Lorna into the waves of the lake. I watch as he rushes the shore, scoops up a squealing Rosie, and walks into the lake carrying her. He dangles her toes in the water as a wave crests, and then he dips her up and down in the rolling water. She clings to him but continues to squeal in delight.

"He's really good with her." A smile fills Anna's voice. A soft hum is my only response. I don't know how to react to a man who so openly addresses my girls. He referred to them as his girls in the kitchen. He constantly calls Rosie "princess" and keeps his patience with Talia. I heard his conversation with my oldest this morning about bad dreams. Talia is protective of me, and I've taken advantage of a child's comfort to settle vivid nightmares I once had of Ryan's tragic death. Thankfully, the dreams have subsided over the years.

As I haven't been on any dates of worth since Ryan's passing, my girls have never been exposed to a man in my life other than a few of Ryan's friends who check in once in a while and Leon Ramirez, my teacher friend's husband. I'm certain Talia doesn't remember Ryan as she sometimes asks me to describe him in detail despite pictures in our home. For a full year, she was obsessed with death and held the fear I would die as well, leaving her alone. Rosie will never know Ryan other than what she is told about him.

"He's just trying to make up for the other day." The gun-and-porn story isn't something I want to recount to the group, but Anna knows what happened.

Autumn pinches her brows in confusion. "I've never been able to picture Archer with children," she interjects. Ben's sister owns a local café called Crossroads Café that specializes in breakfast sweets, custom sandwiches, and excellent coffee. Of note, she sells the most delicious raspberry bar I've ever eaten. "But now . . . I don't know." The brunette who has her brother's blue eyes gives me a rather questioning glance before her gaze drifts back to Archer, who has Talia on his back while swinging Rosie through the waves.

"Parenthood can hit at the strangest time," adds River, Zack's fiancée and future mother of a baby girl. Zack already has twin sons who are eight and run a bit out of control at times, but River has a handle on them. She coasts a hand over her swollen belly. She has an earthy, easy vibe to her in her bikini and looks amazing as a pregnant woman on the beach.

I agree with River. I never thought motherhood would happen for me as I'd taken so long to find the right man to complete me. I was in my late thirties when I had the girls.

"I'm really sorry you missed Monday manicures and margaritas," Anna adds because I had disappeared for the day. "I could strangle Archer." She narrows her eyes at her brother frolicking with the children in the water.

"It was nice to spend a day with the girls." I wave off her apology, knowing she blames her brother, but he was only a part of the reason we took off. While I spend a lot of time with the girls, especially in the summer months, not all of it is quality time. I welcomed a day to just chill, only the three of us, and let my mind rest from the morning's excitement. "It was one of those great days that reminds you why you love being a mother."

Autumn softly smiles. "I can't wait for baby Ben to grow up, yet I don't want to rush the days." Autumn has quite a story about the start of her journey to motherhood, and I'm glad it all ended as a happily ever after. She rubs her soft belly where life number two begins.

Anna smiles at her sister-in-law. "The time goes so fast. In a blink, they're teenagers and off to college." A hint of melancholy hits Anna as she squints at her sons tossing a football to one another along the beach. They're enduring the day as Anna asked them to spend a little time with their pseudo-uncles and the real one. She's already explained that Uncle Archer is a stranger to her children. They don't know where he's been or what he's been doing, and apparently, Archer is tight-lipped on explaining himself.

My thoughts drift back to our conversation last night and his medallion for protection. What has he endured over the years? What does he mean he's done pretending? He's such a mystery to his family and me. His presence says something, though. He's here, but I wonder why. I haven't missed how he favors his right side, wincing or flinching on occasion with his left leg. Did something happen to him? Why doesn't anyone know anything about this man other than not envisioning him with children?

I glance across the beach to where he's playing with my girls. He's a natural. Or maybe he's just a big kid. Watching him capture Rosie and lift her up, or teasingly splash Mila, he has a playful side he isn't given credit for.

"Mommy, come swimming," Talia calls out to me. Hesitantly, I stand and check all the spots on my bathing suit. Breasts contained. Butt covered. Front aligned. I walk across the sand, sinking into the soft grains, conscious of Archer watching me. Our near kiss lingers awkwardly between us. If Rosie hadn't interrupted, I'm not certain what would have happened.

Actually, who am I kidding? I'd have kissed him. I wanted him to kiss me, yet the moment felt like a tease. Hovering over my lips. Asking me to stop him. Was this part of the pretending he mentioned? Was he joking that he would kiss me but had no intention of carrying through on our lips touching? I was so confused and didn't understand why I cared. I had my girls to consider, my children to focus on. I didn't need to be involved with a man, especially one who had a habit of disappearing.

Still, as he blatantly watches me enter the lake and head toward my daughter, I'm curious if he's ever considered being a father, which seems like a ridiculous thought. Instead, I concentrate on being a good mom and playing with my girls in the refreshing water.

+ + +

By late afternoon, my girls have had enough sunshine, and my head is aching. I don't know if it's the lack of sleep, too much sunshine, or day drinking. Perhaps a combination of all three. Either way, a migraine is working its way over my brain, and my left eye throbs in the socket. As I press my temple, Archer questions me.

"You okay, 'Locks?" I don't know why he calls me such a name.

"I think I'm going to give the girls some shade and rest a while myself." Talia rarely takes a nap although Rosie could still use them on occasion. However, if she does, she has trouble sleeping at night. While I hate that television is the virtual babysitter, sometimes a little downtime is necessary. I need to close my eyes.

"Dinner," Autumn reminds me of the stipulation that all must gather for the meal. I smile graciously. My girls and I are being absorbed into this reunion, but I struggle with my position here. I'm supposed to be supporting Anna but haven't actually been the companion she needs.

I quickly look at my college friend. "You okay if I go?"

"Of course. Rest. Relax. See you later." Her smile reassures me, and I gather my little party of three. The climb of one hundred and fifty steps is a struggle, and Rosie is dragging up each riser. Midway, she wants me to carry her, but I'm juggling an oversized beach bag.

"I've got her."

Archer's deep voice behind me causes me to squeak. *Where the hell did he come from?*

"You don't have to do that," I say, hitching Rosie up to my hip but struggling as the bag slips down my other arm to catch in the crook of my elbow.

"Wouldn't offer if I didn't want to." He scoops Rosie out of my arms and attaches her to him. I'm expecting her to be all clinging and cry as she normally wants only me when she gets tired. With her thumb in her mouth, I'm waiting for the tantrum to start, but it doesn't. She settles into Archer's chest, covered by a T-shirt, and we proceed up the stairs. Surprisingly, Archer's been wearing the tee all afternoon, even in the water. The outline of his silver chain underneath the occasionally wet material has not gone unnoticed by me.

Once we enter the coolness of the apartment, I ask Archer to set Rosie on her bed and guide Talia to a couch.

"What's your plan, 'Locks?" Archer whispers to me, noting Talia's position. He's watching me rub my forehead, pausing to squeeze at my left temple.

"Why do you keep calling me that?"

"Raven-haired beauty feels kind of long. And Goldilocks doesn't fit with the dark hair."

'Locks? Okay then. Heat fills my face.

"I'm just going to lie down." I need a few minutes to get this headache under control. "And let Talia watch an appropriate movie." Tipping up a brow, I glance at him, but that tweak to my left side shoots pain through my eye socket.

"You okay?" His hands come to his hips as he eyes me.

"Perfect," I lie. His dark eyes gleam a bit. A slow curve curls his lips, and I recall once again how he almost kissed me this morning. I'd been dreaming of Ryan, who morphed into Archer, and then woke in his arms, clutching at his tee. Those dark orbs stared back at me. Those pouty lips tempted me.

"Okay if I head back to the beach?" Archer asks, interrupting thoughts I shouldn't be having of how much I wanted that connection with him. But he's my best friend's older brother and a man with a habit of disappearing, and I don't need a fling at this stage of my life. I'm no longer the reckless, free spirit the guys teased me about earlier with that story about Richard Ball.

"You do you." Sarcasm takes over for some reason. Archer doesn't need my permission to go back to his family, and I don't need him to stay here with mine.

"Huh." His lips purse, and he lowers his fists. Then he glances at Talia, tipping up his chin at her. "Be good for your mom, princess."

Talia doesn't respond. She doesn't know what to think of Archer any more than I do. One minute, she's fine to climb all over him in the water, and the next, my five-year-old is a closed door toward this man.

Archer leaves without another word, and I start the movie for Talia, keeping the volume low. I've even shut the blinds, washing the room in dim light. I hate to block out a perfectly good day, but the headache is suddenly raging. Snuggling myself onto the other couch, I curl on my side, back pressing into the cushions, and cover my eyes with one hand, squeezing my temples.

What feels like only minutes later, Archer returns, and the couch depresses near my waist.

"Babe," he softly begins. I don't know why he keeps calling me that name either. "You okay?"

"Headache," I mutter, not wanting to talk.

"Did you take something?"

I hadn't actually, too preoccupied with setting up Talia. I shake my head, and the couch shifts when Archer stands.

He returns within seconds. "Here."

Peeling my eyes open, I slowly sit up, feeling groggy, and take a pill he offers me. Next, he hands me a glass of water.

"Drink all of it."

If I do, I'll need to pee, but his expression warns me he'll hold it to my mouth and pour it down my throat if I don't. He watches my throat roll as I guzzle the water, emptying the glass. When I finish, I collapse back on my side and cover my eyes with my hand again.

I hear the soft clink of the water glass being set on the table before Archer returns to the sliver of space on the couch near my waist. His arm slips over my hip, and his hand strokes up my spine with a soothing pressure along my vertebrae. His thick fingers work their way up to my neck and squeeze tenderly at the nape. With my eyes closed, I relax under the gentle massage. His hand moves, and the pad of his thumb slowly rubs circles over my temple.

I hum.

"Like that, 'Locks?" His voice drops, reminding me of the sound in my dreams, the one demanding I give in to him. My body is in conflict as my head throbs, and another area matches the beat in an opposing rhythm. For some reason, Ryan comes to mind and how he tried to make my headaches go away, sometimes teasing that sex would be the cure. He didn't allow the old "I have a headache" excuse. An orgasm healed everything, according to him. Softly, I smile at the memory while a tear slips free.

"Babe," Archer whispers, but I shake my head, hastily swiping at the drop caught along my nose. "I'm gonna move you to the bed. You need some sleep."

My eyes flip open, and I tip my head to glance at Talia on the other couch. "No, I'm good here."

"Not up for discussion."

"Archer, I can't—" He moves so fast and has me cradled to his chest even faster. I'm not a small woman, but he makes me feel light as a feather. Still, I wrap my arms around his neck and rest against the sunshine heat of him.

"Talia, I'm putting your mom to bed, and then I'll be back to watch the movie with you."

"You don't need to do this," I argue, thinking he's taking me to the girls' room, but he detours to his.

"Archer," I groan.

"You're not sleeping with your child. My bed is bigger, and I can darken the room even better in there."

"This is not necessary," I whisper, grinding my teeth. *What is he thinking?* And what will Talia think? Before I can finish my thoughts, I'm laid on his bed, and the covers pulled free. I sit up, ready to remove myself even as my forehead furrows with the pain.

"I'm not opposed to tying you to the bed." His deep sandpaper voice threatens me, and I still. There is no reason that should sound hot. I should be bothered by the comment and not in a good way, but *holy heat*, my underwear might need a rescue as he levels those eyes on me and his warning lingers. "If you need that."

If I need that? Just this morning, he was telling me what he thought I needed.

I'd start by kissing you.

And where would that lead? I couldn't get involved with Archer. For one, he had a gun. He watches porn. He's a total mystery. Plus, I'm a single mother of young girls, and I don't need a disappearing act like him. He's the type of guy I'd fall for pre-Ryan. The unobtainable one. The one-night-stand man. I am too old for those kinds of things. I am better as the only one in my life.

But are you really? You wanted him to kiss you, didn't you?

I curse my long-paused libido and sigh in frustration.

"What's that sound for?" Archer asks, but I don't answer him. Instead, I simply shake my head, which hurts to do, and my brows pinch. Pressing my shoulder, Archer nudges me to lower to the mattress, and

68

when my head rests on the pillow, he swipes his fingers through my hair, brushing it off my face.

"Keep the door open," I whisper, holding his gaze, wondering why he's being so sweet. Wondering if I can really trust him.

"Not going anywhere," he states. "I need you to believe I wouldn't do a thing to your girls or you, okay?" The hesitation in his eyes, along with the strain of his voice, tells me this is important to him. He needs me to trust him, and I do, to an extent. Anna would string him up by his balls if he did something to us. My shy, quiet friend has another side to her when pressed. I also would never let anything hurt my children, not even a sweet man who plays in the water with Rosie or watches a girlie animation with Talia.

I nod to accept his words, and his hand coasts along the side of my face to my neck, curling around my throat before lowering to my chest. The movement reminds me of our first night when he placed his hand over my racing heart before the whole breast-grab slipup.

"I like this," he whispers as his gaze falls to his hand spread over my skin. I have no idea what he means, and I don't have time to ask before he quickly stands and mutters, "Sleep, babe."

He's not even out the door before I'm drifting off to empty dreams while the heat of his palm lingers over my heart.

8

[Jenna]

I wake with a start, finding the room pitch-dark and the apartment too quiet. Something warm lines my body from neck to knees, curving along my form. Unable to roll to my back because a brick-wall body holds me in place, I realize I'm still in Archer's bed. Slowly I attempt to sit, but his arm snakes around my waist, halting me in place once I'm upright.

"Where're you going, 'Locks?" he mumbles without opening his eyes and hardly moving his lips.

"What time is it?" I glance around the dark space hoping for a bedside clock, which I don't see. Archer rolls to his back and retrieves his phone from under his pillow.

The screen light illuminates his face. "3:33."

Holy shit. I slept for almost twelve hours.

"Did you give me a sleeping pill?"

His head whips to the side on his pillow. "Do you think I'd drug you?" The offense in his voice tells me he wouldn't, but still . . . twelve hours.

"Why am I still in your bed?"

"You were dead asleep."

Quickly, I reach for the covers, finding myself free of restraints before I'm circled again by the strength of his arm around my waist. "Where're you going?"

"The girls—"

"Fed. Bathed. Bed."

"You bathed my girls?" I nearly shriek, and his brows crease hard.

"Babe, Anna did it."

Of course. *Oh my God.* My heart races.

Slowly, his arm releases my belly. "You think I'm some kind of sick pedophile?" His voice cracks on the accusation. "You think I'd touch your girls?" His tone rises, anger filling it.

"I—"

"Get out of my bed, Jenna." There's no 'Locks. No babe. My name clear as day is said with disdain. "You think I'm some sick fuck, get the fuck out of my bed."

My heart continues to race, and I swallow hard. I've insulted him, and I didn't mean to. My mind just jumped to the worst-case scenario. It happens. I'm a mother. I have girls. We think all kinds of things we'd never want to consider and can't help imagining. We protect. We sting. My mama-bear claws are sharp.

"I didn't mean—"

"Get out." He directs his gaze to the ceiling as he growls his command and then rolls to his side, giving me his back.

I pause for a moment, reflecting on the fact he helped me carry my girls into the apartment. He played with them on the beach. He took care of me during my migraine and then took my kids to my friend for help with their needs. I was a terrible mother, and I was an awful friend. Anna asked me to be here for her, and I've abandoned her repeatedly. I'm also being unfair to Archer.

"I'm sorry," I mutter, but he doesn't turn back to me, and I find it best. While silently igniting a long-forgotten fuel inside me, his constant gaze makes me uneasy. I shouldn't be attracted to him, and I most definitely should not be in his bed. Removing my legs from under the covers, I discover I'm still wearing my shorts and tee from yesterday after the beach. I need a shower and something to eat, but I don't want to disturb the girls or Archer in the middle of the night. Instead, I creep out of Archer's room and close the door behind me before collapsing on the couch, no longer in need of sleep.

My thoughts scramble between Archer's kindness and Ryan's devotion. We met through friends of friends, and he was relentless in his pursuit to date me. His desire to spend time with me was a nice change of pace. We fell in line with each other, and the compatibility filled all my empty spaces. He was sexual energy and quiet patience. He was laughter at a difficult moment and comfort when I was in pain. He knew the painful parts of my history and promised me he'd be the best father. I believed him. He would have been, had he lived long enough to keep that promise.

But Ryan wasn't coming back anymore than Ben could return for Anna.

And while I might want to get laid, sleeping with Archer McCaryn would be a different kind of heartbreak, and one I don't think I'd survive.

+ + +

The next morning, I tiptoe through my routine before scooting the girls out of the apartment. Archer's bedroom door remains closed, and I'm thankful for the reprieve. I've had time to consider what happened and the accusation I made, and I feel sick about it. Allowing him privacy in his own place, I lead the girls to Anna's, finding the front door open. I've taken advantage of my friend and her hospitality, and it's time for me to step up and be here for her, so I start breakfast for whoever might appear.

Anna enters the kitchen first, looking rested and refreshed. Her body is newly tan from yesterday's beach day, but one look at me and her expression falls.

"What happened?"

"Nothing." I brush it off, pouring more batter into the waffle maker.

"What did he do now?" Anna exhales, leaning on the counter beside me.

"Actually, it was me," I admit. Setting the measuring cup on the counter, I place my hands on the cool surface as well and hang my head. "It was my fault." I turn my head to look at Anna and see Archer over her shoulder just inside the kitchen entry. Pressing upright, I meet his eyes across the room for only a second. He avoids my apologetic eyes, and the rejection feels like a stab to my belly.

"Coffee?" I offer. As a tea drinker, I don't drink coffee, but I turned on the pot for others. I stare at him a moment longer, admiring the tight fit of his jeans and the forest green tee he wears up top. With his dark features, the color is a nice combination, and I'm reminded of a tree, as in I'd like to climb him like one and beg him to forgive me.

Archer shakes his head. "I'm headed out for the day."

Anna shifts her gaze from her brother to me and back, mouth falling open before snapping shut. If Archer wanted a moment with his sister, he doesn't ask to speak to her. He just tips his head at her and turns away.

He's hardly out the front door when Anna faces me. Her eyes wide. She glances to the side, noting my girls are contently eating before she whispers to me, "Tell me you weren't *with* Archer."

"No." I shake my head. "No, nothing like that."

"He's irresponsible. He's reckless. Jenna, you do not need someone like him in your life."

These are exactly the thoughts I've already had about Archer. "I know. You're right. Nothing happened. It was all me." Then I remember him telling me he brought the girls to Anna last night. "Thank you for last night. I don't know why he didn't wake me. He told me how you fed the girls, bathed them, and put them to bed."

Anna stares at me. "He said you had a headache. It was nothing, but Archer's the one who tucked them in."

My head pops up.

"They had dinner with us, and I gave them a bath, but Archer carried them back to your place with Mila as a helper. She said he tucked them in and read them a book."

What? My neck cranes. I glance toward the front hallway where Archer disappeared and feel even shittier.

9

[Archer]

Yesterday, my reluctant thoughts on a day at the beach changed when Jenna removed the barely-there cover-up and revealed a body-hugging bathing suit that left little to the imagination. In a deep blue color, the one-piece tied at the back of her neck and covered each breast with only a triangle of material. The valley between her ample tits left my mouth watering, and then, there were her damn legs again. She was perfect, but I didn't miss how her arm covered her belly on occasion as if she were trying to hide her body. *Fuck that shit.*

Then there was that story about her and some hairy-balls guy. I hate to admit that jealousy swarmed around me over a tale two decades old. I didn't want her ditching a date because she felt threatened. I wanted her to feel safe and I definitely didn't want to picture her with someone else, although she's been married.

When she said her girls were toast, I hadn't planned on following her, helping her, or finding her suffering from a painful headache. I definitely hadn't expected to sidle up behind her while she was sleeping in my bed, but I didn't like the idea of her hurting—headache or otherwise

After months of sleeping with another woman, whom I'd often roll away from during the night, the desire to curl up against Jenna came as naturally as breathing. She was different than Viviana. Vivacious and vicious, my former lover had been one of the roughest relationships I'd ever experienced. Even though it's over, the things I had to endure still make me nauseous. My upper leg would throb with the memory if it still had feeling in it. Jenna was in a whole other stratosphere than Vi.

So, after all I did to help her get some rest, she wakes to accuse me of something incomprehensible, and I couldn't even look at her.

You're a despicable human. Viviana might have been right, but there were lines I would never cross.

When I saw Jenna this morning in the kitchen, looking contrite and confessing to my sister her fault, I had to get out of there for a while. I was suffocating under the reunion of friends, the notion of family, and the apologetic gaze of a beautiful woman. I hadn't asked for her apology, but she was giving it to me with those eyes, soft and sweet and sincere. She wasn't Vi. Jenna was contrite and I didn't know how to take her being genuine.

In need of escape, I missed my ride—my custom designed Harley Davidson street bike, great for screaming up Lake Shore Drive and barreling down the highway. I don't trust myself to balance her now. Instead, I drive my unmarked car to a locals' bar, despite it being ten in the morning, and spend the day shooting shit while watching baseball on the tube. Even though it's Michigan, there are more Chicago Cubs fans in this community and the television plays the daytime doubleheader.

"Archer? Archer McCaryn." With surprise, I turn in the direction of the person calling out my name. His face is as surprised as his tone. "No fuckin' way."

He looks exactly the same as I remember yet totally different. For one, Noah Weller has aged as we all have. With scruffy fuzz along his jaw, he looks like a young man who hasn't fully developed facial hair. He wears a baseball cap backward on his head and smiles with the whitest teeth I've ever seen, and he's a welcome face on this day.

"Noah. How are you, man?" I stand to clasp his offered hand and tug him in for a guy hug. It's been a long time since I've seen my teenage best friend. Helping himself to a seat on the stool next to mine, he orders a beer.

"I'd heard you were back," Noah begins but pauses like he's got more to say but doesn't know where to start.

I hold up a hand. "I'm sorry I haven't called yet."

Noah tips his head. "You wouldn't have had my number anyway."

Eight years ago, we had an awkward encounter in Chicago. I was checking into the hotel Noah managed and needed to cut him off before he came across as recognizing me. Thankfully, he was quick on the uptake, noted the slight shake of my head. He didn't mention that we were acquainted.

"So, how are things?" He nods at the collection of beer bottles before me. "Woman trouble?"

"What makes you say that?"

"Can't think of anything else that might make a guy get drunk midday on a Wednesday." He chuckles.

"It's not that." *But wasn't it?*

Wasn't I hiding out from a gorgeous midnight-haired beauty who had my insides flipped upside down and a strong streak of accusing me of shit? It just doesn't pay to try to be nice.

"Got my own little bird in my life, so I know all about it." He picks up the beer placed before him by the bartender and takes a drink.

"Oh yeah? Tell me about it."

Noah sizes me up. Maybe he sees I'm not going anywhere soon. Or maybe he decides bars are good places for confessions. Whatever it is, he digs in to tell me his story about working at the Magellen Hotel and how one thing led to another, eventually bringing him back here. When he finally explains the local inn owner that has his briefs in a bunch, I laugh.

"She's so full of piss and vinegar, as my dad used to say." His voice sobers at the mention of his father, and I remember what happened when we were teens.

"Ever hear from the old man?"

"Funny you should ask. He lives around here."

My brows lift in surprise. "You're shitting me?" Robert Weller had turned out to be a crook, but as that was more than twenty years ago, his prison sentence must have been served.

"Nope." Noah purses his lips and shakes his head. I'd love to dig into questioning if he sees him, but something tells me the conversation about his father needs to end here.

"So what about you?" Noah narrows his eyes. "Just what *have* you been up to?"

When we were kids, Noah and I defined trouble. His mother was my mother's best friend and they lived here. With high school sports and eventually summer jobs, my stays became less and less frequent. With Noah as the year-round next-door neighbor, though, he had connections in the community when I did visit. Pot. Girls. Parties. I'd tag along and get up to no good with him. I slowly smile at the memory while my stomach burns at the reminder I've let this friendship disappear.

"Remember when I saw you in Chicago?"

"Oh, I remember," Noah says, giving me a look like he wants all the details, and I decide, *fuck it*. I need to tell someone about all the shit I've been dealing with over the last decade.

"I work undercover."

If Noah is impressed, he doesn't let on. Instead, he says, "I figured it was something like that."

"How?" I tilt my head.

"No one enters the Magellen with Viviana Quintero on his arm unless he's up to no good, and as I figured you were still a good guy, it had to be something other than that."

I should question how Noah knows of Viviana, but I suppose working at one of the most highly prestegious and expensive hotels in Chicago, you'd see lots of celebrities from all walks of life. Even the lowlifes. It's funny how someone who truly knew me, surmised in one chance encounter, that I was still decent. I'd known Vi on and off for nearly a decade, more on than off for two years, and she never picked up that I was a good guy. She liked 'em bad, so that's who I was.

I word vomit the entire story, telling Noah about my relationship with Viviana, the intention of it, and how it all went to hell. Explaining the details, I pat my inner thigh. "As soon as I get myself right again, I'm back at it, though."

I cannot sit still. I'd be no good behind a desk and I don't want to be caged in an office. I'm used to fieldwork and need to return to it sooner rather than later. It's been almost a year.

"Assuming Ms. Quintero isn't the one causing you to drink your weight in alcohol midafternoon, then who is it?"

"Fuck," I groan leaning on the bar. "It's . . . no one." Jenna cannot mean anything to me. I need to get my head focused and my leg functioning. I don't have time for the likes of her, which has me wondering why I'm even upset by her accusation. Still, it hurts that she thinks I'm some kind of deviant. I've played the role for so long maybe

I come across as one. Maybe I am one. I'm out of practice at being decent.

Noah chuckles again, not believing me but letting it slide. "You going to Zack's tonight?"

My head swivels in Noah's direction. Zack is his younger brother and one of the Ben Kulis square of friends.

"Didn't know they were having people over?"

"Zack's trying to take the weight off your sister. Some shit about regrouping for two weeks every year as they promised Ben before he died." Noah shakes his head, lowering his eyes to the bar. Ben was younger than us by three years. "It's sad." That's all that needs to be said about a man who passed from pancreatic cancer barely a year after his diagnosis. That cancer is a mean motherfucker.

"It's funny how they're neighbors again." I learned in brief how Zack ended up with the woman who inherited the house next door. Now, they're engaged with a baby on the way. I don't think I'll ever be a father or a husband. Then my thoughts jump to little Rosie and Talia. Those two peanuts crack me up. One is a mother hen while the other has a mischievous streak waiting to strike. I call them both princess, but Talia is more like a queen-in-training while Rosie definitely wants to be a warrior instead.

"Yeah," Noah weakly replies. Then he reaches over and pats my shoulder. "Come to dinner."

"I don't think I'm invited."

"Anyone at the house is included. You're family, man."

Family.

It's been hard to remember what family feels like, especially as my sister has invaded the family home. My parents sold our childhood home right after my youngest sister graduated from high school. They figured with no one sticking to the area, why should they? Then Anna returned with Ben, but my parents were only a few hours from their beloved grandchildren. I have no problem with my nephews and niece. It was just difficult to hear about them and receive the endless questions. *When will you be settling down, Archer? When are you going to let a woman make an honest man of you?* As if I was a lying cheat somehow because I wasn't married. Then again, lying was a trait of my field. It was a means to an end.

"I don't know," I mumble, feeling the effects of my day drinking having lost count how many beers I've had.

Noah squeezes my shoulder. "It will be like old times, only minus making out with girls and smoking pot in the old tree fort." Noah huffs. "The guys actually rebuilt it last year for Zack's boys. River, his fiancé, calls it a pirate ship." Noah shakes his head. "Man, we're old."

"Speak for yourself," I joke, knowing all my parts other than my leg are in perfect working order.

"Still," Noah pauses. "Come keep me company as I'm surrounded by all the love-sick, newly forty gang."

His comment reminds me my sister isn't love-sick. She's heartbroken at the loss of her love and I should have been here for her. I should be a little more supportive of her current situation. She invited her friend for some reason, and I made a big stink about Jenna being in my place. This morning, I was ready to ask Anna to make room for Jenna in the main house. I couldn't keep sharing my space with her if she didn't trust me. But I heard the concern in Anna's voice, laying blame on me once again, and the reminder of another crumpled relationship hits hard. Then, Jenna defended me, or at least took the fault herself, and now I just don't know what I want.

"Free food. Outdoors. It's got to be better than this," Noah continues on his crusade for me to attend. "No offense, beautiful." He nods at the bartender.

"You're a pain in my ass, Noah, but you tip well." The blonde snickers while shaking her head. She's been eyeing me since I came in and we've exchanged friendly banter as bartenders do with strangers. I was working up to asking her if she'd like to spend some time with me, hoping I could rid my thoughts of one hot mother staying in my apartment. At Noah's persistent invitation, and the flirtatious grin she gives him, I decide dipping my wick into the wrong woman won't help me.

The last time I did, I got shot for it.

10

[Jenna]

When Archer shows up for the cookout at Zack's house, I almost drop my beer. His smile is blinding as he enters the yard chuckling with a friend, who I quickly learn is Zack's older brother, Noah. Where were men like these two when I was hooking up with all the randoms around my hometown? Then again, hotties like Archer and Noah were apparently living down here, some three hours away.

The younger set of kids run around the yard and the older ones linger on a cool-looking lounger that seats more than one person. Mila and Lorna are trying to hang out with Bryce, a soon-to-be high school junior who wants nothing to do with the middle schoolers near him. Lorna wears heart emojis in her eyes every time she glances up at Bryce who continues to ignore his sister's friend and it reminds me of all the unrequited love I witness among the teenagers in my classroom. *It doesn't get any easier, kiddo*, I want to tell Lorna, but I won't crush her spirit at only thirteen.

Archer doesn't come within five feet of me throughout most of the evening, but occasionally, I find his eyes tracking my movement. Standing at the base of the tree fort, I gaze across the yard to find him watching me. Sitting on the double chaise-lounger with Anna, and Archer is staring. Helping Rosie and Talia with hot dogs and chips, and Archer observes. Each time I try to catch his eye, though, he looks away. Then a plate appears before me.

"You need to eat. Sit." His commanding tone startles me, but when I look up, he won't face me. Still, he holds out a plate with grilled chicken and salad. "Don't want you getting another headache." His concern is like an arrow straight to my heart. His hand lifts to my lower back, then drops before touching me. With a nod of his head instead, Archer motions at a seat around the outdoor table. Moments later, he sits beside me but keeps his chair a respectful distance, and my emotions ping-pong all over the place.

I need to apologize for my accusations. Archer needs to understand, though. I'm protective of my girls and I won't be played as a single mother with mocking almost-kisses. I don't know why it's still bothering me that it didn't happen. Maybe because I was so close to something I haven't had in over three years.

"Jenna?" So deep in my thoughts, I miss that someone was speaking to me, and I glance up from staring at my plate to find Mason looking at me. "So how 'bout it?"

I swallow. "I'm sorry. What was the question?"

Mason chuckles good-naturedly. "Ditch the rugrats and come out for a drink with me tonight."

Turning my head briefly to Archer and back to Mason, I use the second to contrive an answer but can't think of a good one other than this: "I can't."

Archer isn't part of this conversation. His body leans in a manner that positions him facing Zack at the end of the table, but his head holds still as if he's listening in my direction.

"Why not? Mila's old enough to babysit. Come out for a bit."

While Mila is twelve and capable of handling Rosie and Talia for an evening, I don't want to go out with Mason. We've already been there, done that, and it wasn't even a date. We hooked up, plain and simple, and it's embarrassing to recall such a thing two decades later. We were drunk, young, and doing what college kids do on occasion.

As I'm formulating an answer, something skitters against the underside of my knee and I flinch. Quickly glancing down at my leg, I realize too late what I thought was a bug were Archer's fingertips. Was his touch meant to get my attention? Or was he warning me not to go out with Mason?

His hand stills, then slowly retreats to his own thigh.

"I can't," I repeat to Mason, looking up to meet his eyes. "I'm here to spend time with my girls."

"Aren't you with your girls all the time?" He softly smiles. Mason has a child of his own. I can't remember her exact age, but her name is Lynlee, and I wonder why she isn't present during this two-week vacation with his friends.

"In the summer, yes, but for nine months of the year I'm teaching." My working mother guilt-cup overflows some days. I'd taken maternity leave when Talia and Rosie were each born and found being home with my babies was more rewarding than I expected it to be. When I first returned to work after Talia's birth, I cried for weeks as I left her behind with a sitter. Carol is great as an in-home daycare provider, and she doesn't charge me enough for what she does, but as a single mother on a public-school teacher salary, I appreciate her discount.

Mason stares at me as if my reason isn't enough explanation.

"For old time's sake." He wiggles his brows, giving me a crooked grin which I'm certain works on many ladies, but not me. Not anymore.

I'm older and wiser to the likes of men like Mason.

"Been there, done that," I playfully tease, but I'm suddenly uneasy when the chair beside me scrapes across the concrete patio and the person within it shifts his body to face Mason more directly.

"The lady doth protest, and she said it enough. No." The tone of his voice is sharper than I've ever heard and his forearm leans on the table, exposing strength worthy of arm porn. I'm almost drooling. Even sitting down, he suddenly seems larger, imposing, ready to leap over this table and shut Mason up. Glancing from Archer to Mason, I immediately try to soothe the sudden tension swirling between the two men.

"I'm also here for Anna," I remind Mason, and his attention turns toward the end of the table where Anna sits near Zack and River.

I'm not certain what I'm doing to actually help Anna, especially after I was gone all day the other day, missed manicures and margaritas, and then slept through dinner last night. I'm hoping I offer silent moral support as the stories about Ben fly around us. Ben, Ben, *Ben*. Anna needs to come to terms with the fact that she is an individual. Her life with Ben might have felt like it defined her, but she's going to need a new definition for the future. She is still alive, and she needs to live for herself.

"You both should come out tonight," Mason suggests. His voice quiets as he peers back at me and reaches for his beer on the table.

"She said no," Archer interjects and the growly undertone of his voice raises the hairs on my arm.

Mason tips back his beer and narrows his eyes at Archer.

Archer doesn't move his glare from Mason. "Take the hint."

"Easy, man," Mason snarks, lowering the bottle to the table but Archer does not back down. His body is rigid. His attention focused. The vibe would almost be scary if it weren't so fracking hot. He looks like he's ready to pounce over the table and tackle Mason. While I don't want that type of aggression to play out before me, I understand he's acting this way on my behalf.

I reach for Archer's forearm on the table and squeeze the firm muscle and warm skin while addressing Mason once more. "Maybe we can all go out one night. Adults only, but not tonight." Steadying my voice, I add a smile, but feel all eyes on our end of the table.

"What are we discussing down there?" Anna teases.

"Nothing," Archer hisses.

At the same time, Mason states, "Adult-only things." He tips up a brow as he grins at me before clarifying his sexual innuendo for the rest of the table. "We should go out one night. Adults only."

Anna lowers her head while River perks up. "That's not a bad idea."

"We can just hang out on my patio," Anna suggests. "The kids can watch a movie or something."

"No, we need to get you out," River explains, reaching over the table for Anna's arm. "We should go dancing."

Vigorously, Anna shakes her head. My guess is she's thinking dancing will be a couples' thing. Zack and River. Logan and Autumn. Me and . . . My head swivels between Archer and Mason. My partner would have to be Archer, pairing Anna with Mason. She can't be matched to her brother.

"Line dancing works," Autumn chimes in, her voice rising with enthusiasm. "Everyone just dances collectively." Autumn's suggestion de-emphasizing Ben's absence and Anna's fear of needing a partner.

"I'm not line dancing," Zack mutters, under his breath, tipping up his own beer and chugging. Zack is more prepster than cowboy, and the silver watch on his wrist hints he's never seen the inside of a country western bar. In Elk Lake City, we have one called Rogue River, and I've been there on several occasions to let loose with teacher friends. Going out on the town when you live in a small one can be risky at times, though. Everybody knows your business.

"I think it sounds like fun," I admit. As a group activity, we could have a good time. Keeping my eye on Anna, I add, "If the men don't want to go, we can make it a ladies-only thing."

"Hey, hey, hey! Who says the men do not want to attend," Logan interjects, holding up his hands. "I got moves." He overbites his lower lip and repeatedly shrugs his upper body in his seat. Autumn laughs and rubs a hand down his arm. "Maybe you should save those moves for me."

"I'll be hard to resist," he teases.

"That's exactly what I was thinking," Autumn playfully mocks back, before leaning forward and giving her husband a quick kiss. The sweet teasing is a reminder of all the things I wanted in a relationship and one of many things I've missed after losing my husband. Those quiet moments between two people. The private jokes. The soft touches. Anna watches her sister-in-law and I know she's missing the same thing.

Fingertips skitter over my kneecap this time. Realizing the soft touch is Archer's, I don't flinch. When his warm palm flattens on my knee for a second, I absorb his heat but, too quickly, he releases me, and the pressure of that momentary touch lingers.

"We should do it," I encourage, drawing Anna's gaze from the too-cute couple. "Remember when we were in college. We'd go out all the time." Of course, half the time, Ben would crash the night, or Anna would leave to find her man once people paired off. Once, I had envied their long-lasting romance, but I also enjoyed my freedom without the constraints of a relationship in those days.

"More ballbusting," Archer mutters under his breath, reminding me of yesterday's revelation.

"I don't know," Anna says, staring down at the table, and I ignore Archer's comment.

"Anna," I softly call her name so she'll look up at me. "It could be fun." Holding her eyes, I hope she also reads my sympathy. *It will be okay*, I try to say without words as she stares at me. I'll be her wing woman. "I'll need a dance partner."

At the same time, two heads shift in my direction. One is Archer glaring at me, and the other is Mason narrowing his eyes. Ignoring both men, I keep my gaze steady on my friend. This is why she needs me. I'm the buffer here. The gentle nudge to take a risk but provide her a safety net. Nothing will happen to her.

"What bar hosts line dancing?" I ask Autumn, making the decision for everyone present.

"I'm looking it up now." Autumn lifts her phone, tapping away at the screen.

"This is going to be so fun," River says, leaning over to wrap an arm around Zack.

"Keep your clothes on," he mutters under his breath, and she laughs.

"You know it's a struggle for me." Her reply makes her fiancé laugh a little harder, easing the tense expression on his face after rejecting the idea.

"Noah, you should come, too," I offer. "Got a girl to bring?"

Noah's been quiet during this exchange, and he looks at me before glancing at Archer. One corner of his lip curls, and he shakes his head at his friend.

"No one you said." He pauses, glancing from Archer to me and back. "This isn't nothing." He tips his beer in my direction before softly chuckling. I don't understand what he means, but he answers me, "Yeah, I have someone I could invite."

"Then it's a date," Autumn calls out.

"A non-date date," I correct, looking directly at Anna. She nods, and I grin to myself. This could be really fun. Then I glance at Archer, who is scowling at me. Shaking my head, I decide I'm not letting him ruin my excitement.

The beer and wine flow. The night grows later. The kids continue to run around until River brings out ingredients for ice cream sundaes. Like she's running a professional ice cream parlor, she has everything in little bowls or containers for the mixing and matching of liquid toppings and candy treats. She also has an assortment of flavors, and I opt for two scoops of black cherry on a sugar cone.

L.B. Dunbar

Now, I'm no dummy, so I know what guys think when they see a woman licking ice cream on a cone. The swirl of a tongue. The suck of the icy treat. Even a soft bite of the cold form can be a turn-on, so I do not dismiss Archer watching me lick and lap at my cone as he sits near me.

"Want a lick?" I eventually say, holding out my cone in his direction.

His eyes narrow in on me. He's been drinking all day, and that should scare me, but it doesn't. There's a certain gleam to his eyes as I offer him a taste of my ice cream, and he gradually leans forward in his seat, lowering his elbows to his thighs. His mouth opens, and I hold the cone closer to his mouth. He sucks at the tip I've made from my last bite, and I watch as his tongue lazily laps over his lower lip, swiping up the residue left behind. There's no doubt I'm wet, but in a place I'm hot enough to melt this cold cream. *Cleanup in the freezer aisle.*

Archer keeps his eyes on me, and I return the ice cream treat to my own mouth, licking around the portion where he just took a bite. I don't have the chance to swipe at my own lips before Archer scoots forward on his seat.

"You've got something..." His thumb finishes the sentence by brushing over the lower swell of my mouth. Then he does the damnedest thing. He forces his thumb into my mouth, and I suck at the sticky mess. The corner of his mouth tips higher.

"You also have something..." His index finger swipes over my upper lip, and he brings his finger to his own mouth next, setting the tip against his lips and licking it clean. This motion could have taken a split second—like those moments as a mom when you lick your finger to rub a smudge off something on your kid's face. But Archer drags it out long enough that the cleanup I requested in the freezer aisle is almost a flood.

My entire body vibrates from watching a man lick ice cream off his finger. Or maybe it's that he put his thumb in my mouth. Or bit the cold cream in a way I imagine he'd take a bite out of me. I'm so hot for him it's ridiculous, and if there wasn't a backyard of people, I have no doubt I'd be throwing myself at him.

This is old-school Jenna 101. No holds barred. No holding back.

86

But I refrain. I'm a mother now. I'm a responsible adult. I don't kiss and tell. Those days of sex and regret are gone.

But Archer . . . just *Jesus*, please.

"Still mad at me," I mutter, checking that no one can hear me.

"Aren't you the one angry with me?" Those are the most words he's said to me all night.

With a deep exhale of remorse, I apologize. "I'm sorry for what I said." I lock onto his eyes.

"For what you thought." He narrows his.

"For what I suggested," I clarify. "I'm overprotective and overreacted."

The words aren't enough. I didn't really think Archer would do something inappropriate to my daughters. He surprised me. Taking care of my girls and letting me sleep off a migraine—the gesture was sweet—and my reaction unwarranted. Without all the facts, I acted on a gut response, not a logical one. Archer wouldn't physically hurt me or them. I'm confident of that. My heart, on the other hand, is blinking in warning. A man looking after me when I ache. A man watching over my kids when I can't. It's like a mismatched blend of ice cream, mixing all I want and all I can't have in one tempting treat.

Archer seems to understand and hums. Tipping up his chin, he says, "I'll have to think about how you can make it up to me." The grin he gives me is a wicked promise of retribution. He's going to collect, and the pleasure might be all mine.

Yep, I'm done. I want to pour this melting ice cream all over me, and I wonder if he'd lap it up if I did.

11

[Archer]

I miss my bedfellow that night and find myself wandering to the couch under cover of darkness, curling up behind Jenna while she sleeps.

"Archer, what are you doing?" she mumbles into the back cushions as she faces them.

"Just want to hold you, babe." I hadn't missed how she flinched when I first touched her during dinner. When that prick, Mason, hit on her, asking her out for a drink. I can no longer decide if he wants to get with my sister or get back in Jenna's pants. Apparently, he's been there before, and I don't like it. Not one bit. Then she apologized. Her original accusation stung, but I accepted her sincerity. She went into mama-bear mode, and I can respect her position. The strange new reality for me is I'd kill someone who harmed those little girls.

"Don't want me touching you?" I mutter into her scented hair, inhaling the fruity freshness and finding myself relaxing after twenty-four hours of tension. I don't know how she's doing this—having this power over me. I want to be close to her. I want to hold her. I want to inhale her, breathe her in. She smells clean—like innocence, comfort, and a place I can only dream of calling home—which is a weird thought. After two years with Viviana and her high-priced perfume, I didn't think I'd ever be able to unclog my nose of the stuff or her strong stench of money and privilege.

"I didn't say that," Jenna sleepily whispers. I'd like to take her to my bed where we have more room to spread out, but the tight conditions of the couch might be better. She can't slip away from me on the slim depth of this seat.

"This okay with you, then?" I mutter into her hair. With my arm over her waist, she doesn't move. She doesn't scoot away, but she doesn't melt into me like she's done on other nights. I recall her tugging me to her, clinging to my shirt. Her leg over my hip and my hand under her thigh. Fuck, I want this woman. I want her in this position and over me and under me.

Slowly, she relaxes and rubs her hand up my forearm, leading my hand to her upper chest until my palm rests right over her heart. Fuck, I like this position. I like feeling her heartbeat, and it hits me. It's more than wanting her. She could eclipse me. Her light could brighten my darkness. Someone like her could restore a poor man's spirit and allow him to believe he can deserve someone good, happy, and whole.

Just be.

Be home.

I haven't lost someone like Anna has, but I want my leg functioning and my job back. I feel just as empty inside as my sister but from a different kind of loss. Jenna might miss her husband, but she isn't hollow like Anna. Jenna still laughs. She teases. She offers a spark of life, tempting even me to want to be a better person. Showing me what I've been missing, and just might need in my life—the love and understanding of a good woman.

Fuck, I'm delusional.

Jenna quickly falls back asleep while I remain restless. My dreams are filled with the wrong woman.

You don't deserve to be loved. I hate when Viviana enters my head. She hadn't been wrong, though. I steeled my heart and played a part with her. I pretended. It didn't make me a good person. It also didn't make me the worst. Doing my duty called for extreme measures, and I'd pulled it off. And then . . .

I wake with a start, the sound of gunshot echoing in my head. Twitching, I tug the woman in my arms tighter, overwhelmed with a need to protect her. Her hand slides up my forearm, stroking tenderly over my skin until I remember where I am and who I'm holding. She's actually soothing me, making me feel safe and secure, something I've never felt before.

Jenna. The sweet, single mother who I have no business clinging to as I am. Begrudgingly, I peel myself free from her and roll off the couch. Returning to my bedroom, I give another glance at her curled-up form, tucked into the cushions. My darkness would only block out her sunshine. That was how eclipses worked.

Viviana had been right. I was a despicable man and didn't deserve a good woman in my life.

But, oh what I wouldn't give for a woman like Jenna.

+ + +

During the day, I ask my nephews to have lunch with me. Admittedly, I didn't know them well. We were family, but I'd been a piss-poor uncle, according to my sister. She wasn't wrong, but I wasn't at liberty to share where I'd been or what I'd done. However, I wanted these two young men to know I was here for them and would be better in the future.

According to my sister, Calvin was desperate to return to the Chicago area, where he'd spent his entire life minus the past two years. He was currently undecided in his future studies but leaning toward police work. His mother hoped it was a phase, but I wanted to talk to him about the brothers in blue.

"So, your mother tells me you might want to be a cop," I say to Calvin once we're seated at Driftwood, a popular tourist restaurant in town. I wanted to get the boys away from the constant Ben chatter. Some days were difficult, listening to Mason, Zack, and Logan talking about Ben, recalling their college days like guys who have never moved on. They were forty-two, not in their twenties, but I suppose those good ole days became more nostalgic the older we grew. It wasn't much different between my buddies from the force and me. Jokes about mothers and sex ran rabid between the guys and me. I missed my team, and the ache in my leg reminds me why I'm not with them anymore.

"I'm still undecided. Do I go forensic science or protective services? I've heard it's better to have a degree either way, easier to get into the police academy."

Times had changed, and I agree; a degree is good, especially if the academy doesn't accept him. There is plenty of independent contracting related to police work. Fortunate for Calvin, he'd had an in. He'd have a legacy.

Leaning forward, I glance around the restaurant before speaking. "I can get you in if you want. I can give you the references and recommendation you need."

Bryce's eyes widen, and his eyebrows pop upward when he looks at his older brother. He looks just like Ben, while Calvin looks more like Anna, which means he reminds me of me when I was eighteen.

"How?" Calvin asks.

"I was on the force for a while." I shrug. It isn't quite that simple, and my position became much more complicated than any local division. Still, I know people.

"You were?" Bryce exaggerates the questions. Looking at both their curious faces, I wonder how they don't know this about me. Has my sister never mentioned me? Being a cop once upon a time isn't a secret.

"I was. I can't share all the top secret stuff. Confidential and all that, but I worked for CPD for years." Bryce still looks at me in amazement, while Calvin looks skeptical.

"Mom said you were a vagabond. Like a hobo or something."

Hobo? Is that even politically correct? And why would she think that?

"I wasn't some wayward wanderer." I've certainly traveled, mainly to Central and South America, but it wasn't some uncharted adventure, and most times, it wasn't pleasurable.

"She said it's why you never came around. Always off somewhere." Bryce waves his hand to emphasize the great unknown while Calvin continues to stare at me.

"I wasn't at liberty to tell her anything, although your father knew a few things."

This has both their attention, although Calvin scowls at me. "Like what?"

"He knew how to contact me in an emergency."

"So why didn't you show up when he was sick? Or come to his funeral?"

Aw, man, this is tough to answer. Ben told me about his diagnosis in a secure email. After my father passed away, I'd learned my lesson and wanted someone in the family to be able to reach me in an emergency. Ben even prefaced in his message that he held off as long as he could before telling me about his condition. He just thought I should know.

At the time, the department was so close to the end of the investigation. I was tighter with Viviana and her father than I'd ever wanted to be. I wanted that assignment completed. I hadn't responded to Ben until he was deeper into his diagnosis. I'd asked him to pass the email address to his sister, not mine. *Have her email me.* It implied what I couldn't say—tell me when you're gone. I should have come home to see him before he passed.

"I just couldn't get here." It's a lie. I was present. Slipping home for the funeral to pay my respects, I slid back out of town just as fast. My attendance was risky. I should have skipped it entirely, but I didn't want to disappoint my sister again, even if she didn't know I was present.

Calvin huffs. Bryce just stares at me.

"Look, I know I've been a shit uncle." *I'd be a worse father.* I choke on air with the thought. Where did that come from? "So, I get it if you don't trust me, but I want you to. I want you to know I'm here for you."

"How can you be if you're off doing top secret stuff? Confidential and all that," Calvin mocks, sounding strangely like his mother with that tone.

"If you join the force, you'll understand. There are some things you can't discuss."

"Even with family?" Bryce questions.

Especially with family. Most times, it's better not to even think about family and what you're missing out on. Or their safety as you see the craziest shit you've ever seen.

I shrug. "It's a price I'm sorry I paid." I missed my own parents' funeral. I almost missed Ben's, and I've missed most of the lives of my family who remains.

"Can't get a refund," Calvin mutters.

I'd love to tell him to cut the crap, but I remember being mouthy and eighteen. "One day, you'll make sacrifices, and then you'll understand."

You might even give up your morals, your ideals, and your body to get a job done, and it doesn't mean you'll feel good about yourself. The only saving grace will be knowing a dangerous man was caught, and maybe his demise saved someone else's life, even if it ruined a bit of your own.

Calvin looks away from me while Bryce glances down at his menu. "We already made a sacrifice," Bryce says to the page in his hand, and I realize my misstep.

They gave up their young lives to move here for their dad. Anna has already explained how the decision to move came about and how they ended up in the house. We own it collectively, and I should be upset, but I hadn't been present for a discussion.

And adding Bryce's comment to my pile, the guilt shit keeps getting deeper.

+ + +

After an awkward lunch with the boys, I return to the house midafternoon. Anna tells me that Jenna's girls are next door playing in the tree house with Zack's twin boys, and she thinks Jenna might be doing some laundry. When I enter the apartment, Jenna isn't on the couch nor is the door to the girls' room closed. Wondering where she is, I hear water running in the bathroom like it's filling the tub. The idea of Jenna getting naked on the other side of the door develops a hum under my skin.

Like a creepy stalker, I press my forehead against the closed door, waiting on the liquid to stop filling the basin. With a sharp shut off to the rushing sound, the telltale sign of a full tub ripples through the barrier with a sluice and a whoosh of water.

Walk away, Archer.

Leaning away from the door, I dig my fingers into the trim around the frame, and I prepare to call out her name, telling myself I'm only letting her know I'm leaving. She'll have the place to herself. For another second, my hands grip the doorframe, holding me in place, wondering why I feel the need to tell her I'm going anywhere. Let her figure it out on her own that she's alone.

Step back.

Only, another sound occurs, echoing off the tile of the bathroom. The rip and zip of a coiled pipe suggests Jenna has pulled the ancient handheld showerhead from the holder. The subtle hum of droplets spraying against water, like rain splatter against a puddle, resounds through the door. The hum is lower in tempo, a heavier plunk of beating water. My forehead furrows, thinking it strange for half a heartbeat until I consider what she might be doing with that pulsing showerhead.

Preparing to step away once more, I hear a soft but distinct purr. "Archer."

Freezing in place, I fist my hands and lean forward once again, connecting imaginary dots between the pulsing vibration and the lusty sigh. Without hesitation, I reach for the door handle, expecting the door to be locked.

It's not.

"What are you doing?" she shrieks as the door swings open. At the same time, I ask a similar question in a deep, strangled voice. My eyes glance toward the tub from the open doorway, and Jenna sits upright. She wraps an arm over her ample breasts in an attempt to cover them, which is fruitless. The swell is the only hint I need to conjure the image of sharp nipples peaking against her fitted bathing suit the other day. I'm working my way from semi to full-on hard.

Her other hand is hidden beneath the tub's lip, but the gurgle of bubbles suggests the showerhead is underwater. Jenna's mouth hangs open. Any second, she's going to scream for me to get out, but her expression is stone. It prompts me to close the door—behind me—sequestering both of us in the small, steamy bathroom.

"I asked you a question," I snap, my patience barely contained. It isn't that I'm angry as a lack of patience often equates. I'm the opposite—high strung to join her in that tub. *I'm* practically vibrating myself.

"I could say the same," she snarks, and that bit of sass pumps my dick from half-mast to full steam ahead.

I take another step toward the tub, invading her privacy, encroaching on her personal space, and briefly lower my eyes for the water. Her legs are clamped together, but there's a rumble of water under her closed thighs, giving everything away.

"You called my name." My eyes laser in on hers, fighting the pull to glance down once more and further inspect where her limbs press together.

"I—" Additional words catch on her tongue, and I watch the roll of her throat as she swallows. Shame and something else scribbles over her face. I lower to my haunches, place my forearms on my thighs, and dangle my hands between my spread knees. My eyes never leave hers.

"Whatcha doing in there?" Softening my voice, I tip up my chin, focusing on her face and struggling with my eyes, which desperately want to look downward.

"I…"

I've interrogated thousands of suspects over the years. Come face-to-face with hundreds of criminals and their cohorts, but I was battling words as well as I stared into those expressive eyes. They said everything. They admitted her crime and subjected her to guilt, but I didn't want her to be embarrassed. I was actually a little honored, flattered while shocked.

"Let me help." I reach for the edge of the tub, and I slide my hands outward along the cool porcelain as I shift to kneel beside the tub. Jenna watches me, her gaze drifting from my hands to my face. She seems just as afraid to look lower at my body where there is no disguising the bulge in my jeans.

Both her legs are bent upward, knees pressed together. The strain of her position is apparent as the showerhead is below her thighs. Gently, I place my hand on one knee and pull it toward me, widening a gap.

Jenna only stares at me, swallowing hard while her eyes well with liquid. I'm not certain if those potential tears are fear or need. I reach for the collar of my shirt behind my neck and, with one tug, pull it over my head, dropping it behind me. Her eyes fall to the medal dangling against my chest. Bracing my hands on the edge of the tub once more, I nod toward those slightly spread knees.

"Let me watch." The strain in my voice is unavoidable. The water is a jet stream straight at her pussy. With a shaking hand, I press at Jenna's shoulder, guiding her to lean back against the slant of the tub. I've never seen anything sexier. "Continue," I command, holding her eyes with mine. They soften, and something I can't read fills them.

"This is so wrong," she whispers.

"But a few seconds ago, it felt right, didn't it?"

She doesn't answer. She swallows once more, and while focusing on her eyes, I slip my other hand between her thighs and seek the handle of the showerhead. The water whirls as I lift it higher, watching as she tips her hips upward. The spray hits her just right, and her lids struggle against the pleasure, drifting to half-mast. I rotate the wand in my hand, shifting the position for maximum stimulation, and Jenna bites her bottom lip.

"Say it," I groan, staring at her mouth where she works the sensitive skin with grinding teeth. "Say my name again."

Jenna shakes her head, the base of her skull moving against the tub ledge.

"Say it like you just did, like you want it to be me touching you, pleasing you."

Jenna slowly releases her lower lip, and her mouth slightly opens, but no sound travels over the lush pucker.

"Say it like you want me to take you in this tub. Suck you and fuck you and—"

"Archer," she chokes out. Her eyes close.

"Open," I demand.

"I can't look at you." Her voice is strained.

I want to question why she can't face me, but I also want her only thinking of what's happening between her legs, against her clit, at her channel. The thought has me jealous of a fucking showerhead and any fantasies in her head. I want to turn this thing off and replace it with my fingers, my tongue, my dick. My imagination runs wild with additional ways to use this device on her.

"Look at me," I command, and hesitantly, her eyes open. "You said my name, so look at me as you fall apart."

Those bright but dark eyes hold mine, and we pause on the pull between us, an electric spark like lightning cracking over the lake. Her legs spread until her knees hit the sides of the tub. Her mouth hangs open.

"That's it, baby." Watching her has me as solid as the porcelain, and I want to touch her, feel her bare, slick skin, under the water, but I won't break the trance she's fallen into. Quickly, she grips the edge of the tub, splashing water around the basin as her hips rock in sharp, quick surges. She bites her lower lips so hard it turns white, and she groans against the shout wanting to escape.

"Oh no you don't," I hiss. "Fucking scream."

She shakes her head to deny me, and I wonder how many times she's had to hold her tongue from releasing a cry of delight. Her fingers curl over the side of the tub as her back arches before lowering to the slanted porcelain. She came; I'm certain of it, but it wasn't enough. She rolls her head on the hard ledge, giving me the side of her face. A hint of disgrace washes over her expression again, and a hand covers her mouth as her eyes close.

"I am not done with you," I warn, retracting the pulsing showerhead and reaching for the faucet to cut off the water source. Pressing on the edge of the tub, I use it to help me stand upright. *Damn my leg.* I unbutton my jeans.

"What?" she gasps. "What are you doing?" Her glazed eyes drift to my waistband, and whether conscious or not, she licks her lips. I've already pushed the limit with this woman, but I can't stop now.

"You've got me all worked up." Some space behind my zipper is necessary as my erection strains the fabric. Jenna's gaze remains on my upper body, unabashedly scanning the firmness of my abs and lowering to the unmistakable bulge behind my zipper.

"I—" She swallows around the singular word once again as I step into the tub, still wearing my jeans and placing my feet between hers.

"We really need to work on your vocabulary. As an English teacher, yours seems rather limited," I tease, dropping to my knees and hitching her legs up and over my thighs.

"Archer." She hisses as my palms finally meet her inner thighs, and all the reserve I had goes down the drain.

L.B. Dunbar

"Let me touch you. Let me make you come again. You can do better."

"Better?" she chokes. Her eyes fixate on mine as I slide my hands down the inside of her firm legs, squeezing, kneading.

"Say yes, babe," I command, holding her gaze. Her teeth find that lower lip again, and her eyes spark. "I knew it." She needs to go another round, and she wants this. She wants my fingers on her, in her, guiding her.

"This is insane," she whispers, but I ignore her as I coast my fingers to her center, spreading the pretty pink folds before sliding through her slit. I double-team her as a thick finger slips into her primed channel, and my thumb finds her clit. Watching her once more, I swivel my wrist and reach deep within while her hips rock. The water ripples around us, splashing up my thighs and soaking my jeans. I'd love to remove everything, allowing nothing between us. I'd tug her onto my lap, have her straddle me, and let her ride out what she needs, but this is all about her. This tired mama needs some relief. She needs to scream and holler and rattle the walls with her release.

"Be loud," I demand.

"I can't. I'm-I'm used to staying quiet." She chews at her lips, and the pause reminds me why she hides her pleasure.

"We're alone. It's only you and me."

Our eyes lock, saying so much more. She better be thinking of only me in this tub with her. I add a second finger to make certain she knows *I'm* present. I'm the one touching her. I'm the one pleasing her. When she closes her eyes, it better still be me behind her lids, filling the fantasy, acting out the reality.

"I don't know if I can do it again," she whimpers.

"You can. You will, 'Locks." Jenna tilts her head, narrowing her eyes. "I can read it in you. Once is never enough."

Slowly, her lids widen, and I've hit the mark. For some women, the initial orgasm is only a warm-up. The pleasure is satisfying, but they want a second go immediately after completing the first. I'm happy to oblige, especially in this case. In this turn of events when I'm fingering Jenna in the tub, and we haven't even kissed yet.

Fuck. I'm not treating her like the lady she is, but something tells me Jenna's okay with how things are happening. At least for the moment.

Within minutes, she jackknives forward. Her hands grip my biceps, forcing my fingers deeper within her, and she groans. It isn't the scream I want ringing in my ears but a hard-pressed, long-humming moan of relief. When a hand comes to my wrist, I slow my motions and hesitantly pull back my fingers.

"Better," I mutter. "But we still have work to do."

Standing, I hitch my thumbs into the waistband of my jeans on the final thread of my restraint. Her eyes widen again, and something in them stops me. Is she still afraid of me? Doesn't she trust me?

"Jenna, if you don't want to keep going, you need to get out of this tub." Her eyes lower only briefly to the heavy length protruding behind the denim, wet and plastered to my body, outlining my thick form. Quickly, she stands to her full height, and my breath hitches in anticipation that she'll take over. She'll shove down my pants and tug me forward, reciprocating what's been done to her. Water cascades down her body like a steady stream, rippling over her peaked nipples and dripping off her ample breasts in the best waterfall I've ever seen.

To my dismay, Jenna steps out of the tub and reaches for a towel. Her back remains to me as she secures the fabric around her body before she spins to face me.

"Archer." My name is a choked sob on her lips, and everything in me says to reach for her. Pull her to me and reassure her that what we did was all for her. I don't need more, but I'm a selfish man. I want it. I want her. Instead, I feel played and old haunts slip between the cracks as I warn her.

"Out. Now."

12

[Jenna]

After I returned to my room on shaky legs, I collapse to the bed before giggling into a hand over my mouth.

Oh, my God, what have I done? Reckless and wild, the situation reminded me a little bit of my old self—pre-forty, pre-children, pre-Ryan. However, along with the giddy sensation comes a heavy wave of heartbreaking emotion.

What have I done? The question slowly repeats as reality settles in. I'm no longer young. I'm no longer without those children. I no longer have Ryan. I let a man I hardly know use a pulsating showerhead on me in a bathtub, and then I went again with his thick fingers working their magic on me.

You slut, I silently shout as I roll to my back and stare up at the ceiling. My fisted hand hits the mattress once. I definitely don't want to be that girl again, but I couldn't help myself with Archer. His eyes ensnared me. He wanted me. Every graveled word and smooth movement said he wanted me. I couldn't deny him.

Why did I let him do that to me? The answer comes fast and clear. I wanted it too. I wanted him. I've had three years of self-love, and I wanted the touch of his thick fingers.

My legs snap together, and I roll to my side once more, squeezing at the phantom sensation of his solid digits inside me and the pad of his thumb rubbing right where I needed him. He knew what he was doing, and I have no doubt it's from years of experience. As far as I know, Archer hasn't been married and hasn't dated anyone seriously. Even Anna isn't certain of any information she shares about her brother.

He's a total mystery, and I'm clueless what to think about what we just did.

Still puzzled, I stand and slip on a lightweight dress and flat sandals, dismissing all thoughts of a repeat performance with Archer. The bathtub was seven minutes in heaven. Or more like seventeen, but who was counting? And isn't that the point of what I'd done? For only a few minutes, I wanted to pretend I wasn't who I am and get lost in my head. I wanted to disappear into who I once was—carefree and unencumbered.

Only, that isn't my life.

Talia and Rosie await me.

I peek around the bedroom door and find the bathroom one still closed. Slipping from my room, I race across the living room as quietly as I can and sneak out of the apartment like the coward I am. I don't know how I'll face Archer ever again, and I still have a little more than a week of sharing this space with him.

+ + +

"Can Archer read to us?" Rosie asks in her innocent little three-year-old voice.

To my surprise, Archer was at dinner at Anna's and hung out with the reunion crew, as he calls everyone, until the sun slowly set. As it was late, I excused myself to get the girls to bed, and Archer followed me.

"He does the dragon voice better than you," Rosie adds. My heart breaks a little bit as I'm the only one to read to her for the three years of her life, and it's one of my favorite times of the day. However, my insides are equally warmed that Rosie wants Archer. She likes him.

"*The Warrior Princess* again?" Archer asks, and I turn at his voice, finding him leaning against the doorjamb. *How long has he been standing there?* His familiarity with the princess tale reminds me that Anna mentioned he read a story to my daughters the other night. With only momentary hesitation, I step back, allowing him space to further enter the room. Lowering himself to the floor, Archer places his back to the nightstand between the beds. He holds up the book, allowing the girls a view of the pictures, and the girls each tip their heads to the edge of their mattresses. I sit on the foot of Talia's bed as Archer reads, throwing his voice in ways I don't. His tenor is mesmerizing.

"I want to be a warrior," Rosie interjects around her thumb in her mouth as the princess nears the dragon.

"Want to be a warrior princess?" Archer pauses.

"Not princess. Just warrior." Rosie drops her sweet voice to something gruff and rugged, and Archer chuckles. He gives my daughter one of those smiles I rarely see but call glorious, relaxing his face and buffing the hard edges. I can only imagine it's a weapon of mass destruction, melting panties and breaking hearts wherever it beams.

"You can't be a warrior, Rosie. You're a wimp," Talia counters.

"Ah, but wise master, Rosie is only pretending to be weak. It's a warrior move." Suddenly, it sounds like Yoda invaded Archer's throat as he looks at Talia, and I chuckle.

"Wise master?" Talia questions.

"Yes, you are an expert teacher," Archer answers, still using the voice of a green Jedi trainer. As he gazes at Talia, his head rests on the nightstand behind him, which can't be comfortable.

"Mommy is a teacher," Talia says, her voice perking up. "I want to be a teacher, too."

"I can see that." His voice returns to normal, and he quickly glances up at me. He hasn't exactly avoided me since what happened earlier, but I find it hard to look directly at him, slightly embarrassed that I walked out, slightly mortified that I let him do what he did.

"And I can be a warrior," Rosie adds.

Archer turns to Rosie. "You can be whatever you want, princ—er . . . *warrior*." He winks at her, and she smiles around the thumb still in her mouth.

As he continues the story, the girls are enthralled by his voice and his interpretation as he rattles the book in parts, causing both the girls to flinch then giggle. His storytelling is rather animated, and he's fun to observe and listen to. Watching him read to my girls, my heart warms more toward this mystery man. He's so good to my girls, and he's been more than good to me. Migraine care and orgasm relief rank up there. But it's also the little things. He fixed me a plate the other night. He kept my wineglass full tonight. He's there, circling me, watching me, and I don't want to misinterpret what I see, but the yearning in his eyes is hard to dismiss. It's a reflection of my own feelings. I want to know more about him because just like Rosie, I like him.

When the book is finished, Archer sets it behind his head on the nightstand and uses his hands on each bed to pull himself upward. Only, he stumbles as he rises, and his left knee gives out.

"Whoa," he cries out as he pitches forward, and I stand to catch him. His face contorts for a second as if pain rips up his body. He even hisses a little. *What is this all about?* He clutches at the edges of the beds another second, holding his balance in a bent position. Standing before him, I keep my hands poised to touch his shoulders.

"Are you alright?"

In response, his arms wrap around my waist, and I'm hiked up and over his shoulder. Head dangling, my eyes are level with his backside. I screech, and the girls laugh. Spinning in place, Archer faces the girls, and I grip the waistband of his jeans in need of something to hold.

"Archer," I shriek, laughing, which hurts as my belly presses into his shoulder.

"Say good night to Mommy-butt," he teases the girls.

"Good night, Mommy-butt," the girls cry out in unison.

"What are you doing?" I continue to struggle, fighting the laughter while my face heats, blood rushing to my cheeks.

"Sleepover with Mommy tonight," Archer announces.

"What are you saying?" I hiss, my voice dropping.

"What?" he whines, still facing the girls, still holding me over his shoulder. "They get to share a room. I want to share a room."

I can hear the pout in his voice and imagine one on his face. He probably looks kind of cute.

"Will you be our new daddy?" Rosie asks, and everything stops. My laughter. My heartbeat. Slowly, Archer lowers me before him, and I quickly spin to face Rosie, swiping at my hair which has fallen before my eyes.

"Why would you say that?" My voice lowers, softens even, while Archer remains stone-still behind me. He doesn't offer a sound of rebuttal or shock.

"Because only daddies go to bed with mommies," Rosie explains.

"Who told you that, sweetheart?" She isn't exactly wrong. I don't need to go into the explanation of how when two people love one another, and the timing is right blah-blah. Let her think for now it can be only moms and dads married to one another who sleep in the same bed.

"Trevor said it," Talia explains. "He says his daddy sleeps with Miss River because she's going to be his new mom soon, and when she has the baby, she'll be a real mom."

Out of the mouths of babes.

Archer remains in place, silently behind me. His hand came to my hip when I quickly turned to face the girls, settling me from a sharp spin, and his fingers remained there. Whether to continue steadying me or him, I'm not certain.

"No, sweetheart. Archer isn't going to replace your daddy. Mommy will be on the couch again." I try to assure both my girls, feeling very awkward discussing this before Archer. Stepping forward, I reach for Rosie's wild, blond curls and brush them back from her forehead before kissing her cheek and rubbing my nose to hers.

"Love you, warrior. Time for sleep."

"Love you, 'Locks."

I giggle as she meant *love you lots*, but she's been hearing Archer call me 'Locks. I straighten her covers, which will only be disheveled within minutes of her falling asleep. Crossing the space between the beds, I lean over Talia next, swiping a hand down her cheek as our eyes meet. Hesitation and question fill those young eyes matching mine. If only she knew inside me felt the same as her. I don't know what to think of Archer.

"Good night, my angel," I whisper to her as she is that to me. She's the miracle I never thought would happen. Then I got lucky, and it happened a second time.

Archer remains during this final ritual, and when I stand, he slowly backs out the door, hitting the light switch before we both exit the room. A small night-light in an outlet offers the girls a hint of light so they won't be frightened in an unfamiliar bedroom.

Closing the door, I lean my back against the wall to the side and tip back my head. "I'm sorry about that," I whisper to the ceiling while addressing Archer. I'm afraid to look at him after the daddy comments. Then I remember he started that conversation with his statement.

Sleepover with Mommy. My head snaps forward. "But what were you thinking?"

Archer steps up to me, closing the distance between us. His fingers capture a strand of my hair and brushes it over my ear. "I was thinking I gave a woman an orgasm, two in fact, and I can at least let her sleep in my bed with me."

I swallow the sudden lump in my throat, fighting between thinking he's sweet and wondering how many women he's given multiple orgasms to and allowed in his bed next to him.

"Why did we do that?" I whisper, focusing on his throat instead of his face. I can't look at him as I recall earlier. How brazenly I'd spread my knees for him. How vigorously I practically humped the showerhead. How open I was to him touching me.

"Because you wanted it, babe." His voice drops as he repeats the motion of stroking my hair, although the strands are already behind my ear. His fingers scoop around the lobe and lower to my neck. Then his hand slips to my chest. I'm wearing a lightweight robe I found over my summery pajamas of a tank top and shorty shorts. Archer's palm pushes aside the material to continue touching my skin, and he pauses over my racing heart.

"That's it," I stammer around his explanation.

"Babe. Be real. You wanted it. I wanted to give it to you."

"Archer," I groan. I have so many questions with answers I don't want to hear. I don't want him to regret earlier. *I* don't want to regret it. I don't want to call it a mistake. However, it certainly wasn't smart. It wasn't responsible. It wasn't motherly.

"It's only sleep. I've been good so far," he mutters, referencing his comment about sleepovers and sharing bedrooms. "The bathroom seems to be the danger zone with you."

For some reason, this makes me chuckle, and I shake my head.

"Let's watch a movie," he suggests, and I tip my brow. He doesn't seem like a hang on the couch, watch a movie kind of guy. There's so much I don't know about him. "I know you have a penchant for porn, but I was thinking we could find something a little more PG."

This only makes me laugh harder, brushing away my lacking knowledge of who he is, where he's been, and what he's been doing. He's here now, for some reason, and I focus on that as the important part of Archer. With his hand still on my chest, his palm vibrates against the heaving motion. He slowly smiles, one side of his mouth curling more than the other. His eyes drop to where his hand rests on me.

"That's a nice sound," he whispers, and I stop mid-laugh, surprised by the comment.

"Why do you do that?" I glance down at his fingers spread above my left breast.

"It reminds me I'm alive, and so are you."

Well.

13

[Archer]

The daddy comment didn't freak me out as much as it should have. I wasn't even surprised when Jenna eventually asked me if I ever wanted kids.

"I guess I figured someday I'd have them, but it hadn't happened." We're sitting on the same couch even though there are two in the room. She's tucked into the corner, and I took the middle cushion to be closer to her. She made popcorn but isn't eating half as much as I am. I can't remember the last time I had microwave popcorn or watched a movie with a woman.

"You aren't too old. Mick Jagger from The Rolling Stones has to be like a hundred and he keeps getting women pregnant all the time."

I snort. "Yeah, well, I'd like to be young enough to still enjoy my kids." I'm only forty-five, but some days I feel over a hundred myself. Especially when my leg seizes up as it did, simply lifting myself off the floor between the girls' beds.

"Never been married?" Jenna asks next, and I roll my head on the back of the couch, catching her eyes.

"Are you fishing for information?"

Her brows lift, and her forehead gets a cute wrinkle across it. "Hoping this is a soft topic."

I chuckle. "No to marriages." I tip a brow and add, "No to current girlfriends, as I'm assuming that's the next subject."

"Long-term girlfriend?"

Ah, that gets a little more complicated to explain, and leaning toward the hard topics. And I'm not interested in sharing that story with Jenna.

"How about you? How long were you married?"

Jenna purses her lips at my avoidance. "A little over three years when Ryan died." I already know he died when Rosie was a baby.

"So you got pregnant right away." I wiggle a brow

"We found out I was pregnant after we were engaged. Immaculate conception and all." She smiles at the biblical reference to the Virgin Mary.

I laugh. If there's anything I've learned about Jenna Davis, she's a sexual being, and there is no way she didn't have sex before her husband. Still, I'm curious. "Was he your first?"

"Hard topic for you but not me?" She arches a brow and then gives a heavy snort, answering my question. I don't need to know the rest of her history. We're both old enough to have experiences we regret. Viviana immediately comes to mind. Next comes the memory of Jenna in the tub. She was an experience and not one I'll ever regret. Even losing her mind, she smelled good, looked sweet, and was incredibly sexy. It wasn't an act; it came naturally to her. I'd been the actor with Vi.

"Right, the ballbuster," I tease, recalling the story I'd heard the other day on the beach.

"I prefer heartbreaker," she proudly states, but then her face falls. "Although, I really wasn't that either. More like a love 'em and leave 'em gal, and most guys were on the same page as me." The sour expression on her face proves she isn't as cavalier about her past relations as she wants me to believe. As for those guys agreeing with one and done, they were idiots. Jenna isn't someone you leave. You love her. You love her hard and soft and every topic in between.

When the first movie ends, we decide to watch a second one. Jenna slips lower and lower on her cushion until her head lays awkwardly on the armrest and her backside presses into my thigh. Tugging at her ankles, I stretch her legs over mine and rub my hand up her spine. I wait only a few minutes before I toss the cushions off the back of the couch and tuck myself behind her. Jenna's back rests at my front, and I stare at the movie playing on the screen.

"Okay with this, babe?" I ask after I'm in position, holding my breath, hoping she won't kick me off the couch.

"Yeah, this is good."

Two little girls sleeping in the other room. A woman stretched out before me. A silly romantic movie playing. Some would agree it feels pretty good. I'd say it's fucking fantastic, but I don't allow myself to

Loving at 40

think such thoughts. I'll slip into a role I can't ever have. I can't even pretend for a second that it's what I want, or I'll be lost in something that isn't an act.

We fall asleep on the couch again. While Jenna was originally at my front, we've shifted during the night. I wake to cool fingers tickling the skin of my waist just above my jeans. The top button of my pants is undone, my morning wood straining to the side, and her knee rests between my legs.

The heat of Jenna's center presses on my upper thigh, right through the denim, as her knee subtly moves up and down, knocking against the underside of my balls.

"Whatcha doing, 'Locks?" I tease. Jenna stops, and I slip my hand into my pants, adjusting the position of my dick to line up with my zipper. "I didn't say you had to stop, babe."

Her head is tucked into my shoulder, and my hand slides down her back, scooting under her opposite hip and hiking her over me. As I roll to my back, she gracefully straddles my body and lands with her hot center over my thick bulge. We both groan at the connection. Her fingers dig into the tee covering my chest as her hips roll forward, dragging her over my stiff shaft. Her hair topples forward, hiding her face a bit as she rocks against me. She is wearing some shorty robe over her equally skimpy pajama shorts and tank top, and the material slips down her arm, exposing her shoulder. Jenna reaches for it, attempting to put it back in place, but I swat the cotton off the top of her arm.

"You're so fucking sexy, Jenna."

Her eyes close as she undulates over me, hair wild, clothes disheveled, chewing her lip. She's rocking faster, rubbing harder. She's going to get us both off by dry humping me. My hands come to her hips, resting there as I follow her lead. Thrusting upward into her motions, I try to give her everything, try to get her there, despite the barrier of clothing.

"Mommy, I'm wet."

Jenna stills for only the pulse of a heartbeat before jumping off me. My own heart races. My chest rises and falls with sexual excitement and sudden disappointment.

"Shit," Jenna mutters, swiping at her hair and adjusting the fallen robe. Her eyes meet mine only briefly—an apology in them—before she focuses on her child. Rosie might need to be called the interloper, not warrior or princess.

"Okay, baby, let's head to the bathroom first."

I tip my head upward to see Rosie standing in the doorway, sucking her thumb. Sleepy and a little stinky even from here, I recognize what's happened. She peed the bed.

And although it might be wrong to think it, even that feels a little perfect.

"I'll get fresh sheets," I groan, rubbing two hands down my face before adjusting myself in my jeans once more and rolling off the couch.

+ + +

At night, we go dancing. Well, the women dance, and the men, minus Logan, grumble. He's out there with his wife, yukking it up as he tries to follow the calls. Noah had to back out at the last minute, and Zack keeps a sharp eye on his pregnant fiancée, who moves despite carrying a watermelon on the front of her. Anna and Jenna are actually pretty good at following instructions, and I fight the pull to keep my eyes on her swaying hips and her tight ass in those short shorts exposing those long, lush legs. She's giving Daisy Duke some competition.

"It's good to see Anna smile," Zack says to no one in particular. Mason simply nods and lifts his beer to his lips. Despite being the man who suggested we have an adults-only evening, he's been exceptionally quiet tonight. I half expected him to be out there on the dance floor, hitting on women *to the left, to the left, to the right, to the right,* as the song calls out the steps.

"How is she doing?" I feel like a schmuck asking about my own sister, and my thoughts immediately race back to my lunch with Calvin and Bryce. They wanted to know where I'd been and why I wasn't there for their father. Distrust was written all over their faces, and I'd put it there. I could make the wrong person believe in me, and my family . . . they didn't have faith in me.

"Some days are good. Some aren't," Zack speaks. He's been living next door for the past year, Anna's first year without Ben. Mason lived in my apartment for the months Ben was the sickest, and I could accuse him of leaving when Anna needed him most—which was after Ben was gone. However, what did I know? "She's found an unbiased friend in River."

My head tips, wondering what Zack means.

"All of us are constant reminders of what she had before. River's new, and when Anna goes out with her, she feels like she has a friend that's only hers, even if she is my soon-to-be wife."

I guess I get that. We all watch the girls for another few minutes. Anna laughing. Jenna following the dance calls like a pro. Autumn and Logan kind of doing their own thing.

"How is your venture going?"

For the next half hour, I listen to Zack and Mason discuss their new passion—Four Points. It's a joint venture between the four best friends capitalizing on each of their specialties: design, construction, landscape, and legal.

"How do you feel about landscaping?" Mason eventually asks me, reaching out for my shoulder and pressing at me.

I shrug him off. He's such a wanker. "I don't," I admit. I've never owned a home. After living in a place for two years pretending I was someone I wasn't, I now have a dump I use for sleeping and eating. I'd kill an innocent houseplant if I had one.

Zack laughs, dangling a beer bottle from his fingertips. "I told you Archer was a no."

"A no to what?" I ask.

"With Ben's death, we need a new fourth."

"I'm surprised you'd let anyone into the sacred realm." I wiggle my fingers, lowering my voice as I mention the tight friendship these men have had for twenty years. I had the same things with the guys in the force until I had to act like I didn't know anyone. I'd been a loner for too long, forgetting how to interact with people. I've been working on it in therapy.

"We *aren't* just letting anyone in," Mason stresses. "We want someone close to us."

I'm a little surprised he's even asking me as I've been more out than in with my family over the years. "Yeah, I don't think it's for me." Working on someone's lawn isn't how I see my future. I need to get back on track and be assigned another investigation. My fist falls against my thigh. I need my leg to heal.

With that thought, I glance up to find a man sidled up behind Jenna. His hands are on her hips. He's moving her side to side with the sway of his own. Her ass bumps into his front, and his palm coasts up under her arm. Her head twists to the side, and he leans into her neck. Her eyes meet mine across the distance.

Before I know it, I'm out of my seat faster than one can say *landscaping*. This man will not touch what belongs in only my yard.

Jenna looks at me, all dance-crazed, a little seductive, and possibly tipsy. The girls were going at it pretty hard when we first arrived, doing some crazy named shots called blowjobs and lollipops. It didn't take a genius to know who named those, but it took a freaking saint to watch Jenna open wide to rim the shot glass, then tip her head with hands behind her back and swallow.

Handsy-Dancer gives me a chin tip as I near Jenna and him and returns his attention to Jenna's lush body. She freezes in place. Her eyes lock on mine, and I hold out my hand.

"Babe." The word says it all. *Step away from this guy and come with me.*

Only Handsy-Dancer shifts his body, blocking me with his back as he moves Jenna before him. "Get your own slice of perfection," he mutters, giving me another chin tip over his shoulder and a tight grin.

"She *is* my perfection," I say, reaching around him to catch her upper arm.

"What do you think you're doing?" Handsy addresses me, but I'm only watching Jenna, who tugs her arm from my grasp. Her flinch should say it all, but I'm not letting up. My fist lifts, and I'm this close to clocking this guy. *This close*, until Jenna steps before him.

112

"What are you doing?" she yells at me, holding up her hands like I'm about to hit her, which I would never, ever do.

"You want him?" I snap, lowering my fist.

Of course she'd want him. Some small-town guy, living a decent life and making an honest wage. He'll love her right and raise her children, and I'm going to fucking bury him.

"What are you talking about?" she shouts over the music. My eyes search her face. My heart races. Is she trying to bait me? Is she purposely trying to make me jealous? We aren't even together. So what if I gave her an orgasm or two? I gave them freely. She wants this putz, so be it. Let him get her off.

I wave up my hand. "I'm outta here." Turning on my heels, I stalk through the crowd, not even needing to force my way as the vibe coming off me reads *get the fuck away* from me. I press through the front door with a heavy shove and stomp onto the gravel drive.

"Hey," a feminine voice calls out behind me less than a minute outside. "Hey, I'm talking to you."

I stop and spin, finding Jenna closer than I expected. She halts before bumping into me.

"Oh yeah, 'Locks. Sure you wouldn't rather talk to him?" Wouldn't she rather dance with some guy who can? Wouldn't she rather be with some handsy man who could probably commit to her? Wouldn't she rather be with some schmuck who can give her everything she needs? She should want those things. I want them for her.

But I don't want it shoved in my face.

"What do you care?" Jenna snaps.

We glare at one another. My eyes search hers, taking in the depths of that brown, the spark of her anger, and the innocence behind them. Instantly, I remind myself she isn't Vi. She isn't playing games. She isn't trying to bait me into jealousy.

I don't need to pretend I am because I really am.

"What's that supposed to mean?" I growl back at her, forcing her to step back from me as I lean forward. A new dance begins of her stepping back and me following until her back hits the side of the building after three long strides.

Her eyes hold mine. "You can't be jealous of him," she snaps.

"I sure the fuck can," I huff.

"Why?" Her voice softens but strains. "Why, Archer? I don't understand you. You're . . . you're such a mystery."

Swiping a hand over my hair, I stare at her. "Too many hard topics."

"But what does that have to do with tonight? With that guy? With me?"

How can't she see it? How can't she feel the pull she has on me?

"You haven't even kissed me."

I—*What?!*

"You wanna be kissed, 'Locks?" I cup her face so fast, her mouth falls open, allowing me the perfect opportunity to crush her mouth with mine, invading the opening with my tongue. My lips sip and suck at hers like she did with that damn tempting ice cream cone the other night. Her mouth is all heat, though, and I crave the warmth as her tongue swirls with mine. My entire body gets into the kiss as I pin her against the building. My lower body presses against her as my fingers delve into her hair, cupping her head. I thrust my hips forward, forcing the bulge in my jeans into the seam of her short shorts while I clutch at the softness of her locks. *My 'Locks.*

"You don't think I wanted to kiss you?" I mutter against her mouth, moving down to her chin and scraping my teeth over the hard edge of her jaw. I suck at her neck. "I want to do everything with you, Jenna."

I want to fuck all the nonsense out of her. Take away that occasional flinch. Settle those wary eyes. Fill her up and watch her explode as she did yesterday. Two times. *Give her three.* Maybe four.

Hell, I'd be happy to kiss her for an eternity, which is the craziest thought I've had since meeting this woman. This incredible woman who's feisty and protective, sweet and sassy. She's a good friend, an excellent mother, and this kiss tells me she'd be the best of lovers.

My mouth quickly returns to hers, sucking at the swell of those lips and tangling my tongue with hers. She moans into me, and I swallow the sound, allowing it to curl down my throat and settle in my belly. I want to eat her up and live off her. And this mouth. Her taste. Her sighs.

"Whoa, not seeing anything."

We part on a gasp at a voice we both recognize. Our breathing is jagged. Our hearts race. Turning our heads, we find Logan standing just outside the bar door, holding up his hands like he's surrendering to something.

His head turns sideways, his eyes averted from our position. "Nope, didn't see a thing." He blindly reaches for the door and tugs it open, cutting him off from our sight again.

I turn back to face Jenna, lowering my forehead to hers. My hands haven't left her hair, but one slides down her neck and finds its place above her left breast. Feeling that heartbeat under her skin. Knowing it beats for me, for her. We are both living, but I want that heart to love me.

My eyes close on the dangerous thought.

She'll break me if she does. Heartbreaker and ballbuster all rolled into one. This woman could shatter me because I've never wanted anything more than to deserve her.

14

[Jenna]

Whoa! My heart races, and my lips want more. I've never been kissed the way Archer kissed me. His entire body was in that kiss. Hands in my hair. Bodies lined up. Chest to chest. And his mouth—it was sin, seduction, and something between. Unfortunately, Logan's interruption brought us back to reality.

Once upon a time, I might have let some random guy take me up against a building, but that isn't the direction I want to go with Archer. As he leads me back into the bar, I'm still catching my breath.

Noticing Anna sitting near a petulant-looking Mason, I yell over the music. "I should stay a little longer." The comment has Archer spinning to face me. He's holding my hand, and the shift of his body blocks my view of the table.

"You don't want to go, babe?" Calling me babe would be sweet if he weren't saying it every five seconds. It feels like an act, like he's forcing the term to keep me in some sort of place.

I want to do everything with you, Jenna.

When he actually used my name, a shiver rippled up my body from my toes to my head, picking up steam in my midsection. My name in his strained voice was like a mini orgasm. That rough tone. His heavy breathing. I want him, but I can't leave Anna. Plus, I need to get my head on straight. I am not here for some fling with my best friend's older brother. That is so romance novel, and while I'm not opposed to the fantasy, the reality is . . . I can't leave yet.

"For your sister." Archer looks over his shoulder at his sibling, and the tension in him slowly releases. "I'm here for her," I remind both him and me, hoping he understands. I talked Anna into this night. I can't ditch her.

Archer's eyes return to mine, and just like they did in the parking lot, they narrow and burn, but it isn't desire. He's questioning me, questioning something about me, but I can't read him. And I still can't believe he almost punched a guy for dancing with me. If he wanted to dance, why didn't he ask? Just like if he wanted to kiss me, why hadn't he before?

He certainly made up for it, kissing the bejesus out of me outside.

"Yeah. Team Anna," Archer weakly mocks.

"Hey," I whisper-scold. "Don't be like that."

Archer tips his chin up once to agree and squeezes my hand. Only I pull mine back, and he stops, glancing down where I struggle to be released.

"What's this, 'Locks?" A mixture of hurt and apprehension fills his tone. He isn't as angry as he was outside but still . . . upset, and I sense another eruption coming.

"I'm just . . . I'm here for Anna." I don't want to rub in Anna's face whatever it is we're doing, and we're definitely doing something. Kissing her brother was not part of the vacation manual, yet I don't want a refund on that kiss. I want more. More of him. More *with* him. However, everything about Archer says unavailable, and that's not what I desire. He needs to be all in. For me . . . and my girls.

The music shifts to something softer, and the dance floor clears while we stand only feet from the table. A slow song comes on, giving people a break from the collective mash of country music involved in line dancing.

"Dance with me, babe." He isn't asking. He never asks. He just tells me, and I easily follow his command.

I place my hand in his, and he leads me out to the dance floor. I don't even have to glance at the table to know all eyes are on us. Thankfully, Logan brings Autumn out to the floor, and Zack follows with River, keeping her back to his front to accommodate her belly. Mason and Anna remain at the table, and my heart breaks a little.

"It's difficult to lose someone," I say as Archer holds me close. My hand curls over his shoulder while his arm wraps around my back. "She's lonely."

Archer huffs at my ear. *Aren't we all*, the sound says, but I can't be certain he really is alone. He's assured me of no girlfriend but avoided the hard topic of a long-term one. He wasn't married, and something tells me commitment is an issue for Archer. In a relationship. If I knew what his job was, I'd say he might be married to it, but I have no idea where he's been or what he does. Either way, I'm only a layover for him. Like the frequent flyer who makes a pit stop every once in a while to enjoy the local culture for a few days. The thought sours my stomach.

"It's difficult to put yourself back out there," I continue, uncertain why I'm explaining all this to him. A man I just kissed outside a country bar. Maybe I'm speaking more about myself than Anna. "It's a risk to love again, or even to be involved with someone else. Anna has the addition of her kids to think about." As do I. It's why I haven't dated since Ryan's death. I don't need a man on a layover. I need a man willing to be grounded. Archer remains silent, so I pull back to look up at him. "She can't think about only herself. She's a package deal. Family style on the menu. Party of more than one. She's—"

"I think I got it," Archer snips with a soft chuckle. His eyes stare back at mine.

"But she's still human. She still has needs and desires as an individual. Not mother, wife, or teacher. She deserves to have those needs met." I pause for a second, still wondering if I'm referring to Anna or myself. "Me time, I guess you'd call it. Personal time to be . . . free. Or maybe just be."

Archer continues to look into my eyes, and we hold one another in that manner for a long minute.

Does he understand how to just be settled?

"When you've been alone for a long time, craving company becomes your thing. Companionship becomes your desire. When you can't stand yourself, you want someone else to stand you," he says, surprising me.

We aren't talking about Anna anymore. Who hurt him? Why doesn't he like himself? Can he mean what he says? Does he want to be with people or just one person?

"That's what marriage is. That's what relationships are. That person who stands beside you and sometimes carries you. We all want those things." I glance back at his sister. "It's just harder to get there a second time around. That is, if the chance even arises."

Everything is still too new for Anna, but she's still young. I don't want her to give up on things like love and life. I don't want her to dismiss the desire for what she misses, like sex and holding hands, and hanging out and kisses. We've talked about a few of these things, but she isn't ready to hear someday it might happen again. *Maybe, someday.*

Gazing up at Archer, I'm reminded of how *I* still want those things as well. I just need to be selective in who and how I choose to fulfill my needs.

"Never had a first love," Archer states, his voice dropping as his gaze drifts to my mouth, pausing a minute. "Do you really believe in second chances?"

"People say lightning never strikes twice, but stranger things have happened." Like meeting the man holding me, being kissed like I've never kissed before, and wanting a chance to do it again.

Archer eyes me. His lips curling at the corner, and that gravelly voice lowers even more when he says, "Yeah, stranger things."

+ + +

After the slow song, Anna said she was ready to leave, and as much as I begged her to dance again, the excitement for a night out fizzled. We returned to the house, but before Archer and I entered the apartment, he has me up against the exterior wall, kissing me once more like he did outside the bar. Savoring the lower swell and upper curve of my mouth, he's equal parts hard and tender, rushed and patient. His entire body flattens against mine, holding my wrists over my head and stretching him out to cover me. We line up everywhere. Lips. Hips. Knees. Mine are weak when he pulls away, as he bites the lower curl of his mouth and lays his forehead against mine.

"Just wanted to pretend it was a date and give you a good night kiss on the landing." My God, there's so much sweet in that gruff voice.

"We don't need to pretend anything," I tell him, causing him to pull back and just stare at me. I'd love to know what he's thinking, but he won't tell me even if I ask. His thoughts are a hard topic, which leaves me wondering what that means for his heart.

Of course, a kiss isn't a commitment, and I remind myself to live in the moment. Actually, I can pretend, too. I'll be his layover a little longer.

He kisses me again—all tongue and a little teeth—until he's smiling against my lips. "We should probably get inside." Mila and Lorna are waiting as they babysat the girls for me.

Once we enter the apartment, Archer offers to walk the young teens to the main house, which is really only a few feet across the driveway. Again. Sweet.

While I wait for Archer to return, I still ponder his reaction to the man dancing with me. Admittedly, that guy was getting a little handsy, but Archer's admission of jealousy had surprised me. He didn't answer my question, though. *Why?* Where did that initial anger come from? He wasn't the Archer I'm slowly growing to know but someone else for a few minutes. Until I questioned him about not kissing me, and he launched himself into proving he wanted to.

We have things to discuss, but when he returns to the apartment, he speaks immediately.

"Babe, I can't do that couch again." He nods where I'm seated. "We need to go to bed." We'd fallen asleep on the sofa last night. I like this old thing. It's the kind you can really sink into, but it isn't the best for your back.

"You can go to bed. I'll stay on the couch."

Archer gives me a scathing look like I'm speaking some language he doesn't understand, and something tells me he's not in the mood for interpretation.

"I'm giving you ten minutes to do what you need to do."

I interpret his meaning. *Be in his bed.* He's so pushy.

Allowing him to use the bathroom first, I change in the girls' room. After I use the bathroom to remove my makeup and brush my teeth, I find Archer laying on his stomach, pillow tucked under his head. He's shirtless with the sheet up to his waist. Without having to imagine it, the thick band of boxer briefs tells me he sleeps in only his underwear or at least, he's doing it for me. I stand next to the bed for a second, looking down at him, noting the tattoo on his back.

My best teacher friend back home is married to a man with a ton of tattoos. Ryan even had a few, but Leon Ramirez's are different. From what his wife Tricia has told me, he was in a gang as a teen and part of his adult life. The giant snake down his spine. The crown, raised and marred like something branded him over it. The ink has meanings I don't want to know, and Archer has something similar on his left shoulder blade. As I've only seen him a few times with his shirt off, I hadn't noticed. All the times we were in the apartment, and I've only seen his chest. He keeps himself covered at the beach.

"What does it mean?" I whisper, standing beside the bed, admiring the muscular sculpture of his back.

Archer rubs his nose into the pillow before twisting his head back to the side and speaking. "Hard topic, babe."

He won't explain, but I need something from him. Is he in trouble? Is he in a gang?

Stepping back, he shoots his arm outward, sharp and fast, latching his hand to the back of my thigh. If I thought I could escape to the couch, I wouldn't make it two inches let alone the few feet necessary to reach the other room. He tips his head to look up at me. "'Locks. Bed."

"Give me something, Archer." My voice shakes. He doesn't want to pretend, he said nights ago. I don't want him to keep avoiding subjects. We stare at one another for a long minute. Me standing over him. Him with his arm around my legs. "You almost punched a man tonight."

"Yeah." His sandpapery voice drops low, and he props himself up on an elbow, slipping his hand free from my leg. The sheet adjusts, hardly covering his boxer briefs, but I won't be distracted by the dark fabric below his stacked abs or the trail of hair leading lower.

"Why'd you do that?" I whisper. *She is my perfection.* The words come back to me.

"I was jealous, babe."

The fact he outright admits it again surprises me. "Why?"

"I wanted to dance with you."

L.B. Dunbar

"And you did. Eventually." I tilt my head, ready to ask another question, but he interrupts me.

"I didn't want him dancing with you, though."

"So you should have asked me to dance."

Archer falls to his back and glares up at the ceiling. "I can't dance."

My mouth falls open and then snaps shut. He did dance, though. "You were fine with me." We danced to the slow song together. Actually, two of them played before we left.

"I—" He stops himself.

"Do not tell me this is a hard topic." I bitterly chuckle, staring at this man who's a mystery to me and to most everyone else at this reunion. My eyes fall to the medallion lying against his firm chest. *Protection.* There has to be something he can tell me.

When he doesn't answer, I press in a whisper thin voice. "Tell me about the tattoos."

"Jenna." When he says my name, it's a warning. It also feels like I'm getting the real Archer. Not some tough guy act with the babe and the 'Locks nickname. Not the one with short sentences and sharp commands. Saying my name is when he's honest. The truth is he doesn't want to tell me. He's *afraid* to tell me.

"Fine," I mutter, leaving the lamp on the nightstand still glowing and round the bed. Roughly, I pull down the sheet and flop onto my side, giving him my back. The bed is big enough we can keep our distance.

It was only a couple of kisses. We were caught up in the heated moment. They don't have to mean anything, but my chest aches with the thought, and my eyes burn with tears I refuse to shed.

"Fuck it," Archer says behind me, and the bedsheet shifts behind me. My name is a whisper.

"What are you doing?" I question over my shoulder, peering at him from the awkward angle. The sheet has been lowered to just above his knees, and I stare at his thick legs.

Then I see it.

An ugly-looking scar, deep red and puckered. Angry and severe.

I can't be certain, but the skin looks like a healed wound . . . from a gunshot.

122

15

[Archer]

I stare up at the ceiling, holding my breath and clutching at the bedsheet lowered enough to expose the ugly divot on my upper thigh.

Jenna shifts, moving from giving me her back to facing me on her side. Her hand reaches for my leg and then retracts.

"What happened?" Everything in her voice expresses her concern, maybe even her fear. It's a hideous scar and a constant reminder of who I am and what I've done. The mark is a permanent stain of Viviana in my life.

"It's a scar." I state the obvious.

"It looks fresh." The redness around the dip in my skin looks much better than it did months ago. "Eight months old." Bitterness fills my tone. The puncture is forever, and counting months won't make it better.

When Jenna doesn't speak, I roll my head on the pillow and stare over at her. Her eyes flick up to my face with a silent command. *Speak*.

I can deflect every hard topic, but something inside me wants to tell her this story. Maybe this will frighten her away from me, and I need to frighten her. I need her to be the one to walk away because the pull to her is too difficult for me. I need her to step back because I'm struggling to find the strength to do it myself.

That kiss sealed my fate.

"I was shot."

Jenna's hesitant fingers reach forward again. Her hand lands just below the puckered wound. She scoots closer to me on the bed, so the stretch isn't as far. Slowly, her thumb and forefinger spread, almost as if cupping the spot. Her fingertips travel around the crooked circle before her entire hand flattens over the scar. The heat of her palm is like a soothing balm over a silent ache, and I close my eyes.

"I'm certain the aim was for my dick, but the bullet hit my upper thigh instead. It nearly knicked the femoral artery. If the bullet had been in a slightly different position, I wouldn't be sitting here." Doc said I'd been lucky. If the main arterial supply to my thigh had been hit, I could have bled out within minutes. I don't need to explain the particulars to Jenna. Her husband died from something similar. "I have femoral nerve damage instead."

"Does it hurt?"

"Sometimes. It's like a constant burn just under my skin."

The numbness in the front and inside of my left thigh is a constant ache I've learned to live with. I have to remind myself I'm alive when I should have been dead. If the aim had been better, if the bullet lodged deeper, *if, if, if*... The firm fact is I'd been shot and lived to tell about it. To meet this beautiful woman who doesn't seem afraid of a little scar tissue.

Jenna's fingertips move, smoothing over the skin as if spreading an ointment, a salve to help me heal. My chest tightens. My eyes remain closed as I melt into the tenderness of her touch.

Doctors warned me I could also have a tingling sensation in my groin area and loss of genital function. Jenna's soft strokes prove my dick still works. Her tender touch is making me hard. My cock hasn't been half as alert in eight months as it's been in the last week with this woman.

"Sometimes my knee gives out when I move too fast from up and down, but it all depends." I speak to distract myself. Now isn't the time to be aroused, but I can't help my body's reaction to Jenna's affection. She's still circling, and tracing, and softly touching my damaged skin.

"It's why I can't dance." I laugh a little, hoping the subject is now closed, but I should have known better. Once I opened the lid a little, Jenna's going to want the entire jar.

"Who did this?" she asks next, her voice even lower.

"Hard topic," I whisper back because I don't want to talk about Viviana tonight. It's safer for Jenna if she doesn't know. I also don't want to bring Vi into this bed with Jenna beside me. I'm already cursing myself for even showing her this wound when all I wanted to do was hold her again. And maybe kiss her. More kissing would be nice.

It's been so long since my mouth merged with another, since I've enjoyed the pleasure. Hell, even remembered the desire to kiss someone. I didn't kiss Vi. There was something about the way she kissed that turned me off, or maybe it was knowing why our mouths met. Maybe it felt too much like a commitment, like I'd be part of her family forever. I was only so good as an actor.

And I didn't want to be one of them.

They made certain I wouldn't.

"Are you in trouble?" Her voice is wary, and that tightening in my chest loosens a little at the genuine concern in her question. "Are you in a gang?"

I softly chuckle as my eyes open, and I turn my head in her direction again. Reaching around her propped elbow, I play with the ends of her hair, which dangle over her shoulder and down her back. Her fingers continue to stroke around the scar.

"Why would you say that?"

"The tattoos."

"Not every person with ink is in a gang, babe."

Jenna nods once. "I know, but my friend's husband is a former gang member, and you have something similar to his tattoos on your back."

My fingers in her hair still, and I pull back my head to get a better look at her. "Who are you hanging out with?" I chortle then hold my breath on her answer. I don't want to go into an explanation about how some tattoos can look similar to the untrained eye, but minor details set one crown apart from another. It's about angles and curves, points and stars, color and even texture, not to mention placement. I plan to get mine removed as soon as I can.

"Tricia Ramirez is one of my best friends." Her eyes narrow, and her fingertips still. A protectiveness fills her voice. "She's one of the best people I know, and Leon is . . . He worships the ground she walks on. She was his second chance, and he's hers. He had a rough life, but he's different, he says. And I believe him. And she had a few rough years and deserves the love he gives her."

Her defense of her friends is admirable. She obviously idolizes her friend's relationship, and it has me wondering if she could love a man like me? Could she love a man who's done bad things but had decent intentions? Just as quickly as the questions cross my mind, I erase the thought.

No woman will love you like I did. The female voice negates the possibility. I didn't need that brand of love anyway.

"I'm not in a gang, 'Locks." My fingers return to toying with those soft raven strands. "I'm one of the good guys."

But was I?

You're a despicable human. Viviana's voice returns. The glare in her beady eyes. The sneer on her face. She had no idea. I hated myself for what I'd done, but I hated her more.

"What does that mean?" Jenna asks, and my thoughts return to the present. Can I tell her? Can I trust her? Her innocent eyes beg me for answers, and I decide to give her a little more of me.

"I work for the DEA."

"Drug Enforcement Administration?" she clarifies.

"Yes. I've been undercover for years." Just admitting that feels like a weight off my shoulders. A small one, but a relief nonetheless.

"And that's why you've been absent all this time?" She continues when I don't respond. "You weren't missing. You were working." Her brows pinch. Her expressive face tells me more questions are rolling into that smart brain of hers.

"I was on assignment for the past five years." In a relationship that nearly killed me for two of them.

"And that's when this happened?" She points at my scar as if she can no longer touch it.

"Yes. It's been eight months." New Year's Eve. We'd just announced our engagement. I didn't want to marry Viviana, but I would have. I'd do whatever it took because we were getting close to cracking the investigation.

Jenna's eyes wander back to the bullet wound. "And you've been in recovery since then?" Her voice drops, shaky and rough. Suddenly, it hits me. This must be difficult for her. I was shot but survived. Her husband had been killed. The innocent dead. The guilty still living.

Fuck.

"Yes." I clarify, "Physical and mental."

Her head shoots up again, eyes meeting mine. "I'm glad you're getting help." She glances back at the puckered skin.

"Why haven't I noticed this before?" Jenna seems to be asking herself as her eyes focus on my thigh. Maybe it's because I wear longer shorts, along with T-shirts at the beach to cover the tats. Maybe it's that I've worn jeans more often than anything else, having grown used to pants covering the scar along with the thinness of one leg compared to the other for a while. I'd worked hard in physical therapy and then on my own to strengthen and rebuild what I could.

When I don't answer her, Jenna leans over my thigh and presses a kiss to the permanent mark.

I gasp.

Her lips linger, and my eyes close.

Fuck, that feels good, and I don't deserve someone so good, so innocent, so sweet in my life.

Then her mouth moves. Soft sips and the tip of her tongue peeks out, working over and around the puckered patch. She shifts, slipping her body between my legs and kissing my scar over and over again. With a hand on the side of my thigh, her other hand strokes the short distance to the bulge in my boxer briefs. The palm of her hand cups my balls before her fingers squeeze the thick length.

"Fuck, Jenna. Babe." My tongue tangles, and my mouth dries. Her lips continue to pepper my thigh while her hand massages my hard dick. "What are you doing to me?" I groan, but I don't want her to stop. With every kiss, with every stroke, she's erasing the ugly memories and building new ones I'll never want to forget.

Her hand squeezes harder on my cock, and her mouth opens, sucking at my skin again, lapping at the wound, offering it healing. My fingers delve into that hair of hers, combing through the length and curling it around my hand until I can't take it anymore.

"I need that mouth."

Jenna's fingers curl into the waistband of my boxer briefs and tug downward. As much as I want those lips sucking on me elsewhere, there's something more important to me tonight.

"No, babe. Up here." I tap my lower lip with my finger, hoping she catches my meaning. I need more kissing. When she doesn't stop on my thigh, and her fingers tighten in my waistband, I take action. I fist her hair and remove her from my leg with a gentle tug. Then I jackknife upward and capture her mouth, cupping her chin and forcing my tongue between her lips.

God, I just want to kiss her all night.

I want this to be the way she erases all my pain, all the aches and burns, and bad memories.

She follows my lead as I open wider, dip deeper, sweeping inside the cavern of her mouth to tangle with her tongue. Slowly, leaning back, I pull her with me until her body blankets mine. Her breasts, free of a bra, crush against my chest under the thin material of her tank top. One of her legs slips between mine, pressing her thigh against my rock-hard cock while my thigh rests under the heat seeping through her short shorts, but I only want her mouth right now.

Her head tilts and mine shifts, allowing us to continue exploring with lips and tongues until teeth nip and grins grow. I move down to her chin and scrape my teeth over the hard ball. She angles toward my cheeks, peppering them with kisses like she'd given my thigh. I seek her jaw with my lips, sucking at it before dragging my teeth along the edge. She rubs her face against the prickly stubble on mine. Her breathing comes heavy, and her breasts swell against my chest.

"I swear I only want to kiss you, but I want you to lose the shirt, babe. I want to feel your skin." She slips back only enough to wrestle out of her tank, exposing the lushest breasts I've ever seen—ripe and round with bright pink nipples peaked and pointy.

Shit. I want to kiss her there as well, but first, I bring her mouth back to mine and sigh as her warm skin meets mine. Those full tits flatten against the firmness of my chest, and the heat between us soars. Our kissing grows frantic, desperate even, as my hands slip into her hair again, fingers fisting clumps of her smooth locks. Her hands skim over my biceps and up my shoulders, circling my neck with her arms. She holds me to her as our mouths refuse to separate.

Holy shit, I could love her.

I could also fucking come from only her mouth on me.

As if sensing how close I am, Jenna spreads her legs, straddling me, and rests that hot center of hers over my hard length. Our mouths remain attached as the rest of our body lines up as well.

"Jenna," I groan against her, her name vibrating into her mouth. Her thighs clench, forcing her thinly covered core to drag over my dick. My hands instantly release her hair and slap down on her ass, holding her still over me.

She purrs against my lips, causing the hum to dance against my tongue. I swallow, and Jenna releases me.

"No," I moan, not wanting her to stop kissing me. I place one hand back in her hair.

"Archer," she softly cries in that way she did the other day as I held the showerhead at her clit.

"Yeah, babe?" I tease, questioning her but swallowing her answer as I seek her mouth again. Her hips rock, and my eyes would roll back if they weren't already shut. I don't need to see her. I feel her. I feel her everywhere. On my cock. In my chest. Burrowing toward my racing heart.

"What are you doing to me?" I groan as my balls tighten. I don't know that I've ever been this hard.

She doesn't answer but dives into my mouth again, forcing her tongue against mine and sucking at my lower lip before giving it a teasing bite. She pulls back, but I lift my head, not allowing her to retreat far before meeting her mouth again. Her hips rock forward. I thrust upward. My hand holds one ass cheek and her fingers dig into my shoulders.

"Fuck," I mutter, releasing her. "I'm so close."

"I'm gonna . . . You're gonna . . . make me . . ." Jenna stills, clenching her entire body tight. Her thighs squeeze my hips, and her pelvis tips the slightest bit. Warm wetness soaks her shorts and seeps against my covered length, and I can't hold back. I come like a teen on his first time, spewing in my boxers and loving every second of the release. Jenna shifts, but I grip her hips, keeping her over me until my dick stops pulsing and the final drop drips.

Our eyes meet. "You made me come from a kiss."

129

Her dark eyes light up, and a slow grin curls her swollen, red lips. "You kissed me until I came."

We both chuckle, and her body jiggles over mine until I roll us to our sides. Our legs tangle together as my arms wrap around her, keeping her close to me. There's so much I want to say, words piling up on the tip of my tongue that I've never said to anyone before. Words that feel too soon and too easy to give to her.

Instead, I just look at her. Those dark eyes. That raven hair. Those kissed lips. I try to memorize everything about her to carry deep inside me on my next mission.

16

[Archer]

In the morning, I wake alone but hear the subtle sounds of the television. My bedroom is still dark. Dang, those princesses are early risers. Speaking of an early riser, I have something that needs attention and no warm woman to attend to it. I smile to myself with thoughts of last night.

Then I consider my actions. I kissed her.

What was I thinking?

I answer my own thought. I was thinking I wanted to kiss her, and she didn't disappoint. Everything about Jenna surprises me. I'm the guy who doesn't want to be close to another woman for as long as I continue to live, but I can't fight this attraction between us. However, I can't go through what I went through with Viviana. I need to keep my head up, stay alert, and heal to prove to the department I'm ready to return.

Still, I can't seem to keep my hands off Jenna or my mouth . . . which waters just thinking about kissing her again.

On that note, I flip back the covers and sit upright, rubbing my left thigh, which aches. I can't believe I told Jenna part of my history. Then again, it felt good to get some of that off my chest to someone other than my therapist. Sure, I told Noah some things as well, but Jenna, again, is different. Sitting on the edge of the bed, I scrub two hands down my face.

"Did they wake you?" Jenna's sleep-rough voice from near the door is like an electric current to a part of me already erect and standing at full mast. Her presence startles me, and I turn to glance at her while trying to adjust myself. It's hopeless. One look in her direction destroys any chance of my morning wood lowering its salute.

"Hey." My own voice croaks. "No, I didn't hear them." I should have heard the girls. My ears used to be perked for the slightest sound. I used to sleep deep but in short spurts, but something about sleeping next to Jenna lulled me into relaxed comfort. A strange peace surrounds me when I'm near her.

Leaning on the open door, she tilts her head against the wood. "I was going to make breakfast. Want to put in a request?"

My request would be for her to return to this bed and be my meal, but I understand the princesses need their mother, and the queen takes on a new role. From sympathizer and seductress last night, Jenna slips easily back into caregiver, protector, and breakfast provider. I chuckle at the thought. She's a pretender, too. *Or is she?*

I stare at her a second longer, deciding Jenna plays many roles, but she isn't faking any of them. She's multitalented and can multitask. She's going to tend to her girls—and me if I let her. And I haven't had someone take care of me in a long time.

"Come here." I tip my head at her, beckoning her to cross the room. I just want a sip of her sweet taste this morning.

Jenna stands before me, and I wrap my arms around her thighs, tugging her between my spread knees. Her hands lower to my shoulders, and I peer up at her.

"How'd you sleep?" she whispers, giving me that caring I didn't know I was craving.

"Like a log." I mean it. No bad dreams. No nightmares that woke me. Just peace. Her hand swipes over my hair as I look up at her, like a puppy begging for a treat. "Kiss me."

She leans forward, giving me one that's too quick and incomplete. Pulling back, I clutch her thighs tighter to me. "What's this?" The question comes out harsher than I intend, but I don't understand her brush-off and hesitancy now that it's morning.

"I think we should establish some ground rules," she states, hardly meeting my eyes.

"Why?" I snap.

"My girls," she whispers. I remain quiet a second, assessing her, and she continues. "They aren't used to seeing me with anyone, a man, in any way, and I'm not certain what we're doing. So maybe we can treat this like Vegas. Keep it in the bedroom and keep it between us." Her lips twist, and her nervousness is kind of cute.

"Okay," I answer, gruff and low, but understanding her. "But as we're still in the bedroom, kiss me."

I reach for the back of her head and tug her down a bit to capture those lips in a kiss that will need to last me all day apparently. Our mouths instantly open, tongues coming together. She's brushed her teeth and tastes of mint and a hint of tea. She also tastes like a craving I've had my entire life and never indulged.

I want all of her.

I pull back first, hearing the faintest sound. Releasing her legs almost as quickly, she falters forward, hands falling on my shoulders again to prevent her from crashing into me.

"Mommy, when can we have pancakes?" I glance over my shoulder to meet Talia's sleepy eyes. Jenna chokes on a laugh and steps back, bringing her fingers to her mouth.

"Just give me another minute, honey." She swallows hard, trying to recover from this morning's greeting. *Yeah, I'd kiss her every morning like that if I could.*

"Why is Archer naked?"

Oh, man.

"He's not naked, Talia," Jenna shrieks. "He's wearing underwear." The sexy single mother's eyes return to my bare chest. She takes another step back from me, but her eyes focus on my body, and something passes through them. Something dark and longing. Her fingers are twisted in the tie of her short robe, tugging at the length and squeezing as if she's holding herself back. Everything in me wants her to launch at me. Tackle me back to the bed and continue to kiss the fuck out of me until we're fucking, but I glance back at Talia, waiting on her mother.

"Go, babe."

"I'll be right there," Jenna directs to her child again, and Talia disappears while Jenna lingers.

"I wanted to tell you last night. I'm sorry all that happened to you." Her eyes lower to my thigh. "So, so sorry, and I'm so glad you're alive." Her genuine grin of gratitude sparks a reaction inside my chest. My heart flutters faster.

"I'm happy to be alive, too." Staring at her makes me feel more alive than I've felt in a long time. I feel human again, decent even.

My thoughts drift back to the mission. I'd fucked up everything. We hadn't gotten the man like we wanted. We'd lost the girl. However, we had enough information to move, and the team had to work fast. Since

I was compromised, I was off the scene. The only intelligence I'd been given was the little bits the department wished to share, which wasn't much. I was discharged to rest and recover, and not give a care about the Quinteros. The higher-ups kept close tabs on me, though, wondering if Viviana would return. If she would seek retribution. If she'd want me back despite everything. I hadn't seen or heard a hint of her in eight months.

My hand comes to Jenna's upper chest, seeking that place over her heart, feeling its beat to remind myself how alive I am.

"Thank you for telling me everything. For sharing it with me," she says, bringing me back to the present. Her hand curls around the side of my face, holds for a second, and then releases me. She doesn't step more than twelve inches before I'm wrapping my arm around her legs again and tugging her back to me, kissing her hard and deep once more, taking another minute with her to shore up the longing I'm certain I'll feel the remainder of this day. I've done a lot of things under cover of darkness. I can hold out until tonight to continue this mission—the one where I explore more of this woman's body.

"Pancakes sound perfect," I whisper, breaking off the kiss but not lowering my gaze from her face.

She's perfect, and I would never deserve her.

17

[Jenna]

After all that Archer told me, I have trouble wrapping my head around it. Shot. Undercover. Therapy. He'd been through so much, and no one knew. His family thought he was some wayward uncle and ruffian brother, and all this time, he'd been working. The Drug Enforcement Administration was no joke, and if he worked undercover, that had to mean he was investigating something *or someone*. Did that someone shoot him? When? Where? Why? I had so many questions, but I also felt he'd already offered more than he intended to tell me.

I was honored he trusted me with the sliver of truth he gave me.

"Why does Archer have drawings on him?" Talia asks. The small galley kitchen in the apartment has a peninsula cabinet with two tall stools. Talia sits on one, and Rosie kneels on the other. I've been letting them each pour ingredients into a bowl for pancakes.

"Those are tattoos, like Mr. Ramirez." My girls are familiar with Leon and his artwork.

"I want a tattoo," Rosie says, lowering her thumb in order to speak. My eyes meet Archer's, who is creeping up behind the girls. His index finger against his lips warns me not to give him away as he sneaks forward.

"I want that thumb," he teases, pinching Rosie's sides, and she shrieks. Archer chuckles at her response, but Talia smacks him. I flinch as well even though I expected the surprise.

"You scared me," Talia yells at him.

"Hey. We do not hit people," I warn my daughter and glance back at Archer. What he told me last night explains some things. His aggression. His edginess. His gun.

With his hand still on Rosie's side, he meets my eyes. "Things gonna be weird now, babe?" The return of his voice to that sandpaper sound rescues me from staring at him.

"Nope. Not weird," I mutter. Instantly, I peer down at the mixing bowl, trying to remember where we were in the recipe. Lifting the next measurement in a teaspoon, I hand it over to Rosie. "Rosie's turn." She takes the measuring spoon from my hand over the bowl and dumps the baking powder.

"You made waffles the other day," Archer states. It hasn't even been a week of knowing him, so I easily remember a few days back and what I suggested of him mixes with what I now know of him. My shoulders fall. He'd never harm my children. He'd never hurt me. *He's a protector*. "You know how to cook?"

I softly chuckle. "If frozen fried chicken and pasta from a box counts, then yes." Nodding at the bowl, I add, "But this is baking. It's a different skill set."

"Mommy can make pizza bagels, too," Talia adds, as if singing my praise.

"Also frozen, and from a box," I clarify, laughing at myself. Ryan had been the chef, not me. My talent lay in baking, and I loved that part of TeasMe!, a local tea shop in my hometown where I worked a few summers ago. I keep my summers free now.

"Doesn't matter," Archer states. "You're a great mother."

For some reason, his comment makes my face heat. It's a simple compliment but not one I often receive. As I don't know how to respond, I busy myself with finishing breakfast. Archer remains quiet behind the girls on their stools as they take turns with the remainder of the ingredients, dropping them in the bowl before I mix everything together. When I step over to the griddle, I feel his gaze follow me.

"What are you princesses up to today?" he eventually asks.

"Bike ride," Talia calls out.

Her enthusiasm has me glancing over my shoulder. "We're going for a ride this morning." I pause to look directly at Archer. "You can come with us if you'd like." While I tried to keep my voice even, it's too cheery, too hopeful, and instantly, I hear my mistake.

"I'm going to have to pass. Bikes aren't my thing."

I nod, weakly grin and turn back to the stove. *What was I thinking?* Of course, he wouldn't want to go on a bike ride with a single mother and her little girls. This man has had adventure and danger in his life. The simple things must feel . . . simple. Basic. Plain. I'm so ridiculous.

"Still want pancakes?" I'd doubled the batch as he's a large man.

"I'm going to bounce over to Anna's and check in with my nephews, see if they want to do something this morning." His voice remains casual, but something in his tone is off. *Now who's being weird?*

My head shoots up, and I glance at him over my shoulder again. His eyes are still on me, and I chew at my lip. I don't know what to think of him or what to make of what I now know, but there's no doubt I want him. I want him more than I should, and he's never going to want simple bike rides, small towns, and pancakes on Sundays.

Good thing it's Saturday. What a rebel I am. I used to be wild and carefree, floating through men and ripping up weekends, but that stuff got old by the time I was thirty. By the time I was thirty-five, I didn't think my life would ever be different. Then I met Ryan. The love of my life, Ryan.

Do you really believe in second chances?

It took me so long to find my first love, I don't hold out hope for another round, and a man like Archer McCaryn will not volunteer as tribute. He is . . . *Vegas.* He's my layover—a little enjoyment of the local scenery. What we do will be between us, and then I'll go back to who I am come next Sunday.

Suddenly, a hand rests on my lower back, and I jump.

"Where'd you go?" His deep, rough voice at my side turns my head.

"Lost in my head, I guess. Sorry, did you say something?"

Archer stares at me, giving me one of those looks like he's trying to read me, decipher me. Can he see how I feel about him? Does he know I can no longer separate emotion and sexy time as I once did? Already his kisses mean so much more to me, as much as I want to pretend they don't.

"You can be kind of jumpy sometimes. Flinching even. What's that all about?" His fingers reach for my hair and tuck strands around my ear. I glance over my shoulder and lower my voice.

"Back in my twenties, I was in an abusive relationship." I check once more that the girls are not listening. "I knew it was stupid, but I just didn't see it. I didn't want to see it until one night it went too far." I shrug while Archer hisses.

"He said he loved me." Every girl's foolish belief and worst excuse when in that kind of relationship. "The night you and I met, I didn't know you, and it was an instinctual reaction. I'm over it now. Like I said, I was stupid." If I've flinched at other times, it's just a response to surprise.

"Don't say that. Whoever raised his hand to you was a frickity piece of shit." Archer shifts his eyes to the girls and back to me. "What's his name?"

"Why?" I softly chuckle. "Gonna beat him up for me?"

"I have connections." His tone says he's one-thousand-percent serious, and my thoughts race back to what he told me last night. "What I told you last night freaking you out in the daylight, 'Locks?" His voice drops. His gaze wavering over my face.

"No. I'm honored you told me," I remind him.

His hand slides up my spine and cups the back of my head, and I'm waiting on him to tug me to him and kiss me senseless despite our agreement to keep things out of sight of the girls.

"Who wants the first batch?" I call out as if there's any question. The griddle holds four, and I'll give the girls two each.

"Princesses first," Archer says, turning toward the girls who are both yelling, "Me."

His hand squeezes on my scalp. "You have a good life, babe." The statement isn't directed at me but blanketed around the small space. He turns to gaze back at me. "Don't let your past mess with your head."

Would that advice work for him because it's not my head I'm worried about.

It's my heart.

+ + +

After breakfast, Archer disappears, and the girls and I go on our bike ride. We add Anna and Mila to the trip. As Mila rides ahead with Rosie and Talia, Anna and I keep together, coasting more than pedaling.

"She's getting to the point where she doesn't want to spend as much time with me," Anna states of her pre-teen daughter. We both know it happens. One day, Rosie and Talia won't want to hang out with me as much as they do. For now, as I'm all they have, they cling sometimes, and I have to remind myself they won't want to be with me one day.

"She'll come back." As high school teachers, we've seen kids buck their parents only to become best friends with them again later in life. We've each been teaching long enough to have former students graduate college, get married, and become parents themselves. Some of my former students have children older than mine.

"I never appreciated my mother enough," Anna states, but it's simply not true. Her parents were once only hours away and often traveled to Chicago to experience all they could of their grandchildren. She'd been close with her parents, who have now been gone for awhile. "I need her through these years." She softly chuckles, dismissing the statement that rests heavy with truth. My own parents moved to Florida years ago. Originally snowbirds, they eventually made Florida their permanent home.

"You're actually doing great," I remind her.

She doesn't have to mention how much she needs or misses Ben. I know he's next on her list. Her boys need a man to guide them, and every little girl needs her daddy. What she says next does surprise me, though.

"I wish Archer was more present."

"I don't remember you mentioning him much, other than being absent in your life. Were you close at one point?"

Anna chuckles, focusing on the girls ahead of us. "When we were younger, we actually were closer. Archer and Noah were friends as Zack and I were, and the four of us would hang out together, especially here. I was so shy, and those guys just kept me under their wings. Archer wanted to kill every boy who looked at me sideways, and Noah wasn't any different. When Ben came along, he slid under their radar. Maybe because he'd befriended Zack so quickly. Ben made me stronger, bolder. Archer eventually told me Ben was the sword to my stone. He'd be my protector but strengthen my shell as well."

I softly laugh at the brotherly protection, reminding me of my own thoughts earlier this morning. Archer is a protector.

"What happened between you and Archer then?" I ask.

"Archer was older than me and eventually didn't want much to do with his younger sister. He went to college while I was still in high school, then went off to the police academy while I was in college. He worked locally for a while, and then he disappeared."

"And no one knew where he was?" I can't believe he hadn't told his family anything, but he must have had his reasons.

"No one told me." Anna shrugs. She mentioned her dad might have known, and possibly Ben. "Did you know that Ben sent my brother a letter after his death?"

"What?" I squeak.

"He wrote a directive of sorts to each of them. Logan, Mason, Zack, and Archer. My brother who'd been away from the family for years." Anna scoffs. "Ben left him a message. Autumn sent it to him. My sister-in-law knew how to reach my brother when I didn't. And then when he called me *last summer*, telling me he was coming home, he took an entire year to actually appear." She huffs. "What an asshole."

I bite my lip, knowing it isn't my place to tell Archer's story. "I'm sure he had his reasons."

Anna wobbles on her bike as she peers over at me. "I'm sure he does. Probably had his dick up in some chick."

"Anna!" I can't believe she said that.

"Well, who knows where he's been?"

"That doesn't sound like something you'd say, though."

Anna's quiet for a second, squinting off in the distance. "I don't know who I am anymore."

"Anna." My voice softens, expressing all the sympathy in the world I have for her situation. "It will get . . ." *Better? Easier?* Those were both terms I hated to hear when Ryan died. What was better than my life with him? What was going to be easier in my life without him? Taking a deep breath, I decide to be honest. "It's never going to be the same. *You're* never going to be the same, having loved him and lost him too soon. It isn't fair. It isn't right. It isn't any number of things people want to say to soothe you. But it is what it is. There is no way to bring him back."

The hard, cold truth is that Ben is gone. He didn't leave her. He didn't divorce her. He's well and truly gone. My own eyes prickle.

"I know," she softly says beside me. "It's just so hard."

"Yes, it is." I can't disagree with her because it is difficult. I didn't expect to ever fall in love. Then I found Ryan and lost him too soon. I didn't think I'd be a single mother and navigating this life as a single parent. "But eventually, you learn how to deal with the difficult and make life a little less hard."

"I need a manual," she jokes without a hint of humor.

"We're teachers, but we're also learners. You'll figure it out. You'll learn how to live as you are now because of your experiences, because of having loved and lost."

Anna bitterly chuckles. "I feel like you're prepping me to write a personal narrative."

"Maybe I am," I jest. "It's still your life, your story. What happens next is going to be based on what happened before, but it doesn't mean you don't have control over the future." Suddenly, I do feel like I've gone into teacher mode, coaching my student to understand her past and learn from it for what lies ahead.

"Ben had this crazy life cycle he told the guys. You live, love, lose and learn."

Thinking about it a second, I snicker. "He was onto something."

"I'm definitely in the loss cycle," Anna states, sadness filling her voice.

"Well, up next is the learning one. It's where you let go."

Her head snaps in my direction. "I'll never be able to let go."

"You know that's not what I mean. Ben will always be a part of you. Always." He's even divided further into her children. "But at some point, you'll cycle through those phases in order to live again." And love, maybe. As I said to Archer, we all deserve a second chance. Whether we get one this late in life might be a different story.

Never been in love. How can that be? Archer is forty-five. Surely, he's loved someone along the way.

"Do you know if Archer has ever been in love?" I'd never make it as an investigator or detective, as I was hardly subtle in shifting topics.

"I doubt it." Anna snorts. "Autumn found him on social media once with a woman. She swore it was him although he was tagged under a different name. She was some socialite. The woman looked like a *Real Housewives*-wannabe from somewhere fancy, like someone who would film her life for scripted television."

Socialite. Housewives-wannabe. Scripted TV. My heart sinks as I recall asking Archer if he wanted to go on a bike ride with me and my girls. *So stupid.*

"And speaking of Archer, I don't want him making any false promises to my boys, telling them he'll be here for them and pushing Calvin toward police work."

"Did he do that?" My bike wobbles as I abruptly glance at Anna.

"He did, and he's with the boys again today. I don't need him trying to insert himself into their lives only to slip back out of it."

I understand her concern. I have the same ones. While Archer told me about his previous line of work, he didn't mention if he was still working. If he's undercover, will he disappear again? How soon? For how long? I need to keep my heart guarded and my head smart when it comes to Archer. He isn't going to stick around, and I knew that from the beginning. I will not allow myself any fantasies of Archer becoming part of my small family. My heart can't take another loss.

18

[Jenna]

On Sunday evening, the girls and I return to the apartment early for a movie and some downtime. After two long days of sun and fun, Rosie is crabby, and Talia is overwhelmed. They've made friends with Zack's boys, Oliver and Trevor, but sometimes the boys are too much to handle for my tamer daughters. Oliver is actually a little sweet when he isn't minion to his alpha brother, Trevor. I'd catch him comforting Rosie or helping her, but it's only because he considers her a baby compared to him. Talia likes to put Trevor in his place, telling him how to behave or warning him to watch his language. She's so bossy at times, mother-henning anyone who will listen.

Since yesterday morning, Archer has been distant. He was with his nephews during the day, and the reunion crew guys included him in their bar crawl last night. He came home late, picked me up off the couch, and placed me in bed next to him but didn't speak. Other than his arm around my waist, curling into my body, nearly blanketing my back, we didn't touch. When I woke early, I left him sleeping. The girls and I went for a walk, and the day kept us separated again.

So I am surprised to find Archer entering the apartment early Sunday evening after me. I'm even more shocked when he folds to the couch, slouching back to get comfortable, and asks, "What are we watching?"

"*Frozen*," Talia calls out. She loves this movie as do I. I've analyzed it with my teacher brain, and it's a good story about sisterly love and the strength within an individual. It also speaks to the bond of family as an important line of love in life. I don't have sisters, so watching my girls interact with one another is fascinating to me.

"Popcorn," Rosie reminds me, and I snap out of staring at Archer next to my girls.

"Right," I quip, pressing play for the movie while circling the couch for the microwave. When I return, Rosie has climbed onto Archer's lap, and Talia has moved closer to him, brushing her shoulder against his bicep but not leaning into him. His hands fist at his sides, next to his thick thighs. Archer's eyes meet mine, and something like panic fills them.

"This alright, 'Locks?" His voice strains a bit. "She just climbed into my lap."

My gaze falls to Rosie, where her head is tipped back on his shoulder and her little thumb rests in her mouth. Her legs are crossed at her ankles as her legs stretch forward. She's made Archer her personal cushion.

"I can tell her to move," I say, lowering my voice as I sit next to Talia, squeezing myself between the couch armrest and my daughter. His eyes stay fixed on mine.

"She seems comfortable." His voice still hesitates. Is it weird for him to hold a child? He's played with Rosie in the water and hugged her after she held his gun.

"Are you uncomfortable?"

His forehead furrows as he takes a second to respond as if contemplating himself and his position. "No. No, actually, I'm not."

The hand between his thigh and Talia relaxes, and his other hand lifts for Rosie's belly, keeping her steady as she balances on his legs. He releases my eyes and turns toward the movie, and we begin watching an animated film with a strong message about love conquering all.

My thoughts wander once again, wondering about the types of situations Archer has encountered. What dangerous people has he met, and what bad things have been done to him? On another thought, what are some of the things he's had to do? He's killed men. I don't have to ask to know he has. In his line of work, he must have done such a thing. The question is how many, and another question is if I really want the answer.

I don't.

While I want to know more about Archer, some things are best left unsaid unless he wants to share those details with me. *Don't-ask-don't-tell* mentality. This might be one of the best cases to apply that concept.

"I can't decide who's who in this movie," Archer softly states. "Are you Anna or Elsa?" He wiggles his leg, and Rosie jostles on him. My head turns to him, watching him hold my child while my other one

144

slowly tips toward him, leaning her head on his arm and noticing his pinky resting on her little leg. He's patient with Talia, allowing her time to warm up and be comfortable with him.

"I'm Elsa," Talia firmly states. "Because I'm older."

"But you have brown hair," Archer states.

"I'm the ice queen, so my hair will be snow-colored one day."

My eyes widen at Talia's comment, and I meet Archer's gaze over Talia's head.

"I have to protect Rosie if anything happens to Mommy. Isn't that right, Rosie?" Talia sits upright and pats her sister's belly. She leans toward her sister, rubbing her nose on Rosie's, but Rosie pushes Talia away.

"Stop," Rosie whines around her thumb, her voice sleepy. My best guess is Rosie will be sleeping on Archer before this movie ends.

Archer is still watching me, and I lean over Talia, kissing the top of her hair, understanding her fears. "Mommy isn't going anywhere," I whisper to her. "Nothing is going to happen to me." I glance back at Archer as I pull away from Talia. Placing my hand on her little thigh, I offer reassurance with my touch. I realize anything could happen to me at any time. I can't be one-hundred-percent certain in my assurance to Talia, but I hate that she lives in fear that I'll disappear like her father. She had a hard time understanding that Ryan died. To her, he disappeared, and she once thought he'd re-appear. Her understanding of death evolved, and she now knows it's permanent. That knowledge adds to her panic that it could happen to me.

Archer lifts his arm, stretching along the back of the couch to wrap his fingers in my hair.

"I'd never let anything happen to your mom, princess," Archer says, holding my gaze while trying to comfort Talia.

"Ice queen," she corrects like the label is an honor instead of bordering on something negative.

"Shh," Rosie groans around her thumb, and a song begins. Talia starts to sing along, and Rosie sits upright, adding her voice. Archer chuckles at their enthusiasm. When the song ends, Rosie settles back into Archer's chest, turning her body sideways and watching the movie over her shoulder through half-mast lids. His hand has moved to her back, and within minutes, Rosie is sleeping against him, thumb in mouth, comfortable as a clam without a care in the world.

I only wish my Talia girl could relax half as easily. Instead, she leans over to me, and I tug her into my side, holding her against me while Archer toys with my hair, and we finish the movie like a family enjoying movie night.

Ryan never experienced moments like these, and I wonder what Archer thinks of our wild and crazy Sunday night ritual. Could he see himself doing such a thing weekly? Just like the bike riding invitation yesterday, it's a ridiculous thought. He isn't going to want animated movie nights with stories about princesses. He's probably dated one.

"What?" Archer whispers over Talia's head. I didn't realize I'd huffed at the thought of him with some socialite, beautiful and worldly, unlike me. I shake my head to dismiss a response and pretend for a few minutes Archer joining our family could be a reality and not some fantasy like an ice castle on a mountain in a child's movie.

+ + +

After the girls are put to bed—Rosie never stirred from Archer's lap— Archer and I watch a movie called *The Adjustment Bureau*. It's an interesting story about fate, how it's beyond our control, but *if, if, if* we knew someone was messing with our lives, we might try to change things. In this movie, the main character's desire for love is so strong, he's not willing to let fate dictate his life. He asks the woman he adores to trust him, essentially saying he won't let anything happen to them.

"Who do you trust?" I blurt, and Archer pauses the movie. If he's never loved anyone, who does he trust with his secret desires?

"What?" He chuckles apprehensively, turning his head to look at me.

"Who do you trust? Who do you share your life with?"

"Jenna," he whispers, a mix between a warning and something more.

"This can't be a hard topic. You said you don't have a girlfriend."
Was he lying?

"I don't," he states adamantly. "I guess I don't have anyone I really trust." He gazes back at the television screen, and his eyes narrow. The statement would hurt if I knew him better. Deep down, I want him to trust me, but we just don't know enough about one another.

"Who defends you, Archer?" My eyes lower to the chain hidden beneath his tee. He glances at his covered chest as well, and we both think of the medal we can't see. "More than St. Michael. Who watches out for you? Who safeguards your heart?"

His brows pinch when he looks up at me. "I don't need my heart protected."

"We all need our hearts protected." I pause. "What's your fear?" I don't even know where this line of questioning is coming from.

Archer looks away again, taking a long minute to think. "That I'm not worthy."

"Not worthy of what?"

"Of love."

My hand reaches for his forearm. "Why would you say such a thing? Everybody deserves love, Archer. It's what you do with it when it's given that might be the harder decision." Do you accept it? Do you reject it? Do you question it? Do you trust it?

Archer doesn't answer my question but reaches out to tug me to him. I snuggle into his side, further pretending he could be my reality.

Unfortunately, ragged-run, single mothers fall asleep early on Sunday evenings, even on vacation, so I doze off. When Archer jostles me, I sit upright, realizing I'd passed out before the most important part of the movie. "How did it end?"

Archer swipes his fingers along the side of my face, brushing back my hair around my ear. "He adjusts. For her, he alters everything."

The explanation sounds profound and romantic in his deep voice. His gaze stays on me a moment too long, where it turns uncomfortable, and I don't know if he'll kiss me or stand from the couch and leave me behind. He does a mix of both, leaning forward to press his lips to my temple before standing and leading me to his room, where we make out again like teens, and pretend for a little longer we could be something other than what we are—a simple layover.

+ + +

The next morning, Archer enters the apartment minus a T-shirt and covered in water droplets. He swims in the lake, and I better understand this form of exercise for his leg. My eyes lock on his chest. I'm standing behind the peninsula island cabinet in the small kitchen area as he slowly approaches me. My lips are still swollen from another night of kissing, and my body aches for more from him. Since the bathtub slash showerhead incident, he hasn't touched me in a place that weeps for his attention.

A corner of his lip lifts as I can't seem to pull my gaze away from appreciating his body. Glistening tattoos on his arms. His protective medallion at his chest. Solid legs. With a steady pace, he stalks toward me.

"Where are the girls?" he asks, noting the quiet of the apartment

"Next door. River's giving me twenty minutes for a shower." I saw River after another morning walk with the girls, and she offered to take them to her backyard, so I can have a few minutes alone.

"Twenty minutes, huh?" He comes closer, rounding the counter. In the small space, he's quick to back me into the corner of the cabinets. My smile matches his growing grin as I'm turned on by the sight of him. My heart races. My palms sweat. I don't have time to blink before Archer has a hand holding the back of my head, fingers in my hair.

"Want something from me, babe?"

"Yes." I don't finish the single syllable word before his mouth is on mine, wild and wandering. He's kissing me like I'm the air he needs to breathe, only he's filling my lungs with the oxygen of desire. My hips thrust forward, seeking more connection with him. His other hand lowers to cup my backside, squeezing one globe, tugging me against him as his mouth continues to conquer mine. Lips. Teeth. Tongue. He's drawing me into him, taking what he wants from me, and I'm just as desperate. While kissing him is amazing, I want so much more.

My arms wrap around his back, palms flattening on his shoulder blades. Using his back muscles as leverage, I tug myself against his chest, the coolness of his skin seeping through my T-shirt. While one hand remains on my ass, the other slides down my body, like water cascading over rocks. He lowers his mouth to my neck. He's slippery and a little stinky, but I want him. I want his mouth, his fingers, his thickness. He's slipping his hand into the waistband of my shorts, stretching for the promise land when I moan.

"Ryan."

Everything freezes. Archer's hand at the top of my private curls stops. His mouth on my neck pauses. My hands on his shoulders stiffen.

"Shit," I mutter. "I don't know—"

"You thinking about another man when you're with me, 'Locks?" Archer's voice is hard, as rough as the night I accused him of something with my girls. He pulls back quicker than a match striking flint and stares into my eyes.

"He was my . . ." I never know how to label Ryan. He's not my ex. I hate to say husband, as he isn't that either, other than in my heart.

With his arms raised, hands above his head, Archer takes a giant step back.

"My husband's name was Ryan." The explanation is little concession, and I don't know why I even spoke his name. Something in my brain must have triggered at the wet warmth of Archer's skin. Ryan would sometimes rub up against me all sweaty and gross after a run, and I'd always tease him, pushing him away. However, I was pulling Archer closer, which confuses me about calling out my deceased husband's name.

"I don't know . . . I didn't mean—"

"Whatever, babe." I don't get to finish my sentence, defending how I wasn't thinking of Ryan. I'm very aware that Archer was the man in my arms, making me wet and pressing up against me, ready to take me against these kitchen cabinets. But I don't get to explain myself before he's spinning away from me, entering the bathroom and slamming the door.

I hang my head a second before tipping it back and blinking at the ceiling. Tears fill my eyes, and I don't know if it's from the mention of my husband or the fact I'm so turned on by another man who left me here feeling ridiculously embarrassed and totally rejected.

Then again, I imagine how Archer feels. *Who protects his heart?* My own is torn in two, but both halves belong to Archer McCaryn.

19

[Archer]

Fuck that shit. I jerk off in the shower, taking out my anger on my dick while picturing Jenna on her knees, taking my punishment for calling out her husband's name. *Dead husband,* I remind myself. With my forehead pressed to the tile, I take a deep breath, blinking at the stars dancing before me after the vigorous rubbing.

I have to remember Jenna isn't Viviana. She isn't playing a game by calling out someone else's name. She isn't acting coy like it was a slip. Her eyes expressed her own horror at his name crossing her lips, but it has left me wondering.

Has she thought of him when we're kissing in my bed?

The thought makes me sick, and I flip to my back, tapping my head on the steam-moist tile. I don't want to believe it, though it's a strong possibility. Maybe she's still missing her man and using me to recall things they did together.

Why would she consider me deserving of her love? *You're a despicable human being.*

I hate how much Viviana's words still sting or how often they seem to return whenever I'm with Jenna. Maybe I'm just as bad as her, thinking of my past relationship. Then again, different scars for different hearts. Jenna's thinking of her *husband,* and while my anger still simmers at an old lover. I get it. She loved him. That's the difference between Vi and me, and Jenna and Ryan.

Ryan. His name on her lips was like a shot to my leg. I can't fault her for loving someone before me. I don't even blame her really for wanting to get lost. But I really wish it'd been my name on her lips instead. Because the instant she said his name, I was out. Old triggers returned, restoring memories of Viviana's games, and I reacted.

Maybe I overreacted.

Turning off the shower, I step out of the tub, swipe the towel down my body, and wrap it around my waist. Not caring that droplets cling to my skin and my chest is on display, I open the door, hoping to seek out

Jenna and . . . ask her to explain, talk about what happened. Just what do I want?

It doesn't seem to matter as I find the apartment empty. She had twenty minutes to be alone, and I'd taken her time.

If only I could have a sliver of her heart.

Last night, she asked me who protected my heart, and all I want is Jenna to take mine.

+ + +

Knowing Jenna went to River and Zack's, I head there, seeking her out when I should just walk away. Why am I chasing this woman? She wants us to keep what we're doing to ourselves. She doesn't want anyone to know, especially her girls, but I'm finding it harder and harder to contain my feelings. Even though I've tried to stay away from her, I can't. As for her calling out her late husband's name . . . well, I need to accept it was a fluke. Something triggered her, and I'll just need to learn what I did.

With this thought on my mind, I enter Zack's backyard, and my heart stops with what I see.

Jenna was my sole focus, so it was simply by chance I looked up. Or maybe something made the hackles on my neck rise, pulling my gaze toward the tree house.

Three things happen at once.

I touch Jenna's forearm, cover her mouth with my other hand, and as calmly as I can, I call out to Rosie.

"Whatcha doing, princess?" Little Rosie is standing on the edge of a narrow beam extended from the tree fort platform. Underneath her is a swing and her tiny toes grip the edge of the board that isn't any larger than her feet. All the while, her thumb rests in her mouth.

Time stands still as three *more* things happen at once.

Not wanting Jenna to startle Rosie, I warn her not to scream.

However, I hadn't warned River, who shrieks.

At the same time, Oliver's little head pops up from within the tree fort, and *he* yells Rosie's name while pushing his brother aside, who happens to be standing inside the fort as well, watching the little princess balance on a thin board.

I release Jenna, running faster than I ever thought capable before catching Rosie in a tangle of her small limbs and the metal chains of the swing.

"Holy shit." I exhale. My chest heaves while Rosie nestles against me. Jenna is at my side in a heartbeat, scooping Rosie from me and holding her. My leg gives out from the rush, and I collapse to the ground, landing hard on my butt and covering my face for a second before swiping down it and bracing myself on shaking arms.

"Holy shit," I repeat.

"What were you doing?" Jenna shrieks at her daughter while holding her tightly to her chest, and I'm reminded of the morning Rosie held my gun. She's such a wild one, and standing on the edge of a two-by-four some twelve feet off the ground is definitely reckless.

At the same time Jenna is waiting out an answer, Oliver and Trevor leap down from the tree fort.

"Are you okay, Rosie?" Oliver asks, his small voice full of panic.

"What happened?" Zack questions. Where did he come from? He might have been in the house and heard River's scream. Quickly assessing Rosie in Jenna's arms and his chagrined-looking sons staring up at her, Zack heavily sighs and swipes a hand through his hair. "What did they do?"

I've watched his sons inspire trouble in one another for the past week, pushing each other's limits. In some ways, their behavior reminds me of Noah and myself when we were young.

River places her hand on Zack's forearm while her other hand covers her extended belly. Her face is pale. She's still in shock, as we all are. Her mouth opens and then closes, struggling for words.

"He didn't do anything," Trevor defends his brother, which instantly has Zack looking at Oliver.

"What did your brother do?" Zack asks the second child, and I see he knows the gig. One defends the other while the one defending is the guilty party.

"I don't know," Oliver admits. His small face looks perplexed and stricken as he stares at Rosie. I'd like to say I clearly saw the surprise on his face when he noticed Rosie on the board or even heard his strangled cry of fear mixing with her name as he pushed his brother out of the way, but I took off so fast, anticipating her fall, I hadn't thought of anything else other than her little body *not* hitting the ground.

"I think it's time we go home," Jenna says, still holding Rosie to her.

"Please don't leave," River begs before turning to Trevor and bending as best she can with her expanding waist. "Trevor, baby, what happened?"

Zack tips his head back toward the sky and puffs out another breath before glancing back at Jenna. "I'm so sorry. Whatever happened, I'm sorry. We're really working on things but . . ." He shakes his head, unable to finish.

"No tree fort," River says, standing upright when Trevor hasn't responded.

"But, *Mom,*" he groans while River shakes her head at him.

"That's the deal. If we don't play nice in the tree fort, we don't play at all." She pauses as Trevor looks off to the side of the yard. "Do you know how dangerous that was? She's so tiny, Trevor. How could you let her walk that beam? Do you understand how hurt she'd be if she fell?"

My own body trembles at the thought. How did these little girls get under my skin so quickly?

I can't take my eyes off Jenna until something brushes against my arm. I flinch at first, a natural reaction until I see it's Talia. Fear fills her eyes as she stares at her mother, still clutching Rosie to her chest. Instantly, I reach out for her, wrapping my arm around the back of her knees. For a second, I expect her to fight me, but I'm relieved when she falls into my lap. I need to hold on to something myself, and Talia is shaking as badly as me.

"What do you say to Rosie?" Zack addresses Trevor. I'm not certain either River or Zack is getting through to the kid, but Oliver still focuses on Rosie. His face is drained of color as reality might be settling in for him. Whatever game these two concocted up, Rosie could have died if she fell the wrong way. It's extreme but not impossible, and we all know it.

"You're a real pirate," Trevor states which is not what any of us wants to hear. Even if he apologized, the words would be fruitless as far as I'm concerned. Apparently, Rosie approves, though, as she pulls her thumb from her mouth and tucks it into a little fist. She leans her head back from her mother and looks down at Trevor.

"What?" Zack barks, and Talia flinches, so I clutch her harder to me.

"She walked the plank. Now she's a pirate." Trevor doesn't bat an eye at his explanation. He doesn't lose color in his face or even look regretful. He just stares up at Rosie and winks. The frickity-frack trucker-mother little shit winks at her.

With that, Zack places a hand on Trevor's shoulder. "Time. Out."

Trevor looks at River, but she holds equally firm that Trevor needs some time to reflect on what he's missing. As the little guy walks toward the house, he looks over his shoulder at Rosie with a devious smile. Rosie watches him over the shoulder of her mother.

"I'm so sorry," River says, stepping over to Rosie and stroking a hand down her small spine while Jenna continues to hold her daughter.

"It's not really an excuse, but we've had a lot of adjustments in the past year. He's doing so much better, but sometimes, I swear, I don't know what he's thinking," Zack adds, placing his hand on the back of Rosie's head. "I'm sorry, Jenna."

People might want to argue boys will be boys, and this one certainly has some imagination. However, Rosie is five years younger than Trevor and so tiny compared to the twins. Even at eight, he should know better, right? Then again, what do I know about kids? Either way, my heart is still racing.

"We'll be talking to him again," Zack adds, placing a hand briefly on Jenna's back.

"You okay, princess?" River states, still rubbing up and down Rosie's spine. She stole my nickname, and I'm about to interject when Rosie does instead.

"I'm a pirate," she announces, and River softly chuckles while Jenna presses a kiss to Rosie's cheek.

"You're a brave girl," River encourages, offering a soft smile as the color slowly returns to her face.

"The pirate ship is grounded, though," Zack adds, which forces Oliver to look up at his dad. His mouth falls open and then snaps shut, as if deciding against any argument. He walks over to Rosie and wraps a hand around her delicate ankle, swinging her leg a little.

"You shouldn't be a pirate, Rosie. You're a princess," Oliver says.

"I can too be a pirate," she argues, looking down at Oliver from her mother's arms. Then she kicks out her leg, and Oliver releases his grasp. If I didn't know better, I'd say the little boy just had his first experience with heartbreak. His ashen-colored face turns bright red with hurt.

Yeah, it's going to happen, kid. Women will disappoint you many times in life.

On that thought, Oliver stalks away and. after pressing a kiss to River's temple, Zack follows.

"What can I do?" River asks, meeting Jenna's eyes. "Offer treasure? How about forbidden booty like a c-o-o-k-i-e?"

"I know how to spell cookie," Rosie states around the thumb she's returned to her mouth.

"Brave and smart," River teases. "Good combination for a pirate-girl." She winks at Rosie.

"We're just going to go," Jenna mutters, and River nods, but apology still fills her expression.

I pat Talia's leg, and she unfolds from me.

"Help me up," I jest, holding out my hand as if I'm going to use her to leverage me off the ground. Instead, I press up on one hand as she tugs me with all her might. "Wow, look how strong you are, ice queen," I praise.

"I'll go back to being a teacher princess today."

Once standing, I softly chuckle, knowing Talia will definitely be teaching boys like Trevor a thing or two as she ages. Stepping over to Jenna and Rosie, I rub a hand up Rosie's back and lean forward, pressing a kiss to the back of her head. Her soft blond curls tickle my nose, and my eyes find Jenna watching me.

Tears fill them as she mouths, "Thank you."

"Anything for you," I remind her, not giving a second thought to our earlier position. Even if Ryan is in her head, she and her girls are in mine, and I'm at great risk of them taking over my heart.

20

[Jenna]

I'm coming out of my skin. Once we return to the apartment, I don't want to be confined inside, but the thought of a day at the beach, sitting still and reliving my daughter falling off that board above a swing is not something I can handle. I need to get out of here. I know River is upset, and it wasn't her fault Trevor dared Rosie to walk the plank, but I need some separation from the group and an activity to settle my brain.

I'm afraid to let Rosie out of my arms or out of my sight, but I deposit her on the couch, telling the girls I need a minute. Archer is on my heels, entering the apartment. He follows me into his bedroom, where I leave the door ajar but stand behind the barrier it makes, pressing my body against the wall.

Immediately, Archer is in my face.

"Not now," I breathe out. "I just can't . . . ." I can't deal with him and what happened earlier, any more than I can imagine how I'll ever repay him for rescuing Rosie.

His hand cups the back of my head, stopping my words as he pulls me into him. His large arms surround me as my chest heaves. I'm fighting off a delayed reaction of breaking into tears.

Holy shit, my baby girl is going to be the end of me.

"Just breathe, babe," he whispers near my ear in that growly voice.

"I-I can't." My heart is still hammering, and my eyes burn. Archer's other hand comes to my chest, covering that spot he likes. His flat palm is like a slow-releasing balm, attempting to soothe my racing heart and lower my blood pressure. His mouth lowers to mine. Soft. Gentle. Tender. He sips once. He kisses twice. Then he swipes his tongue across the seam of my lips.

"Archer, I just can't—"

"Babe, shh," he whispers, and he brushes his lips over mine again. "Kiss me."

"Archer . . . I can't . . . and the girls . . ." They're in the other room, but the door blocks where I'm hiding, and Archer doesn't relent. His lips keep coasting over mine, teasing them to open but not pressuring me to rush. Another suck of my bottom lip. Another stroke of his tongue. Finally, my arms wrap around him as I hadn't noticed I wasn't holding him in return to his embrace. Then my mouth falls open, and I kiss him as I had earlier. Mouth wide. Tongue seeking. Teeth looking for the ledge of his lip.

"Archer," I whimper against him.

"Like when you say my name, Jenna," he grunts in that voice that makes my name an endearment all its own. When he makes me sound like I'm important to him. My name makes me special, like a two-syllable love song.

"Keep kissing me," he groans, giving back to me what I give, allowing myself to fall against his body in gratitude and relief. He continues to kiss me, distract me, rid my thoughts until my heart comes down from one high only to stir up another. Sensing the shift, as my body clings to his, he slowly pulls back, offering softer kisses as he retreats. A final swirl of his tongue. One last pull at my lip. Then a grin against my mouth.

"Better?" His forehead rests against mine.

I close my eyes. "I don't know," I honestly admit, wondering how I could be kissing him like I don't have a care in the world when my baby just dangled and fell from a tree fort.

"What do you need then?" His fingers absently stroke my hair over my ear.

Him. I need him to bring me down and stabilize me when stuff like this happens. I need him to catch my daughter when she falls and kiss me like crazy to distract my racing thoughts. I need him to say my name like it means something to him. Mostly, I need him to forgive me for this morning, calling out a name I didn't mean to say. I'm not thinking of Ryan. I'm thinking of Archer. All. The. Time.

"I need to get out of here. I need an activity. Something to burn off this . . . this energy." I wave a hand, finding myself slowly rebuilding the tension of Rosie's situation.

"You up for an adventure, 'Locks?"

I don't know how much more *excitement* I can handle, but I need something to concentrate on.

"What did you have in mind?"

"You trust me, babe?" His eyes search mine, and for a second, it feels as if he's asking me something deeper than merely to partake in an activity.

"I trust you," I whisper.

"Then put on your bathing suit and pack some snacks." He presses off the wall with a mischievous grin and rounds the open door, entering the living area to address the girls.

"Princess and pirate, how do you feel about a water park?"

+ + +

Spending the day at a water park is the last thing I expected Archer to recommend. I hadn't even known of the place, but I don't question how Archer did. I followed his lead. He drove my SUV because of the car seats needed for Rosie and Talia, and we spent the day with squeals and laughter, flinging ourselves down spiraling slides and splashing around in the tidal wave pool.

It was exactly what we needed.

"Such a beautiful family," an older woman eventually says to me, nodding in the direction of Rosie and Talia with Archer, and I can't find it in my heart to correct her.

We aren't a family. *But could we be?* Archer fits too seamlessly with us.

I can already see a bond between the wild spirit of Rosie and Archer. He encourages her risk-taking nature under his protection while nudging Talia to take chances with his guidance. Rosie relaxes around Archer, allowing him to fling them down the tall slides with her on his lap for safety. Talia gives in to his assurances he wouldn't let her drown as he tosses her into the tidal wave pool and quickly rescues her to prove his point.

He's so good with the girls, and I dismiss all the worries that occasionally creep into my head. The ones that remind me Archer is limited in his time with us. The ones that tell me that allowing my girls to get closer to him is a bad idea. The same ones that warn me not to open my heart to a man kissing me senseless and snuggling me into him.

By late afternoon, the girls are water-logged, and we decide on a pizza dinner before we return to the large cottage. Monday manicures and margaritas are on the docket, but I don't have the energy.

"Just go, babe," Archer tells me after our early dinner. "I've got the girls."

The husbandly-sounding statement pinches my heart. I still don't understand how this man wasn't married and why he doesn't have children of his own. He's been undercover and absent from his family, but he's trying to work his way back to them. He spends time with his nephews. He hangs out with the reunion crew. Is it all temporary to him? Or could this time be more permanent? He's a good man underneath the gruff voice and tough act. He could be a decent family man.

"It's been such a long day," I remind him as he's pulling into the driveway at Anna's. I don't want to disappoint my friend by missing her weekly girls' night with River and Autumn, but I don't have the heart for manicures or margaritas tonight.

"But you're here for Anna. She wants you to go with her." His comment has me tilting my head as he parks my SUV. Suddenly, he's more Team Anna. I'm skeptical and suspicious.

"Why are you pushing so much?"

"I'm not pushing. I just think you should go. It's been a long day. Take some time off for yourself. Pamper your pretty toes and drink a margarita or two to keep you out of your head."

More distraction tactics? He must have been good undercover. That soothing tone. That solid stare. I can't read him. Like the use of *babe* in every other sentence. Is that a throwaway word or an affectionate term of endearment? When he says my name in his rugged voice, it feels more genuine. It feels like I mean something to him.

"Mila and Lorna *are* set to babysit again," I admit. "And I know my girls are looking forward to hanging out with the older ones." They'll have their own pampering time as Lorna and Mila promised to paint fingernails and toenails and have a craft project to do with the girls.

L.B. Dunbar

"Then don't disappoint them either," he says.

Will you disappoint me? I hate the thought. He can't disappoint me because we aren't together. We aren't a couple or even friends with benefits. I don't know what we're doing, other than playing Vegas.

Too bad my heart isn't good at pretending.

+ + +

An hour later, I'm ankle-deep in bubbling water. Autumn is babbling about being pregnant again, and Anna listens with her eyes closed. Maybe we all need this moment to regroup from responsibilities or long days or whatever else might be on our minds.

"I'm so sorry again," River says once more beside me. "Trevor. . ." She sighs after his name. "He's come a long way from where he was when I met him. He's just—"

I hold up a hand to stop her eighty-seventh apology. Knowing a little bit of River and Zack's story, I don't fault him or River. What I really believe is Trevor should have known better, and I dislike the old adage, the situation was kids being kids. However . . . "My Rosie has a warrior spirit and a desire to scare the shit out of me. Even without Trevor's dare, she might have climbed up that board and walked the plank to prove to herself she could do it."

She's still young, but I've had time to reflect that Rosie could have climbed that beam on her own. While Trevor encouraged her or dared her or whatever he said to coax her onto the board, my own little daredevil can be just as willful, and she knows how to say no to something if she *doesn't* want to do it. Her personality is strong enough she would have walked away if she didn't want to prove she was a pirate, and she's clearly pleased with the outcome of walking the plank. "We both know it only takes a second to look away, and kids can get into all kinds of predicaments. I'm just grateful Archer was there."

"I'm still new to being a parent," River adds, glancing at the swell of her belly.

"Aren't we all?" I'm certainly not saying I'm the perfect parent. Every day is a new experience with Talia leading the way for me and then Rosie twisting up what I learn because she's so different from her sister.

"I heard about Archer's reaction," Anna interjects.

"It was pretty incredible," River admits.

One minute, he snuck up next to me, startling me by covering my mouth while warning me not to scream, and the next, he was across the yard with Rosie in his arms. The entire experience felt like it was happening outside my existence. As if it were dream-like instead of reality. Just as I said to River, it was one of a million moments as a parent when you look away, and something happens.

Once again, everything plays out in slow motion in my head. I don't know how I'll sleep tonight, but it's also a reminder of Archer's promises. He'd never let anything hurt my daughters. *His princesses.* He plays along with their whims to be warriors, ice queens, and pirates. He really is dad material, even if he doesn't want to be a father.

Glancing over at Anna, she's watching me, and I try to school any expression on my face that might suggest how strongly I feel about her brother. Because I do feel something for him. Something strong. *And wrong?*

"You said you spent the day at a water park?" Anna asks, seeking clarification. I should have invited her and Mila to tag along or even Autumn and Lorna. Even River and her boys might have been included in an invitation if it hadn't been Archer's suggestion.

"Yes, Archer wanted to give the girls an adventure." Instantly, I realize my misstep as River whispers, "Oh," and Autumn's mouth falls open. Anna stares at me. Not a glare but a question. I wish I had answers. I wish I could explain myself and my reaction to her menacing man brother.

"So, Archer was with you all day," Autumn states, seeking her own clarification. I nod, biting my lower lip.

"And how is Archer, besides rescuing your daughter and holing up with you in his apartment?" Autumn teases, and heat creeps across my face.

"He's . . . fine." The hesitation costs me.

Autumn's smile widens.

Anna's mouth gapes. "Jenna," she whispers.

"Nothing's happening." I sit upright while my feet dangle in the soothing water. "I'm only here a few more days."

"Famous last words," River mutters.

"I remember that feeling," Autumn adds, giving me a knowing look.

"I'm not Archer's type, and he's not mine." Instantly, I regret the words. In so many ways, Archer and I seem opposite, yet there are things about him I really do adore.

Pancakes. Princess movies. Water parks.

"Does Archer have a type?" River asks innocently enough.

"I've seen him on social media. That last woman was some mafia princess or something." Autumn glances down at her toes being painted.

Mafia princess? My blood runs cold. He'd told me he was undercover, but he hadn't mentioned anything specific. Had he been involved with someone?

"How do you know these things?" Anna turns on Autumn before I can ask for details. "Like you had that email address for my brother for his letter from Ben."

Autumn turns to me. "Ben gave each of the guys a directive, like a mission, to complete within a year of receiving them."

"Do you know what the letters said?" I ask as the nail tech taps my leg to move a foot out of the water.

"I only know Logan's message as it relates to me," she states.

"Zack's was related to love, and he told me finding me fulfilled his mission," River explains, a smile gracing her voice.

"That leaves Archer and Mason," Anna clarifies. "I doubt Mason will share his, and Archer . . . well, he's Archer. He'll do what he wants, when he wants, if he wants." Bitterness rings through Anna's tone, and my hackles rise in defense of him. *He had his reasons.* But it isn't my place to explain his past.

"And who was this woman? How did you find him with her?" I ask Autumn unable to hold back my curiosity.

"Some social media post or trending news popped up, and I swear it was Archer although he wasn't named as Archer in the picture. When

I scrolled the woman's social media page, images of Archer and her filled her photos."

"Oh." Remaining quiet, I wonder about this mystery woman and questioning even more of Archer's past.

"I need a margarita," Anna eventually mutters, tipping back her head and closing her eyes. I imagine she doesn't want to talk anymore about Ben and secret directives or her wayward brother, as she thinks of him. I'm here for her, I remind myself, feeling a little selfish that I want more time with her brother and a little irritated that she doesn't know him better.

"I wish I could have one," River pouts, rubbing a hand over her belly.

"Same," Autumn groans while smiling to herself about baby number two. She hardly has a bump, but I remember that feeling. Knowing something is growing inside you. Life forever changes after the birth of a child, and I glance among the four of us, knowing death has changed us all as well.

21

[Archer]

While the little princesses had plans with my niece and her best friend, and the queen went out with her girls, I met Noah at the inn where he works. Bluebird Hollow Inn was a family-owned place, inherited by its present manager, a feisty brunette. The old hotel was quite a change from Noah's majestic Magellen Hotel in downtown Chicago, but I wasn't there to chat about the hospitality industry. I was there to get my head on straight about a certain raven-haired beauty with long legs and sweet baby girls.

Unfortunately, while I'm hanging out with Noah, I get a call I was hoping to never receive.

"Archer, Braxton here." Braxton Hawes is another operative. Occasionally, he's fed me information I'm no longer privy to from the Quintero case. "We got a tip on Viviana."

"Fuck," I hiss through the phone after stepping away from Noah.

"My sentiment exactly. Funny story, she was spotted at a marina in Chicago."

Noooo. That's too close for comfort.

"I wanted to give you a heads-up." There's an unspoken message between the lines—in case she contacts me

I snort, deep and rich. Braxton knows there isn't a chance in hell Vi would reach out to me. She wouldn't have a way to find me. Burner phones destroyed. Fake social media accounts wiped clean. No official place to call home in my history.

Hunter Gray no longer exists in this world. As him, neither did I.

"You know that won't happen." Braxton knows the facts. My assignment was to infiltrate the Quintero family. My task is over. Viviana and I are done.

"You were in deep, Archer. Where there's a will, there's a way."

"Her father is gone," I remind him.

"We always suspected she'd take over once we had him. That's why we needed her as well."

Vi told me she had no interest in taking over Daddy's business, but I'd never trusted her. While she'd rather revel in her daddy's riches, she knew how to play dirty, and I had no doubt she'd take over if her father disappeared forever.

The hint of my failure rests in Braxton's statement. I'd botched the investigation and had gotten shot in the interim.

"Think I'll be put back on the case?" I hold my breath, knowing there's nothing I want more than to complete my mission and nothing I want less than to get involved with Viviana Quintero again.

"Hell no," he grunts. "But I thought you should know. And let me know if you see or hear anything."

"Aye, aye, captain," I snark.

Braxton huffs. "How's the leg? Getting the rest and recovery you need?" If I thought Braxton was being compassionate, I'd be appreciative of his asking, but a touch of sarcasm underscores his tone. Five years on a case. I'd sold my soul to the devil and his daughter, and it still wasn't enough.

"Yeah. I'm right where I belong." The response surprises me. I've been bucking emotional support while pushing hard at the physical recovery. I wanted to get back in the field and finish this sentence of a year-long furlough. However, hearing my own words, there's a hint of truth in them.

Being back at Lakeside might be more than I originally thought this place would mean for me.

Be home. Ben directed in his two-word letter.

I might understand his request after all.

+ + +

When I return to the apartment, it's early enough I don't expect to find Jenna back from her girls' night out, but she is. She's also in my bed.

"Hey." My voice croaks with emotion for some reason when I see her under my sheets. Jenna lies on her side, her upper body almost twisted to her belly. One leg stretches its full length while the other bends at the knee, separated from the other, acting like a support beam. She's holding a tablet, reading off it, but shifts to glance at me over her shoulder.

"Hi." Her eyes hold mine, beckoning me forward, and I can't resist. Today has been a strange day, starting with her calling me someone else's name, then rescuing her child, spending time at a water park, the phone call from Braxton, and now this, coming home to her in my bed. It's too much and not enough, and I crawl over her in this position. Her gaze stays on mine as I slip my legs over the straightened one of hers, straddling it and forcing her bent leg higher, stretching it as my thigh presses under hers. My hard on is flush with her center.

She chuckles. "Archer?"

"You drunk?" I ask, knowing she went out for margaritas.

"Only had two. I'm buzzing but nothing more."

A buzz I can handle, and I glance down at her body beneath mine.

"You're so fucking sexy, babe." She's wearing another pair of tiny pajama shorts and a tank top minus a bra that hugs her sweet tits. My arms cage her upper body as I balance over her, tapping my zipper region against the heat between her thighs.

"Whatcha doing?" she teases, knowing where I am and what I want.

"Keep trying to stay away and find I can't. Thought I'd scare you off eventually, but after earlier, I need to be close to you, 'Locks."

"Tried to stay away?" Her brows crease, giving her a stern look that's cute. I imagine her in her classroom of horny teenage boys all wanting to date the MILF in the room. I'd kill each and every one of them for looking at her. "You don't scare me, Archer."

Maybe she scares me.

Her eyes hold mine, telling me she trusts me. Earlier, that trust was only a water park, but now, the honesty in those transparent eyes speaks volumes. She believes I'd take care of her. And I'm not play acting this time. I'm not looking for blind faith, like Viviana. I want to be here for Jenna. "Don't need to fuck you, but still need to be close."

Her breath hitches, but she isn't stopping me. Slowly, I crawl back and remove my shirt and pants. I had already kicked off my shoes when I entered the apartment, adding mine to the collection of tiny pink and yellow flip-flops by my front door. Thinking about shoes on a rug by an entrance and how right mine look mixing in with those child-sized ones might be a silly thought. Considering my big feet might walk anywhere those little ones travel might be just as ridiculous, but I want to consider it.

Jenna shifted to watch me undress. Climbing back over her, her eyes tell me she's hungry, and she licks her lips before digging her teeth into the bottom one.

She wants me, and I want her.

Pressing her back to her side, I strip her of both panties and shorts, then reset her legs in that open scissors position with one leg bent and one straight. I swipe my hand over her bare hip and along the side of her upper thigh.

"So sexy, 'Locks." Her skin is warm under my palm. I'd spank that ass if I thought she'd like it. Vi loved that shit, but Jenna doesn't seem like the type, and I'm okay with that. I don't need to see her skin pink and puffy from a sharp smack. I love the contrast of her pale white globes and long tan limbs.

"You okay with this?" I ask, knowing I'll stop if she asks, but I really don't want to stop touching her. Skimming my hand back to center, I swipe a finger through those luscious lower lips and her breath catches. I want to kiss her there and bite her firm ass. I want her to lose control like she did in the tub days ago. I want her out of her head like she kissed me earlier after Rosie's rescue. I'd been the one to distract her thoughts. I want to do the same thing now for a different reason.

I want her head only full of me.

You aren't worthy of love, Archer. Quickly, I shake my head.

Dammit, I want to be worthy. I want to be everything for the woman beneath me. I only need her . . . love?

My fingers play her like a fiddle at first, loving her little gasps. Then, I slip two at once into her heat. She's so warm, so wet. Her lids lower, and the sound of her arousal sings as I stroke in and out of her.

"Hear that, babe. You want me. *Me*," I enforce, dipping deeper.

"You, baby," she says to me, and my head snaps up.

Her eyes are on me. Yeah, she sees me, and I read the apology for earlier in her lusty gaze. Whatever caused the slip, whatever the trigger,

I'll ask her later so I can prevent it from happening again. She can keep her memories of her late husband, but I want her to make new memories with me.

Of us.

"Want to kiss you everywhere, Jenna." I'll make out with her like a horny teen again tonight if that's all she'll give me, but I really want a taste of her. When her fingers clutch the sheet and her leg shifts offering me a better view of where she's dripping with desire, I have my answer. I lower to suck at slick folds and tongue her slit until her essence coats my tongue. Her breath hitches again, and I take her until she's breathlessly whimpering my name.

"That's right, baby. Say my name 'cause you know it's me making you feel this good. It's me winding you up and wanting you to let go. Wanting you to spill on my tongue."

My mouth returns to her, lapping and licking until her legs stiffen, and a long, strong hum fills the room. She comes, and I savor what she's giving me. Her body. Her trust.

With a final scrape of my teeth to the underside of her thigh, I press upward and kneel back to slide down my boxer briefs. I'm so fucking hard, and my tip weeps, but I don't need to fuck her. I don't need to be inside her. *Yet.*

I flip her leg so she's on her back and spread wide open for me. My fingers re-enter her, and she slowly smiles at the return. Our eyes hold a second as I work her in and out while stroking myself and tugging at my length. She's looking at me like I could be her whole world along with her little girls, and damn, do I want to be everything to her.

"Gonna need to be closer, but I won't enter." I'm not opposed to coming in my briefs, as I've done two nights in a row, but tonight, I need more.

"Why?" The question catches in her throat, and her brows crease.

"Need a little extra tonight, but I don't want your mind cloudy."

"I'm not drunk," she says, almost a little too adamant.

"Not saying you are, but it's been a day. I want to do it right when we do, and we will be doing it, 'Locks. Just not tonight. Tonight is this."

I work my fingers faster, mimicking what I'll soon do to her with my dick. Her channel is begging to be full, but I fight the urge while enjoying this woman coming apart a second time under my attention. This woman letting me play her lush body and accepting my touch.

"Archer," she whispers. "Baby." She calls me sweet names, and I'm going to lose it sooner than expected, but I want her to go again. I want to feel her on my fingers. With a flick of my wrist, my thumb meets the right spot to push her over the edge. Her back arches. Her lids lower. Her mouth falls open. I want to hear her scream, but the girls are in the other bedroom. I better understand her need to be quiet and appreciate it a little more.

With her coming alive on my fingers, I wait out her release. Stroking myself, I'm damn near close to exploding. She's soaked, and it's just what I need once she's come down from the high. I lean forward, lining up the tip and stroking through those seeping folds, coating myself in her essence. She's watching me, but I'm watching how I glide through her heat, slicking up my length. I'm not going to last long. My lower back tightens. My legs stiffen.

"Gonna make me come," I warn her. She's taking away my breath, and I place a hand on her upper chest, feeling her heart racing in a way that matches my own. As I balance on my other hand, slipping through the wet heat of her, my lungs clog as an orgasm rips through me like a steam train at high speed. My balls swipe over her. My shaft gives out like the rocket it is, and I explode just over her entrance, coating her pubic bone. Her heart hammers under my palm. With a ragged breath of my own, I glance down at my seed on her lower belly, and it's all I need to see to know I can't walk away from her or her girls.

She's mine, and I'll do everything to make certain she accepts me as hers.

22

[Jenna]

While Monday seemed long, the days have caught up to me, and time speeds up. By Wednesday night, we've had more beach time, more dinners with Anna and company, and Archer has stuck close through all of it. We've had additional sexy times in his bed in new positions involving my mouth on him while his is on me, and I squirm whenever I think about it.

Whenever I think of him, warmth fills my insides.

Being with Archer, it's hard to pretend my heart isn't screaming for more when we promised to keep things only between us. Only we know what we're doing under the darkness of night and the seclusion of his bedroom. We haven't had sex, but the orgasms he's giving me are enough to fog my brain and tease my ovaries. I'm thinking things I should not be thinking—like how sweet it would be to give this man a little boy.

After another night of drinking wine on Anna's patio, watching the sunset, we each return to our respective places. I haven't mentioned that Zack and Logan never did stay at the main house. Anna couldn't have had an ulterior motive for keeping me in Archer's apartment, but I've become grateful I stayed put.

The upcoming weekend entails a memorial to Ben with a fire on the beach. Anna says she isn't part of the ritual the friends—Logan, Mason, and Zack—participate in, and she doesn't expect to be a part of it this year either. Archer will join them instead.

"I'll visit the cemetery alone, earlier in the day, and then spend some time by the fire before the guys do their thing," Anna had explained during margaritas on Monday.

Archer has been included in this year's activity, and Noah might be attending as well. For tonight, Archer and I snuggle on the couch once the girls are asleep. He's been quiet today, distracted even, and I shift when he doesn't laugh at something funny on the romantic comedy I conned him into watching.

"What's wrong?" I tip my head to better look at him then sit upright.

"Nothing." But his eyes tell the truth. Something's on his mind.

"You can tell me." I tease, nudging him with my shoulder, but when he doesn't respond, I add in a more serious tone, "You can talk to me."

Archer turns his neck to look at me, his lips twisting a bit to the side.

I read the struggle in his eyes. "Another hard topic?"

When he doesn't say more, I reach for the back of his neck, cupping his nape in my palm, and massage the tightness. He's so tense. As I work at the strained muscles, his head slowly lolls forward.

"Feels good, babe."

"Scoot forward," I say, climbing on the couch to wedge behind him. The fit is snug with my back pressed against the cushions as I straddle the outside of his thighs. My hands slip under his T-shirt and swipe it upward.

"Whatcha doing, 'Locks?" He glances at me over his shoulder, but when my hands hit his shoulder blades, kneading and squeezing the taut muscles, he has the answer. He reaches over his head for the collar of his tee and pulls it forward, removing the covering. We stay quiet for a few minutes while I work at the tension in his upper back. With my legs nestled against his outer thighs, one of his hands comes to my knee.

"Loved my motorcycle." His hand strokes up my leg. "Would love to have taken you for a ride on it." His voice drifts, lost in thought, and I don't miss the use of past tense.

"What happened to the bike?"

"My leg." He has already explained the nerve damage. He'd need control of those powerful legs. Riding is a risk.

"What did you love best about riding?" I ask, hoping maybe telling me something positive about the experience will lessen the sadness in his voice.

"It's going to sound silly, but the wind in my hair, sun on my face. Just being free to roam and race."

My fingertips move upward, pressing harder at the base of his skull and working upward to the top of his head. He doesn't have long hair, keeping it close to his scalp with hints of gray everywhere, especially his temples.

"That feels so good, babe."

"Bet the women loved to ride with you." Archer stiffens under my touch. I pause for a second before slipping back to his shoulder, using both hands on the left one to dig into the tight muscles.

"Not many women on my bike, babe."

My stomach still drops because the implication is clear. He's at least had one or two. *Never been in love.* I found it difficult to believe. Certainly, women fell for him. He was fit and sexual and growing older has enhanced his good looks. How had he gone so long without that special woman at least once in his life?

"But there was at least one?" Someone important had once been behind him on his bike. His back flexes under my touch in answer to my question. His hand continues stroking up my thigh, back and forth, rubbing at my skin more than massaging me. I switch to his right shoulder, working it with both hands as well.

"No one important," he whispers, giving me the hint there was someone. I lean forward and press a kiss to the back of his neck without missing a beat in my massage. Then I separate my hands and use my thumbs at the top of his spine. He cleared his throat. "Sometimes being undercover, you do things you aren't proud of, say things you can't unsay."

I remain silent, allowing him to tell me what he will.

"The job called for pretending, acting if you will. You had a position to fill and be empty of your emotions. What was fake had to feel real." His voice drops. "It could get confusing."

"Did you fall in love when you weren't supposed to?" I've read my share of forbidden romance novels, and I was working off a hunch.

Archer twists at the waist, and my hands pause on his back. "It wasn't love." His voice is frost, his tone sharp as his dark eyes narrow at me, imparting a truth he doesn't need to clarify. This topic is hard.

I nod with a weak smile and return to massaging him, digging my thumbs into his back as I examine the tattoos on his shoulder. A crown. A snake. Insignias that could mean anything. Had Archer been undercover in a gang? Had he gone that deep into a role? The idea was like something out of a movie.

"She was just a woman," he mutters. "I try to wipe her from my thoughts."

I don't like that Archer is thinking of her, as I sensed he is from this conversation, and I better understand how he must have felt the other day when I said Ryan's name. It stings to think someone else is on his mind when my hands are on him. Still, the heartbreak in his tone has me reacting. I press another kiss to his back. And then another. And another. Working my way from left to right, shoulder to shoulder, I suck at his skin, sipping at the ink until I tuck into the juncture of his shoulder and neck. I nip him there, and he tips his head, softly chuckling.

"Tickles, babe."

I purr in response but continue my stream of kisses until pausing to slip my hand under his arm and around his body to his upper left pec. His heart races beneath my hand, and I'm reminded of what he said when he does this same thing to me.

Reminds me I'm alive.

Between the gunshot wound and what I can only assume was a broken heart, Archer *is* still alive as am I. Still, who hurt him? How? Why?

What's fake can feel real. It can get confusing.

Who did he have to pretend with? Did he fall for her? Or her for him?

I lay my head against his back and breathe him in. His heart still hammers under my palm, beneath his warm skin.

"Let me protect you, Archer," I whisper behind him. *Let me protect your heart.* He's so quiet I don't think he hears me, and I clutch at his firm pec before lightly scraping my nails over him and leaning back, peeling myself off him.

He said his fear is he's not worthy of love, but he's so wrong. I see it in his attempts to connect with his nephews. His longing to right old wrongs with his sister. The laughter with Ben's friends and the way he is with my girls. He's desperate to be home again from wherever he's been, whatever he's had to endure.

I've barely righted myself when Archer spins and captures the back of my head, bringing his mouth to mine and crushing me with a kiss so fierce, so intense, I almost come just sitting behind him. Our tongues meet. Lips move. His hand skims up my arm and lands over my heart. We stay in this twisted position, kissing like tomorrow is our last day when we still have a few more nights.

Our kisses heat, and our bodies rock with more urgency.

"What are you doing to me, 'Locks?" His voice is strained, like a new fear fills his thoughts.

"Same thing you're doing to me." Scaring the crap out of me, making me want things I didn't think I'd ever have again.

We return to kissing, mouths seeking, speaking without words. We both want more. I feel it in the racing of his heart angled near mine in our seated position. My hand slips back to his.

"Let me be the one to take care of you. At least for tonight." I don't want him thinking of someone else when he's with me. I want to be the one to erase all those memories of whoever she was and replace them with us. "I don't care where you've been, Archer, or who you were with. I don't care about the hard topics. Just let me be the one tonight. Be with me."

"Not going to pretend with you, Jenna." My name is a plea, a prayer, a worship.

"Not pretending with you," I admit because my heart is in this one-hundred-percent. I want him inside me. I want to feel myself surround him. I want us to lose ourselves in one another. "This is real."

"Jenna."

He's already under my skin and burrowed into my heart. Now, I want him in my body as well.

Slowly, I climb up and over the back of the couch. Archer's eyes never leave me, and I hold out my hand over the back of the sofa.

"Come to bed with me." My voice cracks. *Be with me.* My body hums.

He looks up at me, surprise and something else written in his expression. He accepts my hand and stands, holding it over the back of the couch. He doesn't even break our connection but climbs up and over the second one in his way. We enter his room, and he slowly closes the door behind him. I go still, continuing to hold his hand.

"You okay with this?" I ask of him like he's asked of me. There's no doubt what I mean and where I want tonight to lead.

"You're the most beautiful woman I've ever known, Jenna."

That's all it takes for me to leap for him, latching my arms around his neck and kissing him once more like I never want him to leave me. His hands race up my sides until one settles in the middle of my back and the other rests on the back of my head. Our bodies line up, and we move toward the bed. He twists, and we fall back onto the mattress, my body landing on his. He doesn't make a sound at my weight, buffering it as my legs spread and straddle his lap.

"Want you so badly, babe."

I feel the same, and it's a rush to sit up and remove my shirt and then slip off his legs to shimmy out of my shorts.

"Everything," he says, and I slow my movements to release my bra, letting the material drag forward and down my arms. Archer sits up, enjoying the striptease until he can't take it. Gripping my hips and tugging me forward, his mouth surrounds a breast. The attention he gives the achy swell is the same as how he kisses me. Everything is in that mouth, tongue teasing my nipple, lips sucking my skin. He releases me with a pop, and I step back again, taking my time once more to shed my underwear.

"Dammit," he hisses, tugging me back to him before I'm even upright and latching onto my other breast, kissing it, loving it the same as he'd done to the first.

"You're a fucking goddess, Jenna." Despite the profanity, there's so much reverence in his voice when he says my name the way he does. His hand skims up my belly, and he watches as he outlines my body, coasting over one breast and down to my stomach. Back up again and over the other one. If I didn't know better, I swear he just drew a giant heart over my midsection.

He returns to massaging my breasts, testing the weight, squeezing the fullness, and pinching the nipples in tandem. He's paying me the homage he'd give to a fictional goddess, and everything in me believes him. He is not pretending with me. This is real.

Reaching down, I struggle with his belt until he quickly stands, catching me at the hip, and one-handedly, he works his belt, button, and zipper. I take over, shoving down his briefs and jeans until he steps out of them. We stand facing one another, body to body, just breathing each other in. His hand comes to the back of my head again, and he kisses me—tender, soft, sweet.

Slowly, he lowers to the mattress and takes me with him, keeping us attached by our mouths. Once my body covers his, we still.

"Condom?" I'd spent years being the provider or the one to remind my partner of such a thing, but this . . . feels uncomfortable. "I'm not on the pill."

My head dips, embarrassed to admit the truth. "I haven't been with anyone in three years. Not since . . ." I hadn't considered I'd have sex again, and I never renewed my prescription after Rosie's birth. I didn't think I'd ever be in this position again. I shrug, dismissing the awkwardness of this conversation.

"Jenna, baby," he whispers, tightening his hand in my hair. "I'm clean. I've been triple-checked since everything." *Since he's been shot.* "But we should still be careful."

He reaches over to a small drawer in the nightstand and pulls out a small foil square. He's quick to cover himself and guide me back over him. With his hands on my hips, we line up, and he pauses, eyes meeting mine. There are so many questions in those dark eyes, and I lean down to quickly kiss his lips.

"Archer," I whisper, answering all his concerns.

Yes, I'm okay with this.

Yes, I want him.

Yes, I could love him if he'd let me.

He enters me with a slow, measured pace when I expected him to rush. Then again, nothing has been as I expected with this man. A man I've misjudged, misread, and almost missed entirely in my life. We come together, him filling me in a way I haven't been in far too long. For a second, my eyes lazily close at the sensation.

When he's full to the hilt, he pauses again, and I swallow around the lump in my throat. It's too much. The way he's looking at me. The way he feels inside me. The way my heart wants to burst. His eyes seek mine, searching my face. I've never felt more alive, more beautiful . . . more loved.

"Move, babe." With his rough voice, the strain in it has me sliding up his shaft, teasing him at the edge before slamming back down. Holding this position, we move together with me riding him until he jackknifes upward and flips me over. Remaining inside me, he brushes back my hair, taking another moment to get his fill of looking at me. Then he drags back but thrusts forward. Short jabs. Sharp rushes. He takes over, and it's nothing like I've ever felt before.

My hands climb his chest and curl over his shoulders, feeling him everywhere as he rocks into me. Gradually, his pace increases, and my palms cover his shoulder blades, slipping down the dip of his back until I cup his firm backside. Holding him, I press my heels into the mattress and buck upward, losing myself in the thrill of him filling me.

"Archer," I whisper a warning. I'm so close. This never happens. I can't get there without attention to my clit, but the way he moves, the drag of him, the rush of him, his length hits me in a way my orgasm ripples up my legs and across my belly. I brace for impact. The eruption bursts, and I clutch his backside, squeezing him inside me, groaning his name. I never want it to end.

"Jesus, Jenna. Just. Fuck." He moves faster, driving harder, letting loose a little more as my release teases his from him. Propped on an elbow, he lowers his hand, touching that trigger point on my body. "Give me another one."

The command is too much. He's too much. "I can't."

"You can, 'Locks. Do it again for me."

We're two bodies out of control as I thrust upward, and he surges inward. Eventually, the climb tosses me over the edge a second time, and Archer joins me with soft encouragement.

"Never knew it could be like this," I groan. With him pulsing and pumping inside me, my release drags onward. My lids flutter closed as if I can capture this feeling like a snapshot. My hands roam his body, touching him everywhere I can, as much as I can, memorizing his body over mine, in mine. Our hearts race, and my hand pauses on his chest, covering that sacred spot.

"It beats for you," Archer whispers, and my breath catches.

"Same with mine," I whisper back. His mouth takes mine, drawing us together while he's still inside me. Our heads tilt, and lips move, holding this sensation of togetherness as long as we can.

Archer pulls back first, rubbing his nose along mine as I do with my girls.

"Give me twenty minutes, and we're doing that again," he warns in his growly rough voice. I giggle until I see the spark in his dark eyes.

I'll be with him as many times as he'd like. I want to just be. With him.

23

[Archer]

"Let me take you to dinner tonight."

Jenna is making breakfast for the girls, and my hand sweeps up her spine. I want to pull her to me, press her body to mine like we did three times last night. I haven't had a workout like that since I was in my early thirties, and I'm not as young as I once was, but damn, this woman. She keeps me rock hard and wanting.

Her eyes shift to the girls sitting on the stools at the counter before answering me, and I read her thoughts.

"I'll take care of everything. Ask Mila and Lorna to watch them. Make a reservation. You just take some time later to get ready." I can't remember the last time I went on a genuine date. One I actually looked forward to planning and not one facilitated by my position in an investigation. We'll have a sunset dinner, some wine, and a romantic walk on the beach. In my head, the night is a perfect way to appreciate this woman who has given me her body wholeheartedly and repeatedly.

I want to ask her if there's any way to see her again. After this vacation. Before my next assignment.

While Jenna is beautiful as she is, nothing prepares me for the light makeup, loosely curled waves, and hip-hugging dress she wears tonight.

"Babe," I groan as she exits the girls' bedroom. The little princesses are already over at the main house having pizza and movie time with Mila and Lorna. Jenna said her good night to them earlier so she could get dolled up, and she is dolled the frickity-frack up. "I'm going to get in a fight tonight."

"Why?" She laughs, smoothing her hands over her hips.

"Because no matter where we go, men won't be able to keep their eyes off you."

Jenna slowly smiles, and I step forward, pressing a soft kiss to the corner of her mouth.

"You clean up nicely yourself." Her eyes roam my black dress shirt, rolled up to my biceps, and dark jeans. The days have been warm, and

181

despite a breeze tonight, it will be humid on the restaurant's rooftop. A pair of flip-flops tone down my dressy apparel.

"Seeing you look at me like that makes me want to spread you out on this couch," I warn, feeling the hunger in her eyes like a live wire down my center and spiking up my rod.

"Later?" she whispers, biting her lower lip.

"All night," I tell her, reaching out a hand and leading her from the apartment.

Driftwood is the most popular restaurant in town and a bit of a tourist trap, but its rooftop view is incomparable, and it will offer a pretty setting when the sun lowers. They don't take reservations, so when we check in, it's a forty-five-minute wait, and I register my phone for a text alert when our table is ready. I'd suggest a drink in the bar, but I don't want to share Jenna's attention.

"Can you walk in those shoes?" Her high heels make my girl's long legs look even longer, and the way I see it, Jenna is mine.

"For a little bit. What did you have in mind?" She's holding my hand while her other hand curls around my forearm. We look like a real couple. We *feel* like the real thing.

"Let's walk through the marina. Check out the boats."

Jenna wrinkles her nose.

"What?"

"My husband managed the marina in Elk Lake City."

"Not a boat fan?" *Dammit.* It's a reminder there's still so much to learn about her.

"I love boats and boating, it's just . . . it's nothing. Let's walk." She tugs my arm and steps forward.

"Babe, I don't want to do anything that makes you uncomfortable, and I definitely don't want to say something that will trigger thoughts of him when you're out with me."

"I'm not thinking about him," she says, catching my eyes. "Let's walk." She gently nudges my shoulder, still clutching my hand, still holding my arm, and we take off across the street from the restaurant, heading for the marina. Silence floats around us.

"Look, I don't want to be an asshole. You can think about him. You can talk about him. I just . . ." I scrub a hand down my face.

"You just what?"

"I want to be the only man on your mind." My voice lowers, knowing I sound even more like an asshole with that statement.

"You are the only man on my mind. Along with last night."

My head turns toward her, and she sheepishly smiles. After going slow at first, we quickly got creative, and Jenna rode me before I had her facedown on the bed. Our final time was in the early hours of the morning, sleepy and lazy while we lay on our sides. It's how I want to spend all my nights, wrapped up in her arms, slipping into her body.

"If I were a better man, I would not be thinking of you taking off your panties and letting me have you on some random boat deck in that dress," I warn her, fighting my own grin.

"If you were a better man." That smirky curl of her mouth reminds me of her lips wrapped around my dick and her tongue swiping over the head, and just dammit . . . later is not soon enough.

But first, dinner. "Behave," I growl.

We remain quiet for a few more steps until she squeezes my fingers curled with hers. "You know, I think you are a good guy, though, Archer. I mean, you came off a little gruff at first, but deep down, you're a good man."

The conviction in her voice does something to my insides, and I rub my sternum. She has no idea how much I want to believe what she says. I want to be a decent guy again, but that phone call from Braxton has my head all over the place the last couple of nights. I have some decisions to make after speaking to my therapist today. I finally have the all clear to return to work. I can start back up in January.

The only thing is, I'm no longer certain I want to go back.

"Can I ask you something?" We're strolling, taking it slow in her high heels and knowing we have time to waste before we need to turn back toward the restaurant.

"Sure." Her voice rings with excitement.

"You know Ben left these letters for us. Like a statement or something, and I've been puzzled by mine." No matter what the meaning of Ben's letter to me, I'm late in completing his directive. I've failed *his* mission.

"What did it say?"

"Be home. I think he meant to write *come home,* as he'd often ask me when I planned to return."

"But . . .?"

"I just don't know. It feels like he meant something else." I've been tinkering with potential meanings, but decoding shit was not necessarily in my wheelhouse.

"Can I ask you a question?" she teases.

"Suuure," I elongate the word, mimicking her.

"Why did Ben have access to you while Anna didn't?"

"It was safer for Anna and the kids. I didn't need Anna messaging me for every minor detail on the house. Ben would only make contact when it was absolutely necessary." Jenna already knows the three McCaryn siblings own the cottage and not just Anna, though she seems to have commandeered it.

"Do you really think your sister would do that?"

"I don't know." I sigh, not certain if my sister would actually abuse the contact information. *Or just worry about me.* The afterthought is something I hadn't considered.

"Anna told me you were once close. I think she's missed you, and she just wants to understand her big brother."

I exhale again, feeling guilt wrap around my chest. "I know." I haven't been fair to the responsible sister. The one who looked after our parents for years, handled their funeral, and takes care of their house.

"So back to the note. What do you think he meant?" Am I reading too much into it? Maybe Ben did mean come home, and it's been that simple. Ben wasn't complex, and he didn't mince words. If he was lucid enough to write a directive, he wrote it with intention.

"Well, my best guess is family meant everything to Ben. He loved his wife and his children above all else. But he also loved his parents and sister, and then add in his brothers from other mothers." She softly chuckles. "And I guess he might not have meant only to come home but stay home. Be home. *Be* involved with your family. *Be* a family again.

Or maybe . . ." She pauses. "Maybe he meant to just be. Be happy, content, whole."

I nod, pursing my lips as I think about what she's said. It sounds simple enough.

"If I go back to the department, it won't be easy." I hadn't planned to mention the all clear yet, and Jenna's head swivels toward me, pausing us in our walk.

"Are you returning to active status? Are you going undercover again?"

"I'll go where I'm assigned." I don't know if undercover is on the docket for me. Although, if it's a desk job, I can't do it. I need to be out in the field and involved in a case.

There's a slight burn in my leg, stinging like a reminder that fieldwork may no longer be an option.

Jenna turns her attention away from me, her eyes directed off in the distance over the water. "I guess it would be hard to *be* part of a family if you disappear again for years." Something heavy and rough fills her voice. Her head lowers, but she quickly licks her lips and looks up again.

"I don't want to disappear," I admit. "It was . . . fucking lonely at times." While the Quintero parties were spectacular and the lifestyle insane, I was getting older and wiser, and wanted to settle down a little bit. I wanted more than champagne and cocaine every night. Not that I did that shit, but when it was all around you, it definitely got tiresome. However, it was an important part in the image of the Quinteros, which made it necessary for me. Or maybe I was one of them, and I'd never be able to escape the haunting of that family.

"It's your choice, Archer. Be here and be a family or leave them behind again. Leave—" She stops herself and swallows. Her eyes squint, still aimed in the distance. "Maybe this time, tell Anna where you're going, what you're doing, so it doesn't feel so much like abandonment."

"I didn't abandon my family."

"I know that now, but she doesn't. You two should really talk. Trust her. She's your sister."

Jenna might be right. I might have short-changed my sister's ability to accept my position, my line of work. I just thought it best that only my dad knew and eventually only Ben, keeping it in the male line, which sounds chauvinistic.

"I'll have to think about it." As soon as I say it, I know Anna and I need to chat. She needs to know where I've been and why I've done what I've done. Our other sister, Amelia, should be in on that conversation as well.

As we stand still, Jenna glances back out at the water, shielding her eyes to take in something in the distance. We're quiet again, and things aren't going in the direction I'd hoped.

"Babe, I want you to know that I might not always be able to say where I'm going, but it's for your safety." I reach up and swipe the hair blowing in the breeze behind her ear. "I'll never let anything hurt you or your girls."

She turns to me with a soft smiles, but her attention drifts back to something on the water. It's pissing me off a little that I can't keep her attention.

"What are you looking at?" An edge fills my voice.

"That's one big boat."

Turning, I expect to see some shipping barge, not uncommon on the Great Lakes, but instead, there is a sleek white craft that looks large even from this distance, which means it's a yacht, most likely private and pricey. Whoever owns it is one wealthy person. For the briefest second, I recall who I know with that kind of cash, and a shiver ripples up my spine.

Viviana was spotted at a marina in Chicago.

Quickly, I dismiss the thought despite Braxton's voice in my head. Lake Michigan would not be the place Vi would yacht. The Gulf Coast. The Caribbean Sea. The ocean off Colombia. *But a lake?* Not happening.

Still, my eyes can't seem to pull away from the large boat until my phone beeps with a notification that a table would be ready for us in ten minutes. I inform Jenna and steer us back in the direction of Driftwood. As we walk to the restaurant, my mind is skipping all over the place.

Be home.

Big boat.

Family.

Cash on the lake.

It isn't uncommon for homes in this area to be valued over a million dollars. The property alone is worth that much, and then add a huge house, and the price tag might quadruple.

Not to mention, drug running through the lakes up to Canada has increased. It's just something people don't want to consider on the third coast.

My mind drifts, recollecting the Quintero's obscene portfolio. Houses. Boats. Cars. It was crazy. My gaze shifts over Jenna's shoulder, looking out over the water, wondering . . . but it can't be.

Next, I glance at Jenna, long and sleek with her raven hair and sweet lips. She's everything opposite of what I once had—as a small-town high school teacher, raising two little girls on her own and doing a damn good job of it. She's worth more than any yacht, club, or private island.

She's home. She's stability. She's what I need.

Back at the restaurant, the hostess seats us on the rooftop, and we order a bottle of wine. Silence grows between us. An unexpected tension weaves around us. This isn't how I wanted our date to go, but as long as things already feel so tangled, I broach one more topic.

"Sunday is approaching."

Jenna sighs, reaching for her glass of wine and taking a sip while looking out at the lowering sun.

"It was only supposed to be between us," she says quietly, setting her glass back down on the table and lowering her eyes to the linen. "Undercover." She lifts her head and weakly smiles.

Does she think I've been pretending with her? I told her last night how I had to play a role, but I'm finished with acting. I don't want to hide anymore. Crossing my arms on the table, I lean forward.

"Is that all you want it to be?" What happens in the bedroom stays in the bedroom? Can she walk away that easily? I'll never be able to sleep in that room again. Her scent will linger. Thoughts of what we've done will dance through my memory every time I'm in that space.

Her reluctant expression says she's fighting her own thoughts.

"What if I said I wanted to see you again?" I ask.

Her brows arch. "How would that work? Especially if you went back to the department?"

How *would* that work? Could I just come and go on investigations? Would Jenna wait for me if I went missing for months or even years as I had before? The Quintero case was the largest, longest assignment I'd had, and I doubted I'd be put on something so intense again, but still, I'd be placed somewhere.

"What if I didn't return to the department?" *What was I saying?* "Hypothetically speaking," I jest, but there's no humor in my voice.

Jenna sits upright, steeling herself, and giving me a glimpse of the woman constantly protecting her children. The fierceness when Rosie held my gun. The strength when Rosie fell from the swing. The shield around her to prevent ever being hurt again. I see it because I recognize it, but I don't want the deflection used on me.

"You know, Archer, once upon a time, I played these games. I could hang with the best of them. Flirt. Fuck. But I'd never fold for a man. I wanted to be someone's priority. And I found that. I had someone who put me at the top of his list and didn't back down, no matter how hard I pushed. Ryan was my person. I want that again. It sounds selfish and maybe a little snotty, but I deserve it. I told you I believe in second chances, but that second time needs to be just as involved as the first, maybe more. I'm not settling for less. I need someone who wants to *be* home. With me." She points at herself. "With my girls."

"Maybe you could be *my* home." I stare at her across the table, finding myself surprised at the admission but strangely confident in the truth. She and the girls *feel* like home, but I can't tell her that yet. I don't know how I'll protect her if I go back to work for the department. I'm also not convinced I'm the man she needs to *be* home with her. "Because I don't have one."

Her mouth slightly falls open before she whispers my name. "You have a home. A family even. They're waiting for you. They want you to return."

"That's Anna's family. It was Ben's. I want my own." I want her and the girls.

188

While Jenna gapes at me, I retreat into my head. Have I misread everything? Maybe she really meant to keep us in the dark. A little dalliance at the lake, and then she returns to her good life while I slink back into my hole, undercover and unknown. Maybe even unmissed.

Sitting upright, I double tap my hands on the table, brushing off the comment. "Forget I said that. That was stup—" Something knocks into my shoulder, pressing me back in my seat before I jostle forward again.

"What the frack?" Quickly, I stand, spinning in the direction of a person I hadn't seen near our table. A woman in a form-fitting white dress saunters down the remainder of the short aisle. Her ass is large and sculpted, and her heels clack on the rough flooring of the rooftop. Long, straight, dark hair slightly sways across the middle of her back.

Viviana? It can't be.

"Are you alright?" Jenna asks, and I spin back to her but just as quickly glance back over my shoulder. The outline of the woman's curvy hips. Those killer high heels. A lingering scent of overpowering perfume. Everything scrambles in my head like a bad video feed as the woman has disappeared down the staircase leading to the first floor.

Turning back to Jenna, I open my mouth, but her phone buzzes on the table.

"It's Mila. Let me take this." She picks up her phone and answers it in a rush. "What's wrong?"

Holding up a finger for me, she mouths, "I'm so sorry."

I shake my head to dismiss the apology.

"Okay, put Talia on?" In that momentary lapse, Jenna speaks to me as she stands. "I'm just going to head downstairs and take this. I'll be right back."

As Jenna passes me, she brushes a hand on my shoulder, swiping it over my shirt in a soft caress where I'd just been hit. As she walks away, I turn to watch her backside, noting the curve of her form in her tight dress. Her heels click lightly on the rooftop floor as she steps toward the staircase leading downward. As she moves forward, the sound of her softer tapping merges in my ears with the harder pounding of the previous woman stomping off in her heels.

It couldn't be Vi. Not here. Not now.

I reach for my wine and down the remainder of the glass. This could not be happening. It's like I conjured Viviana up to push away the possibility of a normal life. I can't believe I asked Jenna if she could be my home. Of course, she couldn't be my rock. The thought was ridiculous to voice.

No one will ever love you. You're a despicable human being.

I'll be going back to the department. I'll be heading undercover again.

Glancing over my shoulder one more time where Jenna disappeared, where the other woman did as well, I accept that the concept of a real-life, romantic hope, and being home is a fucking lost cause.

24

[Jenna]

"Talia, what's wrong, baby?" I say into the phone as I make my way down the stairs.

"When are you coming home?"

I check the time on my phone. "Later, baby. What's going on?" Why is she even still up? It's after eight, and she should be in bed.

"Will you come in and see me when you get home?"

"Of course, honey. When I get home, I'll come in and kiss you good night." Like I would if I'd gone anywhere with anyone. Because my little worrier worries, I always go to the girls' room once I get home and press a kiss to their heads, telling them I love them, even if they are sleeping and can't hear me.

"Are you with Archer?"

"Yes, baby. Mommy's with Archer." I don't know where this line of questions is leading, but I'm standing in the hallway near the restrooms instead of sitting with Archer. The man who just told me he didn't have a home and asked if maybe I could be his. He wants to see me again, but what does that mean? How would that work if he returned to his job? I have so many questions, but I need to soothe Talia right now.

"Talia, I love you. Now go to bed and put Mila back on the phone."

"I love you, too," she says in a small voice, and rustling occurs before Mila is back on the phone.

"I'm sorry about that," Mila says. "I thought if she talked to you, she might finally settle down."

"Is everything okay?" I ask the twelve-year-old I left responsible for my girls.

"She just said she missed you."

I sigh. It doesn't make sense, but I'll tackle that later. I haven't been on a date in forever, and I really had high hopes for this one, but it seems to be one heavy conversation after another, and now this.

"We ordered a little bit ago, so our dinner should be arriving soon. We'll come home right after that."

"Don't rush," Mila assures me. "I'll just get Mom over here if she asks for you again."

What a frickity-frack clustermuck. I don't want Anna involved because she has her own thing going on. Tellinger her Archer asked me to dinner was awkward enough, and I tried to play it off like it was nothing. He was trying to make up for us getting off on the wrong foot. I wasn't certain we were fooling anyone, though.

"I'm sorry she's acting like this," I say again.

"It's okay. Take your time. Enjoy your dinner with Uncle Archer."

Uncle Archer. See, he does have a family waiting for him, but I wasn't opposed to him joining mine. I'd had too many visions of him doing just that, but it seems impossible if he returns to his department. I might have been a bit harsh in stating what I wanted in a second chance. What I need is to get back up to the table and explain myself.

"Thank you. I'll text you when we are on our way back."

Mila and I say goodbye, and I click off the call. As I'd been facing the wall, I quickly turn around and bump into someone standing rather close behind me.

"Goodness. I'm so sorry," I say, glancing up and immediately scanning the woman before me. She's wearing a body-hugging white dress that accentuates every curve and dip of her form along with emphasizing her large breasts and her deeply tanned skin. She's the woman who bumped into Archer, and I don't even know how that happened. He was leaning on our table, not hanging out in the aisle. Her knocking into him seemed rather on purpose, but that wouldn't make sense.

"So, you're with *Archer*, are you?" she says to me with a soft accent I can't identify. There's also a strain of venom in her voice when she says Archer's name. "Is that what he calls himself now?"

"Excuse me?" I blink. "Do I know you?"

"I doubt it." Her eyes appraise me, skimming down my body as I did hers, but her nose wrinkles like she smells something rotten.

"I'm sorry. I don't know who you are." I don't add that she might have the wrong Archer. I'm not giving whoever this woman is anything to go on. I move to the left, to return to our table. Stepping right, she blocks my retreat.

"Excuse me," I snap a little louder and a little harsher.

Her dark eyes narrow, and a smirk curls her plump lips colored in a deep plum. She's strikingly gorgeous while at the same time nasty-looking. Her demeanor screams entitled and arrogant, that she was a woman who gets what she wants.

"Babe." We both turn in the direction of the strong male voice, rugged and rough, and reminding me of the first time I heard it. "Let her go."

My mouth falls open, ready to defend myself, when I realize Archer isn't looking at me. He isn't addressing me either. His gaze is narrowed in on the woman in white, who crosses her arms.

"I wondered when we'd meet again," she says to him, jutting out a hip.

My insides seize. I shiver.

"Not here." His tone is harsh, like a knife through glass. He's cutting her down with his glare, and even though I can't fully see her face, I imagine she's giving it back to him.

"I hate you," she says as Archer steps forward, coming closer to her.

"No, you don't," he states, softening his voice toward her.

I do not want to be a witness to this. I do not know her, and I suddenly do not recognize him. I don't want to be in this hallway near either of them because the way Archer is peering at this woman, *she* is his home. She's his entire world.

"I should have killed you." Her voice drops as Archer invades her space, coming in closer than is publicly acceptable or even privately appropriate unless he plans to kiss her.

My eyes close. I need to get away from them.

She should have killed him? Is she the one who shot Archer? Who is she? And more importantly, why did she shoot him?

"You couldn't do it. You love me."

"Who is she?" While tipping her head at me, her question echoes my own. She's still blocking me and Archer doesn't shift his gaze from her. He doesn't pay me an ounce of attention.

"She's no one."

What the fuck? Not frickity-frack. Just. What. The. Fuck?

Then it hits me. He told me only last night how he had to pretend sometimes. What was fake felt real. And I've misunderstood everything. We hadn't been anything other than some sexy times in his bedroom. *Undercover.* Even this date has been all over the place. Nothing has been real with Archer McCaryn.

"Babe, let's get out of here." He reaches for her hand and tugs her forward. She stumbles and collides with his chest. He cups her jaw, and then he turns them to lead her out of the restaurant. Without an explanation. Without a glance back at me.

And the only thing I can fixate on is how he called her babe like he's been calling me all along.

25

[Jenna]

I didn't know where to go, and I didn't know what to think. We'd driven here in Archer's car, and I had to call an Uber, which is nearly impossible to find in a small, touristy town. I should have called Anna or one of the guys, but I was too stunned to be logical.

What the hell just happened?

Archer left with another woman, that's what happened, and he left me after all his declarations of what-if and being home.

I was a damn fool.

This is why it took me so long to settle on a man. They didn't want monogamous relationships or commitment. *Fling, fling, fling* worked best, but I wasn't that twenty-year-old anymore, and I wasn't without children. I had to be responsible, respectable, and I felt darn rejected.

As I slam the car door of the Uber that drops me at the base of the driveway, I wave off the driver and step out of my heels, carrying them in one hand. I should check on my girls, but I'm still not expected home for another few hours, and I don't want to face the apartment yet. Instead, I stalk around the main house, cross the stone patio, and skip my way down the stairs to the beach. In the time that's passed, the sun still hadn't fully descended, and the sliver of yolk peeks above the watery horizon. I collapse into a chair on the beach, covering my face with both hands. I should cry. I want to cry, but I'm too angry for tears.

"What happened?" Concern fills Anna's voice as she addresses me, and I release my face, falling back into the Adirondack chair. I'm too embarrassed to face her.

Shaking my head, I don't know where to begin or even how to explain what happened at the restaurant. My eyes narrow on the fading sun, a symbol of time running out. The day is done, and I don't know why I thought I could have a second chance at love with a man I'd met less than two weeks ago.

"Did you sleep with him?" Anna softens her voice. I feel her facing me from her position in the chair beside me.

"It's been three years," I whisper, lowering my head and staring down at my fingers in my lap. "Three long, lonely years."

From the corner of my eye, I see Anna nod in understanding.

"I didn't want it to happen." But that doesn't feel like the truth. I did want Archer. "I hadn't planned on it happening."

Anna remains silent.

"He was the first man since Ryan." I twist my neck, facing her. She'll understand what I say next. "It's been so hard to open up to someone else, to let anyone new in."

Her eyes well with tears, and I shrug, dismissing my behavior. My lips tremble and hurt stabs at my chest. "Maybe he's just not out of my system yet." Ryan. My defense is weak as I did give in to the temptation of Archer. It felt like it was time. I felt safe with him.

Maybe you could be my home.

Dammit. Why had I wanted such a thing? Why did I think Archer meant it?

What is fake feels real. It can get confusing.

"May I say something?" Anna asks.

"I'm sorry," I immediately offer, holding her eyes so she sees my apology while I warn against the possibility of a lecture. I've been nothing but reckless and a little thoughtless on this trip. I was supposed to be here for her, not shacking up with her brother, acting like a layover for him or whatever other bullshit we were pretending to be.

Anna shakes her head. "Don't apologize. I saw how he looked at you, watched you."

My brows pinch. "How did he look at me?" Like I was some joke? Some poor single mother, a desperate widow who was an easy target.

"Like you could be everything to him."

I huff and gaze back at the setting sun. "That's how Mason looks at you."

Since we were in college, Mason Becker's playboy ways were a coverup for his true feelings. He was in love with his best friend's girl.

But she only had eyes for Ben. However, the rest of us were not blind to Mason's eyes on her.

I turn back to Anna, and she shifts, slumping back into her seat.

"He doesn't." She faces forward, squinting at the horizon. "He only feels responsible for us because of some secret directive from Ben. Mason is just . . . Mason. Like you just said, it's hard to open up to someone new, and I don't think I ever will."

"I'll never understand men," I mutter, thinking back on all the men I've dated and slept with in my youth.

"I only understood Ben. But I'm angry. I'm so angry. I'm angry with all of them. Their friendship, their business, their secret pact of letters. Just damn him."

There's no comparison for a man like Ben. Even Ryan didn't match Ben's zeal for his family. Ryan was still a great man, a good father, and a decent husband, but he didn't have the consuming passion Ben had for Anna.

Anna swipes under one eye, and I focus on her face. "I'm not really crying. It's just a leak. It happens, and I ignore them."

"You should talk to someone," I tell her, concerned for her mental state.

"That's what River says." Anna pauses for a beat, swiping at her other cheek. Then she waves a hand, dismissing the thought. "So where's Archer?"

"He left the restaurant with another woman."

"He what?" Anna jolts forward, twisting to clutch the arm of the Adirondack. Her shriek echoes across the beach.

"Yep, some woman he called babe." *You love me.* What was all that?

"He calls you babe," Anna reminds me, and I close my eyes. I never want to hear the endearment again, and it's another reminder of the pretending he's done. The disconnect I felt when he used that word. Only when he said my name in that low, puzzled voice did he sound genuine. He was focused on me, saw me. *Not her.*

"Who was she?"

"I have no idea." Her clothing screamed money, and her attitude said wealth. "Maybe she was his mafia princess." There's no humor in my voice at the joke.

"There's someone who might know." Anna stands with renewed energy, reaches for my hand, and tugs me upright. I don't know if I want to know the truth. I'm too burned at the moment. My insides are incinerated, and my heart scorched. Still, I follow Anna, who leads me back up the steep staircase and directly into Zack's backyard.

+ + +

"He what?" Autumn squawks after I retell my tale to the entire crowd. River and Zack. Logan and Autumn. Mason. Noah. We sit among a scattering of chairs, an oversized lounger, and a couple of blankets on the grass.

"We wondered if it might be the mafia princess you mentioned seeing him with on social media," Anna asks her sister-in-law.

"You saw Archer with Viviana?" Noah questions, and all heads swivel in his direction.

"Who?" Mason asks.

"Viviana Quintero. And she isn't a mafia princess. She's more like a drug lord's daughter," Noah explains.

This can't be real. This doesn't happen here or in my life or in the world as I know it.

"And you know her, how?" Anna asks.

"The Quinteros visited the Magellen whenever they came to Chicago. Of course, that's confidential information, and now I have to kill all of you for knowing." Noah laughs, good-natured and teasingly, but the severity of his words isn't lost on most of the group.

"That isn't fucking funny," Zack grumbles, swiping a hand through his hair. The nervous tell is something he'd done in college, and I'm surprised I remember the movement. His voice deepens as he snaps at his brother. "Explain."

"The Quintero family is weal-*thy,* and their money is dirty, but they had some kind of relationship with the head of the hotel corporation. I don't know the details. I just know main office management would call with a reservation for the penthouse suite, and we'd have to clear the floor for the honored guests like they were freaking royalty."

We all stare at Noah, struggling to process what he's said.

"About eight years ago, Archer came in with Viviana. He caught my eye, warning me not to expose him or even question if it was him. I figured he was either in trouble or in deep with the Quinteros for another reason. Archer isn't stupid, so I went with option two. He wouldn't fall to the dark side."

"You never thought to mention this?" Zack snaps at his brother.

"Can't say I recall Archer coming up in casual conversation." Noah is snarky, and he's not giving in to his younger brother's stiff, sharp address or sarcasm.

"I told you how he's been missing for years," Zack states, irritation filling his voice.

"And it's not like I really know where he's been. Being with Viviana might have been a one-time hookup. It wasn't until recently he told me he'd been involved with her for five years."

"Five years?" I shriek. That's longer than I'd been married to Ryan. That's not a simple woman taking a spin on Archer's motorcycle. That's a relationship.

You love me. He had to have loved her. I saw the way he looked at her. She was his everything.

"Are you certain it was her?" Mason asks me.

"I don't know. I've never heard of her before." *She was just a woman. I try to wipe her from my thoughts.* No man could dismiss a woman like her.

"Luscious curves." Noah moves his hands to form the hourglass shape of a woman. "Throaty accent. Gleam in her eye like she could cut you with a glare. Screams entitled." None of these attributes was a question.

"That was her."

"It's Viviana," Noah confirms. "Funny he left with her as she's the one who shot him."

"She shot him?" Anna shrieks, and she glances at me across the space in Zack's backyard. "How do I not know this?" She's still looking at me as if I hold all the answers.

"I only found out the other night." I rub my upper left thigh. "It's why he always wears jeans and long shorts." The admission feels like a betrayal, and the glare in Anna's eyes says she'd like to cut me, although she'd never ever do such a thing. Hurt and fear and a million other sharp things rest in those dark orbs so similar to her brother's.

Anna tosses her hands up in the air. "I give up. I'm the only one who will never know anything." She glances at Autumn, and I'm reminded that Autumn had access to an email address for Archer, not Anna, not his own sister.

"He didn't want you to worry," I try to soothe her.

"How can I worry when I don't know anything?" she snaps at me, although I know her anger isn't aimed at me.

"That might be the point," Logan tosses in.

"Not helping," Autumn mutters beside him but pats his thigh.

"He wanted to protect you," I state, defending her brother once more.

"Is he dangerous?" Mason asks, looking at Noah as he speaks.

"He was trying to protect Anna from dangerous people," I add. This Quintero family certainly sounds dangerous. Shooting Archer. Drug lords. What kind of conversation is this? It's as if we're discussing a movie we've recently seen and not someone's life. *Archer's life.*

"If that woman is here, does that mean you're in danger?" Mason addresses me. "Is her presence putting Anna in danger? The kids?" His voice rises with each addition to his list. "I'll fucking shoot him myself."

"You will not," Logan huffs, slowly smiling at the tough act Mason can't quite pull off with his preppy clothing and model-worthy good looks.

"Fuck you. You don't know the lengths I'd go to for . . ." Mason's voice fades, and he glances at Anna before dropping his gaze. He swipes two hands into his hair and stands, stepping away from the group and stalking toward the cliff's edge, where another staircase leads down to the beach below.

Mason's question does leave me wondering. What are the chances that Archer ran into her at a restaurant in this small touristy town on Lake Michigan? Did she know he was here? Does she know where he's been staying? Had she been to Lakeside Cottage before? Had she been in his bed in the apartment?

"I'm going to throw up." The overwhelming sensation of nausea drives me upward from my seat, and I disappear around the side of River and Zack's house. I brace my hand on the siding as I bend over and heave in the dark. My throat clogs. My stomach turns. But nothing happens. I'd only had wine earlier, which is now sour in my throat.

A hand comes to my lower back. "We'll move you into the house tonight." Anna's reassuring voice does nothing to soothe the ache in my chest or the hole in the pit of my belly. As for my heart, it's obliterated. I'm suddenly trembling, cold to the bone despite the heat of the night.

"I need a shower," I say to her, and her brows pinch. Instantly I recall nights like this back in the day, as people say. College nights drinking too much. Regrets for messing around with a guy. Time and hearts wasted on the wrong person.

Anna nods. "Mason's going to move the girls. I'll help you pack up your stuff."

In a blink, I'm where I should have been from the start—inside Anna's home.

Not Archer's apartment. Not Archer's bed. Not Archer's arms.

I didn't have to worry about being in Archer's heart.

26

[Jenna]

Mason has moved my girls, and I've settled into a room inside the main house with our things when Anna's son Calvin comes to my room.

"Hey . . . uhm . . . this arrived while you guys were all at Zack's place. I didn't think it was important enough to rush over there, but . . . well, here." He holds out an envelope with a return address for Driftwood.

Great, I've been stiffed for the restaurant bill now—for the meal we hadn't eaten—although I don't know how the restaurant found me, but the envelope has my name on it.

Jenna.

A single word.

"Thanks," I mutter, staring down at the envelope and taking it from his hands to find it weighty and lumpy, like more than a sheet of paper is inside. "How did this get here?"

"Tracy, a girl I went to high school with, brought it by. She's the hostess at Driftwood. She recognized the address as mine." Calvin sheepishly glances down at the floor. He looks exactly like Anna with dark hair and dark eyes, and looking at him gives me a glimpse of what Archer might have looked like as a teenager on the cusp of manhood. I would have had a crush on him then, and he'd have broken my heart as he has now.

"Okay, well, thanks, Calvin."

Slowly, he looks up at me. "I'm sorry Uncle Archer is gone. I guess it's what we expected of him." He glances down the hall as he stands just outside my bedroom door.

"You didn't want to expect more of him?"

Calvin scratches the back of his neck. "He made promises that he was sticking around, and he'd get me into the police academy, but yeah, I should have known better. Mom says he's not dependable."

I firmly believe teens can decide their own minds about people. They have the free will to make their own decisions. However, that doesn't mean they always make smart choices. Even adults don't always make the best ones. Still, I ask, "And what did *you* think after spending some time with him?"

"He seemed like a good guy. Genuine even." Calvin pauses. "But maybe he was just a good actor."

My heart, which is already in pieces, scatters into infinite dust.

"Yeah, a good actor," I mumble, realizing I'm clutching the envelope to my chest.

"Well, good night."

"Good night, honey." I close the door. Crossing the room, which has a view of the patio and the lake, I sit on the edge of the bed and open the envelope under the dim light of the bedside lamp.

Turning the envelope upside down, a silver chain with a heavy medallion falls into my hand.

What the frick?

I stare down at Archer's St. Michael medal in my palm. The inverted sword shaped like a cross and the spread wings along the crossbar.

I might not be able to say where I'm going, but it's for your safety.

My protection.

Clenching the medal in my hands, I curse under my breath. As he fed me that line, he called me babe just as he called her.

You love me, he told her. She shot him.

I didn't understand. Glancing back at the envelope, I discover a small rectangular cardstock piece of paper. When I pull it out of the envelope, one side has the scribble of a shaky hand.

Be home.

Ben's message to Archer. Tears fill my eyes. Glancing back at the envelope, I stare at the return address. Did Archer have this card on him at the restaurant? Why did he slip it into this envelope? Why do I have his medal?

Flipping over the card in my hand, more pronounced handwriting is on the back. All capital letters, sharp and thin, look like someone jotted a second note quickly. My eyes narrow in on what it says.

Protect my heart, Jenna.

+ + +

The following night, the guys have their beach fire and their ritual for Ben. I've learned the men each wrote something in response to Ben's letters as this marks the one-year anniversary of their friend's request for each of them. Archer was supposed to join the group; however, he will be missing as he'd been the year before.

Anna and I shuffle between hot dogs on wire sticks and marshmallows on rudimentary twigs before herding the women and children up the cliff to leave Zack, Logan, and Mason behind. River and I convinced Anna to have her own celebration of Ben on her patio, involving wine and her circle of friends.

"What do you think they've written to him?" Anna asks as two of the ladies are involved with Ben's friends.

"I think they'll write how they've done with their mission," River admits without giving away what her future husband wrote on his card. Autumn adds something similar, but I miss her explanation. My thoughts are muddled with Archer.

Wrapping my arms around myself in the cool night air, I glance out at the lake, wondering where he is. With the sun setting on another day, the horizon is illuminated by the vivid blue water and complementary orange glow of a lowering sun. On the other side of this lake is Chicago, and for the millionth time, I wonder if Archer returned to the big city. His home base. His home, which wasn't a home. Or is he off on another dangerous assignment? Is he safe? What is protecting him?

My hand slips over my chest, seeking the medal I've buried inside my sweatshirt, dangling between my breasts, as near to my heart as I can get it.

I hate to ask, but I do. "Would Ben be disappointed in Archer?" I certainly am. Or maybe I'm just confused.

Autumn answers first. "Ben must have had some understanding of what Archer did . . . what he does . . . because he didn't judge him. Ben believed one day Archer would return. He'd need a place to land, and Lakeside was open to him."

Be home. Ben wanted Archer to know this was his home. His family was here, and he'd be welcomed.

Anna lowers her head. We've already discussed how upset she still is that Autumn had a way to contact her brother after Ben. How Ben must have known Archer was in trouble or in deep with the wrong people. The other night, Noah hadn't been able to convince Anna that Archer was one of the good guys. He tried to assure her she had nothing to worry about despite the drug lord's daughter.

Archer hadn't been fully open. He hadn't been honest. He'd been pretending, and it hurts. However, everything between Archer and me felt so real. *How could I be so wrong?*

I try to remind myself Archer has done what he's done in the past to protect them. His family. Their friends. I should be defending him instead of questioning his actions, but I'm struggling.

"If we could have been included in this male-bonding ritual, what might we say to Ben on this anniversary?" Autumn asks, her voice slightly cheerful. "What message would we send after one year?"

"I miss you," Anna says quickly, and I reach for her hand, sympathizing in more than one way.

"I'd say thank you," River adds, staring up at the sky like she has a direct line to heaven. She never met Ben, but she seamlessly fit into this family of friends. "For bringing Zack to me somehow." She rubs her hand over her extended belly, and I smile.

"You were the best big brother. Always looking out for me. And you were right. Things did work out in the end." Autumn smiles to herself as she looks at me.

I'm honored to be included here, but I'm not certain I'm qualified to direct something to Ben's attention. As I feel like Archer's mission is incomplete, my wish into the universe is simple. "Bring him home to me."

Then louder, I add, "Never eat spinach with a stranger on Thursdays, Benny. That was good advice."

At the mention of something nonsensical we used to say in college, Anna spits out her wine while River giggles, and the seriousness of the moment dissipates while the heaviness of my wish still lingers.

L.B. Dunbar

Be home with me.

27

[Archer]

I had two choices earlier that night—get on the boat or not—and only one real decision: get Viviana away from Jenna. Viviana wasn't my concern, but if I didn't follow her, she'd always haunt me. And if I didn't remove her from Jenna, the woman who was my home was in danger.

Viviana had a jealous streak like none I'd seen before. She'd overreact to any woman looking in my direction. A woman spoke to me, and Viviana hung on me like Christmas lights on a tree. A woman got too close, and Vi was in her face. She'd slapped, snapped, and hissed at other women, pissing around me like some cavewoman.

And she loved to flip the jealousy card when I didn't react half as strongly as her. She'd flaunt. She'd tease. She'd act extreme by kissing a guy in front of me or grinding up against someone as if that would hurt me. All head games. All things I struggled to keep compartmentalized inside me.

Fake. Real.

Five years of pretending I loved this woman.

If I went on the boat, I was dead. I had no protection other than my fists and my dick, which wasn't going near her again. My gun was still locked in the safe at the cottage, and I wouldn't be returning to there. I couldn't risk Viviana following me.

Instead, I led her to the small craft that would ferry her out to the large yacht on the lake. I should have trusted the unsettled feeling I had when I first saw that boat. When my first thought was Vi. My instincts have saved me before, but Jenna . . . she's fogging everything up. Making me question everything, making me want things I never thought I'd want. She's been distracting, but I love it.

Viviana, though? Why here? Why now? The Quinteros liked to keep moving; this much is true. Nevada. Colorado. Florida. New York. And that only covered the United States. They had property in Colombia, Spain, and an island off Brazil.

"Come with me, baby," she cooed, curling her fingers into my shirt. Her overpriced perfume burned the inside of my nose.

"Not a chance, Vi," I bitterly replied, pressing my hands to her shoulders. We both knew this new game. I couldn't go with her. She shouldn't be near me.

"What's going to happen then?" she pouted, her voice dropping to a tone I recognized but one she rarely used. Viviana was hardly ever sincere, and she was never scared, but she'd been frightened that night. The night of our engagement party when someone exposed who I was.

"He's DEA."

I shot her father in self-defense. I'll never forget the look in her eyes. The question on her face. Why? How?

Then she laid out the truth. *"You are a despicable human. No one will ever love you."*

She wasn't wrong. For five years, I'd played her to get close to her father. I'd done things I wasn't proud of that I'd have to live with for the remainder of my life. Those actions did make me a poor excuse for a man, but I did them as my duty.

Then she shot me, narrowly missing my dick, which I'm certain wasn't her intention. She wanted to blow my balls to smithereens. Instead, her aim came just shy of an artery that would have killed me.

There had always been a conflict for me with Vi. I could have brought her out of the life, put her in the witness protection program, given her a new identity, and kept her safe and out of the drug industry. I might have even married her as penance, giving her a different life and making amends for how I'd treated her. But I couldn't afford her lifestyle, and I couldn't keep all the promises I'd made her. I didn't love her.

I loved someone else.

"You're going to get on that boat and disappear," I warned Vi.

"And you'll just make a call as soon as I leave," she told me. "Which is why you're coming with me, *mi corazón.*" My heart. Sarcasm filled her voice.

The click of a gun behind my head held me in place. I could have taken out the man, but what would I do with Viviana? I couldn't let her get away. I didn't want to ever see her again. I also didn't want her to keep ruining my life. The department wanted me to go into the witness protection program. New identity. New location. New life. I'd been away from the real me for so long I refused. Being Archer McCaryn would be my new identity. Lakeside was my new location, although it was now compromised. Jenna and two little princesses were my shot at a new life.

"Babe." The term tasted bitter on my lips. I didn't have to see Jenna's face to know it hurt her to hear me use that endearment with someone else, but I had to get Vi away from her. Now *I* needed to get away from Viviana.

She tipped up on her toes, already matching my height in her heels, and bit the corner of my lip. Not a kiss. Nothing tender. Just a sharp bite that had me retracting and struggling not to react. I fisted my hands at my sides. I'd never hit her. I'd wanted to strangle her, but I'd never touched her like that. She'd provoke me. She'd push me, but I'd never respond. Her punishment came in the form of smacking her ass or spanking her other places. She liked that.

"Follow me like the bad little puppy I know you can be." My bicep was gripped by her newest boy toy, but I shrugged him off, acting as if I'd go willingly. I didn't have a gun, and while I could use my fist, I didn't trust that Vi didn't have a gun waiting to finish what she started.

And I hated her like I always had. "Vi, you're making a mistake."

"No, my darling DEA agent, you made one when you thought you could fuck me and tell me you loved me and walk away."

Her lackey pushed me, and I dropped into the small dinghy. I needed to think. I had to get a message to Braxton. I had to get myself out of this mess, but most of all, I needed to bring Viviana in.

As old habits died hard, I held up a hand to help Vi into the wobbly craft. She refused my offer.

"I hate you, and now, you're going to learn how much."

Which is how I ended up here . . . sitting on the stern as we coast through the large lake, disappearing in the night. I expected Vi to place me in some hull, tied up and sequestered until we reached her destination. Instead, she allows me a seat above deck like a guest. This is all part of her game.

"Let the chase begin," she teases. She loves the thrill of cat and mouse. Most days, she thought I was the mouse, but I proved I was a tiger, capable of handling her. It's how I got in with the family.

As the night passes, utter blackness surrounds us. Running on low lights is dangerous, but this large boat cruises, and then I see it, just off in the distance.

Something small. Something sleek. Something following us.

I'm not certain if Vi notices. She's too busy watching me.

"I should have finished you," she snarls. "Should have blown that cocky cock right off you."

"You liked it too much to ever do such a thing," I snap back at her. Her eyes blaze, and at one time, I knew that's when I should strike. Her anger was hardwired to her arousal, so one touch from me while in this heightened state made her putty in my fingers. I swallow back the bile in my throat at the thought of touching her body so intimately.

"So true, baby. So true. And I'm almost tempted to use it one more time before I kill you."

I'd never touch her again. Never allow her to touch me. Not when I have someone sweet, and good, and clean. Not when I have someone hopefully waiting for me.

Jenna. She's my focus as well as that small dark mass keeping its distance but definitely following us.

Slowly, I stand, walking to the railing and leaning against it.

"Don't do anything stupid, Hunter, or is it Archer now?" Vi questions. She must have heard Jenna use my name.

"Who do you want me to be?" I ask her, spinning to place my back against the railing.

"I wanted you to be my husband. You took me for a fool." Vi's eyes glare with hatred.

My soul matches that look. If I never see her again, I'll be happy, and I'm about to make that dream come true.

"Ms. Quintero, we have a problem," another lackey on the yacht claims. "Eight and four." I recognize the coordinates. Two boats are following us. Hitching myself up just the slightest bit, I sit precariously on the edge of the railing.

"Don't do it," Vi states, holding my gaze. "I'll shoot you without a thought."

"Here's the thing, Vi. You don't think, not with your heart, and that's been your problem. And now, thankfully, you're no longer mine." I pause, inching back just the slightest and praying this works. "Take your best shot, babe, because we both know your aim sucks."

"Shoot him," she demands of the man close to her.

With that, a shot rings out.

Then the world is cold and dark, and I hold my breath, envisioning the only thing real in my life.

Jenna.

28

Three months later

[Jenna]

Fall brings a familiar routine. I rush through the mornings to collect what I need for a day of teaching and prepare my girls for daycare. Talia is attending full-day kindergarten this year, and it's another change for all of us. My baby girl isn't a baby but a school student. I'm elated while melancholy that time passes so quickly. Once again, I struggle with the fact Ryan missed out on these milestones for his daughters.

To my surprise, my girls are fighting one night in the room they share. Our house is small and simple. I'd purchased it before I met Ryan, and the ease in our relationship moved him into my place. We'd hoped to find something bigger, something more forever further down the road in our marriage. However, my little cottage-style home near town might be where I'm planted for a long time.

"He's not dead," Rosie yells as I enter the bedroom, surprised by the shrill of her voice and the redness in her face.

"Who's not dead?" I ask.

"Archer," Rosie pouts, glaring at her older sister from across the space between their beds.

Frickity-frack! "Why would you say such a thing?" I ask.

Rosie points at Talia with enough anger to seriously poke someone's eye out. "She said he's dead."

"Talia," I snap, turning toward my eldest daughter, rushing to the side of Rosie's bed to soothe her while lowering her hand where a single finger is aimed at her sister. "Talia, why would you say that?"

"Because he disappeared just like Daddy did."

Goodness. "Oh Talia, baby. No, it's not like that." While Archer did disappear from our lives, he isn't dead. *I refuse to believe he's dead.* Shaking the thought away, I address her again while rubbing a hand up and down Rosie's back. "We've talked about this. Daddy's in heaven."

"Where I can't see him," Talia reminds me, and I rub at my forehead. Death is so difficult to explain to a young child.

"He's gone, but he didn't disappear. Remember, Daddy can see you. He's thinking of you and watching you, but not in a creepy way. He's not hiding in the closet or under the bed. He just knows things about you. Like a guardian angel." Like a silent protector.

"But why can't I know things about him?"

"Because it doesn't work that way, baby." I've never been great at explaining death, and sometimes I'm surprised by these conversations as Talia doesn't seem to remember her father as much as she knows she had one once. Rosie doesn't understand the concept of a dad other than other people have a daddy and she doesn't, at least not one physically present. "You need to keep living and let Daddy see all the great things you'll do and become."

"Can Archer see me?" Talia's question surprises me. Not because of this death discussion but because she was so cautious of Archer at first. She didn't trust him, but she was slowly warming up to him when he vanished.

"No, honey. Archer can't see you."

"Because he isn't dead," Rosie interjects with the wisdom of a three-year-old.

"It's not because he's not dead." I sigh. "Archer has an important job, and he had to return to it sooner than I thought. He's sorry he didn't say goodbye. Do you remember Tricia's friend, Levi Walker? He didn't disappear. He just went away because he has an important job on the other side of the world." My best teacher friend was close to her ex-husband's younger brother, who is now an adult and proudly serving in the United States military.

"Or Lys, your favorite babysitter. She didn't disappear. She just went away to college. She's been gone for a long time, but she isn't dead. Just because we no longer see someone does not mean they died." I narrow in on Talia, disappointed in this fear she's put in her younger sister, but I also understand that when people leave our lives, it's difficult to explain why or where they went, especially in this case when I don't have concrete answers.

L.B. Dunbar

Plus, I have no idea if I'm telling the truth about Archer's return to work, or his sorrow at not seeing the girls one last time. For now, it will have to be the truth. The alternative is accepting he ran off with his drug lord princess, and he's off doing nefarious deeds I don't want to consider him doing.

"He'll be back," Rosie states, and I swear her voice sounds like Arnold Schwarzenegger from the *Terminator*, but she's decades too young to know the reference. "He can't die. He's a warrior."

Oh boy. "Who told you that?" I ask, chuckling at how confident Rosie is about both Archer's return and his occupation.

"Archer did. He told me warriors are invincible, and he's a warrior. He isn't dead." Her little lips puff and her eyes well. "He wouldn't leave another warrior behind, and I'm a warrior, too."

"Oh, Rosie." I swipe my thumbs under her eyes, which spill at the thought of him leaving her.

"I'm sure wherever he is, he misses his princesses."

"I'm a warrior," Rosie states again.

"I thought you were a pirate," I tease, recalling how proud she'd been this summer when Trevor called her such a thing.

"She's only three, Mom. She doesn't know who she is yet."

I chuckle at Talia's motherly tone. *She* could be a warrior, falling second-in-command to me.

"We're our own team of warrior princess pirates, right?" I reach for Talia's hand, wiggling my fingers for her to grab them in the space between the beds. "We're doing okay, just us three, right?"

It hasn't always been easy raising two little babies on my own while working full time and trying to keep up with the bills on my salary, but we've made it this far. We have our home and each other. We don't need more.

"I still miss Archer," Rosie whispers.

"Me too, baby." *Me too.* Because despite not needing him, I'd still like him to be here with us. I'd like to think we could have built something together. I saw us as a family. Maybe that was just wishful thinking, though. Like believing in something you can't see—like the father my girls don't remember.

214

I don't want them to forget Archer.

+ + +

Winter comes early, and it's so frickity-frackity cold, but it's also nice to be out of the house. We have a long weekend now that the first-semester parent-teacher conferences are over, and while I'd hoped to head to Lakeside for a visit with Anna, the predicted snowstorm arrived. Everything is covered in a thick blanket of the white stuff. I shouldn't bother shoveling, leaving it for another day and allowing myself and the girls to stay trapped in the house. We'd sit before the fireplace, watching movies and scarfing popcorn, but today, I need this. I need to burn off some energy as I'd had the most vivid dream about Archer last night.

I know better than to drink tequila to celebrate the end of conferences.

Despite a slight headache, the cold doesn't bother me, and I'm reminded of a song from *Frozen*. The girls decided to stay in the house so I could at least get the front stoop and the walkway to the driveway cleared. My back is to the street as I heft thick piles of snow to the left and right, recalling when I used to grumble that Ryan needed to do this job. Whenever bad weather struck, it seemed he conveniently was out of town at a boat show or convention, and I'd be the one shoveling this shit or calling in a favor from a friend's husband who has a plow on the front of his truck.

I hated asking for help, though.

"Jenna." Hearing my name in a masculine voice doesn't stop my lifting the shovel as I assume it's Archer whittling his way into my thoughts, shoving Ryan out of the way. I recall Archer telling me how he didn't want me thinking of Ryan when I was out with him and then retracting the statement, telling me I could think of him, even talk about him if I wanted. Archer just wanted to be in the forefront of my brain. I understood in some ways. You can't keep living by loving a ghost.

Did he love a ghost? Had he been thinking of that Viviana Quintero woman when he'd been with me?

215

"Babe." This time, I pause and slowly stand upright, my mittened hand gripping the shovel's handle. God, I hate what that word, in the ruggedness of his voice, did to my insides. Even though he called *her* that term in that same tumbled tone, the endearment triggers something inside me. I ache for Archer.

"'Locks, turn around." A soft chuckle follows the command, and I spin so fast I nearly slip on the icy ground where I've cleared the snow. I stare at the mirage before me because I must be dreaming. He can't possibly be standing here looking sexy as hell in a dark brown, Sherpa-collared jacket. I've only seen this man in T-shirts, but dressed in winter attire, his appearance says outdoor adventurer, and I want to climb him like a mountain.

Instead, I resist going to him.

"Archer," I whisper still not believing he's standing here. In my town. In my yard. I take another moment to wonder if I've conjured him from that dream last night. The one where he appears in the middle of the night, climbs over me in bed, and tells me how he loves me. How sorry he is he left me behind and makes it up to me by plying my body with his tongue and teeth and lips. My body shivers, and it isn't the cold but his sudden presence and the things I know he can do to me.

Like break my heart.

"What are you doing here?" My voice is edgier than it should be. I should be asking about his welfare. How is he? Where has he been? But if I ask those questions, I'll start to lose it. I'll become a raging banshee of anger and relief that he's standing before me. Even if he isn't mine, I'm so relieved he's alive. He isn't dead like Rosie defended.

"I want to be home."

I stare at him, slowly registering his words. *Be home?* Does this mean he's completed his assignment? Is he back at Lakeside? Why didn't his sister tell me?

"Anna must be so happy to see you."

"She doesn't know I'm back yet."

I stare at him again, using the propped-up shovel for support as my knees tremble.

"What do you mean she doesn't know you're home?"

"I came here first."

"Why?" The word bursts forth like a snowball launched at a moving vehicle.

"Because I want to be home."

Shaking my head, I lower it a moment. "Then what are you doing here?"

He steps forward, and I drop the shovel, stepping back. He stills, and his hands slowly lift upward, palms outward. Those hands. Those fingers. The tips of them. *Oh, God.* I close my eyes, feeling too warm despite the cold around us.

"Let me be home . . . 'Locks." The catch in his voice has my eyes springing open. Did he struggle against calling me *babe*? Is he playing a role again? "Please."

The soft plea in his voice twists my belly, and I glance over at a large pickup truck parked on the street near the end of my driveway. Shiny, black, and looking brand new, it's not the temporary car he was driving last summer. The one he explained had been given to him by the department and was unmarked for his protection. I didn't understand the depth of that security. I still didn't understand anything about the man before me.

"I don't have anywhere else I want to be."

My shoulders fall, and I glance back at him. His hands have slipped into his pockets. His face is still that edgy, rugged man of three months ago, but his dark eyes have softened. He doesn't seem the type to beg, but those eyes . . . they are down-on-his-knees pleading with me to let him . . . what? Spend a night? Land a little while? Stay forever?

"What do you want?" My voice croaks around the question.

"You. And the girls."

My breath hitches.

"They've missed you." The words are meant to hit a mark. He didn't just walk away from me, he walked away from them, and it's been a bumpy road explaining his disappearance.

"I'm sorry." The apology isn't enough, but I read in his eyes once again that he knows how weak the words sound. "Give me time, ba—"

My glare cuts him off, and I turn away from him. Forget the shoveling. Screw the snow. Frack Archer.

My elbow is suddenly caught.

"Jenna." My name. That voice. It's better than any endearment, yet I don't trust it. "Let me explain."

Although I'm greatly relieved he's alive, I'm not certain I can trust what he'll say. Three months ago, there'd been news of a yacht exploding on the big lake. Everything in me worried Archer was somehow involved and lost to me in the most final way.

"Let me see the girls."

He's already playing me because he knows if the girls accept him, I'm toast. At the very least, I'll hear his apology or his explanation.

"Archer, I can't do this," I mutter, afraid for them. I need to guard their little hearts. They don't know their father. They've missed the man standing before me. His disappearance wasn't fair to them or me.

"You can, ba—" He pauses. "Jenna. Please."

Shaking my head, I look off down my quiet street, covered in feet of snow.

"I don't know if I can trust you."

Archer sighs, hanging his head. "Just give me time to prove myself."

"I can't take any more pretending."

His head pops up. "I was never pretending. Not with you." He steps closer to me, and I step back, kicking the low stoop with my heel. Blindly, I step up on it. "Everything between us was real."

"Was it?" I just don't know. I know how I felt. I know he sent me his medal. The weight of it rests buried beneath my winter outerwear and a sweatshirt underneath. Every night I've clutched it in my hand, but for what, I'm not even certain.

"Wasn't it for you?" His gravelly voice lowers, uncertain and almost afraid of my answer. Unable to offer him the truth about my own feelings without hearing his, I glance away again, crossing my arms over my midsection. Maybe hearing him out will bring us the closure we all need. The girls will see Archer didn't disappear into thin air, and I'll be able to stitch up my heart again, living with the knowledge he's alive even if he's not mine.

29

[Archer]

Jenna's house is small but warm. Despite the cramped space, love is evident the moment I enter. The kids' artwork decorates the walls, framed in pride and hung to become a focal point. Child-sized chairs rest near a couch, aimed at a television set. A fire crackles behind a protective screen. A staircase divides the entrance area, and a dining room is to the right. The table contains a laptop and a stack of papers, plus coloring sheets, crayons, and a bucket with scissors, a glue bottle and yarn hanging over the lip.

"Archer?" Talia says, eyes wide while I'm unbuttoning my jacket.

"Archer!" Rosie calls out, plucking her thumb from her mouth while tipping back her head on the little chair where she sits. Then she bursts into tears.

What the . . .?

Jenna rushes to Rosie, scooping her up while Rosie keeps her eyes on me. Tears slip down her cheeks, and she hastily brushes them away.

"I told you he wasn't dead," Rosie mutters to her sister, glancing down at where Talia sits on her bright yellow chair.

"What the . . .?" *Frickity-frack.* "No, I'm not dead, princess." I chuckle, caught between sorrow that they thought I was and relief that I'm alive. I thought I might die—again—at one point, but I clearly did not. "I'm a warrior. Like you."

Rosie kicks out her legs, signaling her mother to set her on the ground, and she rushes to me. I squat, fighting the pain in my upper leg. Suddenly, she's in my arms, wrapping her little ones around my neck and nearly choking me. Or maybe it's the lump in my throat at the acceptance of this innocent child. She's not questioning me or struggling with my presence like her mother. I don't blame Jenna, though. God, I can't fault her reaction. Just the fact I'm inside this house is a step forward, and I have many steps to take.

"Missed you, baby girl," I whisper to Rosie while keeping my eyes pinned on her mother across the room. Jenna swipes her cheek, rapidly blinking away the tears filling her eyes. I lower to kneel and shift Rosie to my thigh. The crouched position burns through my old wound, but I'll take a firestorm over my entire body if these ladies take me back.

A second chance, Jenna stated once upon a time. She was my first and only chance to love the right way.

I glance at Talia next. "Missed you, too, ice queen. Did you send all this snow?"

Was she apprehensive of me as well? She's protective of her mother, and rightfully so. She won't forgive me as easily as Rosie, but she does press out of her chair and come to me.

"Hey," I whisper, reaching out for her little wrist and wiggling her arm, waiting on her to come closer to me for a hug, if she wants one, if she'll give me one.

"Where were you?"

My eyes glance up at Jenna, looking for guidance, but she gives me nothing. I'm on my own here. "I had a top secret job to do."

"I told you he was a warrior," Rosie interjects, and I chuckle softly, jostling her on my thigh while holding Talia's arm.

"And I was called back to finish the job."

Jenna's breath catches, and she shakes her head. Her wide eyes warn me to keep it simple and brief, although I wasn't about to spill the details of my assignment to two innocent minds.

"The job is over now." I hold Jenna's gaze. "And I'm free."

"Were you in jail?" Talia asks, and I look at her.

"What? No?" I laugh a bit bitterly. "Why would you think that?"

"I heard Mr. Becker say you were a bad man, and he hoped you'd stay away." *Mason? That fucker.*

"Talia, that isn't what Mr. Becker meant, and no, Archer wasn't in jail." Jenna peers at me, tipping a brow for confirmation.

"I wasn't in jail. Remember, I told you, I'm a good warrior."

"Like Mulan," Rosie murmurs in awe. I'm not certain who that is, so I suggest someone I think Talia might relate to.

"Like Elsa."

"Elsa isn't a warrior." Rosie snorts, playing with the collar of my jacket.

"Yes, she is. She's tough and strong. She knows her own mind and does things to protect her family." I squeeze Talia's wrist.

"She left her sister," Rosie adds.

"And then she came back because she loved her. Because they are family." I glance back at Jenna, who twists her lips and peers out the window behind the couch. The snow is falling again. The storm last night was hell driving through, but I was determined to get here. Determined to be here.

"Are you staying here?" Rosie asks, and Jenna looks at me once again.

Shifting my gaze back to Rosie, I address her. "I was hoping I could stay here, yes. Since you little monsters invaded my apartment, I thought I'd invade your house. It's my turn." I sneak a peek at Jenna before jostling Rosie. "Maybe I can have a sleepover again with Mommy."

Jenna snorts, and the sound says snowball's chance in hell. I won't push, but I'm also not leaving. The door is closed on the past, and I'm only moving forward toward a future I never saw coming my way.

"Our couch pulls out to a bed. It's really cool. Our grandma stays there when she visits," Talia offers.

"Think Grandma will mind if I sleep in her spot?"

"No," Rosie says, slipping her arms around my neck again. I close my eyes, soaking in her acceptance while tightening my hold on Talia. She takes another moment to watch me, but then she steps forward and wraps an arm around her sister and me, hugging us both. It's more than I deserve and more than I expected, but it's everything I'd hoped for. My eyes close a second, inhaling them both and the bayberry scent of their home. Wintery and comforting, the fragrance conjures images of Christmas trees, presents underneath one, and a future. Something I've never had.

"The question is if Mommy minds Archer sleeping in Grandma's spot," I ask.

Both Talia and Rosie twist in my arms to look at their mother, but they don't move away from me, and I'm thankful for the support. I might be leaning on them more than the other way around, and I hold my breath, wondering what Jenna will decide.

30

[Jenna]

Motherfracker.

How can the girls give in to him so easily? He's a charmer, that's why. He's ensnared them under his spell, and there's no turning back. Archer is alive. He didn't disappear into thin air. He didn't die. He survived wherever he went, whatever happened to him, and he's here.

I came here first.

"You should let Anna know you're back." But for how long?

"I will," he states, and I watch him struggle to stand. His hands flatten on the floor, and he uses more of his upper body strength to press himself upward. Is he hurt? Is his leg worse? Was he shot again? I take a few steps forward and then stop myself once he's upright.

"So what are we doing today?" Archer asks like he hasn't been missing for three months and two days.

"Mommy is shoveling, and we're playing Barbies."

Archer glances up at me. "I can help you with the shoveling."

"I've got it," I say.

"Ba—" He stops himself. "'Locks, I can do it."

"So can I." I need to shovel the snow and give myself a few minutes to wrap my head around his sudden presence and the fact he just weaseled his way into a night on my couch. I also need to dispel this energy under my skin.

Slap him? Kiss him? The struggle is real.

Archer must read the conflict in my face because he says, "Okay, Barbies it is then."

+ + +

After clearing every flake of snow I can remove from the stoop, the front walkway, and my driveway, I have nothing left to clear unless I want to start tackling the street with only a hand shovel. With my muscles straining, I'm a sweaty mess and decide I've avoided Archer long enough. When I enter my kitchen through the side door, Archer is rummaging through my refrigerator.

"'Locks, you've got nothing to eat."

"I have plenty to eat," I snap. Anticipating the snow and knowing I'd have a late night from parent-teacher conferences, I went to the store just the other day.

"Babe, you need substance, not this frozen food crap or processed pasta."

I freeze where I am, hand poised on my zipper pull. My boots are making a puddle on the mat. Sensing the danger in my sudden silence, Archer closes the refrigerator door and turns to face me. Seeing me statue still, his mouth opens then shuts. He props his hands on his hips, and he glances to the side before looking back at me.

"It's going to take time, but in my head, they don't mean the same thing. I'm not calling you babe because I'm thinking of her, and when I say it to you, it feels natural. It feels right. With her, it was all . . ." He leaves me hanging like he did that night.

"Pretend?" My voice cracks. "Tell me what I'm missing because I'm confused. I saw you with her, Archer. I *saw* you. She couldn't look away from you, and you didn't look away from her."

You love me. The memory of how he addressed her rumbles through my head.

"Five years, Archer? For five years, you were with that woman. That's not *some* woman. That's . . . that's a relationship. That's longer than my marriage." I huff, my adrenaline rising. I'm ready to turn back for the snow outside and reconsider clearing the street. "How can that be pretend? How do I know you weren't pretending with me? You were with me less than two weeks."

Less than two weeks and it felt so real. *To me.*

"Whoa, whoa, whoa." His hands lift while his brows rise. "Where did you hear all that?"

"I should have heard it from you," I whisper-hiss

Archer lowers his hands and nods. "You're right. And you will, but first, let me feed you and the girls. Let me make you ladies dinner."

"Using my food?" I don't know why I say such a thing. Him preparing anything causing me not to make dinner would be a treat, but I don't want treats. I want the truth.

"I'll go to the store," he states without hesitation.

"I didn't mean it like that." I'd say I don't know what's wrong with me, but I do. He's standing in my kitchen, and I don't know what to think of him here.

"But you're right. I can contribute. I'll go to the store tomorrow. How about spaghetti tonight?"

"You don't need to go to the store." The store isn't the point. Food isn't the topic. I want to know where the hell he's been and how long he's staying. "And you don't need to make us dinner."

"I'm not leaving, Jenna." His firm voice holds conviction, as if he read my thoughts. "No matter what you think or what you thought, I'm not going anywhere. I'm staying here." He points at the ground, emphasizing his position. Strangely, I feel the role reversal. When I ended up in his apartment, he allowed me to stay. I couldn't have predicted where it would lead, just as I can't say now what this means. *If* I let him stay here.

"A month," he adds.

"A month?" I pause, glaring at him.

"Give me a month. We didn't even have two full weeks before."

"Whose fault is that?" I retort.

He ignores my irritation and continues. "No bedroom-only bullshit. No undercover, only in the dark. All in. One month."

"Because that's when you'll leave?" Because he'll leave. He'll be called away or run away or find he's bored in my little world.

"*If* you kick me to the curb, I'll go. I'll leave that on you to explain to the girls."

"Playing my girls isn't cool, Archer."

"Good thing I'm not playing around then, 'Locks. Not pretending here. So get out of those cold clothes and go take a shower. I'm making dinner."

There is no reason those words should sound sexy. Not the shower demand. Not the remove my clothes command. Not even the fact he's making dinner. Yet every single sentence sends a thrill through my body that I'd like to tamp down but can't. The flame this man sparks inside me ignites just as quickly as he set it the first time, and I'm in serious danger of getting burned. Again.

+ + +

Once the girls are tucked in that night, I find Archer sitting on the couch.

"Here." I hold out a pillow, a sheet set, and extra blankets for him. He didn't pull out the sleeper yet, and he glances up at me from where he sits.

Taking the pile, he sets everything beside him. Then he reaches for my hand. "'Locks, I don't want you giving me that look."

"What look?"

"The one you gave me earlier when I struggled to stand from the floor."

I wasn't giving him a look, but I do have genuine concerns about his physical health. "Did something happen?" I have so many questions. The list feels endless.

"Lots of hard topics, Jenna. And I know I shouldn't ask, but I'm asking for tonight. One night to soak all this up." He looks around my small living room with the embers of the fire dying out and the low light of the floor lamp the only illumination. The toys have been placed back in a basket tucked beside the couch, but a puzzle remains on the low table.

"I'll tell you everything, just not tonight." He tugs at my hand, but I tug back. The remainder of the day had been a struggle. The pull to him, the desire to touch him and prove he's real. The push of my head, reminding me to stay on guard.

"Just tell me if you were hurt." My tone softens with concern.

"If you mean, was I shot at again? The answer is yes. Did a bullet hit me? No."

I slam my eyes closed. This isn't my life. This can't be happening. I feel like I'm in an episode of *S.W.A.T*, only I don't know my lines. I'm missing the mark, and I'm a terrible actress. Not this man, though. He's an actor. He told me how he had to pretend, but there's no pretending he's on my couch, holding my hand and staring up at me with so much emotion in his dark eyes that it's melting the cold encasing my heart. The shield I want to keep in place to protect me from the hurt he could inflict.

"I'm okay." He jostles my hand in his. "I'm here. I'm alive."

Without releasing my hand, he presses himself upright, struggling a bit to stand. I step back, but he doesn't allow me to give us space. His other hand reaches for my neck, and he gently draws the silver chain free from my sweatshirt.

"You been protecting my heart, 'Locks?" His voice cracks as he examines his St. Michael medal. Then his eyes lift to mine.

"I don't know," I whisper. Am I protecting his? Or my own?

With reverence, he drops the medal to my chest and flattens his hand in a familiar position. The heat of his palm seeps through my sweatshirt, and the T-shirt beneath, to my skin. Can he really feel it? Does he know my heart beats for him?

His eyes close for a second, and the corner of his mouth twitches. I stare at his face. His features are still hard. Those cheeks. The cliff-like jaw. The faint scruff peppered with salt. But he looks different. He looks calm, at peace even. He looks like a man who's finally home after a long journey.

"Good night, Archer," I whisper, swallowing a large lump in my throat.

His eyes open, and his hand draws back.

"Good night, Jenna." He emphasizes my name in that manner he has. Two soft syllables, like the rise and fall of a heartbeat. *Thump-thump*. A shiver ripples up my spine. The slow crook of his lips hints he knows what he's doing to me. He's wearing me down, one syllable at a time.

31

[Jenna]

The next day, Archer is quieter than I remember and a shadow around me. However, he entertains the girls. And he cooks. I don't question how a man who's never had a home knows such a thing, but I do question him when he offers to paint the girls' nails.

"I hate to ask, but how do you know how to do this?" Skepticism fills my voice along with the fear of his answer. Did he do these things with Viviana? He isn't an expert manicurist, but he's doing a good job of sticking to the tiny nails and not painting entire fingers like Talia has a tendency to do.

"I have two younger sisters, remember? When they were little, they were close, and I wanted to be included sometimes. Then again, I might have been seven the last time I did this."

The answer is not what I expected. "Oh." I chuckle at the thought of a miniature Archer painting Anna's nails.

Archer's concentration doesn't leave Talia's nail or the stroke of the brush across it. "Not everything is about her."

A moment passes before I understand who he means.

"You're just such a mystery," I say, watching him focus on the color filling in Talia's nail.

"Being mysterious can be alluring. Isn't that what your romance novels say?"

"This isn't fiction," I sharply remind him. This is his life. *My* life. And while I like a bit of mystique, I want the truth.

Archer finally glances up at me. "Want the hard topic now?" His eyes shift to the girls sitting at the table, staring down at their fingers colored Luscious Lilac and What's Up Pink.

I shake my head.

"Later then," he warns and returns to Talia's nails.

I'm left wondering if a good nail polish color for him would be a shade of gray because he isn't black or white. He isn't hard or soft. He's somewhere between.

+ + +

When the girls finally go to bed, Archer brings me a glass of wine as we settle in to watch the first episode of *Schitt's Creek*, but I find my mind wandering.

"What's going on over there, 'Locks?" Archer asks after I shift positions for the third time in my corner of the couch.

"How long are you staying?" My aggressive tone isn't necessary, but my desire to know what this man is doing here outweighs everything.

"I asked you for a month."

"And I asked for answers."

Archer leans forward for the remote. "Are you watching this?"

I shake my head, disappointed that I've lost interest in something I'd been anticipating. Maybe that's what's happening between Archer and me. Am I losing interest in him? Or am I just losing my patience? In less than thirty seconds, I answer the first question. I'm definitely still interested in him, even if I don't understand him.

When the television switches off, only the dim light from the lamp near me illuminates the room. Archer remains sitting forward on the edge of the cushion, his forearms braced on his thighs.

"Her name was Viviana Quintero. Her father, Victor, had been our target. My mission was to get involved with her and infiltrate their organization as deeply as I could."

Instantly, I understand. He was involved intimately with her.

"The best way to get close to the family was to be part of the family. At first, it was chance meetings and casual dates. She was attracted to me." Archer swipes a hand through his hair, which is a little longer than his typical close crop cut. "And I used it to my advantage."

"You seduced her," I clarify.

He doesn't look at me but shakes his head as if disagreeing with me. "How could I do such a thing, right?" He pauses. "And then I just did."

"Did you love her?"

Archer hangs his head lower and cups the back with his thick hands. "I didn't know what to feel. Most days, I despised her, but on rare occasions, she could be human and almost sweet. I knew we'd never have a future. She was the enemy. She was my assignment, but there were brief moments I wondered if I could love her. If I could save her."

Archer scrubs both hands down his face and pauses his fingertips on his lips. "She didn't want to be saved. She didn't have a moral compass. And she didn't love me. Not really." He turns to look at me over his shoulder. "She couldn't love me because she didn't know me. Romance was all part of the mission."

My lips twist, reading the conflict on his face. The stress in his eyes. The strain on his cheeks. He's struggling with his past actions.

"How do you know she didn't want to be saved?"

"I asked her to marry me. More staging. The night of the engagement party, it came out who I was. An undercover agent for the DEA. I asked her to come with me and told her I could protect her. She was confused, maybe even hurt, and everything got all mixed up after that. Her father was suddenly present and threatening me, and then bullets flew. I shot him. She shot me."

His eyes close. "She told me I was a despicable human being. That no woman would ever love me like she had. 'You don't deserve to be loved' were her exact words." His lids flip open, and he hesitantly glances at me over his shoulder again. "That wasn't love."

Who says such a thing to someone? Then again, I sympathize for a moment with *her* position. She believed in Archer. She trusted him. She let him into her bed and possibly into her heart, even if her behavior was unethical. The grief in his face also gives me empathy for Archer. He did what he had to do for the assignment, and it messed with his head. Maybe even his heart a little as well. It definitely was weighing on his conscience.

"While I was recovering from my wound, I was told I was removed from the investigation. Her father was dead. He was the mastermind, but there is always a second-in-command. The assumption Vi would take over was legit, and she was under surveillance. The department didn't want me involved. I was too laid up to be part of the team and spent almost eight months in extensive physical therapy, as I told you, along with counseling." He points at his temple. "They worried the relationship screwed me up."

"Didn't it?" *He was engaged to her!*

"It did to some extent," he easily admits. "I hated myself for what I'd done. She wasn't a horrible person, just a person making bad decisions based on her environment. But she also wasn't a child and could have made new choices for herself."

He takes a deep breath. "The harder part is I believed what she said. That I am despicable. I didn't deserve love. I'd never find someone who loves me. Not that I want someone like her." He huffs. "Just in general."

He side-eyes me but doesn't turn in my direction.

"I believed I didn't deserve the family I had. I no longer had friends. I didn't think I'd ever have a chance with a *normal* woman."

I huff at the statement, and Archer shifts. "But then I met you . . . and you're just, fuck. You're a light at the end of a deep dark tunnel, Jenna. You were so different, and it was refreshing. Fucking reviving." He waves his hand between us. "I just want to soak it all up, but I understand I messed up. I *had* to leave, though. I had to keep you safe, and the less time you spent within Vi's orbit, the safer you were. I needed her to forget you, and the only way to do that was to force her to concentrate on me."

"But why didn't you come back?"

"I couldn't risk her following me or knowing where I'd been staying. I didn't want to put any of you in danger."

It all makes perfect sense. But . . . "It's been three months. You told the girls your job was finished. What happened?"

Archer falls back into the couch cushions and huffs before scrubbing at his face. "She got me on the boat, but it was being tracked. I took a huge risk and jumped overboard."

My mouth falls open. "You jumped off the boat?"

"Well, I actually flipped myself overboard as one of her goonies shot at me."

"Archer!" I shriek, recalling he'd said he'd been shot at again.

231

"The boat when up in flames less than half an hour later. Later, I was informed the department had been watching her, and the Coast Guard had been warned of possible drug trafficking up the east side of the lake. CG wasn't wasting time, so they pursued her as the boat was a dark-moving vessel. Very suspicious. As for the explosion, there was an investigation, and that's why I was detained. I didn't know anything, but the department had to be certain. Plus, I was a good source of information on enemies of the Quinteros. Tampering with the wires would make the explosion look like an electrical malfunction. The yacht going up in flames would seem like nothing more than a boating accident caused by faulty equipment. Viviana wouldn't be missed, and neither would the shipment on board. I wasn't involved, just a barnacle on their plan. But that had to be confirmed."

"So she's dead?"

Archer glances down at his lap. "She is."

Wow. Just wow. "How do you feel about that?" I ask, softening the question.

"Guilty as charged," he whispers. Guilty of seducing her and maybe breaking her heart.

"What she said wasn't true, though, Archer. You must know that. You are not despicable. You are not unloveable, and you are definitely worthy of love."

His head rises, and his dark eyes liquify. He nods, chewing on his bottom lip.

"It wasn't your fault." He didn't tamper with the wires. He didn't pull a trigger. She was involved in very illegal things, and he was doing his job. *His job.* "So you're done with the assignment."

Archer slowly nods again. "The department wants me to go into the witness protection program, but I've refused. I've already led a hidden life, Jenna. I just want a chance at being a regular guy."

As I gaze over his body, there's nothing regular about Archer, and there never will be. For the first time, I see the exhaustion in his eyes and hear in his voice how apologetic he is. I also realize if he hadn't jumped off that boat, he'd be dead in the explosion himself.

Without another word, I scoot closer to him on the couch and slip my arms around him, hugging him from the side. He lowers his face and presses a kiss to my temple, holding his lips there.

"Are you safe here? Are we?" Suddenly, my thoughts leap to my girls, and Archer pulls back.

His arm wraps around my lower back. "I would never ever put you and the girls in danger, and I've already told you I would protect you with everything I had. I was protecting you when I left, but I wasn't gone, 'Locks. I hadn't *left* you."

The note and his medal are my reminders. They were a message that he'd be back, only I hadn't read it properly.

"Someone had eyes on you the moment I left."

I pull back from him, but his fingers fist in the back of my shirt, refusing to allow me to escape. "Someone was spying on me?" I glance over his head, looking toward the window behind the couch. The blinds are closed, but a shiver ripples over my skin.

"For your safety, someone was keeping me informed." His harder voice stiffens my spine. He had someone looking out for us. He was protecting me. He was protecting my girls.

"Are we safe?"

"I had to be certain Vi hadn't made any connections between you and me. Not a hint of her passing on your name to someone else. You're as safe as you can be. She never left my sight once I was on that boat, and she didn't get out of me who you were."

"You said I was no one."

"More pretending." His voice lowers and he leans forward, propping his forehead against mine. "I didn't mean what I said."

It still hurt, and he knows it.

We sit in silence for a moment as I try to catch up on everything. This can't be my life. I'm a small-town high school teacher with two little girls and a mortgage. I'm not part of espionage or drug rings. Archer flattens his palm on my back and strokes up my spine.

"You have nothing to fear. I'm here now." His hand cups the back of my head as he's done so many times before he kisses me or while he kisses me. *Will he kiss me?*

Slowly, his fingers move for my hairline and draw down the side of my face, brushing locks around my ear. He watches his own movement and slides those fingers along the column of my throat before tipping up my chin. His gaze falls to my mouth before meeting my eyes.

"I'm home," he whispers.

I swallow around the lump in my throat. The fear. The relief. Overwhelmed, all I want to do right now is hold him. Without responding, I climb over his legs and wrap myself around him, holding him tight to my chest. Within seconds, Archer tips us sideways until we're a tangle of limbs. Legs entwined. Arms around one another. His face buried in my neck. And we hold tight like the life preserver we are to one another. Breathing each other in. No longer drowning. Now we just need to learn to swim.

32

[Archer]

I wake with a start to the sound of a phone chirping like crickets. Jenna stretches beside me, reaching for the device on the coffee table.

"Hello." Her sleep-filled voice stirs my insides, and I'd be hard if I wasn't already. We're back to sleeping on the couch. For the past three nights, we've fallen asleep clinging to one another on this thing, listening to heartbeats and nestling together like we're afraid to let go.

Daylight hours have been a different story. She remains distant. As Jenna had a four-day weekend from school, we didn't leave the house other than some trips outside to build a small sled hill in her backyard and a snowman. To the outside world, we look like a family, but we aren't there yet, and that becomes evident when Jenna introduces me to the neighbor as the brother of a college friend.

I definitely want to be more than that.

"Shit," Jenna mutters, scrambling to get out from beside me. "Shit, shit, shit."

"You said a bad word," Rosie says near the bottom of the staircase while Jenna hops around looking for I don't know what while still on the phone.

"Okay, give me fifteen, and thank you so, so much for calling." Jenna clicks off the phone, drops it to the low table, and digs both hands into her hair. She takes a deep breath and then goes into tornado mode, scrambling toward Rosie.

"Rosie, run upstairs and wake Talia. You both need to get dressed. Mommy missed her alarm."

Slowly, I sit upright. *Fuck.* "What can I do to help?" Jenna turns to me as one foot hits the staircase. When she looks back at me, it's as if she's forgotten I'm here.

"I . . . I'm so late. I don't have time for a shower. I'll just toss something on. Carol can feed the girls breakfast, and I'll ask her to make Talia a lunch for kindergarten. She's the one who takes her anyway. I'll have to buy mine from the school cafeteria." She's rambling off a list of details like a daily schedule.

"Why don't you let Rosie and Talia stay with me? I'll feed both girls breakfast, make Talia a lunch, and get her to school."

"I . . . you—" Her hesitation says it all.

"You don't trust me with your girls?" The question isn't said with as much ire as the first time I asked her such a thing, but the truth stings.

"It isn't that. I just don't want to impose. I can handle it." She steps up the first two steps, and I'm off the couch.

"But you don't have to handle it. Let me do this for you."

She pauses on the third stair, struggling once more, and I'm thinking she's given up on me. There's no hope of her trusting me if she can't trust me with her girls.

"Okay," she whispers slowly, hesitantly. "Okay."

"Does this buy you time for a shower?" Not that she needs one, but giving her a chance at some semblance of her morning routine might help calm her down.

"It doesn't, but it helps." She steps up a few more stairs, walking backward up them this time. "And thank you."

The corner of my mouth crooks up. "Anything for you, 'Locks." I wink, and she turns on her heels, stomping up the remainder of the stairs. Not going to lie, I check out her ass as she runs up those final steps. Then I smile to myself with how right this feels, even if she is late. Waking up with her. Helping her with the girls. Being here. *Being home.*

Within ten minutes, Jenna returns downstairs looking like a lady boss in a form-fitting dark skirt that hits just above her knees and a deep red blouse plus heels.

"You wear that to work?" I choke out.

"What's wrong with what I'm wearing?" She glances down at herself. Her hair is in a tight twist at the nape of her neck, which adds to the naughty teacher thoughts racing through my head.

"It's not what you're wearing but how you wear it. Damn, 'Locks. Those horny teenagers won't know what to do with themselves." I can think of a few things I'd like to do with her had she been my teacher.

Then again, I don't want those hormone-driven bastards thinking about her like that.

Slowly, she smiles, shaking her head as her shoulders relax.

"Lunch?" I hadn't forgotten. I just don't know what she'd like.

"I'll just do cafeteria food, but oh, you made tea. Thank you." She reaches for the steaming mug waiting for her.

"Breakfast?" Last summer, she often made pancakes, waffles, and eggs for her girls, but in the rush of this morning, complex foods seem out of the question.

"I don't have time. I don't really eat it anyway." She waves me off, turning toward her dining room, where her laptop sat unopened all weekend along with a stack of papers. I follow her, and she continues with orders. "Okay, Rosie and Talia are dressed. Cereal is fine for each of them. They don't eat much this early in the morning anyway, but I usually give them something before Carol's, especially as Talia's in kindergarten, and it's a long day for her. Breakfast is brain food. Lunch can be a peanut butter sandwich, cut-up apple, and one crunchy item."

Crunchy item?

"Chips," Talia calls from somewhere behind me.

"Her school is Elk Lake City Elementary." I watch as she scribbles down the address. "She starts at eight ten. I can get her at the end of the day."

"Does that mean I have to go to after-care?" Talia whines.

"Today, yes," Jenna says, narrowing her eyes at Talia behind me. "I'm sorry."

"What?" I glance from her to her daughter. "I'll pick her up. What time?"

"Two forty-five," Talia says.

"I've got it," Jenna says at the same time.

"*I've* got it." I challenge. "What else do you need done today?"

"I have gym class on Tuesdays."

"It's Monday," Jenna states before remembering it's not. "Shiitake." Her head tips back for the ceiling.

"What does this mean?" I ask.

"She has a gym uniform."

237

L.B. Dunbar

"On it," I state.

Jenna glances at her phone. "No time for the washer."

"You didn't wash it?" Talia groans. The ice queen isn't happy to wear a dirty uniform.

"She doesn't sweat much. It's fine. Spritz it with some of my perfume," Jenna grumbles to me under her breath before looking around her. "Okay. Okay." The wheels spin inside her head as she ticks off a silent checklist of items. Laptop bag over her shoulder. Purse in hand. Stack of papers in another bag. She looks like a bag lady, and a sexy one at that.

"Coat," I demand, and she glances down at the straps looping here and there over her body. She shakes her head, but I quickly have her keys out of her purse, remote start going on her SUV, and her winter jacket in hand. I hold it out for her, and she rearranges everything to slip into it. Rushing for Talia and Rosie, she gives each of them a kiss, rubs noses with them, and tells them she loves them. She adds, "Have a good day. Learn something new," to Talia, and turns for the front door.

While she kissed the girls, I slipped into my boots. I walk her to the car as the sidewalk still looks icy, and she's wearing those killer heels.

"You don't need to do this," she mutters, taking shuffling steps to her vehicle with my arm around her.

"I want to do this, 'Locks. End all." Arriving at the side of her SUV, I open the door, and she tosses her bags inside.

"Shiitake. Car seats."

I glance into the back seat and notice two seats. One for Rosie and a booster for Talia. "Got it." After a brief struggle with the safety belts, I've freed both. Jenna scrambles into the driver's seat, and she's tugging at the door when I stop it with my body.

One-handed, I cup the back of her head. "You have a good day. Learn something new." Then I lean forward and press a kiss to the corner of her lips and rub my nose along hers.

A soft intake of breath follows."Okay," she whispers.

I step back, closing her door for her.

As she reverses, I stand in the driveway and hold my breath for a moment as she pulls away. Then I remind myself there isn't a chance I'll let her get away from me. She's late. She's frazzled, and it's been an honor to witness her morning. I want to experience everything with her, and I'm here to prove myself. With that in mind, I turn back toward the house with car seats in hand to feed two little girls who stand at the door watching me.

"What kind of cereal do princesses eat for breakfast?" And so begins my day.

+ + +

With breakfast done and Talia off to school, I head to the grocery store before returning to the house with Rosie. Once the groceries are put away, I start the laundry and prep for dinner. It's all mundane, and Rosie keeps a watchful eye on my progress, but I'm enjoying the simplicity of it all. I don't like to cook for myself and wasn't as concerned about picking up all my stuff when it was only me in a small-ass apartment. But that apartment is gone, and everything I own fits into two rucksacks. Those sacks are here in Jenna's home. She doesn't have a guest room, just two small bedrooms on the second floor with one full bathroom up there. Over the weekend, she explained how this house was her place at first, and when she married, they had plans for something larger someday.

She needs more space. Her little girls are going to grow into bigger ones, and this house can't hold four adult-sized people. And yes, I'm including myself in that body count.

With Rosie settled, watching a video that teaches the alphabet, I search real estate listings in the area on my phone. I have forty minutes until I need to be somewhere, and I take a moment after the rush of the morning to sit on the couch with little princess number two. Every time Rosie's thumb heads for her mouth, I pluck it away, reminding her warriors and pirates and any other thing I can think of do not suck their thumbs.

Despite the months of recovery, sitting still feels strange, especially as the past three months have been another race against time. I needed to get back to Jenna.

Between Viviana's death and the investigation into the explosion, time moved so slowly. I also had to argue my case again against the WPP by reminding the department not every DEA agent lives in seclusion. I didn't want to be alone anymore. I'd been Hunter Gray for so long, being Archer McCaryn felt like I already entered the program. Disappearing into this small town and returning to my own family would be enough disguise.

Although I was no longer hiding and just wanted to be me again. I wanted to discover who I was without the department. It would be a struggle to sit still, but it wouldn't be that much of a hardship. With the case wrapping up and only six weeks remaining on my one-year mandatory furlough, I took a leave of absence. I didn't have physical clearance to continue hard-core fieldwork anyway, and I couldn't handle a desk job. I was too young to do nothing, but for now, I wanted to breathe in the bayberry scent of this home and the waxy-crayon fragrance coming off the little girl next to me. She tried to color *pictures* on her skin like I have on mine. Thankfully, Jenna doesn't have markers easily available to her now four-year-old. I'd missed Rosie's and Talia's birthdays, but I didn't plan to miss any more important dates, including one I have around eleven fifteen this morning.

33

[Jenna]

"Who is that?" Tiffany Miles asks from across the lunchroom table.

"Hello Diet Coke commercial," Tricia Ramirez mutters under her breath at the same time, and I twist in my seat to find Archer holding Rosie's hand and standing just within the teachers' lunchroom door.

"You know we can't just let anyone in here," Dani, the school secretary teases. "But he had this adorable little lady with him, so I knew he must be okay." She winks at me and then turns starry eyes on the man holding a sack in his hand.

"I brought you lunch." He isn't even fazed by the googly eyes these women are giving him or the sound of ovaries popping from each one of them as they take in his large stature, wearing a suede, Sherpa-collared jacket while holding the hand of my small child.

Slowly, I rise, ignoring the pizza slice with canned pears I purchased for my lunch.

"What are you doing here?" I ask, unable to fight the smile on my face and already forgetting that he just said he brought me lunch. My eyes fall to the bag in his hand, and then I reach for Rosie.

"Hey, baby." I press a kiss to her cheek as I lift her but keep my eyes on Archer. "Maybe we should go to my classroom." I typically eat in the lunchroom because just like my students, lunch is one of my favorite times of the day. Also like my students, I get the laugh I desperately need from my hilarious teacher friends. Feeling the eyes on my back, I already know they have tons of questions about the mystery man looking like a model who just stepped out of a glossy catalog. I haven't told anyone about Archer.

However, Tricia is one of my closest friends, and she knew something was weighing on me when the school year began. Just like I had known something wasn't right in her first marriage years ago. She didn't question me, though. What could I say? I had a fling, but now he was gone. And I had no idea where he went.

Placing my hand on Archer's shoulder, I turn him away from the ladies still drooling over him and lead him to my second-floor classroom. Dani is correct. We don't just let anyone into schools anymore, but seeing Rosie with Archer had to prove he knew me. Still, I'm curious.

"How did you get past security?"

Archer remains dumbfounded. "I just told them I was bringing you lunch."

Rosie interjects. "We wanted to surprise you."

"You did surprise me," I say, rubbing my nose against her cheek. I miss the girls during the day, but I need to work, and we all need a break from one another. I've had to learn to prioritize, and I've become more efficient than in my early days of teaching. Work stays at work. My home life is devoted to my girls. "So what did you bring me?"

I only get thirty minutes, and I'm down to about twenty.

"I didn't know what you'd want, but Rosie said peanut butter works. I threw in an apple as you are a teacher." He winks.

His rough voice sends a thrill down my spine, and I'd love to be anywhere but this classroom right now. I recall our sleeping position for the past few nights. How we cling to one another, and he nuzzles into my neck. How his heart beats in his chest, and he covers mine with that large palm of his, reminding us both we are alive.

My feelings for Archer are all over the place, and I've never felt so conflicted about anyone. I want to be mad at him for his disappearance, but I understand he did it to protect me. While I don't understand the depth of his work, I realize he couldn't follow me when he needed to apprehend *her*. He had a role to play. But was the role over? When would the next mission begin? I couldn't be a layover for him before he had to be involved with another woman. The thought of him sleeping with someone else, even if just seducing them for information, made me feel sick.

A hand on the back of my head has me looking up at him. "Hey."

"Hey," I whisper, realizing I'd zoned out a bit.

"We also gave you one crunchy," Rosie adds.

"Oh, yeah. What's my crunchy?" I tease, rubbing my nose into her neck.

"Chips." She squeals as I pepper her with kisses.

"I love chips."

I glance back over at Archer, who is watching me with Rosie, and there's something in his eyes. Then he smiles, scattering my attempts to read him. His lip slowly curls at one corner before rising on the other, and it's like he's undressing me right here in my classroom. I want him to lay me back on my desk, which are not thoughts I need in my head if I'm going to teach for the remainder of the day.

"So. Lunch." I squeak and then clear my throat. "I don't have much time." I set Rosie on her feet and open the bag Archer set on the corner of my desk. Rosie climbs into my chair, and I open the bag of chips and hand it to her.

"They don't know anything about me, do they?" Archer asks.

"Nope." My teeth bite into the sandwich he brought me, and I chew it with thoughts of taking him into my mouth. I want his lips. I want his skin.

"Gonna change that," he tells me. It's not a warning or a threat. It's the truth. "I told you. Not pretending. I'm not undercover or hiding in the dark. I'm here." He pats his chest.

"How long are you sticking around, though, Archer?" I hate that I ask. I even hate my tone in asking, but he hasn't mentioned what's next. Only what happened in the past.

"I told you to give me a month."

"No, I mean, when is your next job? When do you leave for it?"

"'Locks, just eat your lunch. We can talk about that later."

"Another hard topic?" I question, irritation growing when he just brought me lunch. He *made* me lunch. It's sweet, and I'm being a witch. But I can't shake the thought that Archer *will* leave someday. Maybe not in the next thirty days but soon enough.

"Nope. Just think we should talk later." His eyes shift to Rosie. "At home." His voice softens around the word home, although it's still like sandpaper on wood, and I want that sound to rub against me. I've suddenly gone from irritated to an irrepressible desire for him. I made it through the weekend, keeping myself in check. Despite sleeping next to him on my lumpy old couch. Despite him invading my bathroom and my kitchen and my head. I'm trying so hard to keep him out of my heart because I could love a man who wants to play Barbies with my girls, paints little fingernails, and makes me peanut butter sandwiches.

There's no doubt I'm still attracted to him.

The next few minutes pass quickly as Rosie keeps us both distracted by telling me what they did all morning, and Archer accuses her of not keeping secrets. Then he tells me about her trying to draw on her skin.

"I want pictures like Archer."

His back is a graphic display while his upper arms host a few tats as well. I know what's underneath the long-sleeved Henley he wears, and just the thought of his skin, those muscles, and the trail of hair leading into his jeans enlarges the flame of desire like gasoline was poured on it.

Whoosh. I want him.

"You okay, 'Locks?" Archer chuckles. The redness in my face is a giveaway to my thoughts.

"I'm good," I state, choking down a final bite of sandwich. Archer reaches out for my cheek and brushes back the hairs coming loose from the twist at my nape. He stares at me for a long minute before looking down at the plastic container that held my sandwich.

"Okay, little warrior. Time to pick up and let Momma get back to shaping the minds of the future."

I almost fall over at Archer calling me Momma like he's familiar. Like he's the daddy to this mommy. I don't know why it does something to me. Perhaps it's that I'm already worked up by his presence.

And that flame went from personal bonfire to inferno of desire for him.

All of him.

+ + +

"Girl, start talking." Tricia Ramirez nearly runs to my room once the final bell rings and students vacate the hallways. She tugs my classroom door shut behind her and leans against it like she's hiding out on a covert mission.

"About what?" I tease, shuffling together papers and placing them in my bag. I wasn't half as productive as I'd hoped to be during my planning period, and I will need to read these freshman compositions later tonight.

"That giant drink of Diet Coke who brought you lunch." The Diet Coke thing is based on a decades-old commercial where a group of women gathered at a window to watch a local construction guy drink the cola on his break. He was hot. They were hot and bothered by his sexy presence. A few years ago, I called Leon, who is now Tricia's husband, such a thing when we spotted him outside her classroom window playing basketball on the school courts across the parking lot.

"That's Archer McCaryn," I state as if it should explain everything.

When Tricia narrows her eyes at me, I head for a student desk and watch as Tricia's eyes widen when I take a seat. She steps over to the row opposite me and sits in a desk as well. Our positions suggest this will be a lengthy conversation, and I tell her everything, feeling a wave of relief to explain the story from start to finish to someone.

"And now he's here," Tricia confirms. "Sleeping in your house. Making you lunches and taking care of your girls."

"Yes." I stare as her eyes widen once more, and then her fingers cover her lips. And she laughs. She laughs so hard she bends forward.

"Oh my God, Jenna. He's in love with you."

"What?" I snap while the possibility rushes through me.

"You know this is what Leon did. He walked away but came crawling back. And I was so determined not to let him in. He wasn't going to get to me again, but when I saw him with his family . . ." She sighs. "He just wedged himself right back into my heart." She shakes her head. "Damn domineering man."

There isn't a hint of irritation in her voice. She smiles broader, pleased with that domineering man who has her pregnant once again. She'll have had five babies in nearly eight years when this one arrives.

"You love every bit of that domineering man."

"And so do you." Tricia tips a brow to me, implying Archer.

"I don't know," I whisper.

L.B. Dunbar

"It's okay to love again," she says to me, reaching out across the aisle to touch my forearm. Tricia was married before Leon, and the situation with her first husband was completely opposite of mine. Trent Walker was a grade A asshole. Leon was her second chance.

"I know you loved Ryan to pieces, but it's okay to give all your pieces to someone else."

She's right. I know she's right, but she also knows as well as me that there's a fear in opening up to someone else. As the brazen party girl, I kept up the façade that I didn't need a man. I needed to get laid. But deep down, I'd wanted that man who understood me, stood by me, and loved me. I pushed back for years because of that one relationship early on, but I let Ryan in, and I couldn't go back to being that girl who kept men at arm's length. I didn't have the time or energy for it.

Archer wasn't arm's length away. He was in my space.

"Are you bringing him to the fundraiser this Friday?"

"I already have a date." I couldn't believe I'd asked someone, but I didn't want to go alone when most of my closest teacher friends were bringing their significant others. I never minded before, but this year I did. Although no one had known about Archer and my fling this summer, I didn't want to be the woman going stag *again*.

Tricia tips up a brow. "Well, this could be interesting." She giggles while patting my arm. "But I'm happy for you. You deserve this. You deserve him."

She doesn't mean my date but Archer. The man on my couch. In my house. And wedging his way back into my heart.

34

[Jenna]

"Absolutely not." I hear coming from the front door, which Archer has answered on Friday evening. He's been at my house for a week.

Frick. My heels tap on the hardwood and barely drowned out his next words.

"What the fuck is this?" Archer's voice carries, and I pause as Mason stands on the front stoop looking every bit model-worthy in a dark suit.

"I told you I had a fundraiser to attend." Teachers are invited as a courtesy. *Did I mention Mason was my date?* I might have skipped that detail, thinking Archer would be gone before I left. I'd been encouraging him to take a night off. I had a sitter lined up, and the girls love Natasha, so I didn't want to cancel her. Plus, Archer had turned into a regular househusband of sorts, and he deserved a break.

"And hello to you," Mason says, letting himself into the house and closing the door as Archer turns to me. His eyes lose focus as he stares at me in my deep purple wrap dress. When I came down the stairs wearing it, he couldn't take his eyes off me for an entire minute before he finally told me I was stunning.

"You didn't mention a date." Archer's hands come to his hips as he glares at me. "You said you always turned *him* down." Archer tips his head at Mason.

"When did I say that?" I anxiously rub my hands down my hips, and Archer's eyes follow the motion. The way he's looking at me, he wants to outline my body after he pisses a circle around me.

"Last summer."

I vaguely remember teasing Mason about how he asks me out whenever we run into one another, and I always decline.

"You remember that?" I ask Archer.

"I remember everything." His eyes pin mine, and I hate how my mind races back to images of Archer and me in his bed, twisting and turning and tonguing one another.

"Speaking of summer," Mason interjects. "Where the hell have you been?" If steam could come out of Archer's ears, it would. He's mad enough as it is, and with Mason's reminder of Archer's disappearance, he's pouring lighter fluid on an open flame.

"Working," Archer snaps in response while keeping his eyes on me.

"Couldn't call your sister?" Mason adds. Archer turns on him, and I mutter Mason's name. He ignores my warning tone. "Your sister who has been worried sick once again that you'd disappear. Or worse."

The scolding implies the loss of Ben, and I know how Anna feels. I had my own fears that Archer was dead. Even my girls had questioned his existence.

"Alright," I intercede, stepping up to Archer and smoothing a hand down his chest. "Natasha will be here any minute. Why don't you head out?"

With one final piercing look, Archer steps away from me and reaches for the jacket he'd hung on the hook by the front door. It's been hard to admit how right his coat looks hanging there among our things.

"Yeah. I'm out," he mutters without a second glance back at me, and I hate how my heart drops as he silently closes the front door behind him.

+ + +

"So Archer is back?" Mason says to me as we head to Red Barn Table, where the charity event is being held. Ethan Scott owns the place, which started as only a restaurant in a fieldstone building on the old cherry farm property and eventually turned into a place for weddings and large parties.

"He just sort of showed up last Friday," I state, recalling Archer's face when he turned to me after finding Mason on the stoop. I'd never seen him look angry except that time another man was dancing with me when we went line dancing last summer.

I remember everything.

Archer had me so twisted, and the remainder of the week passed in a blur. He helped out with the girls, making three meals a day, taking

Talia to school, and doing my laundry. He was a dream, but I was waiting to wake up to find him walking away. He never did answer my question about when he was heading out on his next job, and I didn't bring it up again. After a long day of teaching, I was tired, and the winter months wreaked havoc on my emotions. I was like a bear, needing to hibernate yet anxious for spring. I didn't want to fight with Archer. I wanted to just be.

"He was as surprised to see me as I was to see him." Mason eyes me over the console in his car before taking a left onto the highway.

"I hadn't exactly mentioned you." Archer wasn't wrong. I never said yes to Mason asking me out when we'd run into one another in the area, but when I saw Four Points as a contributor to an item in the silent auction, I decided to reach out and see if Mason would like to attend the function with me. After Archer's disappearance, he'd decided once again to stay behind at Lakeside Cottage. He was worried about the safety of Anna and the kids, but he'd been back to business as usual as time passed, and Archer's silence continued.

"Well, you know I'm a sure bet," he teases as we pull off the highway onto the road leading to the restaurant.

"Mason," I groan. "We all know you love Anna."

"What?" he chokes, hitting the brakes a little too hard as he slows to pull into the parking lot.

"Everyone knows you love Anna," I repeat, reaching out for the dash to brace myself against another sudden jolt. Mason pulls into a parking spot, cuts the ignition, and twists to face me.

"I'm not in love with Anna."

"How's that lying to yourself working out for you?"

His eyes squint toward the dark cherry orchard beyond the restored old barn, answering my question with one of his own. "How do you know?"

"It's in everything you do for her. You stayed when Ben was sick, and you stayed after his death."

"Maybe I did those things for Ben."

When I don't comment, Mason looks back at me. I tilt my head, giving him my best mom glare. The one that says—tell the truth.

"You shouldn't covet your best friend's wife, right?" He swallows hard around his guilt, glancing down at the console between us.

"Written in the commandments," I tease. "But when the best friend isn't there anymore, and she's lonely . . ."

"I might be easy," Mason says, glancing back up at me with fire in his bright eyes, "but my heart isn't stupid." On that note, he pops open his door, and I reach for the handle on mine. Before I fully have it open, he's present and helping me stand from the low seat. My heart aches a little for him. He's always been a player, and I don't understand his situation as a dad, but he's a good man deep down inside. Case in point is the donation to the high school fundraiser and being my date for one night.

We enter the old barn converted to event space, filled with rustic chairs and packed with white linen-covered tables. This place once held a Halloween party hosted by Tricia's older brother and his wife, but eventually, the wife's youngest brother took over this sliver of family property and turned it into this well-sought event space. The Scott family has generously donated the barn tonight to the school district's fundraising effort. It's a bit of a dance to avoid parents who all want to discuss their child when they couldn't find time to attend the parent-teacher conferences a week ago, but Mason and I finally make our way to the corner where the teacher tables are sequestered. I don't miss the questioning gazes of my lunchtime colleagues, wondering who the tall drink of water is, compared to Diet Coke commercial man who brought me lunch earlier this week. Bombarded with questions after Archer's appearance, I answered with deliberate vagueness. Tricia provided distractions during lunchtimes when the questions grew too much and offered a reprieve during a curriculum meeting when others wanted to analyze my personal life more than student concerns.

The first hour of the fundraiser is for cocktails, and I'm pacing myself when I'd love nothing more than to down an entire bottle of wine. Mason is a source of interest with his fine-tailored suit and artfully curled hair. He's so good looking it's a crime, only I'm not looking to commit one with him. My thoughts return to the questions in Archer's eyes before he stormed out of my place, and I try to dismiss the idea he might be gone for good.

A call to dinner comes, asking people to take their seats, and Mason holds out my chair for me. As I'm lowering to the seat, a firm, rough voice washes over the table. "Sorry I'm late."

All heads turn to find Archer standing beside the table, hand on the seat next to mine, and pulling it out. He doesn't even spare Mason a glance before lowering into the chair and scooting it forward.

My mouth falls open, and it's not just the audacity of his intrusion. It's the dark suit he wears making him look like he stepped off a mafia romance cover. The bright white shirt underneath the fitted black suit coat contrasts with his slightly tan skin, and my mouth waters. *Where the frickity did that outfit come from?*

"What the . . .?" someone growls across the table, and I turn to find Leon Ramirez, Tricia's husband, glaring at Archer. "You," he growls.

Spinning from my friend's husband to the man taking up space next to me, I ask, "Do you know one another?"

"We've met," Leon grunts, tipping up his chin.

"We have?" Archer questions, narrowing his eyes at Leon.

"Never forget a face."

Suddenly, I'm wondering how these two are connected. Leon Ramirez was in a gang more than a decade ago, and he's done time in jail. Tricia told me these things in confidence, and the knowledge has me wondering if there's some connection with Archer and his line of work. Was Archer involved in Leon's gang somehow? Did Leon deal drugs? The Quinteros were involved in that.

My head twists from one man to another.

"You still a cop?" Leon snaps.

Ah, that might be the connection.

"Was DEA most recently. I'm on a leave of absence."

This is the first I've heard of such a thing, but I'm still volleying back and forth between these men who know one another before I catch Tricia's eye. She looks just as confused as I do. Finally, I glance up at Mason, still holding the back of my chair. Behind him, a woman flapping her arms rushes toward our table.

"Don't you worry. We'll find another chair and get an extra place setting right over here," the harried woman says out of breath. Archer smiles at the woman, and her flapping arms settle to fingertips at the edge of her lips. She lets out a strangled giggle. In another second, she'll be choking on her drool. Then she catches sight of Mason, and I'm worried she's about to hyperventilate.

Finally, she speaks. "Mr. McCaryn just made a generous donation to the school's English Department, and he insisted he sit at this table."

Her eyes move from Mason to Archer before landing on me. She's probably wondering what all the fuss is, and so am I. These two men need their heads knocked together. However, I don't need either one to make a scene. I'm already the focus of attention at this table filled with people I work with, plus Leon glaring at Archer.

"How do you know Leon?" I whisper.

"Later, 'Locks," he whispers, keeping his eyes on Leon a second before turning his gaze to me.

"What are you doing here?" I hiss, leaning toward him like I'm telling him a secret. Archer leans in the same way, placing his cheek next to mine and lowering his rugged voice as best as he can.

"I didn't have a real date with you, and I'll be damned if I let him have one first."

"Whose fault—"

Archer holds up a hand to halt my accusation. "Mine." He pauses a second. "But I'm here now."

"Mason is my date," I whisper, trying to stay quiet myself while all eyes remain on me, including Mason, who is still standing behind me, gripping the back of my chair.

"You know what, I need to make a call." Mason pats my shoulder, and I look up at him.

"Mason." I shift in my seat, but he's already working his way around the crowded tables, waving at someone he knows. He's built several million-dollar houses in the area, and my dream is to afford the type of homes he constructs one day.

A hand comes to my knee under the table, and I stare down at it before looking up at Archer. Nothing in his expression shows chagrin or apology for his sudden appearance or his behavior.

"Excuse me. I think I'll use the restroom before dinner." I hastily stand, knocking into the table with my knee before squeezing through the tight fit between chairs. As I weave around the too-close tables, I sense someone following me but slip into the bathroom before he catches me. Taking a moment, I stare at my reflection in the bright mirror.

What is he doing? What am I doing? A thrill races through me that Archer actually followed me, but I'm equally embarrassed that he made a scene. And what's the deal with Leon? I hate that so many questions remain between Archer and me. Nothing makes sense with him. Not his attraction last summer. Not his presence now. With that thought in mind, I open the bathroom door with more force than intended and find Archer standing in the dim hallway directly across from the bathroom.

"What are you doing here?" I lash out at him.

"I told you. I want my date."

I huff and cross my arms as he's the one who disappeared that night, and he's hardly offered an explanation now. I mean, I know why he was gone, but why is he back? Why is he here?

"How many other men do I need to chase off, 'Locks?"

My mouth falls open. "Just what are you implying?"

"I'm gonna be pissed if the list is more than one."

"I . . ." I don't even know what to say. Then again, I have a whole litany of things I'd like to tell him, like where he can shove his implication.

"I understand if you had to do something to pass the time, but that's over." His eyes lower to my legs, and I don't think my mouth can gape any wider.

"I have not . . . how dare you . . ." I have not slept with someone else in the time since I've been with him. He knows he was my first since Ryan, and he'll be my last for a long time. I can't handle the heartache attached to sleeping with someone, and I don't want anyone but him. However, this argument has me reconsidering my attraction for half a second.

"Have you been with someone else?" I fight the gag reflex at the thought of him sleeping with that woman or any other woman since we've been together.

"Are you insane?" His eyes roam my body, and if I didn't know better, he just mentally stripped me of my dress. His voice hardens when he says, "Are you done yet?"

"Am I done with what?" I growl.

"Pretending this isn't going to be a thing." He points back and forth between us.

"I was never pretending with you." Gritting my teeth, I step toward him. He steps closer to me at the same time.

"And I wasn't pretending with you either."

"Then what were you doing with me?"

"I was hoping you'd love me." His words bring everything to a screeching halt. My heart skips a beat. My belly drops, and all my anger crashes into itself.

"I told you what *she* said. I didn't deserve love, and no one would ever love me, but when I'm with you and the girls, I feel . . . something vibrating all around you, and I want it wrapped around me. For a little while, I felt it coming off you and covering me. When you were in my bed. When you were in my place. When you let me spend time with you and the princesses. It was always there, swirling around you, curling around me. That time was too short. I want more." He reaches for the back of my head. "I want it more than I've wanted anything."

I stare at him, still stunned by his admission.

"It's a lot to ask, but I'm asking, 'Locks. Give me another chance. I'm not going anywhere."

"What about the department?" What about another assignment? Another case where he needs to seduce someone? Mentioning his leave of absence moments ago was the first I'd heard him speak of the future.

"I'm not going back."

"What?" My voice strains, quiet and low.

"I don't have medical clearance for fieldwork, and I can't handle a desk job. It's time to walk away."

I can't believe he's giving it up. "Don't do this for me," I whisper.

"I'm doing it for me. I'm a selfish man, Jenna. I want to be here for me. For what I know you can give me."

I was hoping you could love me.

"And I'm going to try like hell to give it back to you." His fingers dig into the hair on the back of my head. "So I'm asking again, are you done yet?"

"Yes. No. What's the question again?" I whisper.

He softly chuckles. "Jenna," Archer whispers as his hand comes to rest over my racing heart. "I'm sorry." Everything in his tone, his eyes, and his expression says he's truly apologetic for leaving me before, and he isn't leaving again.

When I nod once to accept his apology, his mouth is on mine. This kiss is a claiming and a commitment. Tongue and teeth and lips, and embarrassingly erotic for a bathroom hallway, but I couldn't pull back even if I wanted to. And I didn't want to. I wanted to wallow in his apology and accept his request.

I was hoping you could love me.

I can. I will. I do.

A sharp cough breaks us apart.

Leon stands at the end of the hallway, lowering his fist from his mouth. "I'm assuming she's not under arrest, Officer."

I glance at Archer, who has slipped his arm around me and tugged me into his side. Leon's and Archer's eyes lock on one another.

"She's my future," Archer states, surprising both Leon and me.

Leon's brows lift.

"How do you two know each other?" I ask.

"We don't. At least not as we are now." Leon steps forward and holds out a hand. "Leon Ramirez."

"Archer McCaryn." Archer introduces himself, and I watch as they clasp hands. An entire conversation is happening with those hands clapping together, but I don't hear words until Leon speaks.

"You cause her trouble, and you'll hear from me." The warning in Leon's tone is clear, but his protective stance on my behalf surprises me.

"Noted," Archer says. "But there isn't going to be any trouble." His statement is just as clear. He's here to protect me. I relax a little under his arm, and he reads my body language.

He unclasps hands with Leon, then presses a kiss to my temple.

"Let's get out of this place."

35

[Archer]

I'd nearly had a fucking heart attack when I opened Jenna's front door and saw Mason Becker standing on the stoop. I don't even recall what I said, but I'm certain "fuck" and "no" were in the sentence. Now I have Jenna sitting opposite me in a little restaurant we found called Unsalted Mermaid. The place is quiet and dim and rather empty on this winter evening. From where we sit, the black lake glistens under a dark sky outside the window.

Jenna worried about Mason, but I told her he'd already bailed.

"What a horrible date he is," she teased. "He ditched me."

I would have taken the comment to heart, but she was joking, looking lighter than I've seen her since we kissed in the hallway until Leon interrupted us. I can't place him, but I'm certain him calling me officer means I arrested him at some point in the past.

Once we place our drink order, I don't like my position across the table from her and shift to the chair next to her at the four top where seats are arranged two and two at the table.

"What are you doing?" she asks, giggling at my seating re-arrangement.

"I need to be close to you." With my arm over the back of her seat, my hand cups the back of her head, and I draw her to me for a soft kiss. I'm practically vibrating to be hard and fast with her again, but I'm asking her for patience, and I'm trying to tame mine. Damn that Leon Ramirez for interrupting us in the hallway, but making out with Jenna at a school function probably isn't appropriate for her, and I have some making up to do where I need more privacy. This restaurant is a start because I meant what I said. I wanted a do-over on that failed date from last summer.

"Were you trying to get rid of me earlier with that night off crap?" I don't want a night off. I fucking want a night with her. While every night this week has been dinner with the girls and a television series

Jenna wanted to watch, we haven't talked much. I promised we'd discuss my job, and we hadn't.

"I really meant it. You deserved a break. You've done so much for me this week."

It wasn't nearly enough and not even close to what I wanted to do for her. "What about Mason? How did he end up here?" *Fucking Mason.*

"Four Points donated to the silent auction, and I thought Mason might enjoy the dinner. He has built homes for some of the more prestigious families in the community. I didn't want to go alone and thought it'd be a business move for him to be seen." Her voice drops.

"Jenna, I'm here for you. I could have gone with you."

She shrugs. "But I already had it set up with Mason before you reappeared, and I didn't want to explain what you were doing here. In case . . ."

"In case what?"

"In case you left again." She lifts her glass of wine to her lips.

"'Locks," I whisper, watching her take a drink. My mouth waters to lick up the column of her throat as she swallows down the wine. I don't want her worrying I'm a disappearing act waiting to happen. I don't want her thinking I'm going to leave, but I'll need to prove my staying power. "You're not alone."

"Tell me more about this leave of absence." I hadn't meant to blurt it out like I did earlier, but Leon was pushing me.

"As I told you, I'm done with the Quintero case. I'd been put on a year-long furlough for medical purposes—both my physical condition and my mental instability. I was so pissed off that I'd been shot and angry that Viviana had gotten away." Not to mention that she's the one who shot me, which I did sort of deserve from her. "After this last stint, which wasn't planned, Vi is gone. Her family's business cut off, at least for the moment. But I also don't have clearance to return to the field. Physically, I'm not good." I tap my thigh. "And mentally, I can't handle a desk job. I don't want to just push papers."

Jenna's quiet for a long minute. "I can't see you settling down in one place for long." She cautiously looks at me. "If you can't handle a desk job, you won't want to sit still anywhere."

She means here, but she's wrong. I curl a lock of her hair around my finger.

"Jenna. I'm tired. I've been at this gig for fifteen-plus years, and the Quintero case took a toll. A big one. Mentally. Physically. *My* moral compass was going off-kilter. My faith in humanity was breaking down. I needed to get that job over, but it also taught me a valuable lesson. It's time to step away. Let the younger guys tackle things, if you will, but it's really more about me." I heave out a breath. "I want a life. One that's my own and not deemed by the department. Not one where I'm on stage and no longer recognize myself."

Jenna nods, placing her elbow on the table to shift her upper body and face me.

"Tell me more about the department. What made you decide to become a police officer?"

I tilt my head. I've been playing with the ends of her hair throughout my explanation, feeling more grounded by touching her.

"You really want to hear this?" Our food has arrived, but neither of us is eager to dig into the pasta dish yet.

"I want to know who you are," she says, and I slowly smile.

"Okay." I nod once. "Okay. I was kind of a hell-raiser as a kid. Nothing extreme but still trouble, as my grandmother liked to call me. A little underage drinking. Definitely some pot along the way. Driving too fast. One night, I was pulled over going to a party. I'd been smoking pot and had some in the car. It was reckless. Irresponsible. It was also the 90s. The officer took my license and registration. I was freaking out. He could have taken my ID and called my dad, who would have been pissed." I pause. "But he didn't. He came back to the car and told me he'd follow me home. I didn't have a choice. I was going home. He turned on his lights to further drive the point. So he follows me, and before I enter the house, he says, 'I'd say don't do drugs, but it's gonna happen, I suppose. Just be smart. Don't get hooked on that shit.' Then he stays outside for a while, and it hits me. I was damn lucky. I could have hit someone. I could have harmed myself. And it just clicked. I wanted to be a police officer."

Retelling the story reminds me of a guy when I first earned my badge. One I arrested on the west side of the city. He was stealing hubcaps. It was a thing then. I had to take him in, but on the way to the station, something prompted me to ask him a question.

"How'd you get in?" I'd seen the gang tattoo sticking out the back of his white tank top.

"My brother was shot by Hector Ortego right in front of me." It hit me hard. This guy, roughly my age, was so angry, so vengeful. I saw it in his eyes. *"He was only sixteen."*

I pulled over and turned to face him in the back seat.

"If I let you go, you gonna keep stealing caps?"

"Won't matter what I do, I'll be in there at some point." He nodded to the station, and it just made me sad. He'd given up hope of ever being anything but a gangbanger.

My kindness wouldn't make a difference, but I didn't have the heart to haul him in for a couple of hubcaps.

"Get out," I muttered to him. His head turned back to me. *"I'm pretending I don't see ya."* I turned forward, unlocked the door, and stepped out to uncuff him. He didn't glance back, and I knew I'd had no effect on him. He'd be in the slammer eventually.

Suddenly, I realize why Leon Ramirez looked a little familiar.

"Huh." I huff.

"What?" She smiles, still watching me, and I retell the memory, wondering if that guy was Leon. It doesn't matter.

"I'd decided around that time I wanted into the local DEA. Gangs were wreaking havoc, but drugs were the driving force behind them. I didn't like the idea that some sixteen-year-old kid was shot in front of his brother."

Jenna soaks up the details of my stories between bites of dinner, and I marinate in her presence. She listens to me and asks questions. She learns things I haven't spoken about in years.

"I'm boring you," I finally say when I notice we are the only two people who remain in the restaurant. The waitstaff has gathered near the kitchen entrance, waiting on us to leave.

"No." She exhales. "Not at all. I'm more concerned you'll be bored if you stay here."

"I want to be bored," I tease but notice the hard lines of her face. Her brows pinch, and her forehead furrows.

"'Locks, I want to be where you are. It's not going to be boring. You and me. We cannot be boring." I lean in for a quick kiss but want more from her and decide it's time to let the waitstaff head home. After paying our bill, I help Jenna into her coat, hating to cover up that sexy dress of hers, but she's going to look even sexier out of it.

Once we're back in my truck, I reach over for her hand, holding hers as I have throughout the night. I wanted this evening to be a makeup for that lost date, and with dinner finished, my thoughts race to what else I wanted that night. A second chance to make love to this woman. My desire to fuck her has subsided to a deep need to enter her over and over again, taking my time to fill her up, and never let her go.

"You look stunning tonight," I tell her again. "But as much as I love that dress on you, I want it off."

Her breath hitches.

"I'm not saying it has to be tonight or tomorrow or even next week, but it's gonna happen again between us, 'Locks. You're the lake, and I'm the shore, and I want to feel you crashing over me again and again. I want to fill you up, but not just your body. Your heart. Your soul. I want you to know me, and I want to know you."

I talked too much tonight, but it felt so good to share memories, to remember who I was.

"And I'm hoping you can help me figure out who to be next. Not a police officer. Not a DEA agent. Just a man. Who wants to spend time with you and our girls. Who wants to be here for you."

I pause, and Jenna's head turns toward me, but my eyes stay on the road. I'm messing up again. I should have said all this at dinner. I should be looking her in the eye.

"You told me last summer Ryan was your person, but you believed in second chances." I lick my lips. "I want to be your person. Let me be your second chance. Be my first time at love."

261

Maybe it's too much. Last summer, I asked her to be my home to fulfill Ben's directive. Jenna didn't get a chance to answer me because we'd been interrupted.

But when I pull into her driveway, I hardly have the ignition off before Jenna has crossed the seat. Her hands land on my face, and her mouth seeks mine, and it's exactly where I want her to be, but I am not taking her in the driveway. At least, not tonight with a sitter inside waiting on us or the fact there's a warm bed in that house.

"Damn, 'Locks. Kissing you. There is nothing like it." Sex with her is amazing, but her mouth on mine, taking my tongue, melting against my lips, even an occasional nip—I love it. I love her, but is she ready to hear such a thing? Will she believe me?

We make out for several minutes, taking our time without interruption like earlier, but it's not enough.

"Inside," I demand, reaching for the handle on my door and slipping into the cold night. Jenna scrambles after me, climbing out on my side, and I press her against the side of the truck for another minute of rushed kisses. Her mouth is made for mine, and she shivers under me. "It's fucking freezing out here, baby, and there's someplace warmer I want to be."

Jenna takes my hand and leads me inside the house. Somehow, she finds composure to thank her high school student for babysitting, pay her, and then wait on the girl to reverse out of the driveway. In that time, I've turned off all the downstairs lights and cooled a little, so when Jenna takes my hand and leads me to the base of the stairs, I hesitate.

"You okay with this?" I pause, holding her fingers. "Because as I told you before, 'Locks, I'm not pretending. I'm not hiding. I showed up at your work and at that fundraiser with an ulterior motive. I want to be seen. By you. By your friends. I'm here. For you."

She stares back at me.

"I want this, Archer. I want you." She reaches for my other hand and lifts it to her chest. My palm covers the dark purple silk of her dress, and her heart races beneath the smooth material. "You're already in my heart, and you have been since last summer. When I saw how you were with my girls. When I see you watching me. I'll protect your heart as long as you promise to protect mine. Don't hurt me again."

"Never," I groan, moving up a few steps. "I can't promise I won't fuck up. With you. With the girls. But you can teach me." My voice deepens. "You can show me how to love, and I promise I'll do it in return."

She's a step above me, but she leans down and kisses me, soft and slow. Her tongue sneaks out to meet mine, but still, it's a dance of drags and drops, drawing out the kiss. Her lips suck at mine, taking the lower one between hers before she pulls back.

"Come to bed with me, Archer," she says in that sultry way she'd asked me last summer. A way that pleasantly haunted me until I could get here, to this point when I was going to make love to her again.

She leads me up the stairs, guiding me to her room, where I know I'll never be the man I was.

She's my chance to be a *better* man.

36

[Jenna]

I do a quick check on the girls, and Archer follows me, wrapping his arms around my waist as I close their door. His mouth meets my neck, and we struggle to my room like a three-legged team. Once inside, I hardly have the door closed before he has me pressed against it. His hands find the strings tying my dress at my hip, and with one long pull, they release, and the material slips open. Archer leans back and tugs the fabric wider, exposing more of me. I'm wearing a lacy black bra and matching panty set.

"Tell me you did not wear that for him," he growls.

"I did not wear this for him." I hadn't actually. It was just nice to dress up and feel pretty, but the dressing up backfired when Archer gave me that smoldering look earlier, and my underwear instantly dampened under his gaze. The struggle between my thighs tonight has been real. First, he opens up to me about his past, and then he opens even wider, spilling out his heart.

"I want to fuck you just like this but not tonight. Tonight, I'm reacquainting myself with this body. Taking my time to rediscover every inch of you." His palm flattens over my racing heart, and he closes his eyes a moment, absorbing the rhythm.

He's alive. I'm alive.

It's time to start living with this man. As my breaths come sharp and fast, his hand lowers to a breast, and he squeezes. The pressure instantly has me groaning and tipping my head back to the door. I arch forward, forcing myself into his palm, and his mouth comes to my neck. He scrapes his teeth in a teasing manner against my skin. My flesh pebbles, and a shiver ripples down my spine. My entire body trembles.

"Cold?" Archer teases, nipping me again and plucking at my nipple, which is peaked against the lacy bra. I squeak at the pinch, and his mouth opens, his suction on my skin more aggressive. My knees buckle, and Archer hastily brushes my dress aside, forcing the material to slip over my shoulders and fall to the floor. He pulls back without allowing much space between us and gazes down at my body. Lowering his hand down my middle, he hums in appreciation.

"I meant what I said earlier. You're stunning, 'Locks." His palm skims over my belly and between my legs, where he cups me over the lacy scrap. He stares where his hand covers me before his mouth returns to mine. He's everywhere at once. Tongue invading my mouth. Fingertips rushing into me. A deep groan from me floods the room.

"I've missed you," I whimper.

"Missed you so much, 'Locks." He continues to kiss me, dragging those fingers in and out of me. "You are it for me. You're the one for me every morning and every night, filling my dreams and my bed and my heart."

"Archer." My moan is like a plea and a prayer.

"Kissing you." He kisses me again. "I can't get enough of your mouth." Quickly, his fingers leave me, and he turns me to the bed. Walking me backward, he returns his mouth to mine, and he kisses me like I'm all he'll ever need.

Eventually, the back of my knees hit the bed, and I bend. Archer lowers before me as I sit on the edge of the mattress.

"I don't want you to hurt yourself," I say, noting his wince as he drops to his knees.

"Only thing that will hurt is being separated from you again." Instantly, his mouth is back on mine, distracting me. His fingers find the edge of my thong, and I shift, allowing him to remove it while he kisses me.

"Spread," he whispers, guiding my legs apart and glancing down at where I'm weeping for him. Lowering his mouth, he dives forward like a man on a mission. More teasing teeth. A twirling tongue. Two fingers again. I'm writhing against him, and his eyes lift when I comb my fingers through his hair.

It's powerful to see this man between my thighs, and I feel like a goddess as he worships me with his mouth. When I finally break, my knees clutch at his shoulders, which keep me spread wide. After a final lap at my seam, he pulls back and kisses my inner thigh. With effort, he stands, and my brow pinches at the pain that briefly crosses his face. I open my mouth to speak, but then he tugs his shirt over his head, and I lose all train of thought. Archer's chest was bare of tattoos. Only his upper arms and back hold ink, but I find something new over his left pec.

On closer inspection, I see it's several things. An inverted sword. Angel wings. A wave of sorts, like strands of hair blowing in the breeze. Then I read the faint lettering.

"What did you do?" I ask, lifting a shaking hand and drawing a finger over the wavy tresses. In black is the nickname he's given me, woven along the hair.

"You're protecting my heart."

"Archer," I whisper, but he's already working on his belt and removing his pants and boxers in one motion.

"Bra. Off."

I work the catch myself and toss it to the side, causing Archer to groan before pressing me back by a shoulder. I scoot back on the bed, and he follows me, climbing over my body like that dream I had. Like that first night he found me in his bed. He cages me in with his thick limbs and his hard stare, and my body hums with the anticipation of him pressed against me and him entering me.

His hand rests over my heart once again before he lowers to kiss me there. Then he kisses my mouth, taking his time to tease me and rachet my desire, which is already off the charts. His fingers eventually find folds still wet and waiting for him, and my hand seeks his heavy length, wrapping around the hard shaft.

"Your hand feels so good, but I'm not gonna last. Need inside you, Jenna." My name. A heartbeat. Our hearts coming together.

His hips bend back, and his tip falls into place as I open my legs. He's at my entrance, watching my face when something passes over his. I hold my breath a second, thinking he's changed his mind. With one thrust, he enters me, and I gasp when he says, "I love you."

The revealing phrase is strained and quiet, and I almost think I haven't heard him correctly, but when he pulls back and surges forward again, the words are said louder, with more conviction, with insistence.

"I love you. I love you. *I love you*," he repeats in time with his thrusts, and I can do nothing but let him fill me with his thickness and allow the words to wrap themselves around my heart. So much is happening so fast, but Archer seems desperate to share his feelings. His hips rock faster as he balances over me. His arms are columns around me. Suddenly, he kneels back, forcing my lower half higher up his thighs. He cups my backside and moves me up and down his length, watching where he enters me. His cries of love have subsided. He's focused, intent, and tapping a spot that will drive me over the crest again.

I'm a ragged mess, and when his thumb hits that special spot, I detonate immediately.

"Oh, frickity-*frack*," I groan as my head tips upward and then falls back. Wave upon wave rushes over me, and my legs tremble with the intensity. The elation. The emotion. It's all too much, and when I think I'm coming down, Archer speeds up, teasing me with a second crash on the retreating edge of the first.

This. Never. Happens.

I'm beyond myself, allowing him to play my body, giving in to every sensation. I bite my lower lip against the scream as the girls are across the hall. Even if Archer wanted to hear it, he respects that I can't. I can't holler and bellow and howl at the moon.

Instead, the sound of us coming together fills the space, and then he warns me with a guttural groan and a sharp shift. His hands clap on my upper thighs, and he stills me, holding me against him, blending us as one. He and I. He comes hard and fast inside me. It's a dangerous game at my age, but I'm not turning it down. I don't think I could ever say no to him.

"You made me see stars." He gasps over me before slowly pressing my thighs off his. He falls forward, caging me again and giving me a heavy kiss, taking my mouth like he'll never get enough. Breathing me in through this kiss. He pulls back and looks down at me with so much intensity, so much wonder, so much . . . love.

He loves me. Actions speak louder than words, and his efforts have been to protect my girls and me. He takes care of us. Even when he left me, deep down I believed in him because he asked me to protect his heart and keep his medal for him. He told me if he ever left without explanation, it was to keep me safe. *He* wasn't safe, but he came back to me.

In the end, he's here. *With me.*

"Ask me again if I'll be bored here, 'Locks," he whispers, watching my eyes. Before I even ask, he adds, "Nothing about you is going to be boring, Jenna. Nothing. Ever."

He slowly slips out of me but still pauses to hammer home what he says next. "No more fucking couch and no more sleeping apart."

"Are we having a permanent sleepover?" I tease, sliding my hands up his back before slipping my fingers to his new tattoo.

"We're not a sleepover. We're permanent."

37

[Archer]

I wake to the soft creak of hardwood flooring. Instantly, I shift, giving Jenna a squeeze before sitting upright, prepared to jump over her, prepared to protect her. My heart races as the door gradually opens, and I wish my gun were close at hand. I stashed it high and safe and haven't told Jenna yet where it's placed because I don't want her to be concerned. The girls will never find it.

The room is dark, and I don't have a sense of what time it might be. The Midwest winter messes with my assessment. As the door slips forward, Jenna's hand comes to my hip. She's still lying on her side, her ass pressing into me. "What is it?" she whispers, sensing me on high alert until I see a sleepy princess with blond curls sticking up all over her head.

My racing heart crashes to a halt, and I shift the sheet over my waist, allowing only my naked chest to be on display.

Jenna shifts to her back and perches up on an elbow, holding the sheet to her chest, as Rosie walks to her mother's side of the bed.

"What's wrong, baby?" she whispers to her daughter while I try not to freak out that I'm naked and lying beside her mother with raging hard on.

"I'm hungry." Her voice is groggy with sleep.

Jenna reaches toward her daughter, stroking a hand over her sleep-creased face to brush back the wayward hair covering her cheeks. While I'm still freaking out about our position and trying to calm my heart rate, I'm honored to be a witness to such a tender moment between mother and child.

"What time is it?" My own voice croaks from sleep. Jenna reaches for something on her nightstand and falls back to her pillow.

"Too early," she grumbles. These little girls keep early hours. During the week, it makes sense as Jenna rushes around in the morning, but on the weekends, a few extra winks would be appreciated.

"Rosie, give Mommy a minute to get dressed, okay?" Rosie nods but remains standing by Jenna's side while her mother shifts, dragging the sheet with her to keep herself covered.

I imagine this is a new situation for Jenna. She said she hasn't been with anyone else since me.

Every caveman instinct in me says mine, and that goes for her girls as well.

"Rose warrior, how do pancakes sound?" With her thumb in her mouth, Rosie nods. "Can you meet us downstairs then?" Without another word, she turns toward the door, giving Jenna and me some space. Once Rosie exits the room, Jenna looks over her shoulder at me.

"What happened?" she asks, and I swipe two hands down my face before balancing back on my elbows.

"What do you mean?" I try to brush off her concern, but Jenna reads me better than anyone else ever has.

"You seemed scared."

"Not scared," I state a little too harshly. "Just paranoid, I guess." For a moment there, I worried someone had entered the house and was coming after me. Coming for Jenna.

She shifts even more, placing a hand on my chest over my racing heart. "Are you okay?" Her cool fingers hint at the warmth of my skin and the clammy nerves that rattled me for just a moment.

"I'm fine," I mutter and look at her. "You know I'd never let anything hurt you or the girls. Not ever."

Jenna stares at me for a long minute. "Are we safe? Are you?"

"I don't know if I'll ever *not* look over my shoulder, but as long as I'm near you, nothing will get to you. We're safe." Someone will be keeping tabs on me. A shadow is somewhere out there, but it's a necessary safeguard. I refused the witness protection program, but the department refused to let me go without some security. I reach for my medal against Jenna's chest. She wasn't wearing it with her sexy dress, but she must have slipped it on during the night. My fingers cross over the raised symbol.

"Always going to protect you," I remind her and seek her eyes.

"Archer, you need to tell me if there's something more out there."

I nod. "But first, Rosie needs breakfast."

Jenna groans. "You always have an excuse." She shifts her position, giving me her back and taking more of the sheet with her, but I'm quick to circle my arm around her waist, bringing her to my chest and keeping her on the edge of the bed.

"I promise, Jenna, you'll learn everything, but let's just take things one step at a time. I don't need to cram years into hours."

Jenna stills, her head slightly lowered, and I press a kiss to her shoulder while she remains silent.

"Last night," I whisper into her skin, pausing on the reminder of what I said. I don't expect her to say those three words back to me. I don't expect her to love me as quickly as I've fallen for her, but I don't want her to take what I said lightly. "I don't say those words. Ever."

I didn't say them to Viviana. I said a variation of them. *I adore you, babe. I worship you, Vi.* They were just words, like lines in a movie.

"I figured you were caught up in the moment," she whispers, her voice small and hesitant.

I cup her chin and turn her head to face me. "That's not what happened. With you, I mean everything I say when I say it. No pretending. I told you I haven't loved before. That's how I know this is it. You and I are different than anything I've ever experienced. This is real, Jenna. This. Is. Real." My lips suck at her shoulder before I move in to kiss the crook of her neck.

When I glance up, our eyes lock, and I want to kiss her mouth. I want to assure her that what I feel is legit, but I accept that we need more time. I need more time to prove myself. Tipping my head toward hers, I rub my nose against hers as I've seen her do with her girls. That touch always seems like an exclamation point on her telling her daughters she loves them, and I want her to feel the declaration.

I love you!

Jenna's nose moves in response to mine, and then she kisses me, short and quick. "I—"

I stop her mouth with a harder kiss, one that bears all I feel. I don't want to hear she doesn't feel the same or any other variation of rejection.

I'll take what she does give me, which will include more nights in this bed and more days with her little family.

"Time for pancakes," I announce as I slip out of bed and reach for my boxers on the floor. Leaving Jenna still quiet on the edge of her bed, I stand and pull on my pants before heading downstairs to prepare breakfast.

38

[Archer]

"What's wrong?" I ask Jenna a week later. Something's been on her mind since the moment she came home from school.

Rosie and Talia are in bed, and it's just the two of us. She's leaning into my chest, and I toy with her hair as we stretch on the couch.

"I have a student who's in trouble. He isn't a bad kid, but he's heading down the wrong path. He's smarter than he comes across, and I don't know why he doesn't apply himself or isn't proud of his intelligence. It's like he's okay to skate by."

I chuckle at the description. "Sounds a lot like me as a kid."

My grades were barely above average. Enough to keep me out of hot water with my parents but not on the Dean's list. I did minimum work and still passed the required tests. School wasn't difficult. It just didn't hold my interest when there were girls to chase and parties to attend. Then I'd had that one run-in with the law, and everything had changed for me.

Jenna's concern doesn't surprise me. She's already told me how sometimes she has to remember her students are someone else's child. She can't be their parent. She can only offer guidance as a mentor. She believed that high schoolers had capable minds, and despite hormones and dendrite disconnect, they could make decisions on their own regardless of outside influences. She gave many of them more credit than they deserved and maybe believed in confidence not all of them had, but she was devoted to them. Being a teacher was hard work. I'd seen it in Anna those first years when she returned home, and I was still dressed in blue as a police officer.

"What kind of trouble are we talking about?"

"Drugs," she whispers almost as if she's afraid to mention it.

"Ah. Well, marijuana is legal."

"But he's not of legal age, and he was too high from whatever he took." This was the kind of shit I was trying to prevent in the DEA. Drug trafficking had a trickle-down effect. Those at the top wanted to get those on the streets hooked, and while we weren't talking about a big urban center here in Elk Lake City, small towns still had issues with drug use.

"Want me to talk to him?" Even as I ask the question, I'm kidding until the words are finally out of my mouth.

Jenna twists to face me better. "What would you say to him?"

"I don't know. I could just talk to him."

She's thoughtful a moment. "We do have a mentor program. I could ask the school social worker how to sign you up."

"What does the mentor program involve?" I wasn't a trained shrink or some miracle worker.

"Just talking, like you said. Students meet with mentors during their lunch period. Depending on the case, it can be once a week or once a month."

I nod, considering the commitment. "Well, sign me up."

"Really?" Her face breaks into the first smile she's had since returning home tonight.

"Anything for you, 'Locks." I lean forward to capture her lips as I haven't kissed her enough today. With her distraction, I gave her some distance tonight. Ever since our talk the morning after our date, I'm trying to give her space to sort her thoughts. I'm still in her bed every night, but I've backed off on saying *I love you,* keeping my emotions to myself.

When the kiss ends, she rubs her nose against mine like it's our new secret code. An exclamation point, but I don't know what she's saying.

"I've been thinking more and more about what I'll do next." I can't just sit in Jenna's home, playing houseman every day. I wasn't opposed to making meals and doing laundry, but I needed to do something other than hang out for long hours watching mindless television. The situation reminded me a little bit of when I was first shot and in recovery. With the slower pace, I had too much time to collect my thoughts, replay situations, recall mistakes, and regret how the investigation went.

Viviana's father was dead. So was she. A second-in-command had been apprehended. The department had information and locations on several other key players. I could comfortably step away from the case. I *had* walked away.

"What are your thoughts?" Jenna asks me. I'd already told her I was hoping she could help me figure out what's next, but the decision is really up to me.

"Typical stuff. Security company. Private investigation." However, I didn't see myself entertaining disgruntled wives seeking out the extramarital affairs of their husbands, and as this was a small community, installing home security systems didn't feel like my thing either. The area did offer high tourism, though, and with an increase in drug trafficking on the Great Lakes, the area needs some Homeland Security. But I didn't really want to return to that kind of intensity. Unfortunately, I didn't have another skill set like a hobby. I'd heard of guys opening bakeries, starting coffee shops, and even fishing for a living, but none of that felt like me.

"I guess I'm kind of hoping something will just fall into my lap, which I know is a crapshoot." I pause, swiping a hand over my head. "But I don't think school counselor will be my thing, 'Locks." I don't want to disappoint her, but that's not a career path for me either.

"You don't need to be." She pats my chest. "Most of our mentors are just community members volunteering their time. We have firefighters, the chief of police, a former CEO, a retired attorney, and more."

"Good to know." As she settles back into my chest, I have another question for her. "Why were you hesitant to mention drugs?"

"I didn't know if it would be a hard topic to discuss." I tilt my head, still not understanding her, and she peers up at me to clarify. "Considering your line of work . . . I didn't know how you'd feel talking about drugs."

"'Locks, I was an officer of the law, seeking out those dealing drugs. I'd say that meant I was against them."

She shrugs, which unsettles me a bit.

"Did you think I partook in them? Got hooked on them? Approved of them?" I'd already told her about that time I was pulled over. I didn't get hooked, following that officer's suggestion. And while I'd occasionally been high, it was so few and far between then and now, it was like it never happened.

"I didn't know how deep you went. Maybe you saw an advantage to them. The money. The wealth."

"The most precious thing is sitting right here." I tighten my arm around her and press a kiss to her hair. "You're the best thing that's ever happened to me, 'Locks. Priceless. But I'll tell you anything you want to know. Nothing is a hard topic anymore. The interesting thing about most drug cartels is the people at the top rarely do drugs themselves, so while there was access, I didn't partake." While I'd just admitted no topic was off-limits, I don't know if exposing all that happened with Vi is in my best interest. I'm working on building a future with Jenna, not recalling the past, but I'll give her what she asks for. "I've become partial to bayberry candles, the scent of crayons, and this right here." Her in my arms. I squeeze her again.

She tips up and presses her mouth to my lips, and thankfully, the discussion passes from unwarranted concerns to the connection of our bodies as we make love on her couch before heading to bed together.

+ + +

Thanksgiving arrives without much fanfare, and it's just how I'd like to spend the holiday—only us. Jenna and I fumble our way around cooking a turkey. She makes a pie with the girls. We laugh. We drink wine. We play games with our princesses. For the first time in a long time, I'm grateful for all I have. I'm thankful to be alive and have this woman in my life, sharing heartbeats with me. And I'm happy with two little girls who welcome me into their home.

Be home, Ben said. I think I get it.

At Jenna's gentle prodding, I call my sister. She knows I'm here either from Jenna or Mason, but I haven't contacted her myself.

"Archer." She exhales my name. Is that relief in her voice?

"Just wanted to wish you a Happy Thanksgiving."

"You too."

A heavy pause fills the phone. I'm not good at this part, filling in the silence.

"I was wondering if I could come see you and the kids at Christmas." My heart hammers. Asking is so difficult. "Maybe we could talk then?"

"Of course, Archer. This is your home." *Jenna* is my home, but I know what Anna means. Lakeside Cottage will always be home as well. She, as well as my nieces and nephews, are my family.

"Anna . . ." I swallow around a lump in my throat. "I'm sorry I made you worry."

A quiet sound fills the line. *Is she crying?* Dammit, I don't want to make her cry. I'm calling to wish her well on a holiday.

"Don't disappear again. Please." Her quiet tone tears my heart.

"No more disappearing. I'm here to stay."

"Really?" Hope floats in her voice through the wet noise of tears.

"Really." *I promise.* Home is where I belong now.

+ + +

Jenna's student had been suspended for ten days before I could meet with him, which puts us after the Thanksgiving break. *Don't schools know suspending kids only leads to more trouble?* Their freedom doesn't give them time to ruminate on their crimes but act as rebellious as they already are. I'd been warned he might be resistant and possibly even obstinate to the mentor program. I'd dealt with some seriously messed-up people, though, and I thought I could handle a sixteen-year-old.

"What's up?" I ask, finding the sullen teen tipped back in a plastic chair, reminding me of several belligerent arrestees I've interviewed. His hair is long and stringy, and the scruff on his face suggests he's more boy than man. He wears a short black jacket, black jeans with more rips than fabric, and a black tee. The room we sit in reminds me of a closet. It isn't overly friendly or inviting, and I'd like to bust him out of here because it's just too stuffy. I'm told most mentors meet with their students in the library, but this kid has special circumstances. I'd been escorted to the room and was told someone would come pick me up when our session was over.

The kid doesn't respond to me, gazing down at his lap. His half-mast eyes concern me he's high, but he has a drug test at the start of each school day. He's also in a mandatory rehabilitation program.

I hold out a hand to introduce myself, but he doesn't take the offer or give up his name although I already know it.

Brad Collins

When he still doesn't speak, I shift in my seat. "Nice office you have here." I look around the boxy, cinder block space. A round table and three chairs fill the tight room. If the kid wanted to crack a smile, he's quick to fight it by twisting his lips into a sour expression.

"Reminds me of my days as a police officer."

He shifts when I mention this, moving from his casually stretched body visibly tightens. The legs of his chair clack on the floor when he sits up straighter. I don't have the details pertaining to his drug situation. He'd been high in school, but it wasn't marijuana. That's all the social worker would share with me.

"Of course, I also worked for the Drug Enforcement Administration."

"Am I under arrest?" he asks, leaning forward and balancing his elbows on his thighs.

"Not yet," I state, pretending to be as bored as he is. "But you might be one day."

"But not this day," he mocks, falling back in his seat.

Taking a deep breath, I remind myself I'm not interrogating him. I'm here to mentor him, and I might be shit at this. What do I know about staying out of trouble? I was in so deep on my last investigation I got shot and the experience fucked with my head.

"You have Ms. Davis as a teacher?" While Jenna was married, she kept her maiden name.

"Yeah."

"She's kind of awesome," I say.

He shrugs.

"And she cares about you."

His head turns to the side, suggesting he doesn't care.

"She asked me to meet with you."

He huffs, crossing his arms.

"I'm new in town. Got any recommendations where to go?"

He turns back to face me, and his eyes narrow. "Get out of it."

Okay then. Next. I shift myself, lowering my elbows to my thighs and clasping my hands together. We stay silent for a long time. I'm good at this, waiting out arrestees, letting the silence weigh heavy in the room. We don't have to talk. I'm not here to impart wisdom, lecture him, or detain him. I'm present to be here for him, but starting a friendship with a sixteen-year-old will be harder than I imagined.

Flipping my wrist, I glance at my watch.

"Ready to get rid of me?" he asks bitterly.

Oh, the punk speaks. I bite my tongue when the urge for sarcasm strikes.

"Notice we have ten minutes. How about a walk?" Even I don't want to be in this room, so I can only imagine how he feels. He gives me a long look before reaching down for a bag at his feet.

"What's that?" I ask as he tugs the bag up and over his head, allowing the shoulder strap to cross his body.

"School-issued laptop bag," he states dryly.

I huff at the concept, feeling my age. *Back in my day* . . . computers in schools were a boxy, bland khaki color with a green screen and tiny dots forming letters with a blinking underscore which was a new term then. They sat on desks and were heavy as hell. These kids have it all on their hip and even in the palm of their hand with cell phones, but I don't share with him my back-in-the-day story, sensing he'd care not at all. Instead, we roam the hall, him trudging slowly beside me. The building is your typical school, adorned here and there with the high school's colors and posters of encouragement.

Don't Do Drugs. Yeah, that one probably isn't the most effective. I don't fault the school, though. They bought into programs and were sent samples of the ten-step challenges, six pillars of character, and four-point ideas for bettering students.

As we pass a few other students in the hallway, they dip their heads, not giving Brad a glance. On top of that, I notice they carry regular backpacks, not the laptop bag Brad wears. The official-looking, standard crossbody bag does not fit the rest of Brad's persona, but I know better than to judge a book by its cover. We pass the gym, the cafeteria, an auditorium, and classrooms. Finally, we arrive at the library. Reaching for the door, I open it and wave him inward. For a second, he stares at me, hesitating on the precipice of entering. We weren't allowed to meet in here for whatever reason, but that little cinder block room wasn't the way to get through to this kid.

Once we enter, a woman at a table set apart from other gatherings of mentors and students glances up at me.

"Brad?" she questions, shifting her gaze from the teen to me and back.

"Thought we'd take a walk," I state. "Brad was giving me a tour."

He doesn't respond, but he's fighting a smile and I'm starting to feel a little better about our meeting. Viviana and I had an intense relationship, but the buildup took years of chipping away piece by piece at the armor around her. This kid wasn't going to be any different.

"Well, thank you for your time today," the woman states, holding out a hand to introduce herself as the school social worker. For some reason, I notice Brad's fingers fiddling with the zipper pull on the computer bag. *Back and forth. Back and forth.* The nervous twitch has me wondering what he thinks about this social worker. I'd thought my therapist was full of shit at first and didn't know anything, but my therapy sessions were mandatory if I wanted back in the department, and eventually, I did open up to her. Again, I remind myself things take time, and I was walking into the middle of this kid's situation. He'd have to work backward before moving forward as I had done.

"Thanks for spending time with me, Brad. Maybe we could do it next week?"

Winter break doesn't start for a few weeks, and Jenna and I will return to Lakeside Cottage. We need to go back to where we started, bringing us full circle and restoring the tracks that came unhinged when we were last there. Plus, River and Zack are expecting their baby girl any day, and Jenna wants to see the baby.

"Sounds good," the social worker states.

Instinct has me wanting to clap Brad on the shoulder. Something tells me not to touch him, though. Instead, I put my hands behind my back and take a few steps backward, still watching him *zip-zip* the top of his bag. Without a word from my new mentee, I turn away and head for the door. Briefly, I wonder where Jenna's classroom is and if I could sneak into it. I don't remember the room number from her leading Rosie and I there for lunch a few weeks ago, but I imagine I could find it. Then I reconsider. Even with the visitor pass on my chest, I shouldn't be wandering the hallways unescorted.

The thought has my attention turning back to Brad as I reach for the door handle. His laptop bag is two-thirds open, and he's reaching inside it. The old guy in me marvels again that kids carry around computers.

Then my heart starts racing, and my palms sweat because the item he pulls from the school-approved bag is not the rectangular shape of a laptop.

I don't think before I shout.

"Gun!"

39

[Jenna]

This is not a drill.

Nothing in the world prepares a teacher for those fateful words.

After a brief delay, where my head catches up to my racing heart, I rush to push a two-shelf bookcase full of anthologies in front of my classroom door. Barking orders for students to sit along the wall closest to the door but out of sight of the window, I'm shocked at how quickly they move. Something in my voice expresses this isn't a joke . . . or a drill.

Some of the larger boys stack desks next, flipping them over to balance on top of one another as an additional barrier. Too late, I realize I didn't reach outside my door and lock it. Unfortunately, the classroom doors in my building don't have internal locking mechanisms and require a key insertion from the hallway.

Students hunch on the floor, some huddled together with arms around one another. Others are catatonic. We all seem to be holding our breaths. My heart pounds like a sledge hammer. Someone cracks a joke. A few kids awkwardly laugh. Someone says "That's not funny."

"Quiet," I snap.

While actual drills were frightening, especially to someone like me with an extreme fear of guns and some residual PTSD from the loss of my husband because of one, nothing can equate to the actual terror of a real situation. On top of the responsibility I have for other people's children, adding in the factor I, too, am a mother, this is a moment I truly feared happening. I was never so cavalier as to think it couldn't happen here. There was no measure of location or probability. The deadly action was always the result of someone in deep mental distress. Every day became a risk in a classroom. The only way to bypass fear was to have a plan in mind and trust in a higher power.

Then I think of Archer.

He's still in the building. The bell hadn't rung for the lunch period to end his mentor session.

A new fear takes hold of me.

I cannot lose him.

My fingers hopelessly tug at the medal around my neck, sliding it back and forth over the silver chain. I can't say how long we sit waiting. During the drills, police would use the building, firing off blanks that ricocheted around the empty hallways and stairwells to add to the anxiety. Even though it was pretend, the very real sound was nerve-wracking. The silence of the moment feels worse. *Silence is golden.* I hope it is true.

Eventually, we are alerted the threat is contained, and we are guided through an evacuation plan. Students are not allowed to go to their lockers but must leave the school as directed by the closest exit. Meeting points are positioned off the small campus, separating students because large groups can be a target.

Time moves in slow motion.

As Tricia Ramirez's classroom is next to mine, our meetup spot is near one another. It could have been hours or minutes before Leon suddenly appears, sweeping his pregnant wife into a tight hug and reciting Shakespeare to her. He does that often, and while it's endearing, my heart aches at his expressive relief. He smothers Tricia's face with kisses right before her students.

I've been trying to call Archer, and with each unanswered call, my dread grows bigger, until I reach a panic stage. The all-call necessary to notify parents went out as teachers are on the list as well. Although several high school students drive themselves to the building every morning, in this case, parents are asked to retrieve their child and given instructions on where to collect him or her.

Waiting out the time feels like forever. My concern for Archer grows. My only relief is the elementary school and middle school have not been intruded upon. We don't even know if our building had an intruder or if it was a student. The unknown is slowly eating me up inside.

While Leon isn't technically allowed to be on campus, I welcome his presence as he stands almost as close to me as he does his wife, keeping his arm around her in the cold December temperature. Most students don't have jackets, and some even wear shorts from gym class. I shiver myself, but it isn't the cold making me quake.

When my phone buzzes in my palm, I nearly drop it, fumbling the device as if I don't recognize the vibration at first. Eventually, a quivering thumb hits accept on the call I've been waiting on.

"Jenna." My name is a breath of air.

"Archer, where are you?"

"Where are you?" he asks, ignoring the panic in my question. Quickly, I tell him the meetup location. "Stay." The connection drops, and while I could be upset at his one-word command, I'm not.

Within minutes, I see Archer limping quickly across the empty field, heading to the corner where I stand with Leon, Tricia, and the milling students. Everything in my head says run to him, yet I'm frozen in place. My heart races, but my brain keeps me stationary. I've shut down while processing I should be moving. Then my eyes catch on his forehead, where a large bandage covers half his skin. My focus fixates on that bandage, white and bright with a deep red-colored center.

Soon enough, Archer is before me, stalking into my personal space and cupping the back of my head to bring me in for a searing kiss. Despite students. Despite Leon and Tricia. He kisses me, and everything in that kiss tells me what I most need to know.

He's alive. He's okay.

His hand slips down my neck and over my sweater, pausing where just above my left breast, feeling my heart racing. He isn't close enough. I need his hands on my skin. I need to feel the connection between us.

"What happened?" I ask when he pulls away and rubs his nose along mine. He looks at me, still holding the back of my head, and my eyes leap to the bandage. Shaky fingers reach for it, but I'm afraid to touch him.

"You shouldn't stay here." His eyes shift left and right, noting the students within hearing range. My thoughts race with more scenarios than I should consider. Archer's hand catches my fingers, lifting them to his mouth. He breathes warm air over them before he mutters. "You're fucking freezing."

The cold is slowly hitting me along with relief and shock. I'm trembling uncontrollably. I can't seem to take my eyes off the bandage on his forehead.

"Let's get you out of here," he says, tugging me forward.

"Wait." I tug back. "The kids." Some don't want to leave, lingering even in the presence of their parents, hanging about to offer comfort to one another without even knowing what's actually happened. However, they need to vacate the area for their safety. Plus, I can't leave until they clear out.

"Time to head home, guys," Archer calls out. "An email with information will be coming tonight."

"What happened?" Leon demands, stepping closer to Archer. His large leather jacket is draped around Tricia as well as his arms.

"I need to get back." Archer tips his head toward the school. "But I want you to go home." He directs to me before looking up at Leon and Tricia. "Take her home for me."

Leon gives Archer a long look before nodding once.

+ + +

Almost an hour later, Archer arrives at the house. I've hugged my girls a hundred times in those sixty minutes, almost afraid to let them out of my sight. I need to remind myself over and over again it wasn't Talia's elementary school, and Rosie was at the sitter's.

Leon and Tricia join me in my living room after having taken their kids to her mother's. Archer falls into a small chair in the room while Tricia and I remain on the couch. Leon has Tricia tucked tight to his side.

"You know I shouldn't be telling you anything as he's a minor, so I'm sharing in the strictest of confidence," Archer begins. His gaze falls to Tricia and Leon for a second, silently accepting they won't tell anyone what has happened. "It was Brad Collins. He pulled a gun on the social worker."

Tricia gasps. My eyes well with tears.

Before I can ask the W-questions, Archer continues. "I'd taken him into the library. They had us meet in this tiny little room that felt more like an interrogation room than a place for a mentor and student to bond."

Tricia and I glance at one another, knowing the room well enough. The former closet is cold and unfriendly and used for sensitive cases.

"I walked him up to the desk where she sat, but something made me look back before I left the library. He aimed directly at her."

Tricia grabs one of my hands while I cover my mouth with the other, fighting the bile rising in my throat. Mindy Tarlosa is so sweet, and she works hard to help our students. She's had some difficult cases in the past ten years as teen suicides rise and the number of students with depression increases.

"How did he have a gun?" Leon demands.

We don't have metal detectors at our school. We didn't want them despite a major school shooting years ago. We trusted in our system.

"It was in his laptop bag." Archer's voice drops to incredulous while he shakes his head disapprovingly.

"After warning the others in the library, chaos ensued. I'm surprised how many kids dove under tables, flipping them as barricades. It's almost sad how these future adults knew what to do as if they were on a battlefield," Archer adds. "Brad didn't seem as concerned with them. His aim was the social worker. Keeping calm, I tried to talk him down, telling him he didn't want to do anything rash. He didn't want to risk more trouble. He didn't want to go to jail."

Archer's chuckle is bitter as he runs both hands down his face and leans forward. "He'd asked me earlier if he was going to jail, and I joked *not yet*. He gave me a cocky smirk."

Archer takes a deep breath. "When I was within range, I went for it, tackling him. The gun fired as we collided with the table." He reaches for his forehead, where the bandage remains.

"Did he shoot you?!" I shriek, unable to contain the panic inside me.

Archer shakes his head. "Cut my head on the table taking him down."

"What about Mindy?" Tricia asks.

"The shot went over her head. I was able to knock the gun free of his grasp." Archer imitates the chop to Brad's inner elbow, forcing his arm to buckle and the trajectory of the gun to point upward. "I don't want to say she's okay because there's no doubt it was a scary-as-fuck situation. She's alive, but traumatized." Archer holds his gaze on me.

"It's not a cakewalk having a gun held against you," Leon mutters, and Archer glances at him. Tricia rubs a hand up her husband's back, and I'm reminded of the story Archer told me about Leon and their connection. Then my thoughts race to Ryan, and tears I've tried to hold back begin to slowly slip down my cheek. Archer's attention returns to me.

"He'll need extensive help," he states, referring to Brad. "I'm sorry I wasn't a better mentor."

The room is a cacophony of words as Tricia tries to reassure Archer, and Leon says something along the lines of it not being Archer's fucking fault.

I have nothing to say other than removing myself from the couch and crawling into his lap despite our audience. My arms wrap around his neck, and I hold the back of his head, pressing him to me.

"None of this is on you. None of it. It was bad timing." The wrong place at the wrong time, and it hits me all over again that I could have lost Archer in the same manner I lost Ryan. I shudder and hold him tighter, every part of me wanting to climb inside him and never let him leave me.

I don't hear Tricia and Leon leave, but eventually, Rosie and Talia come down the stairs. I asked them to play in their room while I spoke with Tricia, Leon, and Archer. I didn't need little ears hearing all that happened although we'll be having another discussion about guns and safety. The school district will issue a statement not only for the high school students, but for parents with young children, including instructions on how to have conversations with them, especially if they have older siblings in our system.

"Why did he do it?" I whisper to Archer.

"He's just a messed-up kid. I'd guess homelife or loneliness. Mental health issues, maybe. It could be a combination of things. I'll be checking in on him tomorrow."

"You will?" I'm surprised by this but immediately recall his guilt over Viviana.

He feels responsible. He spent thirty minutes with a kid he doesn't know, and he feels guilty for actions beyond his control. Actions not triggered by his presence but something deep within a troubled young man.

Archer shrugs, and the conversation rests as the girls watch me in his lap. Slowly, I slip off him, and Talia runs to Archer, collapsing into him as his legs spread and he circles her with his large arms. She clings to him, and he glances up at me for a second before nuzzling his face into the crook of her little neck and shoulder and tugging her up to his thigh. Still holding Talia close, he pats his other leg for Rosie, and she scampers over to him, not understanding what's happened but knowing enough that it's something serious.

There's value in hugging a child in times of distress. If nothing else, it makes us grateful for life and gives us hope for the future.

40

[Archer]

"Does it hurt?" Rosie asks, reaching up for the bandage on my head. I needed a few stitches, and I've replaced the bloody gauze with a regular adhesive strip. Rosie's tucked into bed with Talia across from her. I sent Jenna to take a relaxing bath. She needs to get out of her head, and I'll be working to erase all the worries on her mind in just a little bit.

"Sometimes warriors have battle scars," I tell her and then swipe at her nose. "But not you. I'm here to always protect you." I wink at her before sending a reassuring smile to Talia.

"Why can't you be my dad?" Rosie asks, surprising me.

Talia shifts on her bed. Her hug earlier shocked the shit out of me, but I took it. I'll take any slice the little ice queen gives me until she's warmed to me.

"Archer has to marry Mom to be our dad," Talia explains in all her infinite six-year-old wisdom.

"Will you marry Mommy?" Rosie asks.

"Think I should ask her to marry me?" I ask Rosie, who immediately and adamantly nods her head. I glance over at Talia once again. Her wide eyes watch me. I need her approval as well.

"Can I call you Dad instead of Archer when you marry Mommy?" Rosie asks, drawing my attention back to her, and for some reason, my throat swells. My eyes burn. I swear she blew dust in them. She's also put the cart before the horse because I have no idea if Jenna would marry me. She hasn't even said she loves me, but deep down, she does. Or she wants to. She's just scared, and today's situation didn't help.

"I'd like that," I finally say around the lump clogging my throat. Then I look over at Talia. "But I want you to know I'll never replace your dad. He'll always be with you." I pat my chest, thinking of my own father, who I'd been estranged from for too long, and then missed his funeral. "I'll love you just as much as he did." It's my solemn promise to Talia. I'll love her no matter how she feels in return. Just as I'll love Jenna, even if she doesn't feel quite the same toward me.

"I didn't know Daddy," Rosie says. "I just want one."

Rosie's words nearly cause the dam to break. I pinch the bridge of my nose and take a deep breath. *Damn dust.*

"I don't remember Daddy very well," Talia says with a quieter voice. "But I remember him pushing me on the swing at the park." She pauses a beat. "Do you know how to swing?"

"I sure do, baby girl. Maybe we can even put one in the backyard." There's limited space for a swing set here, so I add big backyard with space for a swing set to my list of real estate must-haves.

Talia slowly nods and swipes at her cheek. I'm not certain if it's acceptance or relief or maybe none of those things. After the day I've had, I don't think I can be trusted to read kids, but I want to be here for these two. I want them to always feel loved by a mother *and* a father. I want to support them and encourage them and never have them feel whatever Brad Collins felt to drive him toward drugs, cause him trouble, and think shooting someone would solve his problems.

"Alright, my princesses, time for bed." I tug the blanket tighter over Rosie and lean down to rub my nose to hers like Jenna does. Then I stand and brush a hand over Talia's head, knowing she isn't ready for that kind of affection from me, despite the hug earlier.

We'll get there, though.

I step back from the beds and hit the light switch, submerging the room into darkness minus a night lamp that projects stars on the ceiling.

"I love you, Archer," Rosie says, and I pause with my hand still on the switch.

My heart thuds. My throat clogs again. "I love you too, baby girl," I say to her in a croaking voice.

She quickly rolls to her side, satisfied with my return of her words, and my eyes meet Talia's across the dim room. I'm not expecting her to reciprocate her sister's feelings. I don't plan on pushing her for more than she can give. She's too much like her mother, cautious and wary. I know how I feel, though, and that's all that matters.

"I love you too, Talia," I softly call out to her.

Talia nods, taking in the words, before rolling away from me. Eventually, she'll accept the words coming from me and recognize I mean them. For now, silently showing her my love is enough.

After pulling the door almost closed behind me as the girls like it a sliver open, I press myself against the hallway wall, tipping back my head and blinking at the ceiling.

My thoughts race back to Brad and how lost he looked today. How vulnerable he was under that tough guy act. He was too young to have perfected the shield he needed to resist hurt, and I think back to the kids ignoring him as he walked down the school corridor. The look the social worker gave him, writing him off as trouble while he was in the clutches of something painful, in need of help. He was only a kid, the same age as my nephew Bryce, and I vow right then to do better by my nephews. They might have a crew of Ben's friends as male mentors, but I plan to be in the mix. I'm calling Anna again in the morning.

With this plan in mind, I press off the wall and head toward the bathroom when I hear a sob and know I have another fragile heart to tend to tonight.

41

[Jenna]

I didn't have time to fill the tub, so I opted for a shower. I'd been listening to the girls from the hall, although Archer had pushed me in the direction of the bathroom. I heard Rosie say she just wanted a dad, and that's when I knew I had to walk away. It was either rush to her comfort or succumb to the heartache. The second option won out when I heard Archer's response. He'd like to be their father.

The tears for my own girls mix with the tears for every school shooting that ever happened. Brad Collins is only a kid—sixteen and with a gun. I shiver at that thought and cover my mouth to stifle the sob. He could have killed Mindy, the social worker, and any number of students, but most importantly to me, he could have killed Archer. I bend forward at the waist, gasping for air. I couldn't lose Archer like I had Ryan—where someone's selfish, senseless decision shattered our lives.

Suddenly, I hear the shower curtain slide open, and a fully dressed Archer steps into the tub. He circles my bent body and tugs me upright into him. Pressing me to his clothing-covered chest, he smooths down my soaked hair while he whispers at my ear.

"I'm okay, sweetheart. I'm trained for these things. I'm okay. I'm *okay*."

I nod and wrap my arms around his neck, latching onto him as tight as I can. The words register in my head, but I'm still riddled with fear. I'm still so afraid I'll lose him. He's told me he isn't going back to the department, but he'll never be safe. He feels assured he's protected, but he'll never be truly secure.

"What is this?" he whispers, tender and soothing, still stroking the length of my wet hair as I remain pressed against him.

I can't even put my fears into words. I'm afraid stating them out loud will put them in the universe and bring them to fruition. I shake my head against him, burrowing deeper into his neck.

"Jenna." He pleads my name in his rough voice and plants his hands firmly on my face, pressing me back so he can look at me. "What are you so worried about?"

"I'm worried I'll lose you." I hiccup. "I'll lose you like him." Like Ryan.

Archer's jaw clenches. The mention of Ryan throws a stinger in the moment, but it's not my deceased husband who is on my mind. It's the man in my arms, the one I could have lost today.

My hand slips from his shoulder down to his chest, covering the left pec. His heart thuds under the soaked clothing and tight skin, and I close my eyes a second, breathing in time with his heartbeat. Reminding myself he's still alive.

"I'm not going anywhere. Any. Where." He jostles my face still cupped by his large capable hands. "I'm here for the girls. I'm here for you—"

"I love you." My lips seek his.

Suddenly, I'm ravenous for him. I need him closer. I need to feel his heartbeat against mine, matching mine. While my mouth stays on his, my fingers fumble and struggle to remove his flannel shirt. Archer takes over, nearly ripping it off his body while keeping our mouths attached. Next comes his T-shirt. It's plastered to his skin but quickly removed. My hands travel the dips of his muscles until I reach the waistband of his jeans. He leans back to watch my fingers, shaky and rough as I tug at the button and yank down the zipper. His forehead leans against mine.

"I love watching you take my clothes off." His breath comes out ragged. "It means you're as desperate for me as I am for you."

His head snaps up, and our eyes meet. My hands rest inside his pants, against his hips.

"I am desperate for you," I whisper. "I need to feel you are alive. Make love to me." I'm ready to lower to my knees and beg him. "I love you."

Archer's eyes widen and flick from one to the other of mine, searching, seeking something. "I don't want you to say it because you're afraid."

L.B. Dunbar

"The only thing I'm afraid of is losing you. It's why I've held back. I thought you'd leave. You'd grow bored of laundry and dinners and schedules, but the thought of truly losing you—"

His thumb over my mouth stops the words, but I won't be deterred.

"I love you, Archer. I *love* you."

He didn't believe in such emotion. He wanted it, but he'd been told he didn't deserve it. No other woman would love him according to another, but she was wrong. How could someone not love this man?

"I love you," I say one more time for good measure. Suddenly, he's lifting me, and my legs wrap around his waist. We're a fumbling mess with my slick body and his partially dressed. We exit the tub, and I whimper, "Here."

I need him here, now, in the bathroom, but he shakes his head.

"Bed, baby." He sets me down, reaches back into the shower and turns off the faucet, and then hands me a towel. For a moment, I'm thinking he's rejecting the idea of sex. With the towel around my torso, I'm lifted once again. This time, Archer cradles me to his chest and takes us to our room. Using his foot to close the door, the soft click of it secures the barrier to the hallway, and it's a start signal as we fall to the bed. We're at one another again. Mouths. Teeth. Fingers removing my towel and his jeans. We don't speak. We breathe one another in, absorbing each kiss, each touch, each gasp until he slides into me, and we groan.

"Say it again, 'Locks," he begs while his hips lead our rhythm, and my body rocks in response.

"I love you," I say, looking up at him over me, holding his eyes while my hand strokes along the side of his face. I love this man with everything in me.

"I love you, too, Jenna." My name is that heartbeat of wonder and worship, but I don't want him to wonder. I don't want him to ever doubt my feelings for him. I press my lips to his mouth and we kiss until we no longer can. Our bodies take over, expressing our emotions, keeping us connected until the release reminds us we are alive.

We are in love.

42

[Archer]

While Jenna works the remainder of the week from home, it's a blur of faculty meetings, student check-ins, and parent emails. The time bleeds into her scheduled winter break, and by the weekend, we are out of Elk Lake City. She needs separation from the situation, and I need to see my sister.

A strange excitement hums through me as we travel three hours south. Pulling into the snow-covered drive reminds me of Christmases missed but also the occasional winter visit here as a family when I was young. With the girls in the back seat, I'm hoping to give them similar memories. This will be my first Christmas home in more than a decade.

Jenna rubs a hand up my back as I carry Rosie up to the apartment. My sister knows we're coming, and we'll head over there as soon as we unload our things.

"Looks like someone's been sleeping in my bed," I grumble, noting the unmade sheets and the pillows laying askew like someone had a pillow fight.

"Thankfully, he's not in it, though," Jenna mutters before chuckling.

Mason has been here, but he currently isn't.

"We need to burn them," I mumble, and Jenna laughs a little harder.

It's good to hear the sound, and I'm hoping this week's visit will restore us to the flame we sparked last summer. Not that things aren't hot between us because they are. We make love every night, taking our time. Anna's already promised to take the little princesses overnight for us at least once. We'll spend Christmas with my family and then be home to ring in the new year.

Family. Home.

"I'll get them washed." Immediately, Jenna steps forward, yanking the sheets off the bed while I finish bringing up the bags from my truck. As it's almost lunchtime, we told Anna we'd meet her then.

When we enter the main house, it's strangely quiet. The patter of the girls' feet rushing for the kitchen is all we hear until a rumpled-looking Anna enters off the hallway leading to the master suite. She looks like she just woke up, but I'm quick to dismiss the thought as she rushes for me.

My too-thin sister holds me tight, and I breathe in a fragrance that reminds me of my mother. As her arms wrap over my shoulders, her hug even feels a bit like hers, and for a moment, I'm a troubled boy, a misbehaved teen, a college boy returning home, and a man who's been gone too long without explanations. I blink back the rush of liquid burning my eyes and squeeze my sister before releasing her.

She cups my cheeks, giving me a once-over before speaking. "I cannot lose any more family members."

Damn that water blinding my vision a second. I blink against the potential of tears again and decide it's no better time for the truth than immediately.

"That's why Ben was listed as my next of kin."

Anna's hands lower, and she steps back, keeping her eyes on mine, but I catch her wrists, keeping her focused on me.

"We'd already lost Mom and Dad. I couldn't put you through that again. If you had to claim me." I hear Jenna's breath hitch as she's close, standing near the kitchen island while I spill my reasons for being distant from my sister.

"Autumn had already dealt with her father's heart attack, and Ben said she was handling his prognosis. He didn't want you to be responsible for reaching out to me, so he asked her." It explains how Autumn had my email address when Anna didn't.

"I didn't want you worrying about me."

"So it was better to be completely in the dark?" Hurt fills Anna's voice.

"It was." I nod once. Keeping her safe from my world had been my priority, along with keeping my entire family separate from what I did for a living. It was an adventure and dangerous, but it didn't need to be their journey or their safety at risk. I did what I did for me. Silently, doing it for them.

"But I'm here now," I tell her. "I'm done with the department."

"I don't even know what you did." Her voice softens while confusion and questions still fill it.

"I'll tell you what I can, but later." I glance up at the girls, each sitting on an island stool, waiting on the lunch I promised them we'd make when we arrived. Anna notices Jenna, and quick hugs are exchanged with her and the little princesses. Then it's a flurry of cabinets opening and items from the refrigerator being removed.

"What will you do next?" Anna asks when the girls are settled at the four-person dining table in the bay window looking out toward the lake.

"Actually, I've been chatting with the chief of police and the superintendent of the school this week."

At the mention of my talks, Jenna's head pops up. She's seated at the kitchen island with Anna next to her. I went into food preparation mode and took over sandwich making, and even made Jenna and Anna spiked hot tea to go with theirs.

"The area needs some additional safety measures. I'd already been thinking about safety consulting, so I asked about a director of public safety position."

"I don't think we have one of those," Jenna says, keeping her eyes on me.

"The area doesn't and should. With tourism being its number one draw, thousands of visitors come into the area each year." Drugs running so close to the community through the waterway of the giant lake is reason enough for public safety to be upped. The private sector of neighborhoods and families is also a concern as evident this last week. "So I'm working with the chief to connect me with other departments in the area. I'm going to consult until the position becomes a legitimate position in the protection forces around the county."

Jenna stares at me while Anna glances at my girl before looking back at me. Slowly, my sister smiles, which I sense more than see because I don't take my eyes off Jenna.

"Why didn't you say anything?" Jenna whispers, her face pinkening a bit, and Anna's smile grows larger while Jenna seems embarrassed.

"You had enough on your mind this week."

Her mouth falls open, ready to argue something with me. Then she glances over at my sister. Anna's bright expression lessens the tension on Jenna's shoulders, and my girl turns back to me.

"You're really staying." Her voice cracks. There's no question only confirmation, although I don't know how she still doesn't believe I'm not leaving. I've been at her home for six weeks. I've been in her bed every night. I wake with her wrapped around me each morning. And I spend my days thinking of my girls. All three of them.

"I'm really staying." I keep my eyes on hers until she's off her chair and rounding the island, tossing her body at me. With her in my arms, I peek up at my sister, who gives me a smile of reassurance and pleasure. Most of all, her expression reads welcome back to the family.

43

[Jenna]

A few mornings later, when I enter the main house, searching for tea, Mason exits from the master wing.

"Umm." The soft hum fills the quiet space of Anna's kitchen while I stand there, holding a box of tea to my chest as if I'm the one nearly naked and not Mason. As he's wearing only his boxer briefs, my eyes quickly redirect from the soft black fabric stretched tight over him. *I am not noticing your huge erection. Nope, not noticing a thing.* I've got my own man with a big package in the apartment over the garage, but I'm not a hot-blooded woman if I can't react to the spectacle of Mason first thing in the morning.

"Good morning," I mumble, only I've said it a little too loud and a lot cheerier than I feel this early in the day. I shake the box of tea as evidence of what I'm doing in the kitchen, but everything in my expression asks *what is he doing in here?* Especially as he came from a direction that clearly was not upstairs. He's staying in the house to give us the apartment for the week.

Mason swipes a hand through his hair, nervously looking away from me but not anxious enough to remove himself and put some damn clothes on. Eventually, he peers back at me and hitches his thumb in the direction of the master suite.

"About that—"

"None of my business," I immediately interject, holding up a hand and tilting my head so my eyes don't fall where they shouldn't.

"Yeah, I'd appreciate if you don't say anything." His voice lowers as do his eyes toward the floor.

"Not saying a word," I admit, holding my breath a second. "But if I might say one thing . . ."

"Somehow, I figured you would."

Here's the thing about Mason. Despite his good looks, his seductive charms, and the fact he is good in bed from the one night I remember twenty-something years ago, he has a heart as we all do. He isn't

299

impervious to the reckless one-night stands and failed relationships if one can even call his time with Samantha, the mother of his child, a relationship. He's devoted more than he's been given credit because people look at how he is with women and not how he is as a man. As a friend. As a brother to others. He's great with Anna's kids and has been loyal to Ben's memory. It's his own emotions that have me concerned.

"Are you sure this is smart?" I question, and Mason sighs.

His rigid body slumps a bit. "I'm not a mistake," he defends.

I have no idea what he means by that statement. "I'm not saying you are. I'm asking about you. I don't want to see you hurt."

Mason's feelings are written all over him. The only one blind to his emotions is the one person who should take a better look. While I'm equally worried about Anna, Mason has more to lose here. He's been Ben's friend. He's been in the shadows, and there's a fine line between light and dark. If he attempts something with Anna and it backfires, he could lose them all in the name of that loyalty to Ben. Then again, Anna is still living, and she deserves to move forward. It doesn't diminish her feelings for Ben or her commitment to him, but Ben isn't coming back, and that's difficult to swallow.

I know. I was there once.

She's too young to pine for someone she can no longer hold. And Mason is too old to keep pretending he isn't in love with his best friend's widow.

Mason snorts at my concern for his feelings. He looks away. He looks back. Then he sees I mean what I've said.

"How can I be hurt? I've had years to protect myself. Decades actually." He huffs again, emphasizing how long his emotions have swirled around the unobtainable woman.

"Are you sure she isn't someone you want only because you haven't ever been able to have her?"

Mason levels me with a sharp glare before his brows pinch and his expression deflates. "Don't you think I've tried to tell myself that? Tried to convince myself that must be it. The reason I'm so attracted to her is because she isn't attracted to me, or because she's the only woman I haven't had." His voice fills with frustration as he digs his fingers into his hair at the top of his head. Abruptly, he pulls his hands forward as if ripping out his own hair.

"I've tried everything I can to not think about her." His eyes shift sideways, in the direction of the hall leading to another portion of the house. "And it's never worked. Not another woman. Not too much booze. Not living away from here. Hell, not even having her under my feet, thinking I'd get sick of her and her charts and schedules and need to delegate and dictate." His voice grows louder, and I chuckle despite myself as he's ticking off Anna's teacher traits that filter into all she does, much like me.

"What are you doing then?" My eyes dip to his boxers and quickly glance away.

"Nothing happened." He sighs. "Nothing's happening." The second sentence confirms his frustration. Despite any thoughts I might imagine because he's standing in his boxer briefs, sneaking out of Anna's room, it's evident in his voice that things have not progressed where my wild imagination has taken me.

"What will you do?" Although I've told him it's none of my business, I also want Mason to understand I'm his friend. I'm her friend, too. I want what's best for both of them, but whether that's them together or separate, I don't know yet. "Admit your feelings to her or keep fighting them?"

"Maybe that's a question for Anna." His sudden sharp tone surprises me, and on that, he spins away from me, taking his time to enter the front hallway for the staircase leading up to a bedroom he hasn't spent the night in.

+ + +

Later that day, I'm holding River's newborn baby girl, Lake. She's as cute as a button and so good despite the chaos around her. Mila and Lorna have the twins, Trevor and Oliver, along with my girls in a complicated game of Twister, only the boys are trying not to touch the girls, and it's comical to watch. Logan and Autumn are here, along with Zack and Anna. Mason has disappeared.

I'm swaying back and forth, rocking little Lake in my arms, and glance up to see Archer looking at Autumn. Her belly distended as she's due in a few months with baby number two. Archer catches me watching him, and he sheepishly smiles as his eyes lower for Lake in my arms.

"I'm forty-two," I state, still rocking side to side to keep Lake content.

"Is that old, 'Locks?" He's teasing while the question runs deeper.

"Might be cutting it close."

He nods and gives me a little smirk, crooking up the side of his lips.

Is he suggesting he wants a baby? There's no doubt how he feels about my girls. I've heard him tell them both he loves them at bedtime, and Rosie tells me that's what daddies say to their kids. She's already accepting him as her father when we haven't even discussed the possibility of marriage. I'm not expecting Archer to marry me although it's getting to the point I can no longer say he's staying at my place like he's only there on a visit. He's staying period if he's investing in public safety measures for the county where I live.

"I couldn't promise a boy," I state for some reason as if we're even having a serious conversation, and one that's out loud instead of with our eyes which are locked on one another.

"Don't need a boy, 'Locks. Just healthy, happy kids."

"It's risky," I say, noting the room is quieting around us, especially the other adults within earshot, like River and Anna.

"When have you known me not to take a risk?" Archer teases, allowing that half-cocked smile to grow even larger. A smile softens his hard-edged face, and my insides warm. That might be my ovaries heating up, though.

"For me," I state, clarifying that I'd be at risk having a baby this late in life as would any baby we conceived, but it isn't unheard of. In fact, having a child over forty happens more often than people might think.

Archer sobers after my comment. "I'm happy with the princesses we have." His serious tone does not deter me from noticing he mentioned *we*.

We have two girls. While my heart knows Ryan is their biological father, he didn't have the chance to be a daddy to either of them, and the thought pains me. But that pain is more like a chronic ache than a sudden stabbing as it first was. I'll always love him. I'll always miss him, and I'll always be grateful that I finally found him, and he gave me my two beautiful little girls.

But Ryan isn't here to raise them, love them, and support them, and Archer is.

"What do you think about adopting them?" The words fumble out of my mouth before I realize what I'm saying, although I've been thinking about it more and more lately. Not to mention, I've just blurted it out before an audience of friends. We should be discussing this in private. I should be allowing him time to consider it or immediately reject it, not placing him on the spot, where he'll feel pressured into something he might not want.

"I think you should marry me," Archer states, standing from his perch on the couch.

His face grows serious once more, and I start to backpedal. I shouldn't have said what I said, out loud or otherwise, and I don't want him to feel spotlighted like he has to do something he doesn't intend to do.

For some reason, River shifts closer to me, and Lake is removed from my arms. I'm standing in Anna's sitting area off the kitchen, where I suddenly want the floor to crack open and swallow me down. This is so embarrassing. Archer is staring at me, and tears are filling my eyes because I feel so stupid that I've even suggested he'd want a baby with me, or he'd want to adopt my girls.

"Right. Marriage . . . I didn't mean . . . I meant, hypothetically . . ." The hole I've dug feels like it's getting bigger, and I'm sinking faster into a pit of quicksand. *Just shut up, Jenna.*

"And I mean it literally. Marry me, 'Locks." Archer drops to one knee in the middle of the floor, surrounded by this audience of family and friends. He takes my hand while I stare down at him, speechless for a moment as he slips a hand into his pocket and pulls out a gorgeous antique diamond ring.

"My mother never thought she'd live to see the day I married. She was right." Archer chokes. "She passed before I found the one, but she told Anna if something ever happened to her, she wanted me to have her ring. The one my father gave her, promising he'd love her through everything. Thick. Thin. Times of pressure. Times of pleasure. He promised to keep her safe and happy. That's what I want to give you."

With the tears in my eyes, I can hardly see the antique gold ring with its singular diamond. His hand tightens around my fingers.

"My parents were married just shy of forty years. I want all the years with you as well," Archer states. "Only you, Jenna. You're the one to show me I can have love, and I can give it, and I'm a new man because of it. I promise to protect your heart."

Now I'm just sobbing. My hair tips forward, curtaining my face while my hand covers my lips but not muting my tears. Archer squeezes my fingers again as if he's waiting on me, as if he's asked me something and I've missed the question.

His expectant eyes look up at me, and I blink to clear my own. "Yes. Yes, I love you. Yes, I want to marry you."

The ring is slipped onto my finger, and once more, I don't have the chance to really look at it as Archer stands and cups my head, pulling me in for a kiss that's hard and fast before everyone. Slowly, the whoops, and gasps and clapping register, and I remember who is present.

Rosie. Talia.

Archer breaks the kiss and lowers back to his knee, holding my hand with the ring. I watch as Rosie walks up to him and slips her arm around his shoulder while Talia stands close to him.

"Does this mean I can call you Daddy now?" Rosie says, and Archer wraps his arm around her little back.

"I think it does." He jostles her into his side while tugging at my hand, and I answer Rosie.

"You can call him Daddy," I whisper, pushing back once more the ache of Ryan's loss. Archer gaining the girls is just as worthy.

Talia walks closer to Archer and places her small hand on his shoulder. He looks at her, holding her gaze a second. The girls don't seem half as surprised as me.

"You're going to fight off her bad dreams?" she asks, her voice quiet.

My eyes remain on my child, the cautious one. The worrying one. My breath catches at her question. I haven't had a bad dream since Archer's return. The old ones about Ryan's loss were replaced by Archer's disappearance, but in the last six weeks, nothing.

"That's what dads do," she adds.

I don't understand her meaning, but Archer gives her a nod as if he does.

"I'm going to fight off anything that could hurt any of you. Day and night." With his knees on the floor, Archer releases my hand and circles his arm around Talia's back as he holds Rosie. Though Rosie has easily fallen into Archer, Talia still focuses on his face for a moment while Archer looks up at me. "Only good dreams from now on."

Talia surprises me even more and wraps her arms around his neck. Archer tips his forehead to hers and mutters, "I love you, baby girl."

I don't hear her respond, but I hope Archer knows she does love him. In her own way, and it will only grow stronger as she grows older.

"And I love you, too, Rose warrior." He tightens his hold on both girls and stands, tugging them up with him. I don't miss the wince in his face from the nerve damage in his leg.

"Careful," I mutter, not wanting to draw attention to his weakness but wanting to assure him he doesn't have to carry everything for us, girls included.

I'm here for him as well. I'm here to protect his heart.

"And I love you, Jenna." His tone drops before he gives me a kiss, holding my girls—*our girls*—in his arms. My hand rests on his chest, where I find his heart beating steady and strong.

"I love you, too."

Loving this man is going to be a good dream come true.

Epilogue

ANNA

Mason disappeared days ago, not leaving any information as to where he'd gone. Not that he owed me an explanation, but I wasn't running a hotel for him, allowing him to come and go as he pleased. The thought is harsh, but I'm all kinds of confused when it comes to my late husband's best friend. I try to ignore him most days, but he's always here, just behind me, just beside me, especially lately. You can't deny a man who sneaks into your bedroom and holds you while you cry yourself back to sleep. Or holds you until you wake early in the morning. We've had plenty of conversations without words, staring at one another.

While I question *what are you doing here?* Mason seems to answer in a code I can't read.

I blame Ben for the awkward position we're in. He said something he shouldn't have said. Then he left that damn letter with words I'm not privileged to know.

Fuck you, I mutter in my head while deep down, I don't mean the curse. *Fuck cancer.* I've missed my husband terribly these past eighteen months. I missed him before he even physically left this earth.

I dismiss all those drowning thoughts when the front door slams shut, and the sharp stomp of heavy boots fills my entryway. We're gathered in the sitting area, spread between the oversized kitchen and the two couches, which seems to be the meeting place in this home. My home. Without Ben.

Logan and Autumn are here, as are River and Zack. Along with Archer and his new fiancée, Jenna, we've turned into an impromptu reunion again, and I'm still a lonely party of one among the pairings.

The younger children are present as well. Trevor and Oliver. Rosie and Talia. Being observant, as the token quiet one in the group, I haven't missed the way the now nine-year-old Trevor seeks out the daredevil in four-year-old Rosie. Or the way Oliver protects her from his brother and the way Talia glares at Trevor like he's gum stuck to the bottom of her shoe. One day, she might change her mind. She might open her heart to someone opposite her as I had with Ben. Although he wasn't completely opposite me. Just different. Someone unlike anyone I'd known before.

As I think of unknowns, it's Mason who slammed that front door and stands just inside the kitchen area. His tall form fills the space when all I want is him to go away. I don't want to look at him. I don't want to be drawn to him. I don't want to see that pretty face with artful scruff and perfect hair cascading down his neck and over his ears. I don't want to watch his Adam's apple bob with nerves when he looks back at me or see him lick those perfectly pink lips before he speaks, as if the liquid coating builds a barrier and gives him strength before he opens his mouth. Before he shares words he shouldn't share with me.

Let me in.

I can't, and I close my eyes as I often do to ward off the frustrating feelings chipping away at the wall around me.

When I open them, movement happens behind Mason's thigh, and I squint at his long legs, assuming I'm seeing things. His hand lowers and reaches behind him before a small girl steps to his side. A beautiful child with long dark hair and mesmerizing almond-shaped eyes that are deep, black, and penetrating. She's focusing on everything in the room and nothing in particular until those eyes meet mine.

I swallow at the intensity in them.

"Everyone, this is my daughter, Lynlee." Only from the minimal information Mason has shared do I know the little girl is six years old. Roughly first grade, she's at such a fun age of self-discovery and learning, but the way she clings to Mason's leg by leaning into him says everything. She's shy. She's quiet, and that means she's misunderstood as I had been most of my upbringing.

Mason didn't have full custody, and he didn't bring her around. I'd chastise him for such a thing, faulting his fatherhood as I've faulted many things about Mason, but it was one area Ben warned me never to tease him. *Don't put him down for a situation we can't comprehend.* Like many things about my husband and family, I was in the dark as to the meaning of Ben's words.

Glancing around the room, I notice many people's reactions. Autumn is quick to stand but slow to approach the hesitant girl. River and Zack remain seated. Jenna and I cross gazes before I look at the other children in the room.

Trevor now has his eyes laser-beamed onto the new girl. Rosie's too young to notice the sudden shift of attention, something nearly palpitating off the nine-year-old as he looks at this intruder. I don't think he feels threatened as much as curious. In awe, maybe. She's beautiful, even at six. Oliver's head spins between his brother and Lynlee. Back and forth, back and forth, and then he shifts his gaze to Rosie. Conflict is already written in his little expression. He's only one boy. Who will he protect from the shenanigans of his alpha twin? Finally, there's Talia, daggers in her eyes as her young ice-queen heart turns colder. She glares harder than normal at Trevor before staring at Lynlee. The girls are the same age. They're all too young for the drama of loving and the potential of dating, but if I had to write a book about their futures, how things play out for the next generation of Lakeside Cottage isn't pretty.

It's still complicated among the adults, as Mason and I are now the only single people remaining among this crowd.

The last two standing, as he'd tease.

I'm more concerned with how much longer I can fight off my desire to lie down with him.

+ + +

Thank you for reading. If you enjoyed this romance, please take a moment to leave a review were ebooks and paperbacks are sold.

Come back for Anna and Mason's story in the final summer at Lakeside Cottage: *Letting Go at 40.*

If you love small town romance with older characters, you might also enjoy: _Silver Brewer_.

You can first meet Jenna (and her friends)

in Elk Lake City in the Heart Collection: *Read With Your Heart* and *View With Your Heart* (another prodigal son returns story).

More by L.B. Dunbar

Road Trips & Romance
3 sisters. 3 destinations. A second chance at love over 40.
Hauling Ashe
Merging Wright
Rhode Trip

Lakeside Cottage
Four friends. Four summers. Shenanigans and love happen at the lake.
Living at 40
Loving at 40
Learning at 40
Letting Go at 40

The Silver Foxes of Blue Ridge
More sexy silver foxes in the mountain community of Blue Ridge.
Silver Brewer
Silver Player
Silver Mayor
Silver Biker

Sexy Silver Foxes
When sexy silver foxes meet the feisty vixens of their dreams.
After Care
Midlife Crisis
Restored Dreams
Second Chance
Wine&Dine

Collision novellas
A spin-off from After Care – the younger set/rock stars
Collide
Caught

Smartypants Romance (an imprint of Penny Reid)
Tales of the Winters sisters set in Green Valley.
Love in Due Time
Love in Deed
Love in a Pickle

The World of True North (an imprint of Sarina Bowen)
Welcome to Vermont! And the Busy Bean Café.
Cowboy
Studfinder

Rom-com standalone for the over 40
The Sex Education of M.E.

The Heart Collection
Small town, big hearts - stories of family and love.
Speak from the Heart
Read with your Heart
Look with your Heart
Fight from the Heart
View with your Heart

A Heart Collection Spin-off
The Heart Remembers

THE EARLY YEARS
The Legendary Rock Star Series
Rock star mayhem in the tradition of King Arthur.
A classic tale with a modern twist of romance and suspense
The Legend of Arturo King
The Story of Lansing Lotte
The Quest of Perkins Vale
The Truth of Tristan Lyons
The Trials of Guinevere DeGrance

Paradise Stories
MMA romance. Two brothers. One fight.
Abel
Cain

The Island Duet
Intrigue and suspense. The island knows what you've done.
Redemption Island
Return to the Island

L.B. Dunbar

<u>Modern Descendants – writing as elda lore</u>
Magical realism. Modern myths of Greek gods.
Hades
Solis
Heph

About the Author
www.lbdunbar.com

L.B. Dunbar loves sexy silver foxes, second chances, and small towns. If you enjoy older characters in your romance reads, including a hero with a little silver in his scruff and a heroine rediscovering her worth, then welcome to romance for those over 40. L.B. Dunbar's signature works include women and men in their prime taking another turn at love and happily ever. Along with the #sexysilverfox collection, she's also made Amazon Top 10 in Later in Life Romance with her Lakeside Cottage and Road Trips & Romance series. L.B. lives in Chicago with her own sexy silver fox.

To get all the scoop about the self-proclaimed queen of silver fox romance, join her on Facebook at Loving L.B. or receive her monthly newsletter, Love Notes.

+ + +

Connect with L.B. Dunbar